MW01248733

KELSEY

MOONSTRUCK MATES BOOK ONE

By J.L. WEIL

Published by J. L. Weil
Copyright 2024 by J. L. Weil
www.jlweil.com/
All rights reserved.

Edited by Hot Tree Editing
Cover Design by Orina Kafe

ALSO BY J.L. WEIL

ELITE OF ELMWOOD ACADEMY
(New Adult Dark High School Romance)
Turmoil
Disorder
Revenge
Rival

MOONSTRUCK MATES
(New Adult Paranormal Romance)
Kelsey
Liam

DIVISA HUNTRESS
(New Adult Paranormal Romance)
Crown of Darkness
Inferno of Darkness
Eternity of Darkness

DRAGON DESCENDANTS SERIES
(Upper Teen Reverse Harem Fantasy)

Stealing Tranquility
Absorbing Poison
Taming Fire
Thawing Frost

THE DIVISA SERIES
(Full series completed – Teen Paranormal Romance)
Losing Emma: A Divisa novella
Saving Angel
Hunting Angel
Breaking Emma: A Divisa novella
Chasing Angel
Loving Angel
Redeeming Angel

LUMINESCENCE TRILOGY
(Full series completed – Teen Paranormal Romance)
Luminescence
Amethyst Tears
Moondust
Darkmist – A Luminescence novella

RAVEN SERIES
(Full series completed – Teen Paranormal Romance)
White Raven
Black Crow
Soul Symmetry

BEAUTY NEVER DIES CHRONICLES
(Teen Dystopian Romance)
Slumber
Entangled
Forsaken

NINE TAILS SERIES
(Teen Paranormal Romance)

First Shift
Storm Shift
Flame Shift
Time Shift
Void Shift
Spirit Shift
Tide Shift
Wind Shift
Celestial Shift

HAVENWOOD FALLS HIGH
(Teen Paranormal Romance)
Falling Deep
Ascending Darkness

SINGLE NOVELS
Starbound
(Teen Paranormal Romance)
Casting Dreams
(New Adult Paranormal Romance)
Ancient Tides
(New Adult Paranormal Romance)

For an updated list of my books, please visit my website:
www.jlweil.com

Join my VIP email list and I'll personally send you an email reminder as soon as my next book is out! Click here to sign up: www.jlweil.com

To anyone who ever felt stuck or like they didn't have a choice.
Carve your own path.

PROLOGUE

Cold and shivering, I ran through a dark, frozen tundra of
woods. Snow kicked up behind me, my pounding feet sinking
into the powdery white drifts.

Thump. Thump. Thump.

My heart raced, beating wildly in my ears.

I'd been hauling ass through the towering evergreens for more than
an hour now, and I wasn't any closer to losing the beast that hunted me.
The wind whipped through my hair, blowing flurries onto my already
icy cheeks.

Survival pushed me farther and farther into the dense forest. I was
unfamiliar with this part of the land, putting me at a disadvantage, but I
had other skills that gave me a leg up on the hunter—skills that allowed
me to live.

A shudder skipped down my spine as my ears picked out the
whizzing of an arrow cutting through the trees. I focused on the sound,
dashing to my left before it would have struck me in the back. The tip
sank into the bark of a tree trunk with a definite thud.

I didn't know how he continued gaining ground. He shouldn't have
been, not with my speed and not for this duration, but I had to do
something before the bastard got what he came for.

Me.

Zigzagging toward the distant smell of water, I forced my feet to keep going despite the burning in my lungs. My breath came out in puffs of chilly clouds that disappeared as I zoomed by.

I had no choice but to run—to lead him away.

The moon, regardless of how full, offered very little light. Navigating through the dark was a whole lot easier for me than it would be for the asshole stalking me. And yet he never wavered.

I caught a brief familiar scent as I came closer to the frozen river that looked like frosted glass—woodsy with a hint of mint. A more than recognizable combination. It was a part of me.

No! I screamed internally. *No! It can't be him. He should not be here.*

But, of course, he was.

A string of swear words went off in my head, and I stumbled in the snow, slightly flustered by *his* nearness. The stress and fear I felt amplified a million times as I reached out my senses to find him.

A gunshot rang out over the forest, scattering a flock of birds hidden in the branches.

Instinct took over. I stopped thinking and just acted, lunging through the frosty air.

Fur exploded over my body, bones and muscles transforming. A howl left my lips as I threw my head back, crying to the moon.

I'd never been more terrified in my fucking life. Not for myself—for him.

The wolf I vowed to hate.

The boy I loved.

ONE

T here was something universal about the way all high schools smelled. My senses were heightened due to being a wolf shifter, and the stench of self-loathing, boredom, anxiety, and arrogance permeated the halls of Riverbridge High.

Take the two girls huddled in the corner whispering. At first glance, I could tell they thought they were top shit, dressed in their little plaid skirts and cropped tops, but my interest lay in what they were saying and whom they were talking about.

Me.

Another perk of being a supernatural shifter—superior hearing.

I leaned a shoulder on the concrete block wall and listened, knowing I would dislike what I heard. So why the fuck did I torture myself?

They were nothing. Just two midranking wolves.

The sweet-as-candy strawberry redhead tugged out a tube of lip gloss from her pocket and applied it to her already shiny peach-colored lips. "Did you see what she was wearing? Where does she shop? The garbage dump? And those combat boots." The snobbish redhead shuddered. "No fucking way is Liam ever going to give her the light of day. She is total trash."

Oh, and let me guess... Liam is totally into redheads. It would explain

why her voice smacked with jealousy. I shook my head. The joke was on her. I didn't want Liam. And my so-called trashy clothes were all part of my brilliant plan to make sure he didn't like what he saw.

I should have been pleased it was working, or at least on these two.

Her partner in crime didn't have the legs the redhead did or the height. A good five inches shorter than her friend, she had a bit of left-over baby fat that made her face round and full. Soft, wispy brown hair framed her average face. "Maybe not, but it's not like he has a choice. I actually feel sorry for the prince," she said to the redhead.

I snorted. How sympathetic of them to feel sorry for Liam Castle and not the new girl forced to attend this shithole school and live in a place where she knew no one. Oh, and don't forget expected to mate with the Prince of Wyoming's son when she turned eighteen. These two needed to get a fucking clue... and some brain cells might help too.

My fists curled at my sides, sharp nails digging into my palm as my anger rose. I had to be careful or I'd end up making an impressionable scene on my first day. Nothing like wolfing out in the middle of the hallway.

"Didn't Liam's dad tell him he had to stop seeing you?" the little mouse asked.

Miss Goodie-gumdrop curled her shining lips. "Yeah, but when does Liam ever do as he's told?"

The airheads giggled.

I wanted to slam their pretty faces into the lockers. They wouldn't be giggling then.

I had a temper.

Sure, I tended to be reckless, fearless, and wild. Qualities that were supposed to make me a great alpha... if I learned control.

I was still working on the C-word.

Not that I would ever be an alpha. I was betrothed to one instead.

And it seemed my fiancé had a girlfriend. Not the best way to start out our budding relationship. The entire reason I'd switched schools had been to get to know my future mate.

Fuck that.
Fuck him.
Fuck the treaty.

Except I could do none of those things.

If it were just me, I wouldn't have blinked twice about breaking off this archaic promise between packs. But it wasn't just me. Two wolf packs depended on Liam and me joining our families. Not to mention, the fucking king of wolves himself sanctioned our impending joining.

But apparently, Liam either hadn't gotten the message that his future intended had arrived or he didn't give a shit about me. Obviously, he hadn't spent all these years waiting around for me if he had a girlfriend.

I wasn't jealous that he was seeing someone. That was what I told myself, but I had no right to be. In Hot Springs, I'd dated someone, too, but Huntley and I had both known it would never go anywhere. It had been an experience, something fun, someone to go to dances with, to practice kissing, and not miss out on the whole high school dating thing, but that was all it had been.

I hadn't been *in love* with Huntley. Not that I didn't try to have feelings for him more than friendship. One thing I had learned from dating Huntley—feelings couldn't be forced or faked. They just were.

When it came to my betrothal, I had feelings all right. Feelings of hatred.

I'd heard enough from Liam's *girlfriend*. It was obvious I wasn't going to win any popularity contests during my senior year. Time to scratch off homecoming queen from my bucket list.

Sighing, I shuffled around the corner, hugging my history textbook to my chest as I tried to not let those two bimbos get to me.

Being the new girl sucked.

A quarter of the kids in this school were wolves, like me, and part of the Riverbridge pack. As the daughter of the bordering pack, I was an outsider; however, once I mated Liam Castle, I would be not only a member of the pack but their future baroness—sort of the female alpha. I would hold the second-highest position in the pack, something I'd been training for since birth.

Shaking my head, I spun around to find my next class before the bell rang and smacked into some doofus who hadn't been paying attention. I might have been guilty of the same thing myself, but I had an excuse. I was the new girl.

"Whoa, hey there. What's the hurry?" Two strong hands reached out to my shoulders, stopping us from bumping noses. The deep voice flirted along the line of playfulness.

I glanced up from under my lashes into a strikingly familiar and far too handsome face. An easygoing smile spread over his full lips as aqua eyes sparkled with humor. I cleared my throat. "Sorry, I was trying to figure out where—" I skimmed over the printout of my class schedule clasped in my hand. *Who the hell still uses paper? What a waste.* "—room D11 is."

His lips moved into a crooked grin, a hand running through light brown hair. "Kelsey, right?"

I nodded, nibbling on my lower lip, and tilted my head. The familiarity triggered in my memory continued to linger. Was this Liam? Was that why he seemed so familiar? Did I recognize his scent? It couldn't be. Something was off. I had expected Liam to be taller with more of an alpha presence. This wolf reeked beta, and he was definitely a wolf —*that* I could smell. "Do I know you?"

His grin widened, eyes twinkling mischievously. "You should. I'm your future brother-in-law. It's been a while, Kels."

I released a gush of air. It wasn't *him.* "Leith?" I guessed disbelievingly. Leith was Liam's younger brother by a year. I'd only met Liam and Leith once in my life, at the age of six when my parents brought me to a regional pack meeting. They'd been there with their parents.

I'd been excited to meet this mysterious boy I would be spending my life with. He hadn't been as intimidating as imagined at that young age, but I remembered thinking, *Does he never smile?* I also recalled that Leith had been the polar opposite of his serious, stone-faced brother.

Leith was funny, impish, and warm, and when the day had ended, I had wished it was Leith I'd been promised, not Liam. Seeing Liam that day had crushed those starry-eyed dreams of having a mate, and as I grew, they turned into cold resentment at not being able to find love naturally. Our bond was forced, a political maneuver. I knew its importance as well as the position of my birth, yet it didn't make it any easier on my heart.

As I continued gaping at Leith, a tingle of electricity suddenly charged the air around my skin, causing the hairs on my arms to stand up.

How odd. I shouldn't have any reaction to Leith.

Just as the thought passed through my mind, another body came barreling around the corner, drawing my gaze for a moment. Taller than Leith by two inches, this shifter had dark brown hair with hints of sunkissed blond streaks. It was shaved on the sides but longer down the middle and curled at the ends. Unlike Leith's carefree posture, this guy had the dominating force of an alpha.

His eyes landed on me, and a fierce scowl marred his lips, deepening the dimples that framed both sides of his full mouth. That glower reached his eyes, the same stunning color as his younger brother, but lacked the glimmer of fun.

There was no mistaking. This was Liam Castle.

And that damn electric current I'd felt seconds ago amped up to overdrive. It fucking hummed in my ears, pissing me off. I did not want to feel anything for Liam except contempt.

He had changed a lot over the years. No longer a little boy. His cheekbones were sharp, lips full with a slight scar on the middle of the bottom one, and a jaw so sharp it could cut diamonds. He had filled out, his body nothing but lean muscle. He had an intensity about him that only added to the strikingness of his features.

I narrowed my eyes at him as I folded my arms, waiting for him to say something to me.

It was Leith who broke the silence between us. "Look who I ran into, bro." He put his elbow on his brother's shoulder. "Your future wife. I almost didn't recognize her. It was the scent. She smells exactly how I remember—vanilla and cotton candy."

What the fuck? I did not smell like cotton candy.

Liam's glare darkened before flickering from my eyes to my black lips and moving farther down until his gaze had covered every inch of me, from my goth T-shirt to tattered black jeans and combat boots.

This wasn't my normal attire, but I had come up with a brilliant plan to do everything in my power to turn Liam off. It was a long shot and a foolish idea, thought up by my best friend and me in a desperate attempt to keep me from tying the knot with him.

I knew what was expected of me, but that didn't mean I was going down without a fight. I had this whole other life, a really, really great life that I had to leave behind. To say I was bitter was the understatement of the year. I wanted to make Liam as miserable as I felt about being in a place where people only knew me as his mate.

Looked like he was about as happy to see me as I was him. *This should be interesting.* I hoped he was up for some entertaining months getting to know the *new* me. Heck, I was still getting to know the new me. She wasn't exactly someone I would have been friends with. The goal was to make him hate me, despise me, and find me the most unattractive female on the planet.

I had no idea if it was working.

Liam's perusal had been unsettling, to say the least. Something about his eyes did messed-up things to my belly. I didn't want to admit what that might be.

When our gazes collided this time, it was as if the world stopped spinning. Fucking cliché, but I didn't know how else to explain it. I felt trapped by his stare, by the magnetism of him.

But that wasn't all. Something happened inside me. I was filled with this all-encompassing power. It surged through my body, pumping me full of energy and causing the hairs on my arm to stand up.

"Um, hello, wolf eyes. Not at school," Leith murmured near my ear, but my brain was having trouble processing what he'd said.

Wolf eyes?

I had to stop staring, but I couldn't tear my gaze from Liam's, despite wanting to. This was the first time I'd laid eyes on him since the third grade.

Damn, had he changed.

I kind of wished he hadn't. Why couldn't he have stayed lanky instead of filling out? Where was the teenage acne? Why was his skin so fucking flawless and tan? And those eyes. Forget about it. Bright and glowing like a crystal.

Holy crap.

His eyes are glowing. His wolf eyes.

It was then I realized what Leith had been trying to tell me. Our eyes had changed, something that happened when we shifted. I'd been a wolf my whole life and had only lost my control in school once when Jamie Lancer had pulled my pigtails and called me an elf in the second grade because my ears were pointy. They were, in fact, not pointy.

"Liam," Leith hissed all low and rumbly.

Blinking back the wolf, I schooled my expression to hide any emotion from crossing my face. Liam Castle did not need to see the gnawing anxiety he caused inside me.

It is anxiety. Or disgust. Definitely more like disgust.

A cold expression stole over his features.

I took an involuntary step back, my cheeks warming. I didn't need a mirror to know they had pinkened.

What the hell was that?

"Why don't you do us both a favor, and stay out of my way," Liam said icily. Then the bastard brushed past me without a second glance.

I swallowed hard to gather my composure and rid my body of the tingling that wouldn't go away.

It didn't work.

"Asshole," I muttered under my breath. Wolves mated for life. There was no way in seven hells I could mate and bind myself to him forever.

Leith waited until Liam was gone before he replied, "He has his moments."

I had forgotten he was still here.

My eyes narrowed to slits as I clutched the strap on my bag. "Oh, he's having a moment already. Another one like that and my boot is going to find its way so far up his tight ass."

Leith threw back his head and laughed. It was warm and rich, so opposite from what I expected Liam's to sound like. If he laughed at all. Leith draped an arm around my shoulders, leading me down the hall. "I knew I was going to like you, Kels. And don't think you're fooling anyone in that getup. No matter how much makeup you schlep on your face, sis, you're still hot."

"Thank you, I think," I grumbled, unhappy to hear that my makeup wasn't a deterrent. I wasn't conceited, but I also knew I had what people termed natural beauty. On normal days, I rarely wore makeup, just a bit of mascara to brighten my eyes. "And I'm not your sister. Not yet, anyway."

If I remembered correctly, Leith was a year younger than Liam and me, making him at least sixteen.

He gave my neck a squeeze, arm still around my shoulders. "Come on, I'll walk you to class. Wouldn't want to chance any more run-ins with the *asshole*."

My lips twitched. Now, why couldn't I have been betrothed to Leith? At least he could make me laugh. "And I'll have you know, I'm not trying to fool anyone." Except for Liam. But I kept that part to myself.

"Uh-huh. If you say so," he said, totally not buying my excuse.

I glanced sidelong at Leith, wanting to see his expression. "I take it Liam isn't keen about our situation?"

The corners of his mouth lifted, revealing a single dimple on his right cheek whereas Liam had them on both. "That's a polite way of putting it. He's only thinking about himself at the moment. Liam was never one to be pushed into anything—goes with the alpha personality, I'm sure you understand. Give him time, and he'll see you're just a victim in the same game. Right now, he sees you as an obstacle standing in his way."

We turned a corner, maneuvering around crowds and moving with the flow of students.

"And if I wasn't standing in his way?" I inquired.

Leith shrugged. "Neither of you really has a choice, do you? Two packs are depending on this union, so why dwell on something you can't change? Why not make the best of the situation and get to know each other? Liam might surprise you."

A snort breezed through my nostrils. "Gah. You sound like my mom."

He grinned. "I always liked her. Smart lady."

I rolled my eyes. This whole treaty between our packs started because of my mother and Liam's father. They were really to blame. I only knew my mother's side of the story, but she had run away for a reason, and now Liam and I were paying the price for our parents' choices. What utter bullshit was that? I was a firm believer in one making his or her own destiny.

Leith walked me to my math class and winked as he left, leaving me to the wolves. Literally. Liam's girlfriend and her mousey friend were in my class. They eyed me as I strode inside, making my way to the back of the room, where I hoped I could just fucking disappear.

They weren't the only shifters. My senses picked up at least two others, male. The classroom chatter died, all eyes on me.

I loved being on display.

Due to the close-knit pack community, everyone at school knew who I was and of my arrival.

Riverbridge wasn't a particularly big town. Most of the people living in the secluded, mountainous highlands were part of the wolf pack. And those who didn't grow up hearing about the unusual happenings. Riverbridge had a reputation among outsiders, which did two things: kept them away or drew in curious tourists.

Liam's girlfriend wrinkled her nose as I brushed past her. "God, it smells like dog shit in here," she said, making sure the class heard.

Her friend giggled at the desk behind her.

I halted and slowly turned, slamming my palms down on her desk and sniffing the air around her. "You're right. I'd check your pretty heels." I lowered my voice for her ears only or wolf ears. "Smells like a midwolf to me."

The smug grin faltered, her green eyes sharpening. "I'd be careful who you rub the wrong way. You wouldn't want to make enemies your first day."

"Too late." This girl was going to be a problem I didn't need. I had enough shit without adding a jealous girlfriend to the mix.

"When Liam hears about this—"

Anger flashed through me at the mention of his name. "Tell him," I spat in a challenge. "You'd be doing me a favor."

If I hadn't had everyone's attention before, I sure as shit did now.

Determined to not let them see the nerves that actually fluttered inside me, I lifted my chin, removing my hands from her desk. Someone awkwardly cleared their throat, and a few others shifted in their seat, but most of them averted their gazes as I continued down the row to an empty chair and plopped down.

I hadn't come here to make friends, and from the way things were going, it looked to be a very lonely school year. Sinking lower in my seat,

I thought about the school and friends I'd left behind, wondering if they missed me half as much as I did them.

For the next forty-five minutes, I didn't hear a single word the teacher said during class, my head too full of thoughts. They were like a kaleidoscope, swirling around inside my head. I had to stick to the plan. The only way this engagement ended was if Liam refused to honor his duty, and to get him to do that, I needed him to hate me. The kind of hate that would force him to banish me from Riverbridge.

But to do that, I had to interact with Liam, which I so wasn't ready to do. Not until I learned more about his friends, family, and the wolf himself. For now, I would stay as far away from Liam Castle as possible. He could take his fuck-you attitude and kiss my ass with it.

As first days went, this one was kind of rotten, but a lot could happen in nine months. Shit could always get worse...

TWO

Gravel crunched under my Toyota RAV4's tires as I pulled into the driveway. My nana lived in a remote area. Her ranch house sat surrounded by the tallest evergreens I'd ever seen, or maybe it was just the pitch of the land that made them seem larger than life. Golden maples warmed the front of her house, reminding me that fall was sweeping in quickly.

For the middle of October, the weather was beautiful, a perfect temp with a cool breeze. I loved autumn—the cozy vibe, the shift in the air, the smell of bonfires, simmering apples, and pumpkin fucking everything. It was my favorite season, and while I might not want to be here in Riverbridge, I looked forward to curling up with a mug of Nana's pumpkin latte in front of the stone fireplace my grandfather had built. She had this room with floor-to-ceiling mahogany bookshelves stuffed with books. I could sit in the window seat that overlooked the woods, listening to the fire crackle as I read for hours.

The world ceased to exist in those stolen hours at Nana's that never came enough. They were my most treasured memories of the few times I visited.

Nana wasn't like any other grandma, at least none I knew of. She

didn't have a strand of gray hair on her head, just flowing long locks of obsidian hair like mine.

We also shared the same violet eyes, a trait only the females in our family seemed to receive.

She was a strong woman who refused to leave her home after my grandfather passed away, despite my mother's pleas for her to come stay with us. A respected elder of the Riverbridge pack, Nana still served on the Northwest Regional Council.

I sat in my car for another moment, staring at the cedar home with its stone pillars flanking the front door. Smoke curled from the chimney, and the first real smile of the day tugged on my lips, knowing she was inside concocting something in her kitchen. I never knew if what simmered on the stove or baked in the oven would be edible or a remedy.

She dabbled in both.

Gathering my stuff from the passenger seat, I turned off the car and hopped out. The wolf inside me yawned awake, sensing home. Not the kind of home Hot Springs gave me but still familiar and safe. Here I didn't have to pretend to be anything other than me.

I ducked under a low-hanging willow tree branch and climbed the three steps onto the porch. Smiling, I met Nana's eyes as I leaned against the column. "Hey, Nana."

She sat on the distressed wooden swing at the end of the porch, the fabric of her white dress dancing at her bare feet, a cold glass of herbal tea she'd brewed from her garden cupped between her slim fingers. The sun set behind her, casting the sky in the colors of autumn. "How was your first day, Kelsey dear?" she asked, offering me a genuine smile.

"Dreadful," I admitted, letting my whole body sink against the stones.

Her knowing lips curved. She hadn't batted an eye this morning when she saw the out-of-character way I had dressed. A glint had twinkled in the center of her eyes as if she knew what game I played. She probably did, considering knowing was her gift. That same sparkle appeared now. "Why don't we grab you a glass of tea, and then you can tell me all about this dreadful day."

Nothing sounded better.

I followed her inside the house. Dark hair hung loose down her back, silky and straight. The screen door clunked behind me, and my nose immediately picked up traces of brown sugar and honey perfuming the rooms.

"After we finish our tea and chat, we'll have facials before dinner. Exfoliate all those negative energies," she said, strolling into the hall.

"Is that what you've been doing in the kitchen?" I asked, plunking my bag down in the entryway and padding into the kitchen at the back of the house.

Nana went to the fridge, pulling out the freshly brewed pitcher of iced tea. Lemon slices and mint leaves floated on top. Each of her fingers was adorned with rings, and the metal clanged against the pitcher. "Hmm," she said in confirmation. "Restocking a sugar scrub."

Nana sold her home remedies to local shops in town. Not because she needed to make money but to occupy her time. She truly loved nature and using what we had from the earth to create. My grandfather, who died before I was born, left Nana a lofty sum of money for her to live from. I sometimes wondered if she saw his impending death. Everything I knew of my grandfather came from stories I heard from other people, but he seemed like the kind of man who would ensure his wife's future.

I grabbed a tall clear glass from the cupboard and filled it with ice, noticing the little glass jars lining the counter.

She poured the tea and sat down on a barstool, waiting for me to take the empty one beside her. She braced her chin on her hand, studying me. The bracelets on her wrist chimed as they rolled down her arm. "Did you give them hell?"

I grinned and took a swig of my cold drink. "When don't I?" She was the easiest person to talk to besides my best friend, Tess, who also was waiting to find out how my day went.

Nana gave a throaty laugh. "That's my girl. Seriously, though, was it all bad? Did you make any friends?"

My eyes rolled as I snorted. "It's hard to make friends when most of the girls already hate you." A big part of their less-than-friendly welcoming stemmed from jealousy. Not just because I was promised to the next generation alpha but because I was also an outsider, a wolf from another pack. Some traditions and beliefs within the shifter community were still very archaic.

"What about the guys?" she asked. Knowing Nana, there was an underlying question that she was edging around to.

Leith's face popped into my mind. He'd been the only one who hadn't treated me like a pariah. Leith had been warm, fun, and light-hearted. A hint of a smile touched my lips, which didn't escape Nana's watchful eye.

"You did make a friend. Who? Give me details," she pushed.

"What details?" I pretended to not know what she was talking about, that I hadn't been thinking of anyone.

"Did you see a certain boy?"

I hadn't wanted to think of Liam, of seeing him for the first time after so many years, but her question did just as she wanted it to—brought me back to the moment, to emotions I wasn't ready to deal with. No, it was best to pretend Liam Castle didn't exist... for a little longer, at least. I needed to get my bearings first before I dealt with the heir prince head-on.

But that didn't mean I couldn't have a little fun with Nana. She was too fun to tease. How sad was it that the happiest I'd been all day was right here, right now, with her? "I saw lots of boys. Nothing special," I replied with a careless shrug.

"Is that why your cheeks are flushed?"

I took a sip of my tea. "It's hot outside."

She laughed, and the sound echoed over the kitchen. "Was he that bad?"

"Liam Castle's a jerk. If I see him in the parking lot tomorrow, I'm going to run him over."

"Oh, Kelsey." She grinned, chuckling. "I'm so glad you're here."

We chatted for a little bit longer before I excused myself to get started on homework I needed to catch up on. Transferring in the middle of a semester came with its own set of problems.

Tossing my hair up into a messy bun, I went directly to my room on the west side of the house. Nana's bedroom was on the opposite end. My room came with a bathroom and a private screened-in porch that led out to the wooded backyard.

Cream coated the walls, and a large spindle-framed bed in that same warm, neutral color sat in the center of the room. A large picture window overlooked the expansive view. Nestled underneath the window was a bench with a handful of pillows, flanked by two built-in shelves, one with a desk and the other full of books and knickknacks. A rich wood covered the floors that felt buttery smooth under my sock-covered feet. Everything about the space whispered inviting and... was so me. I could see that Nana put thought into every detail, from the textured bedding to the soft rug under the bed.

More spacious than my room at home, except here there was no annoying little brother knocking on my door every ten seconds. And still, I missed Blake. Eleven years younger than me, my brother was as cute as he was annoying.

But I couldn't deny that I found a sense of peace here that Hot Springs lacked. Maybe I needed a bit of solitude and a change of scenery to get my head straight. While most of the kids in my grade were figuring out what college to attend or what their major should be, I was plotting how to end an engagement.

It wasn't that I loathed Liam. I didn't know him. It was what he represented and the lack of choice in the matter that pissed me off. He could have been the Brad Pitt of wolf shifters and I still wouldn't have been thrilled. My wants and needs were never considered. Well, not in the way I would prefer. I was sure at the time my parents signed the treaty with the Castles, they believed this was a high honor for their daughter. And in the shifter world, it was, but I didn't want to be the wife of an alpha.

Hell, I didn't know if I wanted to be a wife at all. I *was* only seventeen.

Not that our parents expected us to get married the moment we turned eighteen. The treaty stated that the heir prince would claim me as his mate at eighteen and vice versa, but we wouldn't take our vows until age twenty-five, after college.

To be bonded to Liam Castle for all of college sounded like a prison sentence. I didn't want to know and feel everything he did.

My heart grew heavy as I collapsed onto the neatly made bed. One of the decorative pillows fell forward, landing partially on my face. I left it there, too zoned out to give a shit.

What am I going to do?

My backup plan needed a backup plan. Of course, I needed a strategy to begin with. Making Liam despise me wasn't all that solid of a game plan. I needed something... something he couldn't ignore...

Like dating his brother or his best friend.

Better yet, both.

My phone buzzed on the bed, the screen flashing a goofy picture of Tess that I had taken a few months ago at the park. Tess wasn't just my best friend, she was family to me, and I missed her terribly, especially after today.

Tess Bakker and I had been friends since we were babies. She was a member of the Hot Springs pack. That was the thing about being in a wolf pack—our community was close-knit, and Tess and I had always been there for each other.

This was the first time we'd be truly apart, and soon we wouldn't even be in the same pack.

"Hey," I said as her face came into focus on the screen. Video chat made being separated slightly bearable.

Tess lounged in her bedroom. The light lavender walls popped against her dark brown hair and mocha complexion. She had naturally curly hair, which I was insanely jealous of. "So, are you pregnant yet?"

If I had been in her room, I would have thrown something at her.

Stretching out on the bed, I lay flat on my stomach, propping my phone up on a pillow. "I'm not letting Liam anywhere near my babymaker."

Tess giggled, her hazel eyes twinkling. "Is he hot or what? And don't lie to me. I'll know."

I rolled my eyes. "I guess if you're into asshats."

"Typical alpha, huh?" she guessed, scrunching her cute, perky nose.

"Bingo." I overexaggerated the word. "And he has a girlfriend. Can you believe it? Pretty sure she wants to claw my face off." Disgust dripped from my voice.

Was it hypocritical to be upset he had a girlfriend when I had a boyfriend at home?

Yes.

Did I give a shit about being reasonable?

No.

I wasn't waving Huntley under Liam's nose. He probably didn't even know about Huntley, and I'd rather not get my ex involved. Huntley was too good of a guy to be dragged through the mud.

Tess sighed, dropping her head down on her bed. "God, my life is so dull next to yours." Her voice came out muffled.

"Want to switch places?" I asked hopefully. If there was a spell that would allow Tess and me to switch bodies, I was there for it. At least she had the freedom to pick who she wanted to date.

Tess suddenly perked up, lifting her head. "If it gets me an alpha, then hells yes," she replied without hesitation and too much enthusiasm.

I groaned. "You need therapy."

She smiled prettily through the phone. "Who doesn't? Besides, you still love me."

Only Tess could cheer me up when I was feeling low. "I do. How's everyone?" I asked, hungry for any information about home and needing to feel some sort of connection with the life I'd left behind.

Flipping around on her bed so she sat up, Tess chewed on her long pink nails, a habit she couldn't kick. "You mean, how's Huntley? Pining for you. It's pathetic... and cute." Her lips formed a serious line. "It's not the same without you."

I didn't want to lose this short-lived slice of happiness. "Ditto."

Shaking her head, Tess wiped at her eyes before the tears welling in them fell. If she started crying, I would lose it. In true Tess fashion, she pulled her shit together, flipping emotions like McDonald's flipped burgers. "How's the elder?"

That was what Nana was, an elder. "Cooler than my parents."

"Do you think she would help you if you told her how you feel?"

The thing was, I did, but since she had influence not just within the pack but on the council as well, I didn't want to put her in that position. This was something I had to figure out on my own without tangling Nana up. "I don't want to involve her."

"How did I know you would say that? It doesn't hurt to ask for help."

"If it comes down to it, I'll tell her, but only as a last resort. Happy now?"

"Not really, but I'm going to hold you to it. If you won't tell her, then I will." Tess didn't dish out threats she didn't mean to follow through on.

"Fine," I sighed. "But I get until at least my eighteenth birthday." Liam's was at the end of October, a few months before mine.

"So, you really didn't want to immediately jump his bones?"

"Tess!" I shrieked. "It doesn't matter how attractive Liam is. It doesn't change anything."

She tapped on the phone screen. "Wake up, Kels. This is Liam Castle."

"Who cares?" I grumbled, picking at a loose thread on the bedding.

"Every girl with a pulse," she stated.

Liam's popularity among shifters only added to the reasons we weren't suitable. "I hate my life."

Knowing I wasn't serious, Tess laughed softly under her breath. "Love the new look, by the way. I wish I was there to see you make Liam Castle miserable."

"Me too," I muttered. "Me too."

THREE

I was still waiting for that moment when I first woke up and it didn't take me a second or two to remember where the hell I was. This morning turned out to be no different. The only thing I found comforting throughout the night was the familiar howls that echoed in the woods. They helped me fall asleep.

Last night had been rough. Seeing Liam, even for that short period of time, had unsettled me. I was someone who valued sleep. All the tossing and turning last night took hours away that I desperately needed. Just one more thing I could blame Liam for.

When I arrived at school bitchy and ready to rip off heads, it would be his fault.

Just two more days.

That was how long I had until the weekend—when I was free of the disguise, of the murmurs, of being someone I wasn't. For two days on the weekend, I could myself. No one watching me. No one judging me. No one hating me solely because of a decision I hadn't made. No Liam.

The weekends were just for me.

And I couldn't fucking wait.

Dragging my ass out of bed, I quickly got ready for school, brushing my teeth, going to the bathroom, and fixing my messy hair. I dressed in a

pair of jeans and a tee with the word *tragic* scrolled over the front. The whole ensemble was black, a shade damn close to my natural hair color. Adding my accessories took almost as long as it did to get dressed. The rings. The earrings. The fake nose hoop. I had to admit, I kind of really liked the nose ring. I might just make it a permanent piercing.

I didn't have as much time as I would like to do my makeup, but some eyeliner and mascara would do. A quick glance in the mirror and I grabbed my bag, heading into the kitchen. Nana had brewed a pot of coffee for me. She rarely touched the stuff, whereas I couldn't live without it. A soft smile graced my lips at the gesture.

Filling up my to-go cup, I snatched a cookie from the platter and popped it into my mouth. Nana was in the garden when I walked outside to my car. I waved before climbing inside and taking off down the driveway.

I hated to admit that Riverbridge High might be one of the most beautiful schools in the country. It had an old-world charm, mystical, as if the school should have taught witches and wizards instead of humans and wolves.

Yesterday, I'd been too nervous and preoccupied to really appreciate the architectural structure of the school. It was a damn castle—a Gothic one—and maintained very well. The gray bricks weren't weathered, chipped, or falling off as you might expect from a building dating back to the early 1900s. The flat roof had multiple steeples and iron fences around the perimeter, perfect perches for crows and other ominous creatures. It was shaped like a U with a brick-pathed courtyard in the center, and each corner had a small garden full of flowers and immaculately trimmed shrubs. In the middle of the courtyard stood a statue of the school's mascot—a wings-spread hawk. A wolf would have been a bit too obvious.

As if the building itself wasn't magnificent on its own, the school also had a pool, a football stadium with a waterfront view, tennis courts, an indoor track, dozens of labs, a theater, and other educational amenities.

From what I understood, the building was originally intended to be a luxury hotel, but unfortunately, investors backed out, and the builders were forced to sell once their funds had all dried up. Rumors circulated that it was the haunting of wolves that sent the investors packing up and running away with their tails tucked between their legs.

The school got its name due to the river that ran along the western side of the building. Water splashing against the rocky banks greeted me as I stepped out of my car. Under different circumstances, I might have enjoyed attending Riverbridge High.

But once you walked through those front double doors, it became just like every other high school. Not that the interior wasn't opulent and the classrooms weren't unique. It was the halls filled with angsty, often selfish, and hormonal teenagers that linked it to every other school in the country.

By the grace of God, I managed to find my first class without a guide. Walking down the halls, I still managed to draw too much attention, and as much as I wanted it to be my clothes, it wasn't. I couldn't help but wonder how long it would take for the new girl novelty to wear off.

I understood they were curious about me, especially those who were shifters and knew what the importance of my arrival meant. It felt like they were all waiting for something to happen.

I hated to disappoint, but neither Liam nor Leith was present for most of the morning, and I couldn't figure out if that was a good thing or not.

Are they ignoring me? God, I hope so.

But I should have known my luck would run out sooner or later. Liam might have skipped second period, and of course, the moment I finally relaxed my guard during my fifth class, the stupid-ass tingles started. They danced happily inside my chest, blooming with each beat of my heart. It couldn't be excitement that made my pulse race. No, it was definitely dread I was feeling. Definitely.

Liam hadn't even entered the room yet and it felt as if my heart would burst through my rib cage.

Prick.

I didn't want to have this sort of reaction to him. Whatever emotion it was. And I had no intention of picking apart my feelings. I had already made my mind up to hate the heir prince.

My fingers fisted on the desk as he breezed through the door, and I kept my head down, refusing to look at him. I didn't have to glance up to know where he was or that it was indeed Liam. My hyperawareness of this particular wolf gave me all the confirmation I needed. I swore that if I closed my eyes, I would be able to pinpoint him from anywhere in the room. It was as if I could see his shadow behind my clamped lids. No matter what I did, I couldn't run from him.

Awake.

Asleep.

Liam's face was there, haunting me.

Avoiding him was harder than I predicted. Then again, the goal here was to make him hate me. Perhaps getting in his way as much as possible was the solution instead of a problem.

He stopped at the desk in front of me, and I felt his gaze on me, could all but see the scowl on his lips before he filled the seat.

Fucking hell. Too close.

He was too damn close. I didn't want to breathe in his scent, but it wasn't like I could stop breathing. At least not for the entire class period. Woodsy with a hint of mint—that was what Liam smelled like, and with the combination of the rain pelting against the windows outside, I was on the verge of losing my shit.

I needed to take deep steady breaths, but after one inhale, it was out of the question. I could all but taste his scent now.

FML.

I turned my head to the side, my gaze colliding with the person sitting beside me. Her stare volleyed between the heir prince and me. It was then that I noticed a quarter of the class glanced our way, and not long after, everyone else picked up on the sudden tension in the room.

"Psst. New girl."

I angled my head to the kid sitting to my right. "I have a name. Kelsey."

"Brandon." Brandon was human. "If you need some help in class, I'm happy to share my notes." He looked me over in a way that suggested studying was not what he had in mind.

Liam shifted in his seat and shot him a glare that basically said, "turn the fuck around and shut up," which Brandon promptly did as I flipped him off.

My eyes burned holes into the back of Liam's head. He had a scar, just below his right ear. Tautness lined every inch of his body. I could see the veins in his neck, see the pulse beating there. I should be glad I wasn't the only one suffering, the only one in pain.

Fuck. I didn't like what was happening inside me. If I reached out and touched that scar on the back of his neck, would I get shocked? There seemed to be so much electricity charged in the air between us, or perhaps it was amplified by the storm brewing outside.

Sinking down low in my seat, I struggled to focus my attention on the lecture Professor Ellis was giving. I should have been taking notes, paying attention, and making sure I graduated. Instead, I tapped my pen on the side of my desk, plotting how I would piss off Liam today.

The pencil twirling in Liam's hand snapped. I narrowed my gaze. Apparently, my presence was enough to rile the eldest Castle, which should have made me feel good.

It didn't.

We hadn't spoken a fucking word to each other, and yet I felt as if we had this long-winded argument that left me drained. This fucking class couldn't end soon enough.

A crack of thunder boomed outside, seconds after a flare of lightning lit up the forlorn sky. Leaning forward on my desk, I propped my chin on my hand and peered out the stained glass window, watching as another bolt of lightning zipped through the gloomy sky, thick with dark clouds. A storm was coming, and the wolf inside me wanted to play. She hated being cooped up on days like today when you could feel the definite shift between seasons. Fall was creeping into summer, slowly shoving out those long hot nights and sun-basking days.

For the last ten minutes, I'd been trying to decipher what the colors in the stained glass created. A picture, but of what?

Anything to keep my mind off *him.*

But then Liam tilted his head to the side as if he meant to look out the window as well. The movement caused me to glance at him, and fucking somehow, our eyes collided.

I wanted to look away. I prayed I would look away. That he would. Neither happened.

It was as if I were in a trance, unable to break this curse.

The specks of blue in his eyes flared brighter than the green, and my lips parted as my breath hitched in my chest. He heard the slight intake and lifted a brow. My entire body flushed, and I wondered what the fuck he was thinking.

I lost track of time and had no clue how long the two of us stayed frozen, locked on each other. Uncomfortably long, but at some point, it became a battle of wills.

The bell rang, and I'd never moved so fast, not in front of humans, but I needed distance. A shit ton of it. Immediately.

I had no idea where I was going, only that I had to get the hell away from Liam.

In the hallway, I made a mad dash for the stairwell, taking the flight of steps down a level to the main floor. People spilled into the halls, hampering my escape, but I made it out the closest set of doors, which happened to be the west exit.

Liam's scent grew weaker with each passing step, though it never disappeared completely. I would need to leave school for that to happen.

The storm had dwindled to a light drizzle, and I welcomed the cool drops on my face. Drawing in greedy gulps of air, I let the dewy scent of rain and the freshness of the river overpower the traces of pine and mint that lingered from the heir prince.

Wanting a place of solitude, I couldn't hang around the side of the building. It was my lunch hour. The smokers would be sneaking out to grab a puff down by the lake. As much as I wanted to walk by the water, I headed in the opposite direction—up.

On the east and west sides of the building, iron staircases wound up to the roof. For the safety of the students, they were blocked, and a Do Not Enter sign hung from one rung to the other. As if that was enough to deter anyone from entering, especially a school full of troublesome teenagers and shifters. It was almost laughable.

Glancing over my shoulder to make sure no one was around, I hauled myself over the side of the railing and dropped down onto the staircase. The steps were wet from the storm, but I was careful as I climbed, holding on to the slippery railing.

How could I possibly withstand that degree of torment daily? I had to find a way to change my schedule and move every class I had with Liam.

Was that the exact opposite of getting in his way?

Yes.

But there had to be other ways to get the heir prince to hate me so much he would break our betrothal accord.

By the time I reached the roof, the rain had stopped, and bits of sunlight dappled through clusters of moving clouds. I was happy to find the rooftop vacant. This was the solace I sought.

Going to the ledge, I took in the breathtaking view from three stories up. I took in the grounds, the river, and the surrounding woods. This was so worth skipping lunch for. I needed this more than food. Besides, I had a protein bar in my bag. It would suffice.

Being connected to nature was part of being a wolf. I craved the outdoors like I craved pizza or coffee in the morning. It was a necessity to feed the wolf's needs as much as my human ones, and as of late, my wolf had been neglected. She was letting me know it was time I paid attention to her.

Soon, I promised. *Soon.*

For now, this would have to do. I couldn't fully shift and risk someone seeing me, so I let her out a little to enjoy the cool breeze and the dampness that clung to the air.

My nails grew into sharp claws, my eyes sharpening and morphing into that of my wolf. It changed everything around me. The world became clearer, from the dew-drenched blades of grass below to the birds sipping the river's water. I could hear for miles as well.

The beast within me purred in happiness. Eager to explore this new place and get her paws in the dirt, she desired more than just a taste. Unlike me, she had no qualms about Riverbridge. Yet.

The wolf wanted more. Seeing and breathing weren't enough. *A little thrill*, she begged. *Please.*

Seeing as the wolf and I were one being—though sometimes I wondered if that part of me didn't have her own mind—I gave in too easily. Deep down, I longed for danger and excitement.

Climbing up onto the edge, I planted my feet firmly and spread my arms out like a bird about to take flight. My head fell back, my eyes lifting to the sun-streaked sky. I wanted to leap, to feel the rush of adrenaline coursing through my veins as I plunged to the ground. Closing my eyes, I could see myself, and by the time I reached the bottom, I would be in full wolf, my paws sinking into the earth with the power of the moon that sang in my blood.

If only I had the freedom to leap. With a campus full of students and teachers, not the best idea to expose a secret that had been hidden for centuries. Not that there weren't humans who knew about shifters, but most of the human population still thought we were only legends, fantasy, creatures that lived only in movies and books. For our safety as well as theirs, we wanted to keep it that way.

Closing my eyes, I inhaled a deep breath, but before I could release it, something wrapped around my waist.

What the—

Suddenly, I was falling. A silent scream caught in my throat, and for a terrifying split second, I thought I might die.

Such a human thought. How could I forget what I was?

Four

Turned out, it didn't matter if I was human or supernatural. I was not in jeopardy of making a splattery mess on the ground for some poor unexpecting soul to find.

I fell backward toward the roof, not forward. Thank the fucking saints, or I definitely would have been forced to wolf out, secrecy be damned. When it came to my life or protecting who I was, living won.

Strong arms held me tight against a firm chest, twisting in the air so they were underneath me. Right before we hit the ground, those annoying tingles sparkled at the back of my neck. They were becoming far too familiar.

Fucking Liam.

With a hard thud, I landed on the ground. No, not the hard ground but a firm *body*. For a few stolen breaths, the air was knocked out of me. Stunned and a bit disoriented as to what the hell just happened, I didn't move. I just lay frozen, sprawled over Liam's chest.

His heart beat wildly against mine, and I could indeed vouch that his body was hard in all the right places.

So not what I should be thinking about right now.

A million thoughts raced through my head, the top being why the

fuck had he tackled me like I was one of his teammates on the damn football field?

I had every intention of asking as soon as my heart stopped jackhammering in my rib cage. I lifted my head, curtains of dark hair framing my face, falling around Liam's. Together, our chests rose and fell as if we'd just run a marathon or had unruly sex.

I had no idea why that comparison popped into my head when it had no right being there. Sex. And Liam. Never again in the same thought. I refused to think that into existence.

It didn't help that his lips were too goddamn close, barely an inch from mine. Or that I could see the small scar that ran down the center of his bottom lip. If I thought being near Liam had been difficult in a classroom, being on top of him was fucking torturous.

I couldn't decide if I wanted to hurl or—

Nope. Not going there.

Liam had his own uncertainties swimming in his eyes, and it was difficult to decode what he was thinking. His arms were still secured around me, but it was always his eyes that captivated me.

Biting down on the inside of my cheek in an attempt to squash the arousal that tightened between my legs, I narrowed my gaze. *What the hell is wrong with me?* I did not have an ounce of desire for this alpha prick.

Temporary shock. That was all it was.

"I heard you were reckless," he stated coldly as he continued to glare at me.

His accusation snapped me back to reality. "Did you?" I chuckled dryly. "What else have you heard?"

Liam's gaze darted to my lips, and at that precise moment, I realized we shouldn't be having this conversation with me still pressed into every inch of him.

He wouldn't. No way. Liam would not kiss me.

Would he?

The centers of his irises flared, and I wasn't so sure anymore. I'd heard the heir prince went through girls like gum—chewing them up and carelessly spitting them out.

"That you were smart. I guess all rumors can't be true. Is your life really that bad?" he asked in a low voice.

Was that a speck of concern I heard? Or did I imagine it?

It took a blink for the meaning behind his question to sink in. I smacked my palms against his chest as I pushed myself upright into a sitting position with Liam still pinned underneath me. "I wasn't going to jump, you idiot. I'm not suicidal, especially over someone like you. God, get over yourself."

His fingers circled my wrist, keeping me from climbing off him. "Could have fooled me," he sneered.

I stared at his hand. "You forget I'm a wolf. Even if I had jumped, it wouldn't have killed me."

"It would have hurt like hell, and you would have risked exposure," he pointed out, two things I was well aware of.

Pinning him with every drop of disgust I possessed, I replied, "You don't believe me, do you?"

"It doesn't matter what I think." A menacing darkness hung in his words that made me want to shiver.

Jerking my wrist from his hold, I glared harder. "For your information, I don't hate my life that much."

Liam made a noise in the back of his throat as he sat up with me in his lap. "Just me."

Now would be the appropriate time to get off him, yet I remained for reasons unbeknownst to me. "I don't hate you. At least not enough to kill myself. I hate the position we're in." And that was the truth.

"Then you should be more careful."

"I'm not your responsibility. I don't need you to watch out for me," I snapped.

That damn brow of his arched mockingly at me. "Don't you?"

He was referring to having just tackled me off the roof ledge.

"I've survived this long without you."

Liam leaned in, his dark and alluring scent drowning me. "But you're no longer in Hot Springs. You're on my turf now, pup. And there are plenty of people who would like to take your place."

I snorted, trying to keep my head about me. This fucking close to me, he made it difficult to keep my sanity. "Right, because you're such a catch."

"You know it isn't my looks people give a shit about it. They want the power. The title," he said with an edge of foreboding.

He was right, and I didn't want to feel sympathy for Liam and the responsibility of being the next in line to lead his pack. I understood all too well the burdens of being born into a position of power. "I don't give a crap about those things. They can fucking have you for all I care."

He brushed the pad of his thumb over the exposed skin on my lower back between the waistband of my jeans and my slightly cropped top. This time I shuddered. His eyes darkened as he felt my reaction. "And that's what makes you vulnerable. They're going to eat you alive."

When the fuck did his hands come around me again? Why is he touching me?

My chin firmed, a hardness descending into my features. "I'm not weak."

Before he thought about doing something else with his hands on my body, I scrambled to my feet. Something I should have done long ago.

I had no excuses. Perhaps I was testing myself. Testing him.

And I had no idea if either of us passed or failed.

The corner of his mouth twitched. "I heard that too."

I angled my head to the side, regarding him as he pushed himself to his full height, at least ten inches taller than me. I might be small, but I was lethal when I had to be. "Why are you up here?" I demanded, folding my arms across my chest. It did nothing to erase the imprint of his body and the warmth it left behind.

"I imagine for the same reason you are. This is my spot, I'll have you know. You're going to have to find somewhere else to wallow."

My chest heaved in frustration. "I was not wallowing," I said between gritted teeth.

"Whatever." He shoved his hands into his front pockets as if he didn't trust himself not to reach out to me, but that could have been my overactive imagination. "Just don't be here tomorrow," he growled and then walked away. It had definitely been a warning.

"Asshole," I muttered to his retreating back.

Dusting off my jeans and running my fingers through my wind-blown hair, I made a sad attempt to look like I hadn't just been assaulted by the quarterback.

Thank you, jackass, for ruining my lunch.

"Well played."

I whirled around at the sound of a confident yet playful voice and spotted a girl leaning against the door that led inside, smiling. "I don't know what you mean," I responded tightly.

Her golden hair was tied into a wispy knot, loose tendrils framing her heart-shaped face. She had deep brown eyes that, despite their friendliness, looked like they could go cold in a second flat. "Okay, we can keep up the pretense. I'm game," she replied.

How much had she seen? "Who are you?" I demanded. Another wolf, that much I was sure of. Was she one of Liam's fangirls, jealous he had been talking to his future mate?

Pushing off the closed door, she sauntered over to where I stood, and I noticed she favored her left leg, a slight limp that made me wonder if it was currently injured or had been hurt beyond a full heal. It wasn't uncommon for wolves to hunt and be hunted, just like any other living creature. The difference between us and other prey and predators was that something in our DNA gave us the ability to heal. But that didn't mean we couldn't be wounded beyond our body's scope of repair. It happened. As did death.

"After that performance, your new best friend," she proclaimed.

"I've got enough friends," I mumbled, turning my head to look out at the river in hopes she would leave me alone.

She didn't. "Do you? From where I stand, you could use someone on your side."

I glanced back at her warily. "Why should that be you?"

She was dressed in cutoff jean shorts, a white tank with a flannel tied around her waist, and white Vans, her posture relaxed. "Because I think we might have a common enemy."

Blowing out a breath, I found myself intrigued. "Already? It's only my second day."

"Please," she replied with a wave of her hand. "Your existence makes some people hate you."

"But not you?" I replied mockingly.

"Unlike the general female population at Riverbridge, I don't spend my days and nights dreaming of Liam Castle." She rolled her eyes, the exact same reaction I would have had with that statement.

"Really? Just what or who do you dream of, then?" I inquired.

She shrugged. "Getting the hell out of here. I'm Hope, by the way. And we might as well get this out in the open while we're sharing. Yes, I am part of the Riverbridge pack. And before you accuse me again of being interested in *my cousin*, I promise you this isn't Kentucky. We don't hook up with family."

My lips twitched. I had no plans of making friends here, but I liked Hope. There was something about her... "Cousin, huh? Should you even be talking to me?"

"Don't let Liam's facade fool you. He isn't as big a dick as he portrays. He did just save you from jumping off a roof."

So she'd seen the whole exchange. Weird. How did I not notice her presence on the roof? Then again, Liam had come out of nowhere. Perhaps my wolf senses were off—all this Wyoming fresh air.

I snorted. "I think he just wanted to slam me to the ground." The words popped out of my mouth thoughtlessly, but once I heard them spoken out loud, heat stole over my cheeks. I wanted to immediately take them back.

Hope's brow lifted.

"Don't take that the wrong way," I quickly added, trying to talk my way out of the hole I'd dug.

She grinned, flashing me a dimple. They must run in the family. "Your words, not mine."

"Oh God," I groaned, dropping my head into my hand.

We both laughed. It felt so good to laugh, something I hadn't done in days. Freeing. Weight lifting. My life had become far too serious as of late.

"Don't ever tell anyone I said that," I retorted once I got my composure back and smiled at her.

Hope made the shape of an *X* over her heart. "Your secret's safe with me. I'm exceptional at keeping my mouth shut."

I toyed with the gold hoop dangling from my ear. "We might just be friends after all."

"Sincerely, I would like that. Despite being related to two godlike guys at Riverbridge, I'm not all that popular."

I pressed my lips together. "Join the club." I pulled out my phone to check the time.

"You should come to the game tomorrow tonight," Hope offered. "Liam will be playing."

If his presence was meant to entice me, the tactic failed, but I figured Hope knew I would reject the idea based on Liam being there. Riverbridge breathed and consumed football. I had every confidence the entire town would show up for the game, which was the perfect opportunity for some *me* time. "I have plans."

She snatched my phone out of my hand. "Well, if your plans get canceled, text me." After she added her digits and saved her name in my contacts, Hope handed my phone back just as the rooftop door burst open.

Leith halted in the doorway, his eyes shifting from me to Hope. His shoulders relaxed. Had Liam sent Leith to make sure I didn't do anything stupid? Well, stupid in Liam's mind.

I didn't need a babysitter.

Hope wrinkled her nose at her cousin. "See you around, Kelsey."

Leaning my hip against the stone ledge, I watched Hope pass Leith and exit down the stairs leading to the third floor. I had taken the off-limits exterior stairwell only because I hadn't known there was also one that went into the school. When Nana asked if I learned anything today, I could honestly answer yes.

Leith waited until the door slammed closed behind Hope before strutting across the rooftop. He wore a backward baseball hat on his sandy hair and flip-flops on his feet that clattered as he walked. "I see you've made a friend. Not sure if Hope would have been my first choice, but you could have done worse."

"Like Liam's girlfriend, Sabrina Thompson?" I suggested, her face popping into my head.

Leith shuddered. "Don't even say her name. I might get fleas."

Without really trying, Leith had a way of loosening the knot of tension that had resided in my gut since I got to Riverbridge. "You really don't like her?"

He shrugged, sweeping his eyes over the view as he replied, "What's there to like?"

"I don't know. Her legs. Her ass. Her tits. Take your pick."

"I'm totally an ass guy, and I have to say—" His wicked eyes glanced at my butt, checking me out. "—yours is better, Kels."

Leith amused me. Perhaps it was because he was safe that let me lower my guard. "You are so much trouble. Are you sure there's no way you were born first? It would make things less complicated."

He turned so his back bumped against the cool, damp stones and faced me. "For you, maybe, but it would definitely complicate shit for me."

Curiosity had me angling my head toward him. "How so?"

Leith wrinkled his nose. "You'll find out sooner or later, so you might as well hear it from the source. The kids in this school are fucking vultures. Careful who you say shit to. Nothing stays hidden. Hope's cool. You can trust her. She's not a scheming, backstabbing bitch like Brina."

"We didn't talk long, but I got the impression she wasn't a total psycho."

His lips twitched. "That wasn't all I have to say, and since something tells me you want to make my brother's life miserable, you should know that flirting with me will just get me killed."

I pouted, actual disappointment sinking in my belly. "That's kind of a bummer. I rather like flirting with you."

Leith flashed me his single dimple. "Weird. I feel the same, probably because you're safe."

Some girls might like to be thought of as *safe*. I did not. In fact, I wanted to be the exact opposite. "Safe how?" I questioned, my lips forming a straight line.

"Like in you're going to be my sister-in-law. And you're not my type," he added with no real sincerity.

I faked a gasp of outrage like I was offended, my hand going dramatically over my heart. "If you're not into redheads or goth chicks, just who are you interested in?"

"At the moment, no one in particular," Leith admitted while toying with the bracelet dangling from his wrist. "Maybe Riven if he wasn't on a personal mission to bang every girl in this school."

I blinked, taking a second to process what I thought Leith was trying to tell me, but at the same time, I made a mental note to find this Riven character. He sounded like just the guy I needed.

"I'm bi," Leith said, to clarify any confusion on my part.

He watched to see my reaction, as if it would somehow change the way I looked at him. The fact that it probably actually happened to him started a fire of rage deep in my gut. I barely knew Leith, but I already had this protective sense within me that wanted to rip out the throats of those who would hurt him. What he needed was for someone not to give a shit who he slept with, boy or girl.

Lucky for him, that someone was me, because truthfully, I didn't care. This was a no-judgment zone considering I had seriously contemplated using him to make his brother jealous.

How fucked-up was that?

I hadn't stopped to think about how that might affect their relationship as brothers. That was how desperate I'd gotten, that I stopped caring about other people. *So* not me.

Liam was already changing me without him even knowing.

And I had to put a stop to it. There had to be a way to stay true to myself and also make Liam hate me. Right?

Keeping my expression neutral with just a touch of boredom, I replied, "Should I congratulate you?"

Leith laughed, a lightness moving into his features. "It really doesn't matter to you, does it?"

"Should it? You should date whoever the fuck you want. Guy. Girl. Wolf. I mean, I'll admit, I definitely thought about using you to get Liam to break off my engagement. I still might."

"You surprise me, Kelsey Summers," he said, shaking his head. "It wouldn't have worked, though."

I stared at Leith, wanting him to see my sincerity. "I'm realizing that now."

"I don't think you're fully understanding what I'm trying to say. Short of killing Liam, there's nothing you can do that will get him to break his oath. My brother has many savage traits that make him a class-act asshole, but he's honorable. Annoyingly so."

A flare of determination ignited in the center of my chest. "I'm not giving up."

He flashed me a killer thousand-kilowatt smile. "I never thought you would, Kels. I can't wait to have you as part of the family. It's going to make Christmas dinners so much fucking fun."

I rolled my eyes. "Thanks, Leith," I said, flipping the bill of his hat around to the front of his head.

Readjusting the ballcap, he gave me a funny look. "For what?"

I couldn't help but smile. "For not being a dick."

"That's Liam's gig. I'm just here to have a fucking good time and stir up a little trouble."

Something told me he was good at both. "Speaking of trouble, where can I find Riven?"

"Oh no, Kels," he chuckled, looping an arm around my shoulders and pulling me in for a partial hug. "Not happening. Did you not hear what I just said?"

I flattened my palm on his chest. "It doesn't hurt to try."

His expression went serious as he stared down at me. "My brother would kill him. Literally end his best friend if he touched you."

Liam's best friend. Interesting.

"Kels," Leith said sternly as if he knew precisely where my thoughts went. "I don't like the look in your eyes."

Clearing my throat, I cast my eyes down from his, staring at our feet. "Hope's really your cousin?"

"She is." He flicked the tip of my nose and started guiding me toward the doors. "And don't change the subject."

I only grinned.

FIVE

I didn't end up texting Hope on Friday. After the week I had, all I wanted was some time away from school. Away from Liam. Not that he had anything to say to me. We hadn't spoken since the roof. Hell, I didn't think he even looked at me. It was as if the whole incident never happened.

Yet I couldn't get it out of my head.

Or perhaps it was more accurate to say I couldn't get Liam out of my head.

Ever since my encounter with the heir prince on the roof, he was all I thought about. The sound of his voice. The color of his eyes. The curl of his lips. The addicting scent. The feel of him underneath me, his warmth seeping in between my legs.

It was making me batshit crazy.

When I closed my eyes, I didn't want to dream about Liam's mouth or running my tongue along the scar on his full bottom lip, dragging it into my mouth and biting just hard enough to taste his blood.

Fuck no.

Bad. Bad. So fucking bad.

I wasn't here to seduce my mate, to screw his brains out until neither of us could see straight.

It was because of these thoughts that I had to get away. This town, the school, and even Nana's house felt like a prison, trapping me inside. I had to break free.

I needed to run. Hard and fast. How else could I banish these bedeviling thoughts? I would run myself ragged until I could no longer feel my legs or keep my eyes open. Then perhaps my sleep would be dreamless. No visions of my arms wrapped around Liam's neck. No images of my body pressed tightly to his. No wondering what his mouth would taste like.

God, I can't stand Liam Castle.

NANA PICKED up the restlessness humming inside me. I'd been fluttering around the house since I got home from school. She didn't need to ask what was wrong. When I told her I was going out, she only told me to be careful and call if I lost my way.

She wasn't referring to a phone, seeing as I wouldn't have mine on me. By call, she meant howl—a wolf's cry. With the windows open in the house, and assuming I didn't cross the bridge that led out of town, she would be able to hear me.

Not that I anticipated trouble. This was Riverbridge, not the back alleys of Chicago.

Slipping out the back door, I traipsed over the lawn toward the rolling woods. The terrain was both magnificent and challenging. I couldn't wait to sink my paws into the earth, explore the unknown woods, and tap into those animal instincts.

Some people spent their Friday nights drinking, hanging out with friends, or going out to eat. I enjoyed all those things, but this other side of me, the wolf, she loved being outdoors. Loved the quiet of solitude and the thrill of running like she was being chased.

When I got into the coverage of the woods, I ducked behind a hefty tree and did a quick scan to make sure no weirdos were lurking about. Once I determined I was alone, I stripped out of my clothes, folding them neatly in a pile with my shoes. There was nothing worse than destroying a really nice pair of jeans during a shift. I couldn't tell you how many outfits I'd lost due to unexpected transformations while I learned to control it. It was something shifters did at a young age. For whatever reason, mastering the will to transform at my command instead of the wolf's had been more difficult for me than for my friends. Fuck, even Blake, my younger brother, had caught on after just a few tries.

I didn't know what my problem had been, but at the time, I could tell even my parents were worried I wouldn't be able to control the wolf.

Eventually, the stubborn, demanding beast inside me and I came to an agreement. It became about balance. She let me know when it had been too long, and I gave her the freedom to run, to hunt, to be careless. And just like that, the internal power struggle ceased within me.

Thank God.

There was nothing worse than an unruly shifter.

My parents tried not to scare me, but I knew they had been very close to sending me away to a school for troubled supernaturals.

Above me, a crow squawked from a branch. I tilted my head, peering into the bird's watchful onyx eyes. Some of the elders still believed in superstitions, like seeing a single crow could mean bad luck. The crow cocked his head before letting out another shriek.

Fucking wonderful.

Just what I needed. As if I already wasn't shit deep in bad luck. Pile it on.

Banishing thoughts of bad omens, I rolled my neck and closed my eyes, summoning my wolf. The transformation to anyone else but a shifter could seem unnatural, painful even, but that wasn't the case. It felt more like a release. Like taking your bra off after a long day or letting your hair down from a tight ponytail. It made me want to shake off the prickles that sparked over my skin, which was exactly what I did.

The moment my body went from human to wolf, shedding my skin for fur, I stood on all fours and shook out the lingering bits of buzzing energy that danced over me. I wasn't a werewolf. I wasn't lanky or tall, nor did I stand on my hind legs. I was a shapeshifter. I became a wolf.

In my wolf form, my eyes were the same unusual shade of violet, and my fur was as dark as my hair. Similar to that of a black squirrel, a wolf with black fur was rare. A fact that used to make me self-conscious, particularly when you paired it with my abnormal eye color. But now, I rather liked being different.

With a blink, all my senses heightened. In human form, I still had better hearing, sight, and scent than non-supes, but in my wolf, it was a whole different ballpark. The world became livelier and more vivid. In a way, it felt as if I'd been in a haze, walking around in my human skin, and the second I shifted, the fog cleared, allowing me to see the world without a filter.

I gave the crow a wary glance before taking off and stretching my legs. Trotting through the brush and tangle of weeds, I did a bit of exploring, mapping my way and familiarizing myself with certain smells or landmarks. Each hill I glided over and every mile I put between Nana's house and myself allowed the air in my lungs to move freer. The woods were like a maze or an obstacle course for me to conquer, dodging, ducking, and dashing through the terrain.

A mile into my run, I noticed the crow from before followed me. His wings beat through the air as he weaved in and out of the canopy of trees. Occasionally, I heard his caw.

I imagined what this place would look like in the dead of winter, branches dipped in ice and frost, the ground a blanket of endless white snow, fat flakes falling lazily from the sky, and the frigid cold filling my lungs. Such a contrast to the plush ground under my paws covered in twigs and moss. I loved autumn, but the painting of winter my mind conjured made me wistful for those colder months.

The deeper I ran into the woods, the darker the space between the trees and bushes became as the sun disappeared. But it was too fast. I'd never seen night descend with such speed.

What the hell?

My front paws fumbled as I noticed that the lack of light wasn't just the evening falling. It was unnatural—as dark as the unexplained places in space.

I came to a skidding halt, dried leaves crunching under my claws as I dug them into the earth.

What the fuck? Are my eyes fading? Is something wrong with me?

Squawk.

The bastard crow dove toward me, his talons skidding over my spine, not hard enough to scratch but to grab my attention. As if I wasn't already suddenly on alert. I didn't need a bird fucking with me.

Squawk, squawk, the winged asshole cried again with an air of fear or panic, but it was enough to raise my alarm, trickles of unease. He swooped down toward me again, and this time I waited until he got close and then whirled around, snapping at the bird in the air.

It was only a warning. My sharp teeth hadn't touched him. The crow hovered a second before flapping off and perching on a branch above my head.

The woods plunged into silence, and that was when I heard it. Or maybe I felt that I wasn't alone at first. Regardless, someone else was out here in the woods with me. My tail twitched as my ears picked up the breathing of another living creature.

A spot of worry pressed at the base of my spine. Perhaps running in the unfamiliar woods alone at night had not been my smartest idea. I was starting to wonder if there was anywhere safe in Riverbridge. No matter where I went, some form of trouble greeted me.

Whoever lurked in the shadows was doing a fantastic job cloaking themselves. It also didn't help that the moon chose tonight to hide behind the clouds; not a trace of light beamed through the leaves.

The crow started screeching as if he wanted to warn me. I got the fucking message and began to backtrack, relying on my senses to pick up familiar scents on the trail. I wasn't running but simply giving them a chance to follow me. If they did... well, we would have a problem.

It had been a hot minute since I'd been in a tussle, but I wasn't a weak wolf. There was a reason I'd been chosen as Liam's mate. Why it had been me and not any other female wolf in my pack.

And if this jackass kept tailing me, he was about to find out.

I didn't know what the fuck was up with these woods, but I made a mental note to ask Nana. The closer I drew to her house, the lighter the darkness became, lifting like a veil of mist.

When I put enough distance between my stalker and me, I waited until I dipped over a hill and darted behind a tree, waiting for the prick to pass by. Then he would be mine.

I never forgot a face.

The wind chose that moment to shift, bringing with it another new scent—a wolf.

No. It can't be.

Before I had a chance to process that another shifter wasn't far from me, my attention snapped to the whiz of what sounded like an arrow slicing through the air. I had a sinking feeling about where the arrow was headed and who its intended target was.

Fu—

Something rammed into my side, sending me tumbling over the brush, but I didn't topple alone. The wolf rolled with me until we both came to a stop. I pounced on top of him to keep him from running off.

Thud.

Above my head, an arrow embedded into thick bark, bits of debris showering to the ground.

Not an arrow.

A dart.

Pulling my eyes from the syringe that could have ended up in me instead of a tree, I glanced down at the wolf who had saved me and stared into those aqua eyes I'd been avoiding for days.

Liam?

Had he been following me as well? What was the chance that he would be in the woods at the same time, especially since he was supposed to be at a football game? Or had it ended already? Honestly, I had no idea what time it was.

His fur was snow white and made his eyes look like ice crystals. I'd always been a smaller wolf, but next to Liam, I felt like a child. Under my paws, muscles rippled, a show of strength and discipline.

I'd never seen Liam in his wolf form, and as far as I knew, he had never seen me in mine. And now we couldn't stop staring at each other. Not the best time to be enamored by the other when someone in the woods was hunting wolves like he was goddamn Michael Meyers.

I had to admit, though, I did feel like one of those girls being chased through the forest in a horror story. It was time to snap the fuck out of it. I was a predator, not prey.

Despite being an apex predator, wolves were still hunted by other animals like bears or tigers, but our biggest threat was humans. If there was a pack in town, you'd better believe hunters weren't far away. Back home, my father had wolves patrol the woods nightly. It was a kill-or-be-killed relationship. They showed us no mercy, and my father had always had the same attitude in return.

But not all packs operated the same. I didn't know how Liam's father dealt with hunters. Or if they even made an effort to keep River-bridge free of threats. It wasn't easy to pick out a hunter. They were human, after all, and looked like everyone else. It wasn't until situations like this arose that their identity became known.

That reminder had me springing into action. Liam was a second behind as if he, too, had the same realization. We needed to see the hunter's face, at the very least. Catching him would be ideal.

Whirling around, I jumped off Liam as he scrambled to his feet, both of us scanning the woods. Using all my senses, I reached out, looking, listening, feeling, and smelling for something that didn't belong. If Liam hadn't been behind me, I would have used my sixth sense, but because it was something that very few wolves had and I didn't yet trust my future mate, I locked down that mystical part of me.

I doubt it would have made a difference. Whoever this hunter was, he was long gone or possessed camouflaging skills that went beyond anything I had ever come across. Either way, I suspected our paths would cross again.

He'd failed in killing me. Or perhaps Liam had been his target. That made way more sense, seeing as he was the current alpha's son and next in line, whereas I was no one in the Riverbridge pack. Not yet.

When I turned back around to deal with Liam, he was gone. Not a trace of him anywhere, leaving me once again alone with so many unanswered questions in my head.

$$)) \bullet (($$

NANA HAD BEEN in bed when I returned, and although exhaustion crashed into me the last mile or two in the woods, I couldn't sleep. And I fucking tried hard. My body wasn't the problem. Every inch of me was plenty tired, except for my mind. That little bitch was running an endless marathon.

The few times I had managed to doze off, my disturbing dreams woke me up shortly after.

As I tossed and turned, my mind relived those moments in the woods, but the ending always turned out differently and a hell of a lot more terrifying. There was one where I'd been captured. Another had my blood spilling into the earth, dying alone. One where a blade hit Liam's heart, killing the mate I never accepted. Each scenario left me shaken, angry, and conflicted about my emotions.

Why had Liam taken off? Why had he been there at all? Had he been tracking the hunter? Or following me?

I shook my head. I would have felt Liam if he'd been tailing me. Unless he masked his scent, which I could confirm he hadn't; when I'd been on top of him, all I could smell was the heir prince.

What I really wanted to know was who the hunter had been. I cursed myself until morning for not having at least gotten a glimpse of the asshole's face. Not even a whiff of his scent. It was like he was a ghost.

Now all I had to do was hope our paths crossed again so I could identify the hunter who didn't just threaten me but the pack. I might not be a member yet, but Nana was, and that was enough to make me want to sink my claws into his heart. If he got anywhere near her, the bastard would find himself without a pulse.

Still early when I gave up on sleep—early for me, anyway—I tossed the covers aside. Nana preferred the wee hours of the morning over late nights. In that we were opposites.

She had just come in from the garden when I moseyed my way into the kitchen looking like the walking dead, my eyes puffy, my face swollen. With clumsy movements, I dropped into a chair. "Coffee," I moaned scratchily.

"The run didn't help yesterday?" she asked, noticing my zombie state as she washed the fruits and vegetables she'd picked from the garden.

Slouching against the chair, I frowned. "It did. And you were right. The land is beautiful." It wasn't home, but that was also what made it interesting, leaving me eager to explore more. "I just ran into a little bit of trouble."

"Oh?" she exclaimed, lifting a brow. Turning off the water, she left her basket in the sink and moved to the coffee maker. "Do tell, dear. It's been a while since I've had any trouble."

I rolled my eyes. She thought I meant boy trouble, a.k.a. Liam. He was involved, so she wasn't totally off. "Are there many hunters in Riverbridge?"

She set a hot mug of coffee on the table in front of me. "As far as I know, there hasn't been a hunter attack in…" Pausing a stretch to work through her memories, she reached for the sugar and cream set to push toward me. "It's been a while. More than a decade. It actually might have been the year you and Liam were born."

The birth of an alpha would be the perfect time for hunters to come out of the woodwork. That would have been at least seventeen years ago. "That long, huh?" I mused.

Nana pulled out a chair and sat down at the table with me. She had her long dark hair pulled up into a neat bun high on the crown of her head. The white tee she wore scooped at the neckline, a turquoise stone dangling from a gold chain around her neck. Her long, flowy skirt fluttered at her ankles as she crossed her legs. Her cheeks and nose were sun-kissed from the morning sun, and she smelled like dawn, full of warmth, fresh-cut gardenias, and hints of something citrus. I could inhale her scent all day. "Why do you ask?" Specks of worry entered her purplish-gray eyes.

I poured heaps of cream and sugar into my cup, stirring the contents. I didn't want to alarm her, but I would only be putting off what she would find out from Liam's father. He would have gone home and told the regional prince that a hunter was in the woods. I found at an early age that lying when you're in a pack always backfired. "I crossed paths with one in the woods during my run," I informed.

The dab of concern in her eyes spread. "Were you hurt?"

I shook my head. "No," I said, taking a careful sip of coffee and swallowing. "Liam was there." It pained me to admit that.

The distress in her expression quickly turned into interest. "Oh."

I cupped the warm mug. "And before you start jumping to absurd conclusions, we weren't secretly meeting in the woods."

"It wouldn't be that absurd if you were. He's your mate."

I groaned, pressing two fingers to my temple. Pretty sure before the morning was over, I'd have a headache. I didn't want to get into the topic of whether Liam would be my mate. "Regardless, he nearly got hit with a dart. I think."

Her dark brows rose. "You aren't sure?"

I chewed on the inside of my cheek as I thought back. "It all happened so quickly. I'm not sure who the hunter's target was."

Nana rapped her nails over the table, the bracelets on her wrists tinkling. "He might have followed one of you into the woods, but make no mistake, Kelsey, he would have killed you both."

She was right. I knew that. So why had he taken off? Why hadn't he stuck around to finish the job?

"I know your mom doesn't like to talk about this, but do you still have your sixth sense?" she asked, serious yet soft lines crinkling the corner of her eyes.

I nodded. "Yeah, but I'm rusty. I haven't used it in a very long time." Mainly because my mother didn't like it. It had been ingrained in me since I was little how dangerous it was for me to use that extra ability that most wolves didn't have.

"It doesn't matter how little or how often you use the gift. What matters is that you still feel it inside." She pressed a hand over her heart.

My mother didn't possess the extra sense, but Nana did. From what little I knew, this ability had been passed down maternally and often skipped a generation.

"It will keep you safe." Scooting her chair back, Nana stood and made her way to the sink to finish prepping the produce from the garden. "Would you mind running into town for me and grabbing a few ingredients from the store for dinner tonight?"

I took a long drink of coffee, wishing there was a quicker way to get the caffeine into my veins. "Sure. What do you need?"'

She rattled off her list, which I quickly put into my phone so I wouldn't forget. I added one additional item.

Get answers.

SIX

The heart of Riverbridge looked like something printed on a postcard. You wouldn't find a Nordstrom, Bloomingdale's, or any high-end store. The town was damn lucky to have a fucking Target. Yet it did have a charming quality to the streets lined with mostly locally owned small businesses. Part of the allure was that the shopping centers weren't all constructed to look alike and filled with the same stores.

Maneuvering my car through the weekend traffic on Park Street, I pulled into the grocery store, scanning the lot for a spot. Being that it was early Saturday afternoon, the place was busy, everyone dashing to get their groceries before the hectic week began.

I hadn't bothered to put on makeup after a quick shower and had tossed on a comfy pair of joggers with a tank. It seemed highly unlikely that anyone at school would be shopping at Fairway Foods this time of day.

Grabbing a basket on my way into the store, I started for the pasta aisle only to be distracted by the haircare products. I swore they strategically put all the beauty and personal care items in the front of the store, forcing you to walk through those sections first. That way you ended up buying shit you didn't need. It was like the items in the checkout line, tempting you. For me,

the bait was new shampoo, a bottle of nail polish in a shade I probably had ten of at home, or skincare. I was a fucking sucker for face products.

After spending way too much time looking at lipsticks and smelling shampoos and conditioners, I hauled up my basket filled with shit I shouldn't have been buying and turned the corner right into another body.

My nose rammed into a firm chest, smashing it a little too hard. I hissed, trying not to swear as I backed up, except two hands gripped my shoulders, keeping me from moving.

What the hell?

I glanced up and wished I hadn't.

The fingers wrapped around the basket handled tightened as I stared up into Liam's face. His hard gaze pinned mine, a deep scowl marring his lips. Those icy eyes roamed over my face. I forced my focus to stay on his eyes, fearing that I might glance at his mouth again and never look away.

Why him?

Why does my path seem to constantly cross with his?

Most people would probably consider it a blessing to have such an intense and physical attraction to the person you were to marry. I hated that my body betrayed me whenever Liam was nearby. It made me want to fight whatever response this was within me twice as hard. The problem was I never had the time or the clear-headedness to dissect all the things happening to me. Anger often took over. It was the quickest emotion to latch onto, and I clung to it like it was a damn lifesaver in the middle of the ocean during a storm.

My chin firmed, as did the rest of my body. "You can let go of me now."

He blinked as if it just occurred to him who I was, and I remembered my bare face. A silent groan rolled inside me, along with a few colorful choice words.

Liam forked a hand through his hair, letting his other hand fall to his side. "What are you doing here?" he demanded.

I angled my head to the side and lifted my basket slightly. "Shopping," I replied, not concealing the sarcasm in my tone.

Did the corner of his mouth just twitch? Surely not.

What were the chances that I ran into Liam two days in a row? My suspicious nature didn't like those odds, no matter how small River-bridge might be.

"Are you following me?" I blurted.

He let out a bitter snort. "Don't flatter yourself. You're not the only one who eats food in this town."

"It's just that you were in the woods yesterday, and now today... It seems fishy," I said, feeling the need to defend myself.

"What were you doing alone last night?" he demanded, eyes narrowing.

If he thought to deter me with a question, it failed. I still thought he was following me whether he chose to admit it or not. Shifting my weight to the other foot, I dropped the basket on the floor, predicting this conversation would swiftly blow into a fight. Would this be our first or second fight? Did the one on the rooftop count? It didn't matter. What I did, where I went, and with who was none of Liam's damn business. I opened my mouth to tell him just that, but the bastard cut me off.

"And before you tell me it's not my business, it is. What happens to you while you're in *my* town is my concern. You're under the protection of *my* pack, regardless of how much we both might not like it." He took a step closer, forcing my neck back farther to continue meeting his gaze. "And coming from someone who's directly responsible for your safety, stay out of the woods, *pup.*"

I hated the reminder of last night. A snapshot of his wolf clearly came into mind. I poked him in the chest. "Cute, but we're not giving each other nicknames."

A lady and her shopping cart rolled by. Liam waited until she left the row before he replied. "You're right. Pup isn't quite right. Twinkle toes, perhaps?" He flashed me a lopsided grin that did unspeakable things to my heart.

Fucker. "Not unless you want to lose your front teeth. Haven't you heard? I bite."

The bastard actually smiled, a full smile graced with dimples that sparked something like desire. *No fucking way.* "Ah, Kelsey, what the hell am I to do with you?"

I fought to keep my breathing even. "Nothing. I'm not part of your pack."

He lifted his hand, grabbing a strand of hair that had come untucked and wrapping it around his finger. "Aren't you, though? You being here is as good as sealing the deal."

Did his nearness intimidate me? Yes. Was I going to let it show? Fuck no. And I was pretty sure it was intimidation fluttering around in my belly. Not something else. Something like desire. "And that pisses you off?"

"No," he replied with just a hint of snarl. "Yes."

This time I grinned. "Which is it?"

Those striking aqua eyes started to glow as he released my hair. "Clearly I bother you. Why did you come, then?"

The million-dollar question. My face grew somber. "Same as you. It's my duty."

Something in his expression changed. "As long as we're clear on that."

He'd drawn a line in our relationship. I was nothing but a duty to him, like taking out the trash, so I shouldn't expect anything more from him.

"Crystal clear," I assured him, moving around the sudden lump that formed in my throat. It shouldn't be there, and I couldn't figure out why I felt so glum.

Nothing was going according to plan.

I was supposed to get him to hate me, not be so damn practical that it left a sour taste in my mouth. Everything about our relationship felt stiff and informal.

"Can I go now, Your Highness?" I bit out. "Or was there more you wanted to scold me for?"

"I'm serious about the woods. It's not safe," he warned, sounding too much like my overprotective father.

"I'm a wolf, in case you've forgotten." Running in the woods was second nature next to breathing. I needed it as much as I needed oxygen.

"I haven't. It's impossible to forget considering your name is all I hear lately."

"How's that my fault?" I challenged, my voice rising as my blood pressure did.

Liam's bright eyes glanced around the store. "Chill out before you create a scene."

"As if you wouldn't love that," I snapped, frowning.

A cocky brow lifted. "I would, but if our parents found out..." He let the threat dangle. "And I prefer you with the makeup." Then the prick brushed past me, walking away.

My mouth dropped fully open, and I whirled, intending to tell Liam Castle to fuck off, but Leith was there behind me, his eyes volleying between his brother's retreating form and my gaping expression.

"I'm going to kill your brother," I growled, the promise vibrating in my throat.

Leith chuckled. "I'm sure you're not the only person to make that threat."

I had to kick something. Anything. My toe hit the basket I'd dropped on the floor, sending it sailing down the aisle with all my shit in it. "God, he's the most frustrating male alive."

Leith, being the nice guy he was, retrieved my items and walked them back to me. "Are you okay? I heard about the incident in the woods." He shook his head, disbelief dulling the normal sparkling in his eyes. "I can't believe we have a hunter."

"Could be hunters," I added without thinking. It occurred to me that if there hadn't been any attacks since Liam and I were born, then Leith and many of the other wolves our age had never experienced what it was like to be hunted by humans. I was envious of that oblivious fear. They would learn soon enough.

Leith's interest was understandable. "Our father's taking care of it. You don't need to worry."

A chill stole over me. "I wish that were true," I mumbled, snatching the handle on my basket. I had too many worries running like sprinters in my head.

He walked beside me as I made my way to the pasta. "Besides, what can happen when you have my big brother watching over you?"

Smartass. I rolled my eyes. A lot. "I don't need a babysitter."

"Your father was very specific in his request."

"He would be," I muttered, scanning the boxes and bags of noodles. Had my father asked Rowan, Liam's father, to put a guard on me? Was that why Liam was in the woods? Dad had never done so before, but I'd always been in *his* territory.

I finally found the pasta Nana requested, and Leith took my basket from me to carry. I didn't resist, my head too full of thoughts. He followed me as I headed to the bakery for a fresh loaf of bread. "In case my brother failed to mention it, our mom wants you over for dinner."

I halted in the middle of the refrigerated goods and tilted my head at Leith. "Dinner?" I exclaimed, taken aback even though I shouldn't have been. Of course they would want to see me. I was their future daughter-in-law. Though I'd assumed it would be at the moon ceremony where I would be introduced to the pack as Liam's future mate.

He nodded. "It's not a big deal or a formal event, so don't stress," he added, seeing my face blanch.

"Leith," Liam growled a few feet away, looking on the verge of losing his patience, drawing my attention. "Let's go," he told his brother, sparing me nothing but a fleeting glare.

"Wear something sexy." Leith winked, dropping my basket beside my feet. "I'll be in the car," he told Liam. "Don't trash the place."

Liam started to turn to follow his brother.

Oh no. He wasn't leaving. I wasn't done with the heir prince yet.

I stepped into his path before those long strides took him away. "When were you going to tell me about dinner?" I demanded, fisting my hands at my sides.

He scowled. "I wasn't." His frown deepened. "You don't have to come."

"You mean you don't want me to go? Message received," I replied snottily.

His eyes never left my face. It was like staring into a frozen ocean. Cold as fuck and endless. "Why are you putting words into my mouth?"

"Because you don't say a whole lot. Not to me," I snapped.

"Isn't that what you want? Why you dress like you're a vampire slave?" His eyes raked over me from head to toe, reminding me that I had left the house without my guise.

Being called out by him had my blood pressure rising. I scoffed. "Hardly. I like the way I dress." I would rather die than admit the clothing had been a ruse.

His eyes flashed, nostrils flaring. "So do I. And that's the problem."

Stunned, I blinked, unsure if I heard him correctly.

Fuck me. This was not part of the plan. He had to be messing with me, trying to rattle my composure, or using some kind of reverse psychology babble. Well, it wasn't going to work.

"I thought redheads were more your type," I sneered.

"So did I," he said tersely. "Turns out it doesn't matter what you wear, what color your hair is, or how much you loathe me. It's your smell."

My chin jutted out as I swallowed. "What about it?"

He shook his head. "Nothing. It doesn't matter. Seven o'clock. Next Sunday. You're not obligated to be there. In fact, I don't want you there, but I know it would mean a lot to my mom."

I'd been right about the headache. The dull pain had moved into a killer throb. "God, you have such a way with words. Really know how to make a girl feel special."

"Is that a yes?"

"Fine. Do I need your approval on my attire?"

He moved in close, trapping me between his body and the shelf at my back. "Come naked for all I care."

Under the intensity of his eyes, a faint warmth stole over my cheeks, followed by a hot line of anger that cut through me.

Could Liam Castle be any more of a dick?

Grabbing the basket Leith had left beside me, I gave Liam a sinister grin. "You wish. The only way you'll see me naked is in your dreams."

And with that wonderful parting statement, I stomped off to the self-checkout. I needed to get the hell out of Fairway Foods before I destroyed the place.

SEVEN

On Monday morning, I told myself this was just another week for me to do some damage. Liam wouldn't know what hit him. If my appearance alone wasn't enough to discourage him, then I needed a new tactic.

No way would the alpha's son take a slut as his mate. I didn't intend to sleep around; I just had to make Liam think I was hitting it with every guy in school.

The football team seemed like the perfect place to start. Not only were they horny jocks, but they loved nothing more than to brag about their conquests in the locker room. Just how would Liam like hearing my name passed around on his teammates' lips?

Why did the prospect of pissing him off actually make me smile?

Something was wrong with me. I shouldn't take this much pleasure in making another wolf upset—except somehow getting under Liam's skin was fucking entertaining. He had this too-serious exterior that made me want to mess up his orderly life. I doubted he ever had a day of pure fun for himself. How sad and pathetic.

Well, he might not have fun, but I sure as hell would.

I grinned the entire drive to school, giggling to myself like a crazy person.

Right up until I parked my car and got out.

What I hadn't anticipated seeing so freaking early in the morning was Sabrina Thompson clinging to Liam like she was made of Saran wrap.

You have got to fucking kidding me.

And just like that, my good mood went down the drain, much like Sabrina's tongue going down on *my* mate.

I shook my head. Not mine. Okay, on paper, Liam was mine. Did that count?

And she wasn't going down on him technically, but given the opportunity, she would have been all over Liam's dick. It was so clear to see, and her obvious desperation made me sick. Did she actually believe he would make someone like her baroness?

Liam leaned against the side of his truck, Sabrina pressing every inch of her body into his, including her perky tits.

Snorting in disgust, I hugged my laptop closer to my chest. I didn't want to see this, but just as I took a step away from my car, Sabrina's cunning eyes flicked over Liam's shoulder at me. She slid her fingers into his hair, a smug smile curling over her frosted peach lips.

I'm going to choke the bitch.

Sabrina and I had barely exchanged words, but I knew I had made an enemy before I'd ever stepped foot on campus. She had no intention of giving up Liam, and seeing that smug expression on her face kindled my temper.

Sabrina lifted on her toes, a twisted seductress smirk on her lips as she pressed them to Liam's. He didn't push her away, but he also didn't kiss her back—not like a guy who was into her would have, not like a boyfriend. He remained still, letting her rub her mouth over his, trying to draw him in.

His hands remained shoved into his pockets as Sabrina made an absolute fool of herself.

Something hot worked its way up my throat. My fingers tightened against my laptop, nails digging into the metal. If I used any more pressure, I might snap the thing in half—I was surprised I hadn't already. I was supposed to be the one making him jealous, not the other way around.

You are not jealous. No fucking way.

It wasn't that Liam had a girlfriend. It was who she was. Of all the girls in the school, why had he gone for her?

Questions I shouldn't give a shit about.

I refused to let Liam outdo me. This was not how things were supposed to play out.

After what felt like an eternity, Sabrina finally broke off the kiss, letting her heels drift back down to the ground. But the bitch made sure her eyes shifted to mine. The triumph in her expression begged me to slam her pretty face into the blacktop. Or against the glass window of Liam's trunk. Either would work, and my damn fingers twitched. *Shit.* I thought I might have even taken a step forward, murder running through my veins.

Liam followed her gaze, noticing me for the first time, and our eyes met. It could have been for only a mere second, or time could have just stalled. It was impossible to tell, but all I could do was stare at him. How could a single look feel so much more intimate than the kiss he had shared a moment ago with another girl?

I didn't have time to lecture myself, but I would definitely be having a stern conversation with my body, heart, and mind once I was far from Liam Castle.

My heart soared, thumping wildly in my chest.

I shouldn't react. I shouldn't show any emotion. I needed to be impervious. The heir prince had to believe I didn't give a shit where he put his mouth. Nothing he did hurt me.

Too bad I didn't work that way.

Two could play this game.

The jealousy act... I knew this well.

"Kelsey, hey, I—"

I didn't think. My emotions were in control now.

Spinning at the sound of the male voice, I grabbed the front of his shirt and hauled him to me. Right before my mouth slanted over his, I caught a flash of startled aqua eyes, but it was too late to stop myself by the time recognition made its way to my brain.

An f-bomb went off in my head, but there was no point in stopping this charade. It hadn't been my intention to create a problem between brothers, but since I was here, I might as well make the best of it. Perhaps this was the push I needed to shove Liam off the edge. Surely he would hate me beyond reason now.

Leith's lips were warm and soft. He didn't apply pressure, but he also didn't stop kissing me. My fingers stayed on his shirt, but I lessened the intensity of my grip, my laptop smashed between us in my other hand. It was a nice kiss, much like how I had felt with Huntley.

But as much as I wanted to feel something, anything, all that registered through my body was pleasant friendship. It made me want to end the kiss quickly and drop my forehead on his shoulder, seeking support and comfort. Leith was someone you could lean on.

Easing back, I blinked up at him, an apology shimmering in my eyes.

"How did I do?" Leith whispered, the edge of his mouth lifting, drawing my gaze in confusion.

He isn't pissed?

My eyes flicked up. Mischief danced in his. He had gotten over the surprise and understood the real reason for my impromptu kiss. Leith wasn't mad. He hadn't shoved me away or embarrassed me in front of the entire school—in front of his brother and the witch.

"I'm sorry," I replied softly, meaning it. I didn't want to use Leith. He had been nothing but a friend to me.

God, I know how to really fuck things up.

Leith tucked a piece of hair behind my ear. "I told you I'd help you, and I meant it if this is what you truly don't want."

He meant Liam. If I truly didn't want his brother.

I took a step back, and in that fraction of time, Leith was suddenly pinned against my car, Liam clutching his shirt. I stared in disbelief. *What the—*

The heir prince's nostrils flared as he got in his brother's face, the center of his eyes glowing like stars at night. "What the fuck do you think you're doing?"

"I could ask you the same thing," Leith tossed back. "Parading Brina around in front of her. Do you have no conscience? Or is faithfulness not part of the Liam code?"

Liam flinched. "Don't interfere."

"Don't be an asshole and I wouldn't have to," Leith said, shaking his head as if disappointed in his brother.

I didn't want them to fight. Not over me. I might be many things, but a family wrecker was not one of them. I knew getting out of the treaty would be difficult, and I would have to do some questionable things, but seeming Liam and Leith like this... I had to find another way.

They glared at each other, breaths away from a brawl.

"She's mine," Liam growled.

Leith shoved at his brother's chest, hard enough to push him back a step. "Then start acting like it."

I wedged myself between them, careful of the laptop I still had in my hand. "I'm not yours," I gritted at Liam. The denial flew out of my mouth before I realized what I'd said and in front of whom. Fucking everyone. Color stained my cheeks, making them hot. I wanted to drop my head. I wanted a spaceship to fly over and abduct me. I wanted anything other than to be here, making a spectacle in front of the whole school.

Liam's head tilted toward me. "Aren't you?" he countered arrogantly with an irritating lift of his brow.

My chin went up a fraction of an inch. "I'll never be yours," I vowed vehemently.

His lips curled, and I wanted to slap him. "We both know that's a lie. In two months, that's exactly what you'll be. Mine." He made sure to keep his voice low enough so only those who were shifters might hear and understand the insinuation in his warning. No one else was to touch me unless they wanted to deal with Liam's wrath. Everyone else would be left wondering what he said that had my eyes darkening.

Why did that statement sound so damn possessive? Why did his words ring inside me? Why did they make my blood hum? Why didn't I feel disgusted? Why did a trill of excitement ribbon through me?

Unless either of us found a way out of this treaty without tarnishing the relationship between packs, I would, in fact, be claimed by Liam.

Like I'd lost my damn mind, I stepped forward, invading Liam's space. I ignored the sensations dancing up and down my spine from being this close to him. "A lot can happen in two months."

The corner of his mouth tugged in a deep scowl as he murmured, "That's what worries me."

His scent, his breath, it made my head swim. I glanced at his mouth, reminding myself where it had been only minutes ago, needing to hold on to that surge of anger as it rose within me.

We had drawn a crowd. Lingering in the parking lot, our peers watched and waited to see what the Castle brothers or I would do next. I sensed Leith off to my left. "You should be worried," I spat. "And for the record, I don't give a shit who you hook up with. Fuck whomever you want. I plan to."

Liam's gaze went wholly dark.

Good. I'd finally hit a fucking button. One I planned to keep on pushing.

I felt very self-satisfied, like I had somehow gotten the upper hand— I didn't really believe I had, but I was faking it till I made it.

Having put on enough of a show for one day, I tucked my laptop under my arm and pivoted on my heels to leave.

A firm hand latched onto my arm, jerking me back so fast he could have given me whiplash if I were human. The laptop slipped from my grasp, crashing to the ground with a wincing clatter. It split in two, the screen shattering on impact along with what I was sure were other important bits.

Liam imprisoned me between the car and his body.

My eyes closed briefly as I attempted to gain control of myself. This would definitely put a damper on my studies today. One of us had to be levelheaded, and seeing as how Liam's actions were rash and irresponsible, that someone would have to be me. A joke. I was the least calm person. If someone had seen the way he'd moved at speeds faster than normal, we were all screwed. Then again, maybe Riverbridge was used to the strange and unusual. Its reputation for wolf activity was what kept tourists away.

This whole situation was overwhelming.

Liam was overwhelming.

You can handle him. He's just a guy, I did my best to convince myself. It helped not to think of the heir prince as an alpha but as an ordinary dude, like all the other ones in school—the ones now whispering and murmuring.

But staring into his eyes burning like crystals of fire, it was impossible to see him as anything but who he was. Powerful. Strong. Arrogant. Dominating. Alpha asshole.

"Liam," Leith called darkly, putting a hand on his brother's shoulder. "Enough. Let her go."

The heir prince's eyes never strayed from mine. "Leave," he ordered Leith, his tone permitting no other option. "This is between Kelsey and me."

I dragged my gaze from Liam's murderous one and nodded at Leith, letting him know I was fine. I wasn't scared of Liam. He wouldn't hurt me. At least, I was pretty fucking sure he wouldn't.

"You might want to take this discussion somewhere more private," Leith suggested before he left.

Liam suddenly became aware of the crowd. "Get in the car," he growled.

It probably wasn't wise to keep poking the bear—or in this instance, the wolf—but control had always been a problem for me. I had to work too fucking hard not to lose my shit daily. That went for everything. My emotions. Burying my sixth sense. Hiding my identity from humans. The list went on.

Perhaps it was me Liam shouldn't poke too many times.

Had there ever been a fight between an alpha and a baroness? I wasn't sure. I hated history and paid even less attention to shifter legends and the footprints left behind by our ancestors.

I folded my arms, firming my stance as my lips pulled into a straight line. "No. I don't have anything else to say to you."

He took a deep breath, his chest brushing against my arms. "I think we need to set some ground rules."

"I don't give a shit about your *rules*."

His jaw tightened. "Kelsey," he ground out, exasperation in his features.

The bell blared, buzzing loudly and annoyingly over the parking lot. We had five minutes to get our asses to first period. The throng of students began to disperse. It wouldn't be long until I was left alone with the heir prince, something I wanted to avoid at all costs.

"We're going to be late for class. And you owe me a new computer." I ducked under his arm and quickly took off toward school before he could try to grab me again, merging with the herd.

I had to get away from him. Even when he behaved like a total jerk, I couldn't ignore the sheer male of him, his stunning eyes, the golden skin, and his defined cheeks. He was attractive, no matter how much I wished otherwise.

Pissing Liam off had been exactly what I wanted.

So then why the fuck did I feel so... weird about it? I refused to admit that what I felt could be guilt or remorse.

While everyone else piled in through the front doors, I snuck off to the side, edging along the brick wall until I came to the winding stairs that went to the roof. This time I didn't go up but went under, crouching down as I waited for the final bell to sound.

What was the point of going to class? I had no laptop. A pathetic excuse, but it was all I needed to convince myself to ditch school today. Every encounter with Liam left me rattled, mad as hell, and confused.

I waited until the parking lot cleared out other than a few stragglers who obviously had the same thought as me to skip school. It made me wonder why they'd shown up at all. Maybe they each had a Liam in their life too.

Scooting out from under the stairs, I dusted off my clothes. If anyone from my other school saw me right now, they wouldn't have recognized me.

Hell, I didn't recognize myself.

It wasn't just that my appearance had changed, but I was hiding under the stairs and isolating myself. I was social. I loved people. And hanging out with my friends. Parties. I was the never-say-no girl; if something was happening, I wanted to be at the center of it.

Not anymore. Not here.

Jogging back to my car, I stared down at the shattered laptop. With a sigh, I bent down and collected as many pieces as I could to dispose of later. Dread tumbled within me as I thought about having to explain to my dad why I needed a new computer the second week of school.

Not a conversation I wanted to have. He would not be pleased to learn that his daughter and future son-in-law weren't getting along.

Avoidance was becoming second nature.

Liam.

Now my father.

Tossing the broken-ass junk into my passenger seat along with my bag, I got behind the wheel and started the car. I had no idea where I was going. I couldn't go to Nana's, although she would have welcomed me, made me tea, and eventually found a crafty way to get me to tell her what happened. She was damn good at getting people to unload their shit without them realizing it. She should have been a therapist.

I had about five minutes before campus security did their routine check through the parking lot. With no destination in mind, I drove. Taking a right out of the school parking lot, then hooking a left onto River Road, I followed the river. I should have been concerned about the repercussions of skipping, but I wasn't. Detention was no foreign concept to me. Not that I particularly liked spending extra time at school, but sometimes the risks were worth the consequences.

Today it was my sanity at risk.

Four or five blocks later, a prickling sensation ran across my neck, that tickling awareness of being followed—by a wolf, no less.

My eyes darted to the rearview mirror, spotting a truck. And not just any truck.

Liam's.

That fucker.

Can't he take a hint? I don't want to see him. Not ten minutes ago and not now.

What I wanted was a few hours alone with my toxic thoughts. Was that too fucking much to ask for?

I stomped on my brakes without any notice and jammed the car into Park. In two seconds, I was out of the car, storming to the truck almost kissing my bumper. Liam hurled out of the vehicle, slamming the door shut on the truck with such force it shook.

I didn't need to glance at his face to see the anger there; it radiated in pulsing waves, making the air heavier the closer I got to him. Any other wolf would have halted in their tracks, bowed their head, or turned back. Despite how uncomfortable it felt, I pushed forward.

"What do you want from me?" I launched at him like my words were a weapon powered by all my frustrations, fears, and anger. His truck's engine purred, my voice carrying over the gentle rumble.

Eyes sparkling under the sunlight, he declared, "We need to talk."

He'd said so earlier, but I guess my bluntness hadn't been clear enough for him. "What makes you think *I* want to talk to you?"

"This time I'm not giving you a choice."

As if. *A choice!* Who did he think he was?

I opened my mouth with every intention of telling Liam Castle to go fuck himself, but instead of the words spitting from me, a rush of air left my lungs as he picked me up and hauled me over his shoulder.

Appalled and shocked at finding myself upside down and staring at Liam's back, my reaction time was hampered. Otherwise, I would have dropped him to the ground the moment he touched me. That was what I told myself, because I might have blacked out for those few seconds, but my sanity returned quickly.

"What are you doing? Put me the hell down. Now," I growled through the strands of dark hair that had gotten stuck on my glossy lips. The wolf inside me howled.

When he started walking, I started to fight.

"You can scream, curse, and kick all you want, but you're getting into the truck even if I have to hold you upside down all day."

"I'll bite you. I swear to God I will," I threatened.

The heir prince came to a dead stop in front of his truck's passenger door, his body stiffening underneath me, which only made me aware of the muscle under his skin.

Someone give me a damn break.

"If you bite me, pup, just know that I bite back."

Did he have to say that in such a fucking sensual way, like he was dying to sink his teeth into me? For wolves, the matter of biting had different meanings, but there was no mistaking the contrast between my implication and his.

Mine had been a threat.

Liam's sounded like a promise.

If either Liam or I did bite the other hard enough to pierce the skin and draw blood, we'd have bigger problems.

Again, he took advantage of momentarily stunning me and threw open the door, tossing me inside. My head whirled in his direction, a mass of dark hair flying in the air around me. I bared my teeth, letting my wolf show.

Liam chuckled, a deep, sexy rumble. "Stay," he ordered like I was a damn dog, further pissing me off. If I weren't confined in such a small space, I would have brought him to the ground and wiped that smug smirk from his lips.

He slammed the door shut and started to walk around the front of the car. Foolish to think I would obediently stay put. My hand flew to the door handle just as the locks clicked. I jerked my head toward Liam through the windshield. The bastard dangled the key fob in his hand, smirking smugly.

Liam Castle is so dead.

Opening his door, he slid into the truck and blew out a breath. "God, you really are a handful, aren't you, pup?"

Rage burned my throat. I stared straight ahead, watching the smoke from my exhaust curl over the truck's front bumper as I replied, "Do you want me to answer that?"

"No. Why did you leave school?"

"I needed space. From *you*," I added in case he didn't get the implication. "Stop following me."

A car swerved around us, laying on the horn. "You know I can't."

His car smelled like the woods, pine and earthy—like him. A pack of mint gum sat in the cupholder. It was all so overwhelming that my senses scattered, making my cheeks prickle with heat. "Why? Because of my father? Bullshit," I hissed.

He raked a hand through his hair. "You think I like this any more than you do? This was not how I thought I would be spending my senior year—babysitting."

Shifting in the seat, I angled toward him, my gaze landing on him. "Have you ever defied an order in your life?"

Liam's hands went to the steering wheel, twisting over the leather. "I've had seventeen years to come to terms with you being my mate.

Acting out, skipping school, changing your appearance—none of that is going to get you out of your duty. Trust me. I've tried."

I didn't buy for one second that he'd come to terms with having to claim me in a few months. He was just damn good at masking his emotions. Way better than I was. "What will, then?" I asked, a sliver of me hoping he would have an actual answer.

His mouth quirked to the side, a dimple appearing. "I'll let you know as soon as I figure it out."

I studied Liam's profile, trying to see past the tough-guy guise. "You don't want me, do you?"

His nostrils flared. "I never said that, but you've made it clear since the day you got here that you want nothing to do with me. I'm giving you the *space* you're looking for."

I had rejected him and continued to do so. So why did it feel like guilt and remorse were stabbing me in the gut? "Did my father tell you to be nice to me too?"

He snorted. "That would be my mother."

"Won't your *girlfriend* be upset you chased after me?" The jealousy I heard in my voice made me that much angrier. Why did I care so much?

"She isn't my girlfriend," he clarified.

My fingers gripped the sides of the seat. "Oh, just someone you fuck for fun, then? What's the difference?"

The centers of his aqua eyes smoldered. "You're not the only one with an agenda."

I raised a brow. "You thought I would see the two of you together and run home crying?"

"I might have underestimated you," he admitted.

"What do you propose we do?" I asked with sweet venom.

He sighed. "For starters, you could try being nicer."

I almost laughed. "Not going to happen."

"Why was that hunter following you?" he asked, changing topics. It threw me for a loop.

"Me?" My eyes searched his, thoughts racing through my head. So, it had been *me* the hunter had been stalking that night.

"Yes." He gave me a long look. "Did you know he was trailing you?"

"I did, but then when you appeared, I couldn't figure out if you were following me and he was following you or if you were both just stalking me."

Brows shades darker than his hair bunched together. "You have no idea what he wanted from you?"

"The same thing all hunters want. To kill me," I said, shrugging.

Liam shook his head. "It was a tranquilizer. He planned to capture you."

Disbelief caught my tongue briefly. "You're sure?" The idea of hunters capturing wolves turned my blood to ice. A shiver rolled through me, and dark, ugly thoughts circled in my head. I'd heard stories of torture and imprisonment. Being captured by a hunter only prolonged your death sentence.

The back of his head hit the leather seat, his expression somber and bleak. "I went back. I'm sure."

My stomach twisted. I did have a hunch, but I couldn't tell Liam. I had a secret that very few people knew. It was safer if he didn't know.

Tensing, he turned his turned toward me, suspicion edging into his features. "What aren't you telling me?"

As I twirled the bracelets on my wrist, my eyes met his and did not waver or blink, the key to telling a believable lie. "Nothing."

He reached out, taking a lock of my hair in his fingers. "I'll let that slide for now, but at some point, pup, I will find out. What I'm most curious about is what our parents are hiding from us."

Why does he keep touching me? Why do I let him? It was hard for me to remember what the hell he'd said. "What makes you think they're hiding something?" He wasn't alone in his doubts. My father had always been protective, but I thought he'd been exceedingly so months before I left. I'd just assumed it was his way of dealing with sending me away.

"When aren't they?" Liam muttered as he dragged my hair lightly between his fingers.

True. But his response didn't answer my question. Was he holding something back just as I was? What did Liam know about me? What did his family know? The protection of my secret had been so drilled into me for as long as I could remember that I couldn't imagine my father or mother would have told anyone. Not even my future in-laws or my mate.

But the secret would only be that until Liam claimed me. Once we were mated, it would be impossible to keep things from him and him from me. The link would connect our emotions, our thoughts, our hearts, our bodies, and our souls. It was part of the deal when you bound yourself to another wolf. And some bonds went deeper.

"If you know—" I started.

"Kelsey!"

Liam's voice roared in my head, something he shouldn't have been able to do as I wasn't part of his pack. Yet. His eyes went wide, trembling with... fear?

They weren't looking at me but over my shoulder.

I jerked my head to see what spurred such instant alarm and saw an approaching car. The full-throttle sound of its engine propelled my confusion into "oh shit" territory. It was headed straight for us, and all I could do was gape out the window.

EIGHT

We had only seconds before impact. For a wolf, seconds could save our lives if not wasted.

Liam didn't squander them. He reacted.

As my mouth opened to scream and I braced myself for a bone-jarring collision, the heir prince's arms came around me, strong and steady. Only feet away, the oncoming car steered so the bulk of the impact would hit directly where I was.

Those powerful hands lifted me out of my seat and hauled me to his side of the car into his lap. Before I could catch my breath, Liam twisted his body around me like a cocoon, turning to the side away from the impending crash, shielding me.

I squeezed my eyes shut, burying my face in his chest. I clamped onto his shirt for dear life as I reached for my powers, but time had run out.

The car hit the passenger corner of Liam's truck with an ear-piercing shrill, metal grinding and shrieking on metal. The truck lurched, the front of the car spinning like we were on the Teacups ride. Glass shattered, flying everywhere. His arms tightened around me, never flinching or wavering. He was like a fucking immovable force. I clung to him until the truck came to a jerking halt in the ditch.

His unshakable hands kept me secure in his arms—kept my head from hitting any part of the car.

Liam had saved my life. Again.

This was starting to become an unfortunate pattern—or fortunate, depending on how you looked at it.

My heart, which only seconds ago had stopped, now hammered in my chest. A metallic taste touched my tongue. The heir prince's chest heaved under my face. I was afraid to move, but being in his arms wasn't safe either. There was a different form of danger that lurked within the confines of his embrace.

I went to pull out of his hold, but Liam's arms remained solid around me. He inhaled and let out his breath in a long exhale. Only then did he slowly release me. I lifted my gaze to his as I eased back, still fully seated on his lap. Not that I had anywhere else to go. The spot where I had been was sunken in with an imprint of the other car's front end.

Flecks of green and blue glowed in Liam's gaze. "Are you okay? Are you hurt?" he murmured, those wolfish eyes roaming quickly and thoroughly over every inch of me.

Did he really expect me to be able to talk right now? Between the car hitting us and being on his lap, my brain literally stopped working. I needed a few minutes to collect my bearings, but the anguish in his voice told me I didn't have that kind of time. He wanted an answer. Now.

I nodded. It was the best I could do.

He ran his fingers through my hair, sending fragments of glass clattering over the car. "Stay here," he ordered, reaching for the door handle.

He isn't leaving me, is he? My breathing rough, I tried to calm down. "Wait!" I called out, wrapping my fingers around his forearm. "Are you sure you should be moving?" Smoke billowed from the other car's engine, drifting into Liam's truck.

"Don't move, Kelsey. I mean it." Tight tension lined his features. "I'm not asking. This is a direct order."

The *order* shifted something inside me, a slapping reminder of who he was, and despite the fact that he had just saved my life, I suddenly felt anything but gratitude. "Whatever you say, *princeling*," I huffed, irritated not just with him and his fucking orders but also with myself—for allowing myself to worry about him in a moment of weakness.

Liam seemed to want to say or do something more, but his lips turned down, and the door squeaked open. He lifted me just enough for him to scoot out of the truck and then deposited me onto the seat, leaving the door open. My heart faltered a beat watching him through the cracked windshield as he treaded to the other vehicle.

While I waited for a sign or a word from him, I inspected the damage to his truck. It was bad, and I honestly didn't know how Liam and I didn't end up seriously hurt.

He might be stronger than I gave him credit for. It was his quick movements that saved me from being crushed.

Impatient, shaken, and still freaked out, I lifted in the seat to locate Liam and winced. Pain lanced down the side of my leg. It wasn't severe, nothing that wouldn't heal in a few hours with rest. I should have been thankful for the few bruises.

"Are they okay?" I called through the broken passenger window. When he didn't respond immediately, I called his name. "Liam!"

"There's no one here," he finally said as I was about to hop out of the truck.

"What?" I had to have heard him wrong. A car didn't fucking drive itself. Unless it was a Tesla, but judging by the vehicle embedded in the side of Liam's truck, it wasn't that fancy. Not that I was an expert at cars or anything. "Did they get tossed out of the car?" I asked, a semi-reasonable explanation if you overlooked the fact that they most likely would have landed on the hood of the truck.

"I don't think so," he replied, sounding a little farther away. "The windshield only splintered. It didn't fully break."

Screw this.

I jumped out of the truck and instantly regretted it. The world went topsy-turvy, my legs not as steady or sure of themselves as they usually were. I flattened a hand onto the side of the truck for balance and waited for the trees, the sky, and the road to stop spinning.

Gruff fingers hauled me to his side. "What did I tell you?"

"Shhh," I replied, putting my other hand to the side of my head and leaning into his sturdy form.

"Do you ever listen?" The heir prince's voice softened but lost none of its harshness.

His warmth seeped into me, chasing the chill that had taken residency in my bones. "I don't need you to chide me for being concerned about your dumb ass."

His laugh was short and without humor, rumbling his chest. "I'm a dumbass, huh?"

"If the shoe—" I started to say, my gaze rising to his, but I got distracted by streaks of red running down the side of his face. "You're bleeding." My fingers shot to his chin, turning his head for me to inspect how deep the cut was. Once I got a good look, I felt the color drain from me.

"I'm fine," he said, clipped and terse, pulling away from my hand. "You shouldn't be standing. Christ, you look like you're about to pass out."

Am I going to pass out?

The sight of blood never bothered me before. Why did seeing the trickle of crimson down the side of Liam's cheek make me queasy?

He didn't wait for me to argue but swept me into his arms. My head wanted to drop on his shoulder the moment he had me secured against him. I refused. Things were getting way too comfortable between the heir prince and me. That wasn't going to work.

"I don't need you to carry me," I argued, my tone weak and scratchy. Hell, I didn't even believe the refusal, yet still I went on. "You've done enough. *Liam,* put me down."

"You have to stop doing that," he whispered, the side of his head touching mine as if he knew what a struggle it was for me to hold mine upright.

Fully relaxing into him, I sighed. "Now what?"

He turned his head slightly so his lips just grazed my cheek. His hot breath caressed my skin as he replied, "Saying my name."

The twist of my lips couldn't be stopped. "You prefer dumbass?"

His legs started to move, carrying me away from the truck. Humor tugged at his lips. "You're a pain in my ass, pup." Releasing a breath, he faced forward. "We need to get out of here in case they decide to come back and finish the job."

That got my attention, and my head shot up. Wrong move. The world wavered, but I gritted my teeth through it. "Who? Wait. You think the accident was intentional?"

His eyes smoldered at me, and not in a good way. "I'm learning that if something happens when you're around, it's a calculated maneuver."

"Twice." I held up two fingers. "It's only been twice, and you've come to that conclusion?" I didn't want to admit he was onto something. Trouble didn't find me in Riverbridge. It followed me.

And I didn't know how I felt about being the one to bring hunters to this town.

"I also found this abandoned on the seat." My arms tightened around his neck as he paused and reached for something in his back pocket. He held a slim tranquilizer needle, still intact.

My stomach dropped. It was the same from in the woods. A hunter's dart. "I don't understand. Why run away before he finished the job?"

Shoving the capped needle back into his pocket, Liam's hand returned to bracing my back. "Good question. I intend to find out."

Wasn't that dangerous? And why should he care if a hunter captured me? He wouldn't have to claim me if I went missing. But staring into Liam's eyes, I was no longer sure if rejecting me as his mate was what he wanted. I knew my feelings. His were... so much more unclear to me, yet being this blasted close to him didn't help clarify things.

Why was it harder to resent him when we were together?

"Come on. I need to get you somewhere safe," he said.

"As if I have a say in the matter. You won't put me down." I wiggled in his arms but swiftly decided that was not the right tactic. Too much fucking friction.

His damn eyes sparkled like he understood why I'd given up so easily. "At least you're catching on, pup."

My car engine still ran, purring softly where I had deserted it on the road. This wasn't a main road and didn't get a lot of traffic, but the odds were another car would pass soon. I'd never left the scene of an accident before, but I didn't want to be here to answer any questions.

I chewed on my lip as Liam delivered me to the passenger seat and then climbed in behind the wheel of my RAV4. "What are you going to do about your truck?" I asked, guilt gnawing in my gut. If he hadn't followed me, it wouldn't be smashed immobile. If I weren't who I was, then his life wouldn't be in danger.

He adjusted the seat to fit his much larger frame—a pet peeve of mine. I hated when someone else drove my car and screwed up all the mirrors and settings. OCD at its finest. "I'll call it in. The sheriff's one of us. He'll come out with a few of our boys and take a look around, get a hit on the culprit's scent. They'll tow the truck into the shop when they're finished," he explained.

"It might not seem like it, but if the hunters were looking for me, I'm sorry about your truck."

He put the SUV into Drive but kept his foot on the brake and glanced over at me. The way he peered into my eyes was so intense, it was like he could see into my soul. It made me uneasy. "You've nothing to be sorry for. You didn't hit my car."

"No, but I have thought about slicing your tires on more than one occasion," I admitted, needing to make a heavy situation lighter. The tension in the air pressed down on my chest.

He shook his head, the lines around his full mouth softening. "Why can I see you doing that?"

Because I would.

Keen eyes searched my face. "Are you sure you're not hurt?"

I snapped my seat belt into place, feeling weird about not driving my car. Other than being a little achy, I hadn't suffered any real injuries thanks to Liam. I was still in no condition to drive, though. "Nothing that won't heal. Where are you going?" I asked as he steered the car onto the road, making a U-turn.

"Where you should be."

What did he mean by that? Then it hit me. "School? That's your idea of safe?"

"A hunter would have to be pretty stupid to try something in a building full of hormonal shifters," he said, eyeing a car rolling past us. He shifted his attention to the rearview mirror, watching them brake at the sight of the accident. He hit the gas, sending us speeding down the road.

I pulled my eyes from the side mirror and gazed at the river. "God, I hate when you actually make sense."

"So, you always hate me, then?"

"Pretty much." *Did I just admit that his actions made sense? No. That isn't right.* I swore under my breath as Liam chuckled.

Stewing in my seat, I kept my attention out the window and rode in silence. I didn't trust myself to not say anything else stupid.

I hadn't driven far to begin with, and it didn't take us long to swing into the Riverbridge High School parking lot. Guiding my SUV in between the two white lines, he put the car into Park. Neither of us moved.

The silence had gone on long enough. I couldn't stand the tension and sparks of energy bouncing in the confined space. Reaching into the glove box, I pulled out a pack of portable wipes I used to remove makeup on the go. They would have to do.

I angled toward Liam and leaned over the center console. I reached for his chin so I could turn his face to me, but the heir prince caught my wrist in midair.

"What are you doing?" The question came out in a gruff demand.

I rolled my eyes. "Seducing you."

I didn't know who was more surprised by what popped out of my mouth. Nerves made me do and say stupid shit.

His features darkened, and I couldn't suppress the nonsensical lift of my lips. Did Liam honestly believe I was capable of doing such a thing? I might have fooled around and had a *boyfriend*—the label was a loose one to describe Huntley and me—but I was far from experienced when it came to lust and relationships.

I wrinkled my nose. "Kidding. I'll let Sabrina do the seducing. She seems to be quite adept at it."

This time he didn't stop me when I reached for his chin, guiding his face toward me so I could assess the damage. I swore my dad shoved a first aid kit in my car somewhere.

"I told you. There's nothing—"

"I know what you said. And I know what I saw," I interrupted, needing to draw some damn boundaries before my body disobeyed my mind. Biting my lip, I dabbed at the drying blood, and then I made the stupid mistake of glancing into his eyes.

Liam's gaze was focused on my mouth. He gulped as I licked my lips, the centers of his eyes churning like a storm at sea.

Fuck. Why did I do that? Did the temperature in here rise like a hundred degrees? Why is it so freaking hot?

Keep it together, Kels. You do not like Liam Castle. Your emotions are out of whack, and you had a near-death experience. That's all. Nothing more.

"You can't go into school looking like you just came from a murder scene. Do you have a spare shirt?" Then I remembered we were in my car. "Shit," I mumbled under my breath.

"In my locker," he stated.

"You should go there first and change." The wolves would be able to detect the fresh blood, but they should also be able to identify the scent as Liam's. What they did with that information remained to be seen. If they thought he was hurt, chaos would break out. I didn't plan to be anywhere near that clusterfuck. The goal was to fool the humans, anyway, to blend in as best as we could.

Electricity continued to crackle in the air, and I knew I shouldn't touch him. Despite the warning bells going off in my head, I brushed aside strands of his hair, and he jerked as if he in fact had been electro-cuted. I did my damnedest to ignore the shock that rippled into my finger and down my arm. The little bolt of power went all the way to my heart.

I dabbed the wipe gently over the cut alongside his brow. He didn't wince or move, but I saw a flicker of pain in his eyes. It was gone as quickly as it appeared.

With a bit more pressure, I stroked the damp cloth down his cheek, doing my best to erase the streaks of blood. His face angled slightly toward me, mingling our breaths, and my mind failed me because all I seemed to be able to think about was his fucking lips. And how much I wanted to taste them. Just a quick nip.

It would take little effort for me to take possession of his mouth. To find out once and for all if all I truly felt for my future mate was loathing. At the moment, it seemed impossible for me to ever feel what that word implied—strong dislike.

I came here without giving Liam a chance. Did I owe him one? Did I owe myself the same opportunity?

A part of me wanted to give in, to test the waters with Liam. I couldn't deny my curiosity about what it would feel like to have him touch me, to have his lips and tongue on me. Even before I came to Riverbridge, I had thought about it—dreamed of him.

But those had been fanciful dreams of a naive girl.

I was neither fanciful nor a girl anymore.

His nostrils flared as he took in my scent, and with it my desire.

For a heart-pounding second, I thought he was going to drag me into his lap again, but for entirely different reasons this time. If he did, who would save me? Because I was definitely going to need to be rescued from the taste of Liam's lips if kissed me.

And the alpha heir so wanted to press his mouth to mine.

What bothered me was how badly I wanted it as well.

The hand rubbing his cheek had gone lax. Liam reached up, his fingers gliding over the back of mine. Never had a touching of hands ever felt this intense, this sensual—this fucking mind-blowing.

It scared the shit out of me.

I swore a crack of lightning speared across the sky. Or it could have been inside me.

I could no longer tell what was happening outside from within me. The two realities merged, bundling Liam and me in our own little steamy bubble.

Until the bubble burst.

Like an audible pop went off in my ears, I blinked at him, wondering what the fuck was wrong with me. Was I sick? Unlikely because wolves rarely got sick, not with human illnesses. Due to our fast healing abilities, diseases and viruses didn't stand a chance.

A shadow drifted over his features. "I can do it," he insisted, taking the wipe from me, his voice a gruff purr that awakened something inside me, entrancing my body.

I surrendered the cloth without argument, but the fact that I wanted to argue, that I wanted to keep touching him, hit me almost as hard as the car had.

Easing back into my seat, I fisted my hands, allowing my nails to pierce my palms. The pain brought me back to reality.

Liam had better control than I did.

He flipped down the visor mirror and finished what I started, cleaning up the remaining blood. It took more than one wipe, but the cut near his brow had already started to stitch itself together.

I had to get out of the car, out of this confined space with him, and clear my head. Without saying a word, I opened the door and stepped out. I drew in a deep breath, cleansing my sinuses of Liam's scent.

The reprieve didn't last long.

The heir prince exited the RAV4 just as the fucking wind blew. The universe was definitely trying my patience today. It was like fate woke up and said, "I'm going to fuck with Kelsey Summers today."

No matter how much I wished the smell of him repulsed me, it wasn't so. I had to find a way to deal with it and the way he aroused my primal wolf instincts.

Standing at the front of the car, I held my palm out, waiting for him to drop the keys into my hand. The pink puffball attached to the key ring landed in the center of my palm. Awkwardness descended. I didn't know what to say. Cars lined the rows, filling the parking lot, yet it was just Liam and me. That pull inside me yanked. The one that told me to run.

What I couldn't figure out was if it wanted me to run away from or toward Liam Castle.

It didn't matter. I'd already made my decision.

"Is your father going to tell mine about the hunter?" I asked, matching my steps with his long strides as we began to weave through the cars together, heading toward the main campus.

"Probably," he admitted.

That would be a good thing, right? My gut told me no. Knowing my father, he would send a few of his guards, the very last thing I wanted. Less freedom. More rules.

As we came to the pathway, I split off, walking away, not toward school but to the river.

"Where are you going?" Liam called after me.

Spinning around, I kept moving backward as a ghost of a smile touched my lips. "You got me to school, but I never said I would go to class."

The sun glinted off his sparkling eyes. "Kelsey," he growled. His displeasure showed in every feature of his face. The furrowing brows. The downturned lips. The hardening of his eyes.

Why did I find those things so amusing?

"I'm not going to class. Not yet," I insisted, refusing to budge as I turned back around. I could be just as stubborn.

"Did today teach you nothing?" he deadpanned, following me.

A breeze set the branches in the tree over our heads rustling as we grew closer to the water. "I've lived with the threat of hunters my whole life. Next time he tries to kill me, I'm going to rip his throat out."

His hand forked into his hair, a frustrated sigh escaping from him. "I'm not above hauling your ass into school and tying you to a chair."

I'd been in Liam's arms too many times today. My quota had been met. "Try it," I said, flashing my canines. "This time I'll bite. And I don't think either of us wants my teeth on your neck." The double entendre was purposeful. A wolf's bite wasn't used just for tearing shit apart. It could also be seductive and erotic.

Humor danced in his expression. Or that was what I told myself it was. "One day you're going to have to make good on your threats, pup."

So much for shocking him. And the thing was, I feared I just might bite him.

Hiking down the steep incline to the water's edge, I paused when I noticed we weren't alone. A girl sat on one of the hunky stone slabs. Her flip-flops were discarded to the side. She rested back on her hands, face tipped up to the sun.

Hope's head turned in our direction, golden hair tousled by the wind. Her grin twisted into something wicked when she noticed I was with Liam. Again.

"Does anyone go to class around here?" I mumbled, sitting beside her.

She shrugged, gliding her fingers over blades of grass. "We're all running away from something. It's obvious who you're running from." Her gaze rose to a looming Liam.

Was it? The heir prince was obvious, I'd give her that. But what about the hunters? Did she know about them as well? Would she be surprised if I told her? And who or what did she hide from? Someone at school?

Since the dark shadow didn't seem to be moving, I lifted my face to Liam's. "See, I'm not alone. You can go to class."

"Can I trust you not to take off again?"

I gave a halfhearted shrug. "Probably not, but for today, I'll give you my word. Tomorrow, all bets are off." And I would go back to pissing him off and plotting.

"She's not allowed off school property," he said to Hope. "Is that clear?"

"So we're babysitting now," Hope snapped back.

"Until further notice." His order hung in the air, bleak and somber.

I was too damn tired to fight him. I'd concede today, but tomorrow...

"Whatever you say, boss."

Liam ignored Hope's hand salute into the air. He gave me one last scowl before taking off back up the hill.

"God, is he always so uptight?" I mumbled once he was out of hearing distance.

"That's a nice way of putting it. I have to admit I was shocked to see him with you. As you've probably learned, Liam hates to break the rules." Water glided over rocks and pebbles along the shallow shore's edge. "What were you two doing?"

I rubbed a kink at the base of my neck. "Not what you're thinking."

"Uh-huh. Is that why you look like a wolf ready to bolt?"

Did I? I couldn't imagine what I looked like considering fifteen minutes ago, I'd been in a car crash. "Is nearly getting killed a normal occurrence in Riverbridge?" It was meant as a jest, yet somehow the question came out more serious than I intended.

She plucked a piece of grass, twirling it between her fingers. "Are you kidding? Riverbridge must be the most boring town in the country. I'd die for something more exciting than the weekly farmer's market."

She just might get her wish. I'd been here for less than two weeks and had been nearly killed twice, which reinforced the idea that the issue was me, not the town.

Fucking hell.

"What happened?"

I glanced up, noticing Hope studying me. It was pointless to try and wipe the worry from my expression or the frown tugging at my lips, and yet I did try. "Nothing," I quickly dismissed. Perhaps too quickly. I wouldn't be landing any acting jobs in the near future.

"Does this have anything to do with the hunters?" she asked, tossing the blade of grass into the breeze.

"Liam told you?" I guessed.

She shook her head. "No. My father's the pack's beta. I overheard him talking with Liam's father."

Beta was second-in-command to the alpha. And I had a sneaky suspicion that "overheard" was code for eavesdropping. Hope struck me as someone who liked to know what was going on. I drew my knees into my chest and watched the river flow. "Maybe. Liam thinks so."

"And you agree with him." Her brown eyes are soft. No judgment shone in them.

My mouth went dry, a chill skirting over my neck. The horrible sound of the crash still echoed in my ears. "As much as I hate to admit it, yeah."

"Why are they after you?"

She wanted to know what made me different from other wolves. That I couldn't tell her. "I never meant to bring hunters here. And now I've put the entire pack in danger."

"I'm not so sure about that," she replied. "The hunters only seem interested in you. So, the way I see it, the only person in danger is you, Kelsey."

I dropped my hand into my hands. The last time I cried had been saying goodbye to my friends, but I could feel that thick, choking sensation rising in my throat. "This is so messed-up."

"Are you going to tell me why you're skipping classes today?"

She had no idea how grateful I was for the change in topic. I didn't know if she sensed how upset I was, but regardless, it helped ease the pressure clamping on my throat. Lifting my head, I glanced sideways at Hope. "Are you going to tell me why you're here instead of in class?"

"Touché." Her lips curved. "I think you might actually be too cool for my cousin, which does make me curious why you would rather hang out with the misfits."

"Is that what this place is? Where all the freaks get together and skip school?"

Picking up a loose rock, she tossed it at the river. The flat surface skipped once, twice, three times before sinking to the water's bottom. "Every school has that spot."

"Perfect. I'm right where I belong."

Hope grinned.

My lips curled, the tension in my shoulders and neck slowly vanishing.

Snap.

I stiffened at the cracking of a twig, and my head whirled at the sound, seeking out the source. Instinct had the wolf inside me soaring to the surface. Not fully, because shifting at school was a terrible idea, but enough to heighten my senses. This was the type of control most wolves learned at an early age but took me years to master. For the longest time, it had been all-or-nothing with me.

The key had been gaining not just control of the wolf but also the power that hummed in my blood.

A figure stood in the shadows under a towering birch tree.

Dark eyes. Dark hair.

And very human.

NINE

A hunter wouldn't dare come to school. Would they?

The wild hammering of my heart was no longer sure about anything. Perhaps they were getting bolder and more desperate in their attempts. Although I knew why the hunters wanted me, I didn't know what they had planned for me. I could imagine all kinds of torturous scenarios, every one of them giving me a reason to fight, but one thing was certain: If they caught me, I would never see home again. Not my family. Not my friends. Not my pack. Not Liam.

Run! You have to run now! the voice inside urged me into action.

My palms hit the stone underneath me, preparing to shove to my feet, but a gentle hand touched my shoulder. "Hey, it's okay. It's just Gunnar. He's a friend." Hope said.

I flinched, processing her words through the knee-jerk reaction whirling through me. It took conscious effort to get my muscles to relax, my heart to chill the fuck out, and to pull back the wolf.

"Gunnar, this is Kelsey, the new girl," Hope introduced. The calmness in her tone helped.

Closing my eyes, I tightened my hands against my thighs, willing the wolf to retreat. The last thing I needed was a human asking questions about the weird new girl.

"It's okay, Kelsey," Hope assured me. "You aren't the first wolf Gunnar has seen."

My eyes flew open, glancing at her. *Did I hear her right? He knows about shifters?*

Gunnar stepped out of the shadows, wariness pulling at the corners of his mouth. I watched him, not completely convinced he wasn't someone I should worry about. His dark eyes shifted from me to Hope. "The one giving Liam hell?"

She laughed. "The one and the same."

My guard went down a notch. There was no better way to bring people together than through shared dislike of a person. Perhaps Gunnar could be an ally.

Had he heard what Hope and I had been speaking of? It wasn't often that a human snuck on me. My defenses must have slipped.

Thanks so much, Liam.

It had been a long day, and it was barely second period.

Stretching her legs, Hope watched me. "I can see your mind whirling. You don't have to stress. He won't say anything. He's known about us for years. Been my best friend since junior high."

It wasn't all that uncommon for humans to learn about the shifter world. It happened.

Gunnar kept his movements lazy, shoving his hands into the pockets of his faded jean shorts. "Not by choice. Hope more or less bullied me into being her friend."

"True story," she affirmed with affection. I could sense how much she cared about him.

"How's your leg?" he asked her, concern lining his forehead as he sat down on a rock across from the one I shared with Hope. "The forecast said we're in for a storm later."

She rubbed at her calf as if to massage away an ache or cramp. "They're not wrong." A feeble smile played on her lips. "This leg tends to remind me it's weaker than the other when it rains or if it's cold. Makes my limp worse," she explained.

"Does it hurt?" Sometimes my curiosity overtook my manners. It probably wasn't polite to ask. I should have waited until she volunteered the information, as it wasn't my intention to make Hope uncomfortable.

"Not most of the time. It only bothers me when there's a change in air pressure. You're curious what happened?"

"I'm sorry," I said quickly. "You don't have to tell me if you don't want to talk about it. I don't always think before I speak."

Her shoulders lifted in a mellow shrug. "We're going to be family soon. I'd rather you hear about it from me."

"From the scar, I can guess. You were bitten." To the point of mangling the flesh past the ability to fully heal, even with shifter magic.

She nodded. "By a rabid wolf when I was ten."

A rabid wolf was the deadliest of bites. Blind with bloodlust, their only instinct was to kill. It didn't matter if it was a friend, a lover, or a child—they couldn't distinguish anything or anyone but the thirst for the kill. It was a miracle she survived.

"I hadn't heard. Then again, I didn't know Liam and Leith had a cousin." My focus had always been on the boy I was promised to. "Did you see a shaman?" I asked. Often traces of the illness lingered in the rabid wolf's venom. It would explain why her wounds left her leg lame.

"Doctors, shamans, Gypsies, witches," she rattled off. "You name it, my parents tried. It could have been worse if Liam hadn't been there. I owe him my life."

"Is that where he got his scars?" The ones behind his ear and on his lower lip. Imperfections that looked sexy on him. How was that fair when Hope walked around with a wicked mark on her leg and a limp? Not that I blamed Liam. It wasn't his fault. In fact, he was a hero who hadn't walked away unscathed.

A flash of regret passed through her eyes. "His scars are deeper than mine. You just can't see them, not until he lets you in."

"Yeah, Liam Castle is a real teddy bear once you get to know him." Sarcasm dripped from Gunnar's voice.

For the first time since coming to Riverbridge, I was beginning to wonder if that might be a true statement. Liam had saved me today before turning back into a righteous ass. Maybe he had a hero complex?

"Like Hope said, we all have our scars and personal demons," Gunnar stated wistfully. "Liam and I might have our differences, but that you weren't alone, that he was there with you, is the one thing I will forever be thankful for."

Hope wiped a fake tear from under her eye. "Don't get all sappy on me. Enough of all the dark, heavy shit. That is not why we're out here, is it, Kelsey?"

"So, what's detention like here?" I asked.

Hope and Gunnar both chuckled.

⟩⟩●⟨⟨

THE LAST THING I wanted to be doing on a Wednesday night was attending a pack meeting, but I had little choice in the matter considering it was being held in my honor—an official welcome to the family.

So again, I'd rather be doing anything else. I'd eat a plate of wiggly worms. I'd swim in a pool of nail clippings. I'd ride the scariest roller coaster in the world a dozen times. Okay, scratch the last one. Roller coasters might not be much of a punishment for me. My point was I did not want to attend tonight's meeting.

Mandatory or not, this gathering solidified my status in the Riverbridge pack and as Liam's mate, neither of which I had come to terms with.

Over a dozen times I contemplated calling my father and begging him to reconsider and break the treaty. There had to be another way than forcing his only daughter into a claiming she didn't want.

But that would be deemed treason by shifter laws, a crime my father and I could both stand trial for. Our entire pack could be chastised, people I loved. My mother. My little brother. My friends.

I could find no other way around it.

I was going to the Lunar Convergence.

And Nana would be my chaperone, the family representative to give me away.

During this moon ritual, I would be introduced to the entire Riverbridge pack as their heir's future mate. The pack had to accept me, and although I had little hope anyone would object, the possibility was still there, however small. It was also at this time that any other member of the pack could challenge me in my position as the future baroness. Not all challenges ended in death—it depended on the stakes—but a fight for the head of the pack didn't stop until only one wolf was left standing.

I could essentially be walking into my death or walking out a murderer.

The scowl on my lips mocked me as I stared at my reflection. It was almost odd not to see the dark cherry lips. I'd gotten used to the new edgier version of myself, but not tonight. All the makeup I'd worn to school today had been scrubbed off in the shower and reapplied with a lighter, more natural touch. My long dark hair fell in soft waves, the front pieces in small braids that wrapped over the crown of my head like a makeshift hairband.

I shimmied into the white dress I'd bought on a shopping trip with Tess. It had been a splurge, but seeing the simple yet stylish dress on made the purchase worth it. The hem hit me midthigh, showing off my tan legs. Longer dresses only made my petite frame look smaller, but there was short, and then there was flashing my kitty-cat short. This was somewhere in between. At least I could bend over and not worry about my future in-laws seeing whether I wore panties or not.

The dress screamed innocence and sex—a dangerous combination, and just what I'd been looking for. I wanted to make a statement. I would uphold traditions by wearing purity white, but I would do it my way.

I'd bought it with the objective of making Liam want me but unable to touch me. It had seemed like a good idea before coming to Riverbridge. Now... I wasn't so sure. Toying with Liam's emotions and desires wasn't just reckless and cruel; I could find myself tangled up in a web of my own designs.

Talk about poetic justice.

This version of Kelsey was soft and girly. There were no rough edges or prickly thorns to be wary of.

"Kelsey, dear!" Nana called from the kitchen. "We need to go."

"One minute," I hollered back, reaching for my heels. They sat on the floor right beside the combat boots I'd worn earlier. The heels were classy and fit the dress impeccably, but my fingers went for the boots instead. I would be traipsing through the woods at night. Boots were more practical. I needed something to remind me of the toughness I possessed.

Grabbing the clutch off the bed and the earrings from my dresser, I slipped the gold hoops into my ears as I went into the hallway.

"Ah, honey. You look beautiful. Love the boots." She winked. Unlike my mother, Nana wouldn't scold me or voice her opinion on my choice of wardrobe. It was just complete acceptance with Nana and the freedom to express myself however I wish.

I tapped my toes together, glancing down at my shoes. "It wouldn't be me without a little spunk."

"I know this is difficult for you, and I'm not one to dictate someone else's life, even if it's in the best interest of the pack. You give the word, and we're on the first train out of town."

I laughed. Nana and me on the run? What a trip that would be. Adventurous, chaotic, and liberating. A fun idea to entertain for a moment, but that was all it could be—a fleeting idea, no matter how tempting. She would be ostracized by the pack—a lone wolf.

No. She was too important to me. Just me living with Nana put her in danger, and I was figuring out how precarious being close to me put a person.

A factor I had yet to fully scrutinize. But I would, as soon as I got a moment to think.

First, the Lunar Convergence.

Ten

The sun made its final descent below the mountains, cloaking the woods in twilight. Crickets chirped, their song a desperate attempt at clinging to the last morsels of summer. Already the air had shifted, a nip of fall cooling the breeze that pranced through the trees.

My favorite part about being in the woods at night was the moon. Each phase made wolves feel different emotions, and tonight the full moon heightened everything. A full moon held the most power. It was when a wolf was at its strongest, versus a new moon, which weakened our gifts.

But nothing was more powerful or weakening than the lunar and solar eclipses. During these events, we lost control of our shift, forcing our primal side to take full control. As with any magic, there were upsides and downsides.

Amid a lunar eclipse, we were virtually impossible to kill, but when a solar eclipse occurred, wolves were in their most vulnerable state. If a hunter wanted to take out an entire pack, a solar eclipse would be the perfect opportunity to strike.

It had happened in the past—whole packs wiped out, another

reason why our numbers were low. Every year, it seemed there were fewer and fewer of us while the number of hunters doubled.

In the distance, I could make out the twinkling of firelight—torches. They surrounded the clearing. Not all pack meetings took place in the woods. Many were done in the alpha's home. It all depended on the reason and occasion for the summons. Rituals, like tonight, were upheld in the sacred domain staked by the original alpha. Each pack had a place held in high regard—a sanctuary of sorts.

I'd only been to the Riverbridge sanctum once, when I'd been promised to alpha's son. As babies, our little fingers had been pricked, a drop of our blood binding the treaty our parents fortified with theirs.

Couldn't say I was looking forward to my return.

"You have nothing to be nervous about," Nana whispered in my ear. We walked side by side, her long, flowy skirt trailing over the forest floor and occasionally getting snagged on a thorn or a tree branch, but she just gently tugged it free, seemingly unbothered. "You're the guest of honor."

She had no idea how thankful I was to have her by my side.

Lanterns hung from the trees, swinging and twinkling from the branches. Traces of smoke and burning wood filtered through the canopy of leaves. Nana and I started down the torch-lit path leading to the clearing, the amber glow soft and whimsical on the side of her face, highlighting the sheen of her long hair. Voices murmured beyond in the clearing, but I was too in my head to give a shit what they were saying.

A pair of wolves guarded the four entrances to the clearing. East. West. North. South. They bowed their heads at Nana as we passed inside the clearing.

When we stepped to the outer circle, Nana faced me and put her slim but sturdy hands on my shoulders. "You are so much stronger than you know. Now go in there and show them why you're my granddaughter. Show them you're worthy of leading them."

I took a deep breath and straightened my spine. "Thanks, Nana. I couldn't do this without."

"Bullshit. Like me, you never back down, and you keep your head held high." She gave my shoulders a squeeze.

Nodding, I forced my feet to move as I took my first steps toward a fate I had balked at for years. I wasn't giving in or giving up. Not yet. This was me buying time until the day came when Liam claimed me.

Long, craggy branches intertwined from the surrounding trees, creating a shelter overhead that was both eerily beautiful and spookily creepy. I might have been able to shift into a wolf, but that didn't mean I still didn't have phobias, and walking into the center of the clearing, all I could think about was how many spiders and other critters dwelled in those branches.

I moved with unearthly primal grace, representing my parents and my pack. For most this was an honor. For me, it felt like a burden pressing like thousand-pound weights on my chest. Despite how poised and confident I looked outwardly, I feared my knees would buckle at any moment, that I would pass out, but I kept going toward the center where Rowan and Sydney Castle, Liam's parents, waited.

The pack started to gather around, sensing the summons was about to begin. Knowing I had so many eyes watching, judging, and scrutinizing, I was glad I wasn't part of the pack yet. I didn't want to hear their thoughts.

Telepathy was an ability pack members shared. It could be done in both wolf and human form but took less effort when in our animal skin. There were limits as to how far we could project thoughts and receive them. We also had the ability to turn off the frequency, with only one exception—a mate. Because the connection was at a deeper level, a mate was always in tune with their counterpart.

Sydney Castle did not come off as a baroness at a quick glance. She appeared gentle and kind, and her eyes, the same color as her boys, were welcoming. They lacked Liam's cold ice and leaned more toward Leith's, which sparkled with humor. Warm caramel hair tumbled over slim shoulders. Nurturing by nature, Sydney was a nurse practitioner in town.

At her side was her husband—the alpha—Rowan Castle. His presence couldn't be ignored. He stood out in a demanding way. Wide, broad shoulders. Muscles that rippled over his chest. He was larger than life, and it wasn't just that he was way bigger than me. His aura exuded from him, pulsing in the air, resonating through the pack. Rowan wasn't just the badass wolf in town. He gave the pack strength.

Intimidating was only one of the adjectives that came to mind seeing Rowan at first glance. He had a rugged, handsome face that only improved with age. Under his icy blue stare, I felt the pressure of his power, but he wasn't the only one who had power.

Mine might not come in the form of muscles and a vicious bite, but that didn't make me any less lethal.

And knowing he craved power—desired the power my family had—made me warier of the prince.

Pulling my gaze from the alpha's, I scanned the pack, searching for one particular face. Since the accident on Monday, I'd avoided Liam, and despite the two of us sharing multiple classes, we neither looked at nor spoke to each other. I could only assume he was also avoiding me.

Yesterday, the morning after the incident, a wrapped box sat outside my front porch. No note. Not that I needed one to tell me who it was from. Inside had been a laptop, newer and nicer than the one I'd brought with me.

Leith winked at me as my eyes passed over him, but still no Liam. He was nowhere to be found, and I was both jealous and angry. I wanted to be the one who disappeared, yet for my pack, for my family, and for Nana, I took the ceremony seriously, despite wishing I could skip it completely. I hated the politics of pack life, as well as many of the caveman traditions the elders clung to.

As an elder, Nana wasn't required to attend the summons unless her presence was requested. I could go in her stead after tonight.

Go me.

This was the pack my mother had grown up in. The pack that had been her family. The pack that had abandoned her.

My mom had been a member of the Riverbridge pack until she'd been outcasted. On the night she was to mate the alpha, my mother ran off with my father, the alpha for Hot Springs, leaving Rowan Castle shafted.

Obviously, that hadn't gone over well.

She hadn't just rejected an alpha but the Wyoming state prince. That was how the treaty started, to prevent a war between the two packs.

Rowan wanted blood.

But he settled for me instead.

Why?

I was pretty sure I knew why. The same reason he'd wanted my mother—for the magic that ran in her bloodline. She didn't have power like Nana or me, but it was still in her veins—dormant, ready to be passed on to her children.

It hadn't been love that spurred Rowan into choosing my mother as his baroness. No, it was power. If there was one thing Rowan Castle was, it was an alpha prince with a thirst for dominance. I wouldn't be surprised if he had his sights set on the throne.

My mother's actions stained her family's name. Rowan, rightfully upset, demanded punishment beyond being outcasted. My parents were brought forth to the council, made up of fifty princes and the king. The violation of breaking an oath didn't go without punishment, not to a family as powerful as the Castles. And so, the payment for their love had been the price of their first daughter—me.

Rowan found a way to get the magic he sought through his son and me. Actually, I was surprised he hadn't tried to claim me himself. I should have considered it a blessing that the king promised me to Rowan's son. And because this treaty—this moon's vow—was sanctioned by the king, I couldn't break the promise without further shaming my family.

Still to this day, I didn't know if my mother married my father solely to escape Rowan or if it had been because of love. I knew she loved my father, but I could never be sure if she was *in love* with him.

I was almost to the center as I did one last sweep of the clearing. Sabrina gave me her trademark bitchface. My middle finger twitched. I'd love more than anything to slap her with a smug grin and flip her off. I did neither, knowing every single member had their eyes on me. I was being scrutinized, not just for the way I looked or how I held myself but for my behavior as well. I was a reflection of my pack—of my parents.

Conflicted by Liam's absence, I wasn't sure how I should be feeling. Relieved? Or embarrassed?

I halted when I stood in front of Rowan and Sydney. Between them sat a stone podium, the pack's insignia carved into it surrounded by climbing ivy. The treaty my parents had signed to keep the alliance between packs in place lay on top.

"Kelsey Summers, you are here as an honored guest of the River-bridge pack. We officially welcome you into our fold," Rowan announced.

A snort rose up in my throat, and I snuffed out the urge to roll my eyes. *Welcomed guest, my ass.* I had no choice in the matter. Neither did Liam. We were both pawns of our parents—of the king.

A delicate smile touched Sydney's lips as she offered me her hand. My eyes flickered down to the invitation. This somehow felt like a pivotal moment. This was Liam's mother. The baroness. Why did it feel like if I put my hand in hers, I would be accepting more than just an offer of kindness?

I hesitated a fraction too long.

Fuck.

Her fingers twitched, and for a second, I thought she might drop her arm, taking back the extended branch from her family to mine. Why did the thought fill me with such stark panic?

My cheeks warmed as I quickly placed my hand in hers. She squeezed my fingers in encouragement, understanding passing over her lovely features that reminded me of her youngest son, Leith.

Rowan's voice boomed over the clearing. "We offer you our protection, our home, and our loyalty. From today, you will be a part of *our family*. And on your eighteenth birthday, you become one of us, and the peace between our packs will continue for another generation as deemed by the king."

Nothing like being a bargaining chip.

The pack was a place I should have felt safe, but without Liam's presence, I felt exposed, vulnerable, and alone. Even with Nana in the crowd, a ghostly unease ribboned inside me.

"You have been promised to my oldest son, Liam, and he to you. Our bloodlines will ensure a future for our pack," Rowan continued.

Why didn't he just come out and say it? Why sugarcoat it? He wanted my power to pass to his son's children. Did he know it would only go to our daughter? That there was no way an heir of his bloodline would ever possess the sixth sense of my family?

If he didn't know, I wasn't about to volunteer the information. My ability, like being a shifter, was to be protected. The only people who knew were often our mates, but due to the connection packs shared, it had been known to slip out time and again. The skipping of a generation was also a factor.

Those shrewd blue eyes lifted to his pack, searching for someone. Liam, undoubtedly. He was supposed to be here, standing by my side, a united front for the pack.

A twitch went through Sydney's hand, and I glanced at her. She was nervous, I realized. I studied the baroness closer. *Is she afraid of her mate?* So many questions buzzed through my head.

Rowan cleared his throat, the muscles along his neck tightening. Sensing Sydney's distress, I gave her hand a squeeze as the silence over the clearing continued to linger.

Liam wasn't coming. He'd stood me up.

And somehow in my messed-up mind, I was actually hurt and embarrassed by him ghosting me in front of his pack.

When did I start thinking Liam would be there for me?

As the seconds passed, it grew harder to keep my chin up and my head held high. A part of me wanted to bolt from the clearing and keep running until I reached Hot Springs.

But then I wondered if Liam was doing me a favor. I had no idea what it would mean if he didn't show, but it was unlikely to have any impact on our future nuptials. Had he really blown off such a commitment?

No.

He was here. I hated to admit that I sensed him, didn't want to believe I already knew his scent, but it was true. Liam was close. The tingles that were ever present when he was near were all the proof I needed. And now that I was conscious of them, they strengthened, regardless of how hard I tried to block the radiating awareness of him. It was like drinking diet water—pointless.

Sydney's fingers released mine, and the tension crinkling at the corners of her eyes vanished.

Liam stood in front of me. I stared at his shoes, knowing it was him without seeing his face. Inhaling a deep breath, I forced my gaze to rise. No, that wasn't quite right. I was compelled to lift it.

Our eyes locked, and I suddenly couldn't breathe.

Nothing about his presence should have been comforting or familiar. His body stiffened, a frown marred his lips, and his eyes... those fucking eyes.

I'd stared into them numerous times, and it was true they were a breathtaking color, so crisp and clear like the sparkling ocean on a hot day. But his wolf eyes...

Fuck me.

They were too much. The glowing intensity made me shiver. I'd only seen his wolf eyes twice before, and each time I found them hypnotic, to the point where I could see nothing else—think of nothing else.

Totally not a normal reaction. Wolf or human.

Those mesmerizing eyes narrowed on me, and it made me wonder what it was he saw when he looked at me. I knew I appeared different without all the dark makeup, but was it that noticeable? Did he truly prefer me made up like a dark temptress?

A hush descended over the pack, something I'd only just become aware of. Had something happened? I didn't religiously attend ceremonies like this. It wasn't my first, and although I knew what to expect and what I was to do, the whole event seemed odd. I felt out of place, and Liam's fastened stare didn't help.

"Their eyes," Sydney whispered, cluing me in to what had everyone so speechless.

What the fuck about our eyes? I took it my eyes glowed as brightly as Liam's did.

Wolves' eyes often took on a luminous glow, especially in the dark. Although, it *was* midnight, the moon was full, and the circle was lit with candles, casting warmth to the clearing.

"Do you see the marks?" she asked her mate, a look of pure awe shining in her expression.

"Moonstruck," Rowan muttered, a cunning, almost cruel smile curling on his lips as he lifted his gaze to the moon.

ELEVEN

hat?

Holy shit! He did not just suggest that Liam and I were moonstruck mates.

Uh-uh. No fucking way.

Liam recoiled as if the word had left his father's lips and smacked him across the face.

I kind of felt the same way, but mine was a punch to the gut, the kind that stole your breath, making you double over and want to puke your guts out on the spot.

Yeah, I was damn close to throwing up.

My hand pressed to my belly. Murmurs started rippling through the pack, creating a stir in the clearing.

"Is it possible?"

"Do you think they could really be moonstruck?"

"Bullshit. I don't believe it."

"By the blessing of the moon."

"Holy shit."

The musings and speculations of the pack rumbled from one wolf to another. I didn't understand how our eyes alone made people believe I was fated by the moon to be Liam's mate. Being moonstruck was so

rare it was practically a myth. I didn't know of a single pair of wolves who had been moonstruck. I'd heard stories, of course, but they were just that, romantic tales of lovers.

It didn't make sense.

Liam blinked, breaking the spell that trapped us, and his attention shifted off my face, gazing upward. I hadn't noticed it before—my focus had been centered wholly on the heir prince—but now that I was free from those eyes that lured me like a siren, I noticed the soft white glow that haloed around Liam and me like an angel smiled upon us, or a ship of aliens hovered over our heads.

Either way, the light didn't make sense. Despite being in a clearing, tree branches wove and tangled together, shrouding the area in darkness and shadows. Hints of light peeked through the web of nature, and yet somehow the moon found a way to illuminate just the two of us as if we were the lead stars in a drama.

Someone please explain that phenomenon.

Panic clawed in my chest, heat flushing my skin. I had to get out of there. Get the fuck away from Liam. I feared the longer I stayed in his presence, the truer the swirling speculation of our mating might become. The last thing I needed was to speak something of that magnitude into existence.

This time I listened to that voice inside me. I turned and ran. My name rang out after me, but I kept going.

$$\text{))}\bullet\text{((}$$

No one in the pack stopped me. Whether it was an order to let me go or if everyone was too stunned, I didn't know. I also didn't care. The only thing on my mind was running.

The moment my feet hit the outer circle of the glade, I exploded into my wolf, and the silky material of my dress shredded. I continued to run without looking back, deeper and deeper into the woods.

I should have been concerned about hunters, but the possible dangers or traps lurking in bushes or behind the trees didn't cross my mind. I had no space in my thoughts for such worries, not when one word consumed me.

Moonstruck.

Fucking impossible.

The idea was ludicrous. Absolutely insane.

No. I refused to entertain such a stupid notion. Kelsey Summers did not believe in fated love.

Hell, I didn't even know if I believed in love in general. I'd never seen the kind of love they portrayed on TV and in the movies. Not in real life.

The evening air blew through my dark fur as I hurled over a fallen tree. My paws crunched over loose twigs and rocks, sank into patches of cool moss and grass. For miles, I ran, until I came to the side of the highway that led out of town. Standing on the side of the road panting, I glanced at the stretch of blacktop.

What would happen if I kept running right out of town and never looked back?

I would become a rogue wolf, but would that be such a bad thing? Was it better than the alternative—eternally binding myself to the heir prince?

What about the hunters? Did I believe they would stop chasing me because I left town?

No. Definitely not.

I would be on the run my entire life. Never able to settle down. Have a family. Fall in love. What kind of life was that?

Regardless of the choices in front of me, I felt trapped, stuck— screwed. I'd literally come to a fork in the road. Did I turn left and never look back? Or did I go right, back to Liam and the predetermined destiny our parents laid out?

A beam of headlights approached and swiftly passed by without sparing me a glance, but as dark as it was, I blended in with the night, my fur like a starless sky.

It would probably be a good idea to get off the side of the road, but where would I go? Which way should I choose? Too big a decision to make on the spot.

Conflict whirled within me. I had people who would worry about me if I disappeared. My family. My little brother. My friends. Nana. As selfish as I wanted to be and think of only my feelings, I couldn't stop wondering about them.

How would I feel never seeing any of them again?

Never seeing Liam again?

It shouldn't bother me. I should feel nothing but relief at never laying eyes on the heir prince's face again.

So why did my stomach cramp at the idea? Why did it feel like leaving might cause me physical pain?

Fuck! This is such bullshit.

I didn't want this. Didn't ask for Liam. How could we possibly be moonstruck when I didn't even know how I felt about the asshole? Tell me how that made any sense?

Whether I wanted to admit it or not, the fates of the moon didn't consult us before they sent down their blessing. According to the lore, the fates foreordained mates at the beginning of time. There was no escaping or running from a destiny set by the moon gods.

Another set of car lights appeared in the distance. The yellow glow blinded me momentarily as it flew by, but this car didn't keep going. The driver slammed on the brakes, the rear end of the Jeep fishtailing and the tires screeching over the road before coming to a jerking halt.

I should run—it could be a hunter—but the voice of intuition within me remained silent. Had she abandoned me?

A figure jumped out of the doorless driver's side, and his scent registered with my wolf, calming the spike in my blood pressure.

Leith.

The knots in my shoulders unraveled.

He stalked over to me with purposeful strides, fire gleaming in eyes so like his brother's, yet different. "Kelsey," he called, his tone even, contradicting the heat and strain in his expression.

I had never seen Leith upset. Liam always seemed pissed off or arrogant, but I'd grown to expect the opposite from Leith. He balanced the seriousness of his brother with his fun and cheeky attitude.

Was he angry with me? Because I had run off?

No, that wasn't like Leith. Then what? Had something happened after I left?

I needed answers.

Since I wasn't part of their pack, we couldn't communicate with me in my wolf form. I would have to shift, and I wasn't sure I was ready to be human—to face the consequences. There was also the little detail that I had no clothes, but honestly, nakedness kind of went with the shifter territory. It wasn't as big a deal.

Still...

This was Liam's brother. It somehow felt wrong to let him see me naked before my mate did. Then again, I never expected Liam to see me unclothed. I'd been so damn confident I would get the heir prince to hate me. There had also been the possibility that he would hate me and still claim me. That had been the worst-case scenario.

"Kelsey," Leith said again, dragging a hand through his hair. "Are you okay? I wasn't sure I'd find you."

A whimper left me.

"Hang on. Don't go anywhere." He jogged back to his Jeep and returned with a blanket he had stashed in the back seat. "Here. I'll take you home." He held up the plaid material by two corners in front of him and turned his head to the side, giving me a few moments of privacy.

Even in an awkward situation, Leith turned out to be a gentleman.

Though I was unsure about everything else in my life, shifting was the only thing I had control of. I banished the wolf, and when the last tingles of the shift subsided, I stood up slowly, stepping into the blanket.

Leith, sensing my presence without turning his head, wrapped the material around my shoulders. I clutched the fabric in front of me, keeping it secure. "Thank you," I whispered.

"Are you okay?" he asked again earnestly, sounding worried.

"No," I admitted. "But you don't have to worry. I haven't been fine in a while." As if my body wanted to defy everything that came out of my mouth, a shiver rolled through me. It had gotten colder.

"That doesn't make me feel better." The goose bumps covering my arms didn't go unnoticed. "Come on, let's get you inside the car."

I let Leith lead me to his Jeep and tuck me into the passenger seat. He cranked the heat after hopping into the other side. "Sorry about the doors. Hopefully the heat will help."

Clamping the blanket under my arms, I dangled my fingers in front of the vents, letting the warm air chase the chill from my hands. "Everything is such a mess," I mumbled, shaking my head as I scowled out the window.

He kept the car in Park, the engine idling. He flexed his fingers over the steering wheel. "Were you planning to leave town?"

My teeth chattered. *Do I tell him the truth? That I contemplated doing just that?*

"I wouldn't blame you," he added. "I can't begin to understand what you're feeling. And you're right, this is a messed-up situation. Who still enforces things like arranged marriages? I don't know why my father's so decisive about you being Liam's mate. I've never seen him so worked about anything before. It doesn't make sense to me, but then again, little does. I'm the second-born, after all."

Leith's rambling helped, and my anxiety slowly began to ease up. "What happened after I left?"

He released a breath. "My father and Liam and a few choice words, which is a pretty normal occurrence in our house. I didn't stick around long. Liam told me to go after you."

It had been Liam's idea. "Why you? Why didn't he come himself if he was so concerned?" I couldn't stop the tartness from souring my tone.

Leith rubbed the back of his neck as he met my stare. "I don't think he trusts himself to be alone with you."

What does that mean?

Trust himself how?

I gave him a long look. "Leith, I'm so confused," I confessed, my head falling back against the seat. A beat of silence passed before I turned to look at him. "Can you explain what the fuck happened back there?"

"You don't know?"

I fumbled with the hem of the blanket. "More like I don't want to believe it. I want you to tell me that what happened was normal, that there's no way Liam and I could be moonstruck. It doesn't make sense."

His knee bounced under the steering wheel, and in his eyes, I saw a glimmer of doubt. "You're right, it doesn't. And was what happened tonight unusual? Yes, but I promise you, not every member of the pack is quick to jump on the idea that you and my brother are fated by the moon."

"It's not like every time I see your brother, I want to rip off his clothes and bang the shit out of him."

Leith chuckled under his breath, cringing slightly. "I could have really done without the visual, and I don't think that's how it works. Not that I would know. But I can say it's not normal for Liam and you to have the reaction you did."

"The eyes," I supplied.

He nodded. "It's not just that your wolf eyes materialize. You go into this trance. Like the world around you no longer exists. Neither of you seems conscious of it, but as someone who's witnessed it on more than one occasion, it's eerie." He reached over and touched my wrist "It's gone."

"What is?" I asked, brows drawn together.

He lightly ran his finger along the inside of my arm. "The mark. When the moon hit you and Liam, a symbol of a crescent moon appeared at the top of your wrist."

I scoffed, sinking lower in the seat. "Awesome."

"I should probably get you home before my father sends out the cavalry."

"He would do that?" I groaned.

"If he doesn't, Liam will."

I rolled my eyes as he put the Jeep into Drive. "How could we be moonstruck when we can't stand each other?" I tried to rationalize. The question had been introspective mutterings, but Leith chimed in.

"You and I both know that's bullshit, Kels," he said, whipping the car into a U-turn section of the divided highway, then steering the Jeep back into town.

Chewing on my nails, I stared at the lush woods, nothing but tall, spooky figures blurring by. The blanket offered little warmth as the night's air blew over the topless Jeep.

As Leith drove, I couldn't stop my mind from replaying tonight. If Liam was my moonstruck mate, it didn't matter how far or where I ran, he would be able to find me.

Like humans, shifters had a choice in their mate, but unlike humans, once the claiming was completed, there was no divorce. Wolves mated for life—literally until death do us part.

To claim a wolf and create the mate bond, an exchange of blood must happen, most often through a bite. This formed both a physical and mental bond deeper than the pack bond.

Mating with other species wasn't as taboo as it had been in the past and had become a more common practice. Our dwindling numbers had been attributed to this acceptance decades ago, but mating with a human, witch, or other animal shifter diluted the wolf bloodline. In this day and age, few purebloods existed. My family and Liam's were among those few.

Just as many people believed in soulmates, moonstruck was much like having a soulmate but magnified by the same undefined power that gave us the ability to shift from human to wolf.

What were the chances that the wolf I'd been promised to my whole life happened to be my moonstruck mate? I mean, that had to be astronomical odds. Like one in a billion.

Had our parents known?

Was that why we'd been kept apart for all these years, except for that one time when we were six?

I couldn't process this.

Not until I was sure.

And to do that, I would have to see Liam. My impatience and impulsiveness made me want to demand Leith take me to his brother right now and put the question of our relationship to rest. Was it better to know the truth or pretend ignorance? At the same time, I never wanted to see the heir prince again. That urge to run and keep running still whispered within me.

It felt like all I'd done since I got here was run away.

At some point, I had to face my problems.

Perhaps sooner than I was prepared for, but it could have also been the universe's way of pushing me toward a destiny I'd rejected for so long.

Leith pulled into Nana's driveway, parking behind a truck—Liam's.

Did I take this as a sign?

TWELVE

L iam paced in and out of the shadows, glancing up at the Jeep's flash of headlights cutting through the darkness. I hadn't expected him to show up at my house, not after almost ditching me at the summons. That seemed like a loud gesture, but then again, he had come through in the end.

And he'd asked Leith to find me. Plus, my curiosity was piqued. What did he have to say to me that had him showing up at my house?

Squinting against the lights, Liam leaned against his truck, waiting for me. My heart hammered in my chest as I clamped the folds of the blanket tighter. This was not a conversation I wanted to have with Liam while nearly naked, but fuck it.

Why did it feel like the moment I stepped out of the Jeep my whole life would change?

It scared the shit out of me.

The heir prince scared the shit out of me.

"Do you want me to tell him to leave?" Leith asked softly, sensing my hesitation as I lingered in his car.

I shook my head. "No, I think we need to do this."

Brows knitting, Leith dialed the heat down a few notches. "Should I stay and wait?"

A yes rose quickly to my tongue, but I stopped myself before the word left my lips. "It's okay. I doubt we'll kill each other."

A smirk tugged at the corner of his mouth. "That's not what I'm worried about."

Fuck.

Why did he have to go and put *those* kinds of thoughts into my head? I did not want to think about Liam's lips, his hands, his body when I was wearing nothing.

"That's the last thing that will happen tonight," I assured him, but the statement was weak and lacked conviction. I meant what I said. So why didn't I believe it either?

"At some point, Kels, you're going to have to face the truth. Maybe that starts tonight. Maybe it doesn't," he added with a one-shoulder shrug. "It's up to you."

I nodded, offering him a small smile. "Thanks for the lift." Hopping out of the Jeep, I made sure to keep the blanket securely in place as I walked barefoot up the driveway toward Liam.

The Jeep's engine rumbled down the street, leaving me alone with the heir prince on a full moon. Definitely not a wise choice, not with my emotions so close to the surface and the moon only emphasizing everything inside me, including my sixth sense.

It hummed louder in my blood as I drew near Liam.

I stopped a few feet in front of him, and we stared at each other, assessing one another in a new light. Had he speculated that I might be his moonstruck mate? I searched his eyes, wishing the answers I wanted would be right there, swimming in the depths of his aqua eyes.

They weren't.

I couldn't remember when our gazes first collided. It could have been from when I got out of Liam's Jeep. Hell, it could have been before.

Leith was right. Something happened when Liam and I locked eyes.

The flecks in his irises darkened, churning like a storm about to suck me in. What was he doing to me? I had to find a way to stop this.

A kindle of magic sparked in my blood, spreading through my veins until the tingles of power overran the awareness that Liam incited inside me. An invisible shield to protect my heart.

Suspicion flashed through his face.

I had to do something. Say something.

It would be stupid to use my extra gift in front of him. The heir prince was too damn observant. Too damn perceptive. And although we weren't bonded, I got this feeling that he sensed the change in me.

As usual, I said the first thing that popped into my head. "What are you doing here?" I demanded, deflecting with anger.

He had his hands shoved into the front pockets of his black denim jeans that hugged the muscles in his thighs. I refused to admit he looked good. Really good. Smelled even fucking better.

A deep frown pierced his striking features. "Making sure you don't take off again. What did you just do?" he asked, tilting his head to the side as his eyes roamed over my body, inspecting me in a way that made me all too aware of him.

Under the blanket, my nipples hardened, and I prayed he couldn't tell. It was my turn to scowl. "I don't know what you're talking about."

"Your scent changed. Not a lot. Most wolves wouldn't have noticed, but there's definitely a hint of something new."

Of course he would pick up traces of my magic. I cursed him silently. "Maybe you need to get your sniffer checked."

His lips twitched. "We all have our strong suits. I have an incredible sense of smell, among other things." He shoved off the truck, closing the few feet that separated us. "But you... you're different, pup. I've always known you weren't like the rest of us. Your nana too. What is it about you? The wondering has gnawed at me for years."

My chest rose and fell. "What're you talking about? I just got here. It's been like two weeks."

He took another step forward, and ardent warmth traveled through my body. "You've been torturing me since I was six," he said.

Holy shit.

No way could he have noticed something about me from our one and only meeting as kids. Then again, back then, I didn't have the control I possessed today. I hadn't had any at that age, and my gift often slipped out without me knowing. The memory of that day still rang crystal clear in my mind. It wasn't something you easily forgot, meeting your future mate at six.

Liam had been memorable even as a little boy. The dreams that followed also made it nearly impossible to forget his existence.

Had he dreamed of me as well? Did he still have those dreams?

I inspected his face, looking for a telling sign. He wasn't kidding.

"Do you have dreams of me?" I asked, needing to know.

"I wouldn't be surprised if we had the same dreams, pup." He raised his hand, plucking a curl that had fallen over my shoulder.

Shared dreams?

Seriously?

Panic seeded in my chest. I didn't want this. Didn't want him.

Lies. All lies.

Leith's words came back to haunt me. *"At some point, Kels, you're going to have to face the truth."*

Like a cobra striking, Liam's fingers released the curl and snagged into my hair, holding me so I couldn't bolt. And I fucking wanted to. "Don't run off again."

He'd seen the panic spring into my eyes and recognized the look. My eyes narrowed as I lifted my chin. "I'm not."

Questioning brows went up. "You don't have to run from me."

"Let me guess—you want me to run into your arms instead." I snorted, and the movement had the nubs of my breasts brushing against something hard. Our bodies were touching without me realizing, and it was too late to pretend like he didn't stir something within me.

A dark emotion flared in his eyes, and he yanked me into his arms, nuzzling his nose into my hair as he drew in the smell of my shampoo. "Why can't I forget your scent? It's fucking driving me crazy."

Did he mean that in a good way or in an I-want-to-kill-you way? Stilling in his arms, I dared a glance up. I couldn't read his expression.

My hands got trapped between us. If I lifted them, the blanket would tumble to my feet. It was bad enough that just the thin fabric was all that separated Liam from my body.

He stared at my lips.

Warmth flooded my system, going from pleasant to hot like I'd spent all day lying directly under the sun.

If he kissed me, everything would be ruined. I didn't know how, I just knew if I let the heir prince get close, all the defenses I'd worked so hard to keep in place would crumble. "Don't," I pleaded.

His eyes slammed into mine, a speck of annoyance flickering in his expression. "You have to accept this sometime, pup."

"Don't call me that."

He chuckled, his minty breath fanning over my lips. "Is there anything I can do?"

"Let me go," I whispered. That was what my mouth said. A straight-up lie, because the last thing I wanted was for him to release me, not when being in his arms felt so damn good—right.

Liam glared at me, an almost daring stare. "We both know that's not an option. Not even if it was within my power to do so. Whether you like it or not, Kelsey Summers, you're mine."

He needed to stop declaring me his, despite the words making my heart flutter. "I'm not a damn possession. I don't belong to you." I lifted on my toes with only a singular thought.

I had to taste him. Just once.

Only then would some of my muddled confusion become clear. The answers lay within his lips.

"Oh, but you do, pup," he said with a lopsided grin, the scar on his bottom lip taunting me.

That possessive-ass statement curled my toes. How messed-up was that? I shouldn't be having these thoughts, not about Liam Castle, but they made me want to devour every inch of him. This internal tug-of-war started inside me, jerking me from one side to the other.

You hate him. And don't forget it.

Kiss him. You know you want to.

Don't. It'll be a mistake.

Do you want to spend your life regretting this moment? Never taking a chance?

The imaginary devil and angel continued to toss barbs, making me crazy. On the other hand, did I owe it to myself to see if there could be anything between us? Did I owe it to him? To my family? To myself?

The conflict warring felt as if it would split me into two pieces. I had to do something. I had to make a choice.

Fuck it.

I pressed my lips to his in a tentative kiss meant only to test the waters, explore what might be there, what I refused to allow myself to feel.

I captured the sharp inhale of surprise from Liam with the kiss. For an instant, I wondered if I'd made a mistake when his lips didn't immediately respond to the pressure of mine.

Then he made a low sound in the back of his throat that sent a shudder down my spine. The shifter kissed me as if his life depended on it. Thoroughly. Skillfully. Hungrily. Selfishly.

My lips parted with a gasp, and his tongue swept in, seeking out mine. The taste of him exploded against my tongue, and every nerve ending I had burst alive. The shield around my heart shattered. He broke through all my defenses with a kiss, untying all those knots that usually twisted in my stomach.

I had to touch him, but there was a reason my hands weren't moving. I could no longer remember why, and it didn't seem important, not as vital as touching Liam.

He broke off the kiss with a part growl, part moan. "God, you never fail to surprise me."

My heart swelled, beating in overtime. "I need more," I murmured, leaning in to fasten my lips to his in another kiss.

"Kelsey," Liam growled before slamming his mouth over mine. His fingers ground into my hips as he flipped us around, pressing my back into the side of his truck.

The sound of my name with such gravelly hunger unlocked another link in my defense. Electric tingles sparked over my skin, shooting and dancing like tiny stars.

I wound my arms around his neck and dug my fingers into his hair, completely forgetting that they were supposed to be clasping the fabric. With a single hand, the heir prince clutched the front of my blanket as the material started to fall.

I no longer cared about modesty.

Muscles quivered under my fingertips. Our tongues tangled, darting, teasing, and lavishing the other. He molded against every curve of my body. I whispered his name, tightening my arms around him.

A finger slipped into the front of the blanket, inching it down lower over my breasts. They ached, swelling as his finger continued to dip lower and lower. I was about to take his damn hand and place it on my boob when the pad of his thumb brushed over my nipple through the blanket.

My breath caught.

Jesus Christ.

I wanted him to touch more of me, but he only continued to kiss me, the kind of deep kisses that left me breathless and dazed—the kind that made me forget my name.

Liam pulled his mouth from mine, his breath coming out in rough gasps. My lashes fluttered up to see why his lips weren't still making my knees weak. His pupils radiated through the darkness.

Biting my lip, I dropped my head back and stared into his eyes clouded with need.

He dipped his head, teeth scraping over my ear. "What would you do if I took you right here, pup? Would you stop me?" he whispered, the warmth of his breath sending shivers down the side of my neck.

I twisted my face a fraction, letting my mouth graze the high point of his cheek. "The real question is would you stop me?" I pressed my hips against the hardness swelling in his jeans.

Desire blazed in every feature of his face. Nostrils flaring. Eyes darkening. Mouth parting. Fingers tightening. The struggle for control lined the column of his neck.

At that moment, I realized I wanted to be the one to make Liam Castle lose all control. Seeing as I already lacked discipline, there was no doubt that he could do the same to me.

Hell, he already had with just a fucking kiss.

His jaw hardened. A mask dropped over his face. "Has your curiosity been satisfied now?"

Hardly. I was just getting started, but he had to go and ruin everything. I slipped my hands off his shoulders and shoved at his chest. He stepped back, giving us both space to breathe, not that it helped. His taste coated my tongue. His smell taunted my senses. My body buzzed from his touch.

I jerked the blanket higher up my chest, securing the folds together. "You're an asshole."

An arrogant half smile tipped at the corner of his lips. "At least we can agree on that."

"Stay away from me, *princeling*." I spun on my heels and stormed off toward the house, trying to look as dignified as I could in a blanket and barefoot.

THIRTEEN

I hated Liam Castle.

It didn't matter that his lips were fucking wicked and heavenly. It didn't matter that he made me feel things I'd never felt before. And I sure as hell didn't give a shit that we had matching moon marks during a full moon.

I should have known better than to find myself alone with the heir prince on tonight of all nights. It was the damn moon that made us do crazy things—shit we wouldn't normally do sanely. Like devour each other in my driveway.

I wanted to entirely blame Liam, but I couldn't. He might have ended what had been the best kiss of my life on a dickish note, but I'd been the one who started it.

What was I thinking?

Why didn't I just run out of town?

My gut told me I wouldn't have gotten far. Liam would have come after me. His father too.

Silence greeted me when I entered the house. The small light above the kitchen sink Nana always left on guided me down the hallway. She was home, probably asleep, and I sighed, relieved she was here and safe. I had left her at the summons without a word.

She would have worried, but she also knew I needed to work through what happened tonight, and the best way for a wolf to do that was a run through the woods.

Careful not to disturb her, I tiptoed down to my room. Neither the floor nor the hinges squeaked, but it wouldn't matter. If Nana was awake, she would sense I was home. My scent alone would give me away.

Dropping the blanket on my bedroom floor, I flopped naked onto my bed. The thought of a shower crossed my mind, but what would be the point? No amount of soap or toothpaste would scrub away the stamp Liam left on me. He was in my pores. If his father was right, the brand of Liam went deep into my soul.

Those were thoughts I didn't want to deal with, not when my lips still tingled from his kisses, which might make the whole moonstruck all too plausible.

"Ugh," I groaned, covering my face with my hands.

Why the fuck is my body still buzzing? If I didn't know better, I would have thought Liam was in my room.

My head whirled to the window. *Is he still out there?*

Once the thought entered my mind, I had to satisfy my curiosity. Rolling off the bed, I padded over to the window that looked out to the front of the house. Darkness embraced my room, concealing my nakedness. A good thing.

Liam sat in his truck. The headlights were out, the engine running. Smoke from the exhaust curled behind the car. If it hadn't been for the blue-green glow of his eyes, I would have thought the vehicle was vacant.

I sensed his gaze on my window, and I could all but see the cocky smirk on his lips.

I flipped him off.

A husky chuckle floated from the other side of the window before the taillights illuminated and the truck backed out of the driveway.

Resting the side of my head against the glass, I glanced up at the moon. What had always been a sense of comfort to me had become a curse.

Moonstruck. Really?

Why me?

Why Liam?

October's full moon was often referred to as the hunter's moon. How ironic that it was the month that hunters came to Riverbridge. I was no longer sure I could deny that fate, destiny, or whatever name you gave it didn't exist.

My problems appeared to be multiplying.

Climbing back into bed, I went to sleep feeling uneasy, my heart twisted and out of sorts. I didn't want to dream, didn't want to see the heir prince's face when I closed my eyes. And yet, despite clearing my head, he invaded my sleep.

If I was going to dream of the heir prince, I would have preferred an exotic dream over the nightmare. Anything over seeing him hunted... and seeing him die.

$$ ꜜꜜ●ꜛꜛ $$

GETTING up in the morning sucked. I hit the snooze button on my phone at least six times before I finally sat up, still half asleep. The dreams had been too vivid—too real. For a few dazed moments, I believed the whole night had been nothing but a dream. The summons. The moonstruck mates. Taking off into the woods. And the part I really wanted to be a figment of my wild, sex-craved imagination.

Kissing Liam.

But the fact that I was stark-ass naked brought it all back like a tidal wave, nearly sucking me under. I had to find a way to tread through this mess or sink.

Midway through the cold shower, I remembered I had detention today after school for ditching classes.

Just fucking fabulous.

Already running late, I forewent any makeup and only managed to partially dry my hair. Nana sat in the swing as I rushed out the front door, my new laptop courtesy of Liam tucked inside my bag.

"You had an early morning visitor. I asked them to stay for coffee, but they declined," Nana said, lifting her eyes off the morning paper.

"Visitor?" I could only think of two people who would stop over. Liam or Leith. The question was which one?

"Hope, the beta's daughter," she informed me.

"Oh." *That is not disappointment in my gut.*

"Were you expecting someone else?" she asked as she tipped her glasses down the bridge of her nose, looking at me with sparking violet eyes.

"No, of course not. She left?"

Nana crossed her legs as a gust of wind gently swayed the swing. "I figured you needed the sleep."

"Thanks." We still had yet to talk about last night, but Nana wasn't one to push or pry. She would wait patiently for when I was ready, unlike my mother. "I'll be late today after school," I told her.

"You'll be home for dinner?" she inquired.

I nodded, trotting down the porch steps. "I should be."

Doing speeds that would get me pulled over in a heartbeat, I raced to school. Thankfully, the cops in this town were too busy having their morning coffee and donuts to be patrolling the streets.

With the same sense of haste, I jogged into school, entering my first class mere seconds before the bell shrilled. My day seemed to be set at this pace of me scrambling to get places on time. Part of it was due to lack of sleep, making me sluggish and forgetful, and the times my mind was active, my thoughts were distracted by the heir prince.

Riverbridge High was smaller than my other school. Fewer students meant fewer classrooms and too many fucking chances of bumping into the one person I wanted to avoid.

His girlfriend-not-girlfriend also made the list of people I was ignoring.

Sabrina Thompson.

I'd kept to myself all day, and I did not want Brina to be the first person I spoke to. In my current mood, I couldn't be held accountable for what might come out of my mouth, so I kept walking, ignoring her. But if there was one thing a girl like Brina hated, it was being fucking ignored.

She leaned against the locker next to mine. "That was quite a show you put on last night," she sneered, smugness oozing from her voice.

Annoyance entered my blood. I slowly turned my head toward her. As always, Brina looked beautiful. Her red hair was curled perfectly, framing her heart-shaped face. The short, pleated skirt and cropped top showed off her slim frame. I wanted to hit her. She didn't even have to insult me; The feeling was just there, burning inside.

I hated girls like her. It had nothing to do with who she dated. It was her holier-than-thou attitude as if her shit didn't stink.

"Glad you find my life amusing," I retorted tartly. I'd been getting odd looks from people all day. Nothing new, really. I'd gone from being the new girl to being the one who ran out on Liam Castle during a summons.

Her green eyes roamed over my face, scrutinizing me as she bunched up her nose. "You look different. I noticed it last night too."

I took that as a compliment. Anything that made Brina uncomfortable was a win in my book. "Are you afraid I might be prettier than you?" It was clear that she relied on her looks for confidence. Anyone slightly prettier posed a threat.

She snorted. "You could never. Suggesting so is an insult."

Slamming my locker shut, I turned and faced her. "Why are you talking to me? We're not friends." I wasn't in the mood for games. If she had something to say to me, it was best she just came out and said it.

Brina chuckled snottily, flipping strands of hair to the side. "Of course we're not."

"If you came to gloat or make yourself feel better, find someone else to be your ego booster."

The expression of outrage on her features gave me a glimmer of satisfaction, and I started to walk away.

"He doesn't believe you're moonstruck," she blurted.

I halted and counted to five before I spun around. "Your first mistake is thinking I give a shit what Liam believes. The second is thinking you can hurt me. The only one who's going to get hurt in this situation is you."

Anger flared over her face, and I wondered if she would give in to those primal instincts swirling in her veins and attack me. It wouldn't be my first or last girl fight. Perhaps it was time I showed Brina who the fuck she was messing with.

As if she sensed that I was itching to slam her face into the ground, she smiled. "I'm only trying to help."

"We both know that's a line of bullshit. Save your breath. I don't want or need your help."

This time I did walk away, something I seemed to be becoming increasingly good at.

>>●((

WHEN THE FINAL BELL RANG, and the majority of the school rushed out the front doors, I dragged my feet down the hall to the library. I got that detention was a form of discipline—I had broken the rules, and there were consequences for my actions—but why was it still a thing in schools?

This wasn't the first mark on my record, but I also wasn't a trouble-maker. I was a good student, but I also didn't shy away from having fun or taking risks. Sometimes, like a few days ago, those risks cost me, but I would gladly pay the price for a couple hours than let my emotions get the best of me at school.

I gave the teacher my name, and she crossed it off her list and pointed me to my seat, an empty table at the back. Rows of tables sat in front of the main desk, and about half of them were occupied by one person each. Riverbridge didn't seem to have a very high rule-breaking population. Why was I not surprised?

I passed Hope, who shot me a wink as I went to take my seat. Gunnar was also there, reclining in his seat as if he sat there frequently. He did seem like the type who spent more time in detention than he did in class.

He frowned at me, and I wondered if Hope had told him what happened last night at the summons. Was that why he watched me vigi-lantly? Regardless, something in his guarded eyes made my spine straighten.

Then the tingles started as I sat down. But it wasn't Gunnar who made my neck prickle.

Fuck no.

The bane of my existence strolled in, flanked by two other guys, Riven Hayes and Colsen Adams, Liam's closest friends. The three of them together were a sight to behold. Power rippled in the air. It was easy to tell who in the room was a shifter if you paid attention. The wolves wormed in their seats from the charge in the atmosphere. Everyone else just stared, oblivious to who Liam Castle really was—all but Gunnar, that was.

If I thought the frown he gave me had been gruff, it didn't compare to the deep, cold scowl that formed on his lips at Liam's approach. Gunnar's fists curled under the table. Evidently, there was history between the two of them. My curiosity was tickled.

The teacher directed the trio to different parts of the library as if she knew they would cause disruption if too close together. A wise choice. Mischief danced in Riven's eyes.

He had a cocky swagger about him, from his walk to the crooked-ass smirk on his lips. His boyish face made him look like he could be in a boy band. Sunglasses shielded his eyes, making me wonder if he was recovering from a hangover. Probably. Even from where I sat, the distinct scent of booze entered the room with them.

On the other side, Colsen wove around the tables to his seat. His dark hair and eyes made him mysterious and a bit serious. His rich, flawless skin would make any girl envious. He stood an inch or two taller than Liam.

And that left the heir prince heading down the center aisle, right toward me.

Hell no.

Before Liam's gaze landed on me, I dropped my head on the table and groaned, letting my hair curtain in front of me like it would conceal my identity. I wanted to be invisible. For the first time ever, I wished my sixth sense had the ability to do just that—make me vanish.

Not that it would matter. He didn't need to see my face to know I was close by.

He sat at the table in front of mine. I heard the scraping of the chair legs on the carpet, the clattering of his belongings on the table, and the thump as he dropped into the chair. My veil of hair sadly didn't prevent his woodsy scent from reaching me.

I wanted to groan again but bit my lip instead of drawing attention.

Not that it mattered.

"Are you avoiding me, pup?" he murmured.

"I did tell you to stay away from me," I hissed back, my voice muffled by the tabletop.

His chuckle came out warm and annoyingly sexy. "Does that mean you're not coming to dinner on Sunday?"

Fuck me. I'd forgotten.

Lifting my head, I rested my chin on my hands and stared at the side of Liam's profile. He had his head twisted to the side, and I hated that he looked good from all angles. How was that even fair? "Depends. If you don't want me to go, then I'll be there."

"And if I do want you there?"

Fucker. "I'm only going for your mom." And because my mother would kick my ass if I didn't. Plus, I didn't want to disappoint Nana. The baroness had invited me to dinner. In no world could I refuse the invitation. Liam knew it too.

"So you do have a heart," he bantered, blinking incredibly long lashes.

"Of course, just not for you." Gah. Now I needed to go shopping and pick out something respectable to wear. Maybe I could get Hope to come with me.

A long shushing came from the teacher, Mrs. Walker. Her head snapped up, beady eyes zeroing in on Liam and me as her lips pursed, just waiting for one of us to do something.

I averted my gaze, drawing patterns on the tabletop with my finger. Silenced filled the library, except for the occasional shuffling of a book, a sigh of boredom, or a squeaking of chairs. Hope snuck a glance over her shoulder at us, and I gave her a small smile.

Detention dragged. Literally the longest hour of my life. It wasn't that I couldn't sit in a quiet room alone with my thoughts. My hyper-awareness of Liam made it impossible to think about anything else but him. By the end of the hour, I was ready to jump out a window.

The moment the second hand ticked to four o'clock, I shot out of my seat and zoomed out of the library, but as I reached the door, Liam's voice reached me.

"I'll see you on Sunday, then, pup," he taunted.

My steps faltered, yet I forced myself to keep going, and other than the little misstep, I gave no indication that I heard him.

Greedily, I inhaled as I burst outside, hoping to cleanse Liam's scent from my nose, but the fact that woods surrounded the school didn't help. The traces of pine, damp soil, and fresh water in the distance reminded me of him. It was as if he was the earth itself.

I cursed under my breath, and damn if I didn't pick up fragments of Liam chuckling in the air.

It had rained while we'd been in detention, soaking the ground. A light mist clung to the sky, dark clouds shadowing overhead. Wyoming was a relatively dry state, but it seemed to be having a rather rainy autumn. I wasn't complaining. I quite enjoyed the rain and spent many nights running through storms. Something about the thunder, lightning, and rain called to me.

A thrill of excitement went through me at the prospect of a storm tonight.

I sprinted to my car. The parking lot was fairly empty, only thirty or so vehicles compared to its usual hundreds. Hope caught up with me just as I was about to get in my car.

"Hey, what's the hurry?" she asked.

I tossed my stuff into the passenger seat and leaned on the open door, facing her. "I'm currently avoiding all things Liam Castle."

"Enough said. I stopped by this morning to see if you wanted to ride to school together, maybe get coffee," she suggested.

This was the first time I'd seen her today, other than in detention. I'd expanded the concept of staying away from Liam to pretty much avoiding everyone. "Sorry. Nana told me. I woke up late. Long night and all."

"I figured. Maybe tomorrow?" she offered.

I never turned down coffee, but the chance to get to spend some girl time with someone I liked was even more tempting. "I'd like that."

Hope grinned. "Great. I'll text you before I leave my house. I'm not far, just a five-minute drive."

"Great." I was about to say "see you later" when I remembered. "Oh, any chance you want to go shopping this weekend? I need something to wear for dinner at your aunt and uncle's house."

She made a face. "Dinner with Uncle Rowan. That sounds about as fun as detention. Sort of feels like it too."

"Does he always come across so... intimidating?"

She rubbed at her nose. "Always. Is your father not like that? I assumed it was an alpha trait."

I thought about her question. "Perhaps it's because he's my father that I don't see it."

"I'm really glad you're here, Kels. I've never had a female friend before."

"Really? Why not?" I asked, shutting the passenger door.

"Because girls are bitches. No offense. All of the girls here want something from me. Nine of ten times, I'm just a way for them to get close to Liam or Leith. The other slim percentage are forced by their parents in hopes of looking good in front of the pack's beta."

It was sad that I could understand her reasoning. Having a pack did give you an extended family, but that didn't mean it wasn't without its drama. We had all the components: mean girls, bullies, snobs, assholes. Hearing Hope had a hard time made me glad I had Tess in my life. "You don't have to worry about any of that shit with me. Technically, I already have Liam. But don't tell anyone I said that. I will deny it all the way to my grave."

She laughed. "Good thing I'm good at keeping secrets. See you tomorrow."

I nodded and watched her trot off to her car. She glanced over her shoulder once and waved. I returned the gesture, then slipped behind the driver's seat of my car. Today didn't turn out to be a complete waste after all. Funny how things worked out. Making friends hadn't been a priority for me when coming to Riverbridge. My focus had been on Liam and finding a way to release me from the treaty that joined us.

Now... I didn't know what I was doing anymore.

I hit the Start button on my car, but the thing just clicked, no gentle purr of an engine. Nothing.

What the hell?

Blinking, I hit the button again.

Click. Same shit.

Did I drop my key fob? Is that the problem?

It only took a quick peek into the zippered front pocket of my bag to see the little device nestled snuggly inside.

Now what?

A flash of lightning speared across the sky.

This can't be happening. Haven't I taken enough shit since I got to Riverbridge? Now my car's rejecting me.

Like any rational person in this situation, I freaked out and spammed the Start button with angry fingers at least a dozen times.

Click. Click. Click. Click. Click.

And so forth.

I slammed my hands down on the steering wheel, a series of curses tumbling from my lips. From the outside, I had to look like a crazy person. Good thing no one was around to see me on the edge of a meltdown. Well, no one but Liam and his friends as the three of them came sauntering out of school.

Shit.

I had no energy to deal with this.

Dropping my head onto the steering wheel, I inhaled and exhaled, trying to be rational and think of a way out of this situation. Did I have jumper cables? I thought so. Could I ask someone for help? No. Absolutely not, because the only people in the parking lot at the moment were Liam, Riven, and Colsen.

I came up with only one solution that my mind could currently handle: walking. It wasn't that far to Nana's, especially if I cut through the woods. Faster if I shifted and ran. A few miles at most. No big deal.

Pretending to be on my phone, I waited until the heir prince slipped inside a Jeep and gunned his brother's car through the parking lot. I had no right to be disappointed that he hadn't waited until I left first. Or come up to my window. Yet there it was in the pit of my stomach.

Riven and Colsen's cars followed Liam's, and I wasted no time. Grabbing my bag, I did a quick sweep of the car, making sure I didn't leave anything I needed behind. I got out, locked the doors, and slung the bag over my shoulders.

Thunder rumbled in the distance, an indicator that an impending storm loomed in the sky. My wolf could sense it, the hairs on my airs rising.

Sighing, I took off toward the patch of trees instead of taking the road. Why waste time going around when I could cut straight through?

Not to mention, I wanted to avoid any creeps trying to pick me up along the way. Perhaps beat the storm too.

My boots clattered over the blacktop as I ran. In under a minute, I reached the edge of the trees and slowed my pace to a walk. The sunless sky made the woods somber. A light mist sprinkled from the ominous clouds, bringing a cooler wind with it. The temperature had dropped significantly from earlier in the day, creating a ghostly fog that curled over the ground.

Without a second thought, I entered the forest, starting the trek home.

And that was my first problem. I'd forgotten who I was.

The ground, soft and wet from the earlier storm, made me grateful I'd worn boots. A comforting calm lingered among the trees, despite the horror movie setting. An eerie yet beautiful fog danced between the branches and teased the mossy floor.

I hated leaving my car behind, but I'd call someone to look at it tomorrow. Surely someone in the pack was a mechanic. Good thing Hope offered to pick me up tomorrow, or I'd be walking to school.

Plop.

A fat drop of water fell from a branch, hitting me on the head. It might not be downpouring... yet, but I would still get dirty. Each step deeper into the woods called to the wolf residing within me. She all but whimpered, pleading with me to shift.

And I wanted it as much as she did, but what would I do with my bag? I could stash it somewhere, which meant I would have to come back for it—*if* it didn't get stolen. The idea of having to replace the new laptop I'd just gotten didn't sit well in my gut.

A boom of thunder filled the air, rattling the treetops and sending a flock of blackbirds to the sky. I jumped, my heart suddenly zooming in my chest, and almost lost my balance on the slippery leaf-covered ground.

Laughing at myself, I shook my head and carried on. I loved being spooked. Enjoyed scary movies and death-defying excursions like jumping out of planes. Anything to get my heart pumping.

But there was a difference between a good jump scare and pissing your pants in fear. To feel both in a matter of seconds wreaked havoc on my mind and body. I came to a dead stop, ice freezing my blood.

A figure clad in all black stepped out from behind a birch tree only a few feet in front of me. Running into an unknown man who looked like a fucking serial killer alone in the woods was never a good idea.

It wasn't often I regretted a stroll through the woods, but taking a shortcut home might have turned out to be more than I bargained for. As a shifter, I could be ferocious and could fight when I needed, but I wasn't invincible. I could still be hurt. I could still be killed. And I would bet my life that the gun at his side was stuffed with silver bullets.

The one thing a wolf couldn't heal from if hit in the heart.

FOURTEEN

It didn't matter how many f-bombs went off in my head, my situation wouldn't improve. Or disappear. This definitely wasn't a dream, regardless of how much I wished it so.

As if my legs had turned to stone, I stood motionless, my mind doing all the work my feet should have been doing. I had to find a way out of this mess without getting shot, or at the very least not somewhere vital like the heart.

Shit. Shit. Shit.

Swearing didn't help, but it somehow made me a tad less frantic. Only about a mile into my hike, it would be quicker to run back toward school and pray a few teachers or students lingered about. A janitor even.

It was a risk. He might still shoot me. *And* I had to make it the school. The odds weren't in my favor.

Behind a ski mask, flat eyes cataloged every inch of me as if deciding how he would kill me. "I was hoping we'd meet again, little wolf." The mask hid his identity, and the bastard disguised his scent, a feat I couldn't quite figure out.

He was smart. I'd give him that.

"Me too," I admitted, surprised at how steady the words had come

out. "You've been following me quite a lot. I almost think you're stalking me."

"I guess you could say I am." His voice was familiar, but I couldn't place where I'd heard it before. It was partially muffled by the knitted material.

I began backing up, slowly testing the waters. The air in my lungs thinned.

The movements didn't go unnoticed. The hunter sighed. "It would be best if you didn't run."

"I was born to run."

"Believe it or not, I don't want to hurt you."

My eyes flicked to the weapon he held. "The gun in your hand says otherwise."

"Oh, this," he said, lifting the rifle. "This is motivation and security, just in case."

"In case what?" I prompted, not sure why I felt the need for details. I wanted to keep him talking, and words were tumbling out of my mouth.

Behind the mask, I was sure his lips twitched. "You decide to be difficult."

Oh, I planned on being hella difficult. "I've never been good at playing by the rules. This is a game, isn't it? Like a twisted round of tag."

"Fun, right?" It was a rhetorical question.

I bared my teeth in response, my wolf instinctually rising to the surface.

In that case, let the fucking fun begin.

I only had seconds to decide on a plan. Only seconds to execute it.

The hunter notched his finger into the trigger, and I took off running, my heart beating out of my chest. I dashed farther into the woods. My boots slammed onto the ground, my legs pumping as fast as they could in my human form. I was too far in for screaming to be of any use.

I couldn't be sure he was alone. There could very well be another hunter or two waiting for me to fly by. I kept my senses alert, doing my best to pick up any unfamiliar or new scents as I ran, zigzagging left and right between the trees in erratic patterns.

The goal was to make it as difficult as possible for him to get a shot. Firing a rifle while chasing after me didn't make for precise aim, which meant I had to keep moving. It gave me a better chance than fighting, but my predatorial instincts urged me to stand my ground. It was only one hunter, after all. In my wolf, I could take him. If I could knock the gun away or wrestle it out of his hands, it would make injuring him easier.

None of my ideas were solid plans. They would probably get me hurt to one degree or another.

A light drizzle of rain began to trickle from the sky, but I continued to push myself, ignoring the branches that slapped against my arms and face.

Behind me, twigs snapped. He was gaining ground—too close. I had to shift. I was much faster as a wolf. Now was not the time to be worrying about my laptop.

Veering right, behind a massive oak tree, my boots got caught on a root and I stumbled, yet somehow managed to stay on my feet. The deeper I went, the more tangled and difficult the terrain became to navigate. I smelled the sharp metallic of my blood from all the scratches my cheeks, arms, and legs suffered. Thorns dragged over the material of my jeans, tattering them.

Extricating my arms from my bag's straps, I tossed it aside, and the loss of the added weight added speed to my legs. Behind me, the heavy pants of the hunter's breath grew closer.

Now. I had to shift *now* before he caught me. Before he narrowed the gap enough to take a shot at me.

Tingles radiated over my skin as the change in my body started. Kicking off on the balls of my feet, I leaped, summoning the wolf inside me.

Bang.

I heard the gunshot a second before I felt the pain. Shock splintered through me, and I gasped.

Holy crap.

The asshole shot me.

Instead of landing on four paws, I hit the ground on my side and rolled, still in my human form. Pain lanced through my right leg,

making my eyes sting with tears and ripping a cry of agony from my lips.
I might have called someone's name.

My hands immediately went to my leg as I curled into a ball. Despite
the spiking pain, I had to get up. I had to keep moving, or there was a
good chance I'd end up with another bullet, and this time, it might be a
mortal wound.

Blood soaked my jeans, dribbling down my leg, but I didn't have
time to think about it or the pain.

Leaves crunched off to my left as the hunter moved in toward me. I
bit down on my lip to keep from crying out and forced myself to my
feet. I hobbled from one tree to the next, using the trunks to support
myself. At this rate, I'd be dead in a few minutes.

Doing what apparently every girl does when being chased, I glanced
over my shoulder to see how close my assailant was. Big mistake. I saw
the glint of his gun pointed directly at me.

I had no choice. I had to use my gift—the very thing that intrigued
the hunters and drove them to chase me. I would die in these woods if I
didn't expose how different I was from other shifters.

My mouth dropped open, a scream rising in my throat just as a deaf-
ening roar echoed through the woods.

Not mine.

A wolf as pure as snow came charging through the trees, and before
the roar finished echoing, Liam crashed into the hunter from the side,
taking him to the ground. The thud of his body had me wincing, my
ears picking up the crack of a bone. My guess, a rib.

Sinking against a tree, I exhaled, a strong sense of relief washing
over me. I'd been almost certain I was about to die, and now... I still
wasn't certain. The idea of Liam fighting against a rifle made my
clammy skin turn colder. From the massive burning that speared
through my calf like a fiery virus, I could attest the bullets were indeed
silver.

Liam's nails swiped across the hunter's chest, shredding the military-
style vest. The hunter slammed the length of his rifle into Liam's torso,
sending him backward. Tossing his head back, Liam scrambled to his
feet, letting another roar cleave through the forest. This one was different. It was the call for the pack.

The hunter took advantage of the split-second reprieve to stand up and point his gun at me.

Bastard.

Throwing himself in front of me, Liam bared his canines at the hunter. I no longer questioned how he always knew I was in danger. All that was important was he was here, and I wasn't facing the hunter alone.

The hair on the back of Liam's neck stood up, his front paws in battle stance. Aqua eyes smoldered with feral rage and the power of an alpha, his nostrils flaring. He stayed protectively in front of me, guarding me with his body as he glared at the hunter, waiting to see what he would do—and waiting for his pack.

Idiot. He was going to get himself shot. Or worse, killed. And all because of me.

Why does he have to be so damn heroic all the time?

My legs could no longer hold me upright, and I collapsed to the ground, my energy waning. It would be better for my wound if I shifted to speed up the healing process and stop the blood flow, but that would require energy—strength I might need to save Liam's ass if he did something stupid. And I was 99 percent positive he would.

Hell, I was about to do something just as dumb.

Perhaps Liam and I did deserve each other.

The hunter's eyes grew sharper behind the mask. "Two for one. I always love a deal," he sneered, his tone smug and arrogant despite being muffled. He believed he had won.

"Go to hell," I said. Injured leg or not, I wouldn't go down without a fight. Neither would Liam. The crazy son of bitch would sacrifice himself to save me. He was that kind of wolf.

The hunter laughed, the black material curling where his mouth was. "Should we end the game, then? Or maybe eliminate a player?"

Liam snapped at the air, his chest rumbling as he issued another warning to the hunter.

Gritting my teeth, I kept my gaze focused on the prick's eyes. He shifted the end of his rifle a fraction, making Liam the target.

Panic as I'd never felt before clawed like a caged beast within me, desperately trying to rip itself free of my body. "Liam," I rasped. I never thought I would want to be linked to the heir prince. Ever. But right now, I wished it more than my next breath. Not being able to communicate with him telepathically killed me. "I need you to trust me."

His ear twitched, the only indication I got that he heard me.

"I don't have to shoot him if you surrender. It's *you* I want. Not him," the hunter bargained.

Teeth shining, Liam's eyes were glazed over with bloodlust. He wanted to rip the hunter to shreds until he was nothing but a pile of bones and blood.

Rain pelted my face, but getting drenched was at the very bottom of my fucks-given list. "Go fuck yourself."

I couldn't see the features of his face, but I would bet my life he grinned under the mask.

The hunter's finger twitched, and wild instinct took over. I didn't give a shit that I was about to unleash my deepest secret.

My nails pressed into the earth, calling forth my sixth sense. A second shot fired through the trees, the blast booming like a shock wave. I squeezed my eyes shut and released the humming power that sang in my veins. I felt the power leave me and snap into place, and my eyes flung open to see the nearly invisible shield erected in a bubble around Liam and me.

I had no time to breathe. The magical barrier was barely sealed when the bullet hit. It was safe to say I'd never tested my power against a gun, so I had no guarantee it would block the pellet of silver from penetrating.

It held.

A gush of air expelled from my lungs. I felt a small ripple in the ward, but the power remained steady and impenetrable. The ominous growl vibrating at the base of Liam's throat faded.

Lightning lit up the sky, immediately followed by the rolling of thunder. The hunter blinked and yet appeared unfazed that his bullet never hit the target. "Impressive," he whispered. "The rumors are true."

My concentration went solely on keeping the shield in place. I couldn't waver. Not yet.

The storm continued to loom over the woods. "Should we see how much you can withstand, little wolf?"

Jackass.

The heir prince snarled, his eyes glowing as a howl splintered in the distance. His white head tilted a beat to the side, listening. I heard it then, the pattering of paws striking the ground in a thunderous stampede.

The hunter might not have the hearing abilities we did, but he could read our body language and knew trouble was coming his way.

Body stiffening, he narrowed his eyes, realizing the pack had arrived. If he didn't run now, there would be no escaping. One rifle was no match for a dozen or more wolves. They would eat him up before he could get off another shot.

I stared at him, challenging the prick to linger. *Try me,* I said with my eyes.

His gaze flickered, and I could see it went against his internal code—or perhaps it was a hunter code—but he didn't want to leave. Not without the prize he came for.

But if he wanted another chance at kidnapping me or killing me, he would have to retreat.

Lowering his rifle, the jerk winked at me and took off, bolting back the way we'd come from.

Seeing him leave should have alleviated my fear and anxiety. It didn't. I shouldn't have expected it to, considering I was bleeding all over the place.

My leg had gone numb, and I couldn't decide if that was a good or bad thing. The silver was still lodged inside me, yet the intense burn had subsided. I hoped that meant my body was healing. A twisted sense of dread told me otherwise.

Half afraid the hunter might still be out there, hidden behind a tree or a bush, I kept my hold on the shield. He struck me as someone who easily gambled his life and that of others.

Just a little bit longer.

With the immediate threat gone and Liam's life in less danger, my strength sapped out of me. I didn't know how long I could keep my magic intact. Already the hum of power stuttered in my veins.

Liam remained protectively over me, his muscles locked until the first wolf streaked past us, a blur of brown fur. A moment later, a second raced by. And another. The pack was on the hunt.

The heir prince whirled toward me, eyes unreadable as he scanned over my injured leg.

I released the shield, the power retreating within me, and my body sagged farther into the tree propping me up. Without it, I'd be a pile of mess on the ground.

My eyes fluttered closed, exhaustion making me want to sleep on the spot, my body not giving a shit that I was outside, that it was still raining, and the danger wasn't over.

It wasn't sleep that tried to drag me under. I was injured, and despite not being able to feel the lower part of my right leg, I could still smell the fresh blood.

It hadn't stopped.

I had slowed down the healing process immensely. All the energy my body needed to stitch itself together and counteract the silver embedded in my calf had been used to stop the bullet. My body needed rest to recoup its strength.

Problem was... I didn't have hours.

Liam nudged me with his nose, and I forced my eyes open, staring into those turquoise eyes that begged me to stay awake.

Easier said than done.

To do that, I couldn't stay here. I had to move. The prospect of moving sent a punch of dread into my gut, but what other choice did I have?

Liam's nose nuzzled my arm, not once but twice before I got the signal. He crouched down onto the ground, at my side and waited for me to climb onto his back. It wouldn't be easy and required strength I didn't know if I possessed.

But I had to try.

Fisting my left hand into the wet white fur at the nape of his neck, I got up on my good knee and used my other hand to lift my injured leg over Liam's back. *Halfway there.* Knotting my right fingers alongside my other hand, I pulled just enough to get my left foot underneath me so I could push myself the rest of the way. It wasn't easy or fucking graceful, but I managed to drag myself onto his back. Wrapping my arms around his neck, I rested my cheek on his head.

A gentle rumble vibrated under me, and I tightened my grip.

Happy now?

He must have been satisfied, because he took off cautiously at a docile trot, despite the urgency I sensed trembling in his legs. The sounds of the pack hunting drew farther away, but from what I could tell, they hadn't found the hunter. Not yet.

I did my best to hold on and stay seated on Liam's back. With each minute that ticked by, my arms weakened. I had only a matter of seconds before I fell, and no amount of growling from him would prevent that.

"Liam." The heir prince's name tumbled from my lips as my fingers finally gave out on me and I slipped off, landing on my side and rolling once. Pain painted the lower half of my leg. I tried to bite back the whimper of curses and failed, tears stinging the corners of my eyes. Putting any form of pressure on my leg was a big fat no, not if I wanted to stay lucid. However, if I wanted to faint, then all I had to do was step on my right leg.

Crumpling into the soaked ground, I shook my head, unable to speak with the hot stabbing needles of agony coursing at the wound.

Liam's tortured howl sounded through the forest.

I didn't have the strength left to pull myself up a second time. We weren't far from a road. Tires trudging over wet blacktop sloshed up ahead, giving me my first glimmer of hope.

Just a little bit farther.

Liam licked my cheek, the warmth of his breath giving me a heartbeat of respite from the cold that had settled into my bones. Then he took off, dashing ahead and leaving me alone in the woods. I assumed he had a plan and trusted he would be back soon. All I had to do was hang on.

I heard a car door open and the hasty rustling of what I thought was clothes. A minute later, in a pair of unbuttoned jeans and a T-shirt, Liam ran toward me. He hadn't bothered to put on shoes.

"You're going to be okay," he promised, carefully scooping his arms under my legs, hesitant to touch the wounded one. "I'm sorry," he whispered, eyes brimming with guilt.

"This isn't your fault," I rasped, doing my best to breathe through the pain.

He noticed, and an air of urgency darkened his features. "I need to get you somewhere safe and have that leg looked on. Wrap your arms around me," he ordered.

"Why?" I asked without thinking, a ridiculously dumb response. It had become second nature to question him on everything.

"Kelsey," he sighed. "We don't have time to argue. Just do it."

"I'm not thinking straight," I reasoned. Obeying in general was not an easy feat for me. I draped my arms around his neck, but I didn't know how helpful they would be.

Before I could protest, he gently lifted me into his arms, but regardless, the movement caused me agony. I winced.

"I'm sorry," he apologized again as I started shaking. "I tried to make it quick."

I tried not to think about how incredible he smelled, hints of the cool night and the wolf clinging to his skin. It called to me in ways I couldn't explain, causing the wolf inside me to want to come forward.

"It's okay," I gritted out, laying my head in the space between his shoulder and neck. I inhaled, comforted by the familiar scent, and relaxed in his arms. I didn't ask where he was taking me, and I honestly didn't care. I trusted Liam enough to know he would keep me safe, and that was all that mattered.

"Just stay awake," he said, always commanding. "I'll have you in my car in a few minutes."

My fingers involuntarily toyed with the curls at the nape of his neck. Touching him kept my mind off the agony shooting through my entire leg. If I thought about the bullet, then I would think about the blood, and though I wasn't normally a squeamish person, there was something unsettling about seeing my blood. A lot of it too.

"How did you find me?"

Liam angled his head slightly toward me, his breath fanning my cheeks. Those full lips were so close to mine, brushing against the side of my face. "I don't know."

Not the answer I'd been expecting. I assumed there had been some great scientific reason for him knowing I was in trouble—like a pack thing. But I wasn't part of his pack, not yet. "Oh."

"I don't know how to explain it. It was weird," he attempted to elaborate. "I was driving home, and I thought I heard you call my name."

Had I?

I couldn't remember yelling his name, but it was possible.

"I got this sick feeling, and the closer I got to the woods, the stronger it became until I had to pull over. That was when I heard the gunshot. I got this sharp pain. It stole the air from my lungs. And then I heard you scream."

His voice had the ability to calm me. The longer he talked, the more at ease I became until the shaking had nearly subsided. "I'm glad you found me."

We had come to the Jeep parked along the side of the road, idly running. He finagled the car door open while keeping me secured with his other hand. The jostling motion didn't hurt as much, and I hoped that meant my leg was beginning to heal, but I still hissed, because I wasn't out of the woods yet, figuratively.

"Fuck, getting shot sucks."

"You're doing great."

"I don't want to get blood on the seats," I protested when what I was really upset about was losing the protection and stability of his arms. That was how I knew my head wasn't right.

"Aren't you the same girl who threatened to slash my tires? "

"I still might slash your tires," I groaned, stiffening in anticipation of being moved into the car.

He set me in the front seat, lines of concentration on his forehead, and clicked my seat belt into place. I laid my head back against the seat and closed my eyes, riding through the wave of endless pain. It intensified as Liam dashed around the Jeep and hopped in.

Just when I thought things had been getting better, the agony started again. With the loss of his body heat, the chills returned, and my teeth began to chatter.

I didn't want to admit that the heir prince might have anything to do with the way my body was reacting to being shot, but a theory scratched at the back of my mind.

What if...?

Liam reached into the back seat and handed me a hoodie. "Here, put this around you." He shifted the car into Drive as I took the soft material, steering the Jeep onto the road and merging with traffic.

"Thanks." I wanted to ask him why he was being so nice to me, but I couldn't seem to muster the energy.

Not even the heater blasting on high or the doors being attached this time rid me of the damn cold that moved through my veins, and I longed for the warmth Liam had supplied. I shuddered under the hoodie, doing my best not to think about the throbbing that continued to pulse in my leg. I preferred when it had gone numb. Getting shot was nowhere near as cool as it looked in the movies.

"I need you to stay awake. Do you hear me, Kelsey?" he added when I didn't move. "Kelsey," he growled.

"If you want to keep me from drifting off, you're going to have to touch me."

His head whirled in my direction, eyes off the road for a moment. "What?"

Dropping my hand, palm upward, onto the center console, I murmured, "Touch me. I don't know why, but I think it helps."

A moment later, his large hand closed over mine, interlacing our fingers. The fucking relief came almost instantaneously, and a heavy sigh left my lips.

It actually worked.

I had no room in my mind to overthink what it meant, but later, when I recovered...

I didn't notice when the car stopped, not until Liam untangled our hands. Then it was like being jarred awake from a dead sleep by being electrocuted. The air was sucked from my chest, and I wanted to cry out from the lancing burn. I was seconds away from digging the bullet out with my nails.

My car door opened, and Liam was there. He noticed the tortured expression on my face. "We're here. Just hang on a little longer."

"It b-burns," I stammered through the agony that seemed to be traveling farther up my leg. Fear dug into my heart.

He tensed, hearing the evident pain in my voice. "This better help," he murmured under his breath, and I couldn't tell if he was talking to himself or me, but then it didn't matter.

Nothing did.

Liam's lips were pressed to mine.

The kiss was soft and quiet, meant to comfort instead of entice passion. To give strength and steal the cold that trembled in my bones. To make me forget the silver that wreaked havoc on my leg. Embers stirred in the center of my stomach, fluttering and flickering to different parts of my body.

He broke off the kiss, his head whirling toward the house. It took me a moment to catch up.

Someone stood on the front porch.

FIFTEEN

Thanks to Liam, I could breathe and picked up Leith's scent. He leaned against a white column like he had not a care in the world, a phantom of a smile on his lips. His light brown hair was damp as if he, too, got caught in the rain, but his clothes were dry.

"Oh, I get it, a little evening make-out session. I'll just go back inside. Pretend you never saw me," he said to Liam, eyes dancing. Leith turned to walk back into the house but paused, his eyes narrowing. "Why do I smell blood? Liam, did you bite her?"

"No, for God's sake. Where the fuck have you been? She was shot by a hunter. Help me get her inside," he snapped, forking a hand through his wet hair.

Leith's jaw almost hit the ground. "And you thought it would be a good idea to kiss her to death?"

My lips twitched. I couldn't help it. This whole scenario was too damn much. What were the chances that Leith would walk out right then when Liam was actually saving me with his lips?

And now that the kiss had ended, I could, in fact, confirm that the touch of his mouth made the trauma to my calf manageable. I was tempted to try and stand, but why would I walk and potentially hurt myself more when I could have Liam carry me?

God, is the heir prince growing on me?

Just because he saved my life didn't mean I had to start catching feelings.

Liam lifted me out of the car, my legs dangling over his arm. The sight of my blood-soaked jeans was alarming. Could I afford to lose more without needing an infusion? Hospitals weren't places shifters voluntarily went. Our DNA and blood weren't normal to that of humans, and in order to keep what we were from being broadcasted over every news station, hospitals were avoided at all costs.

That was why I wasn't surprised Liam had taken me to his house. Packs strategically had people in all the necessary fields so we could take care of ourselves without jeopardizing our identity.

"It's not what you think," Liam defended the kiss, his long strides taking us to the house. "I had my reasons. Now open the door so I can bring her inside."

Propping the door open with his back, Leith made a sweeping motion with his arm. "By all means. Mom's going to have a shit-fit if she finds out you kept a bleeding girl on her porch instead of bringing her inside."

"Shut up, Leith, and go get Mom," Liam grumbled as he passed his brother into the house.

"Ma, Liam bit Kelsey!" Leith hollered.

Liam groaned as he sat me down on the couch, his expression pinched like he was seconds away from hitting his younger brother. Or, at the very least, ramming his elbow into his gut. Whereas I was afraid I'd ruin their couch, staining the beautiful leather with my blood.

Sydney came rushing down the hall, an apron tied at her slim waist and her caramel hair piled up on top of her head. Sharp eyes assessed both her sons before landing on me. A delicate hand flew to her chest, her lips forming a surprised *O* shape. "This isn't a joke. You're hurt. Tell me Liam didn't really bite you," she said, coming to my side, lines of worry crinkling the corners of her eyes. She shot Liam a stern glare as he huddled on the other side of me.

"I did no such thing," he hastily protested before his mother could berate him.

Leith raised his brows behind his mom, mocking Liam. The

younger Castle had no idea how much his lighthearted reaction to the situation helped. Before, my thoughts had been bleak, the possibility of dying at the back of my mind, yet somehow Leith made the notion silly. I was grateful for him not freaking out; his presence calmed both Liam and me, even if it was done so unintentionally.

"She was shot by a hunter," Liam explained, glaring at Leith.

"I can see that now. Leith, quick, go into the kitchen and get me my bag." Her voice and features softened as her gaze met mine and Leith jogged out of the room. "I'm going to have to cut off part of your jeans. Are you in a lot of pain?"

I lowered my eyes and curled my fingers into the leather couch at my sides. "Not as much as before," I admitted.

Liam cleared his throat, and Sydney glanced from me to her son, picking up on the sudden awkwardness that hung between us at her question. She was curious, but taking care of me took precedence. Later, Liam would be getting the third degree.

I had a feeling I would also be subjected to interrogation, not just by Liam's mother but the heir prince as well. He hadn't said anything about what he saw me do, but he wanted to. Even now, I could sense his eyes on me, studying, wondering like I was a puzzle he couldn't quite figure out.

"I'm going to lift your leg and prop it on the table," Sydney informed. "Liam, can you move it closer for her to comfortably rest her foot on?"

He sprang into action, shimmying the coffee table near me. Sydney ever so carefully raised my leg. Her fingers were light on my ankle as she set forth on the task of removing my boot and sock.

"I'm sorry for showing up like this," I apologized to the baroness.

She shook her head, offering me a warm smile. "You have nothing to apologize for. You're one of us."

Leith came back with a black bag and set it on the floor beside his mother's feet. Sydney sat on the coffee table, digging through her bag and pulling out a pair of scissors. "Try and stay still. This won't hurt, but the wound will protest at being jostled, as you probably already know."

Keeping my head resting on the back of the couch, I nodded, letting her know I was ready.

The baroness made quick work of cutting a line up my jeans, keeping the material as far from my skin as it would allow. Good thing I'd worn stretchy jeans today. She stopped cutting at my knee and rolled the material out of the way.

I was afraid to look, to see how deep the bullet had impaled itself into my leg. Or how much the silver had eaten of my flesh. I looked at Liam's, Leith's, and Sydney's faces to prepare myself. Their reactions would give me an indicator how serious my injury was.

Liam sucked his bottom lip, the scar there disappearing behind his teeth. He did a good job masking his emotions, his expression indecipherable.

Sydney and Leith didn't have Liam's control. Leith whistled, shoving his hands into his back pockets as he rocked on his heels. "You really outdid yourself this time, Kels."

Fuck.

"Leith," Sydney scolded as she rolled up the sleeves of her thin black sweater. Even at home, she dressed classily. "You're not helping. Go get some towels and water."

"Why can't Liam do it?" he complained, leaning over his mother's shoulder to get a better look at my leg.

Liam folded his arms, glaring at his brother.

"Because Kelsey needs him here," she replied calmly, her attention staying on my calf, examining the severity of the wound, but her drawn brows had me concerned. "We need to get the bullet out before your body stitches itself together further."

"It's silver. The bullet," I informed her, my voice breaking.

Sydney's eyes snapped up. "Silver?" she echoed. "Are you sure? Your leg has already begun to heal."

I slid a glance at Liam. "I've never been shot before, but it felt like silver from what I've heard. It burns like hell."

Her lips pressed together, a shadow drifting into her eyes, so much like Liam's. "Either way, it's best we get it out as soon as possible and give your body time to do what it needs to do."

Leith walked into the room carrying an armful of towels and a bowl of water. "Still looks gnarly," he said, giving me a wink.

Liam's face tightened. "Knock it off."

"What?" Leith feigned ignorance.

"Boys!" Sydney snapped sternly like she'd said it a million times before. "You'd think I raised a bunch of wolves." Her eyes rolled.

Liam's and Leith's lips both twitched, and she sent me a motherly smile that made me miss mine. It was easy to see why Sydney had been my mom's best friend. She was the most likable shifter I'd ever met, and she had a way about her that made me feel safe and cared for.

Pulling on a pair of gloves, she got to work cleaning and disinfecting the surface area before removing the bullet from my leg. I was looking forward to neither practice.

The couch dipped on my left side, and I twisted my head to see Liam sitting beside me. Leith had been sent on another errand to retrieve bandage wrapping from the upstairs closet. The effects of the heir prince's kiss were wearing off. My body was in this constant tug-of-war between pain and healing, the silver in my leg hampering what should have come naturally.

"I'm going to give you something for the pain," Sydney said, readying a syringe of medicine from a bottle.

Compared to the open hole in my leg, I didn't feel the tiny prink as she administered the good stuff. It hit my bloodstream quickly, making my limbs heavy.

"You've done this before, right?" I mumbled.

She laughed. "I've had plenty of practice stitching up two particular wolves, and believe it or not, I have removed a few bullets in my day. You're going to be fine, I promise, and I don't lie. Ever."

I couldn't believe the baroness of Riverbridge was removing a bullet from the side of my calf. What were the fucking chances?

I didn't have time to think about it for more than a few moments as the disinfectant bubbled and oozed into the bloody mess.

I dropped my head back and bit down on my lip, hard, drawing more blood I didn't have to lose, but it was the only thing to keep me from screaming as the disinfectant worked its way into the hole. My muscles tensed. The towel placed under the table caught the drippage.

Liam tucked a damp strand of hair behind my ear, his fingers lingering on the column of my neck. I cut him a look, his eyes connecting with mine. It was there, the pull I'd felt from the first day I saw him but refused to acknowledge. I didn't want to admit it now.

I couldn't look away. This boy's eyes felt like a mirror to my soul.

Once Sydney finished cleaning the area, she took a tool out of her bag that looked like a cross between mini forceps and tweezers, and although I caught her movements from the corner of my gaze, it was Liam who warned me.

"Don't faint," he said, our eyes still locked, neither of us blinking as he reached for a piece of my hair.

"Please. Don't insult me."

Sydney took advantage of my distractedness and, without prompt, stuck the tool into the wound at the same time that Leith held down my leg to keep me from moving it.

Holy shitballs.

My eyes widened, a hand flying to the edge of the couch and gripping it as I fought through a wave of pain so fierce tears stung my eyes. The world blackened at the edges. "Okay, I might pass out," I gritted out, my body begging me to submit to oblivion rather than endure any further pain. I'd suffered enough.

Liam reached for my hand, and the swirling blackness that crept into my line of vision edged away, bit by bit.

Sydney gave us a brief glance. She didn't say anything but a glimmer of something flashed in her eyes. Relief? Happiness? Concern? I couldn't tell, but then again, I wasn't in the best shape to be reading people.

"Got it," she breathed, and the room seemed to sag in relief until she said, "Your father will want to see this."

Liam looked away, and his jaw went taut. Pinched between the extractor sat the culprit of my agony—a tiny silver bullet. Sydney and Liam shared a glance that would have made me think they were hiding something if I were in my right mind.

"You're lucky it was your leg the bullet hit and not anywhere close to your heart," Leith said, staring at the thing that could have killed me.

The bullet clattered into a stainless steel bowl. "Now that we got it out, you'll start to feel better," the baroness advised. "Your body will be able to heal faster. I'm going to put in a few stitches to close the wound until then and wrap it up. I imagine tomorrow you should be able to walk on it without pain."

I just had to get through the night.

"I don't know how to thank you."

"You're like a daughter to me, and not just because some treaty signed years ago declares you mate my son."

Liam's fingers fidgeted underneath mine. I'd forgotten that our hands were still intertwined. Perhaps I should release my grip, but I feared if I did, the tranquility his touch offered would dissipate, and I wasn't ready for it to end.

Not yet.

Sydney threaded a funny-looking needle. "Since the day you were born, I wished I'd been able to see you a million times over the years. I will find a way to keep you safe, and right now, there's no place in River-bridge safer than this house."

Leith hovered behind his mother, watching over her shoulder as she worked, but he lifted his gaze at her statement, his brows coming together. Did he find it odd that his mother had used "I," not "we"? Like she would personally see to ensuring nothing happened to me again. Not the alpha. Not the pack.

Homesickness clogged my throat. I swallowed over the lump. "My mother spoke of you often. She misses you."

A sad smile stirred on her lips, and her glassy eyes pooled with tears that refuse to fall. "We'll talk more in the morning after you've rested." Her attention shifted to her son beside me. "Take her upstairs, Liam, to the guest room. I'll call Penelope and let her know Kelsey will be staying with us." She stopped the protest on the tip of my tongue. "And before you argue, it would please me if you stayed. I'd like to monitor you for the night. It would ease my mind."

I nodded. How could I deny the woman who helped me? "Thank you." I was glad Sydney was going to call Nana. She would worry. I chewed on my lip, thinking about Nana alone at her house.

Sydney patted my hand. "I'll let her know you're okay. You're a brave young woman, Kelsey. You'll do well as a baroness. Better than me."

The moment she was alone, those tears she vigilantly held back would fall like a dam breaking. I hadn't noticed before, but cloaked behind her eyes was a well of sadness... and secrets.

Sydney knew something, and it frightened her.

Or the drugs could have been making me see shit.

Sixteen

I couldn't believe I was spending the night under the same roof as Liam. That had to be a horrible idea.

The heir prince carried me upstairs while Leith stayed with his mother to help clean up. Soft, luminous light from the ceiling brightened the hallway, beaming over rich wooden floors covered in a long runner. On the walls hung framed family photos of Liam and Leith at various ages. With curious eyes, I peeked into open doors until Liam stopped.

From what little I could see, the Castles were well-off. I couldn't remember what the house looked like when Liam had pulled in, but the interior reflected Sydney's style—simple, modern, yet also warm. It was a home that was lived-in but not cluttered with unnecessary possessions.

It was also large. I counted at least five bedrooms upstairs. Liam entered the one at the end of the hallway, the floorboards squeaking slightly under his feet.

"Can you stand?" he asked.

In the dark room, I glanced at him and swallowed. "I'll manage," I assured him, more than ready to put some space between us. I was overstimulated at this point. Too much Liam in one day. Being in his pres-

ence was like a drug I needed to monitor in small doses or risk being fucking high out of my mind.

Any more and I might OD.

He set me down on my feet. Careful to keep my weight off my right leg, I balanced to one side. His hands lingered at my waist, making sure I didn't hit the floor, and when I didn't immediately topple over, he moved to turn on a bedside lamp. A soft glow brightened the room with walls the color of oatmeal. In the center, a plush rug sprawled underneath an iron-framed bed donned with different textures of fabrics and pillows of mossy green and white.

A piece of unique artwork hung above the bed that was more like sculpted art that I doubted was sold at any home goods stores in town. It looked commissioned or bought directly from an artist. Not that I was any expert when it came to art, but my mother also had a thing for buying custom designs over manufactured ones. She said it added character to a room.

Everything from the bed to the decor reminded me of home—of my mother. It made me want to cry. Emotion lingered in the back of my throat, tears stinging my eyes.

If I heard my mother's voice right now, I would lose it. Big, sloppy, ugly tears, and I didn't think I would care. I wanted nothing more than a hug from my mom.

Liam watched me. I sensed his attention. He might have thought my reaction strange, but it was easy to rationalize that the events were finally catching up to me.

"My mom wasn't lying. You don't need to worry. You'll be safe here," he softly pacified.

I sniffled and nodded, unable to actually speak. And I didn't want to correct him.

He rubbed at the back of his neck, and I noticed the dark stains on his shirt. My blood. "The bathroom's on the left. It should have everything you need, except for a change of clothes. I'll find you something to wear and leave it on the bed."

"Thank you. For everything. I don't know what I would have done if—"

He pressed his finger to my lips. "Don't say it. Nothing is going to happen to you. I won't let it."

Staring into his heated, sparkling eyes, I began to think the heir prince might not be such a jackass after all. Perhaps he didn't have a million redeemable qualities, but he had one that mattered.

Strong-willed.

He was known for many things. A liar was not one of them. If any other wolf had made the same bold vow, I would have laughed it off. With Liam, it was a promise he would keep at all costs, which should have comforted me instead of sparking nerves.

He left before our locked gazes became something neither of us was ready to handle.

Hobbling on one foot, I used the furniture in the room to help maneuver to the bathroom. I had to pee like a motherfucker.

The bathroom was opulent. Champagne-colored tiles covered the wall from floor to ceiling in the walk-in shower. I looked at it longingly, wishing I could climb in. But as much as I wanted a hot, steamy shower, it wouldn't be good for my wound.

I peeled off the grossest set of clothes I'd ever owned, knowing there was only one place for these jeans and shirt—a firepit. They had to be burned. The stench of my blood covered everything. This was one of those times I wished I could dial down the strength of my senses.

I shoved the soiled clothes into a small waste bin, tying the liner inside into a knot.

Blood had dried in the smallest folds of my skin, under the nails, and in places it shouldn't be. Doing the best I could with a washcloth and warm water from the sink, I scrubbed at my hands, face, arms, and just about every part of me that needed it. I did feel almost human afterward.

The lower part of my leg was swollen and red, and I stared at the white bandage wrapping around my calf. Had the pack been able to catch the hunter? Was he still out there, already planning his next attack? He would try again, I was certain.

I stared at my reflection in the mirror. She didn't look like me. Not at all like I had been a few months ago. The girl I'd left at home. Since coming to Riverbridge, I'd become a different person, pretended to be someone I wasn't, and in doing so, I lost who I was.

I had to stop the charade.

Claiming Liam was no longer my biggest problem.

Looking at the girl in the mirror, I saw the fear in her eyes—my eyes. Without the protection of my pack, I was left vulnerable here and would continue to be so until Liam claimed me.

The real game had started—the hunt.

The way I saw it, I had two choices: I could continue to be the hunted... or I could become the hunter.

I waited until I heard Liam deliver the borrowed clothes and then leave, closing the door softly behind him.

Naked, I cracked open the door and peeked out to verify the room was indeed empty. Favoring my right leg, I padded to the bed, spotting the T-shirt and sweatpants folded neatly on top of the mattress. It took me twice as long to reach the bed, and when I did, I traced my fingers over the shirt, knowing it would smell like Liam. I was going to spend the night wrapped in the scent of him, and it made something inside my chest flutter.

Fucking hell, Kelsey. Don't tell me you're actually catching feelings for him.

So what if I was?

Slipping the shirt over my head, I sat on the edge of the bed and carefully pulled on the sweatpants one leg at a time. The whole ensemble was big on me but in an extremely comfortable way. As expected, the crispness of pine, cedarwood, and hints of juniper clung to the clothes. If I closed my eyes, I could deceive my mind into thinking Liam sat beside me.

The wolf within me woke up, called by the scent of another wolf— her mate.

A longing to see his face knocked against my heart, a longing I didn't want. It was stupid to say I didn't feel something for the heir prince, but how deep those feelings went was still unexplored, territory I wasn't sure I was ready to chart.

Not yet.

Shaking all the forlorn and heavy shit from my head, I pulled back the covers and climbed into bed. The tableside lamp still offered a cozy glow that I found both comforting and relaxing.

I had just settled in when someone quietly knocked on the door. A moment later, it opened, and the baroness glanced inside.

"I thought you might be hungry." She carried in a tray. "It's nothing fancy, just some pot roast I had cooking in the oven and a slice of bread."

My stomach growled at the presence of food.

Sydney smiled, hearing my eager belly. "I take it that means you're hungry."

I nodded. "Thank you. It smells delicious."

Setting down the tray on the bed beside me, she placed a glass of water on the nightstand. "I also wanted to let you know I spoke with Penelope. She was understandably very concerned about you, but I assured her that you were fine, safe, and recovering. I'm sure she would love to hear from you once you've rested and feel up to it."

I dropped my gaze to the bed, where my fingers fidgeted in my lap. "I don't want to worry her."

"As a mother, I can tell you that some things are unavoidable. But Penelope knows how strong you are." Sydney tucked a strand of hair behind my ear. "You're special, Kelsey."

"Does Liam know?" I asked, wondering if she'd told her son about my powers.

She patted my hand. "It's not my secret to tell. That's up to you." Her expression held such understanding and a touch of awe. "I brought a few pills for pain in case you need them, but take them after you eat. If you need anything, please ask. I want you to feel comfortable here."

After she made me promise, the baroness left, leaving me to devour the food she brought up with her. I didn't know if it was because I was famished, but Sydney made the best damn pot roast, and my body needed the fuel to regenerate all the energy that had been sapped from me.

As I finished off the last morsel of buttered bread, I sensed someone outside the bedroom door. The shadow of their feet moved under the doorway, pacing back and forth. I set the tray aside on the table, the tingles only Liam could entice dancing on the back of my neck.

He continued hovering outside the door, neither walking away nor coming inside, and I watched, curious about how long he would torture us both.

Finally, I couldn't take it anymore.

"Liam," I called, my voice a hushed whisper, but he would hear me. Any louder and the entire house would know.

The shadowy feet under the door paused. Another long moment passed before the knob turned and his body filled the entrance.

He'd showered, his hair now clean and no traces of my blood anywhere to be seen or scented. In clothes like those I wore, he lingered in the doorway.

"I thought you might be sleeping. I didn't want to wake you." All those questions he'd refrained from asking were in his eyes now.

"Not yet," I replied, my head tilted to the side. As tired as I was, I couldn't sleep. Too many factors contributed to my racing mind. I didn't know how I could get them to quiet down.

"How are you feeling?" he asked, his gaze drifting to my leg for a brief glance before returning to my face.

"Better." Was it my imagination, or were things weird between us suddenly? It made me almost miss the angered tension. At least then I knew where we stood. This uncertainty made me anxious. "How long are you going to darken the doorway?"

His lips twitched. "I haven't decided yet."

I needed to clear the air. I wouldn't be able to fully relax until we got this out of the way. "You have questions. I get it. Just ask me. I might surprise you by actually answering." I patted the bed, signaling for him to sit.

He didn't immediately react, which meant he hadn't decided whether he should stay. I could practically see him weighing the pros and cons in his eyes. Saying nothing, I watched him work through whatever debate went on in his head.

Slipping into the room, he closed the door softly behind him. My eyes never left his as he crossed the room, stopping in front of the bed. He didn't sit but stood, hovering over me. Darkness shielded half his face, the other warmed by the lamp.

Liam studied me. Not in the same way as someone who just found out I was a shifter, hesitant, curious, and slightly afraid. The heir prince's expression came across as confused. "You saved my life," he murmured, sounding not altogether pleased.

I swallowed hard, hating the memory that flashed through my head, the bullet speeding straight for Liam. "I guess we're even now. Well, technically, you've saved my life three times now. I'll make sure to catch up."

"This isn't a game, Kelsey." He tended to only use my name when he meant business. "No one is keeping score."

Cutting a sharp glance at him, I replied, "The hunter is. This whole thing... it's one big game to him. And I'm the prize."

With a frown on his lips, Liam said, "Good thing I never lose."

I rolled my eyes. "Arrogant much?"

A shoulder lifted in a lazy shrug. "How did you do it, pup? How did you stop the bullet?"

The urge to play dumb or pretend ignorance climbed into my chest, an automatic response for something I had protected my entire life. I might not always like Liam, but I could trust him. My instincts were buzzing for me to tell *him* the truth.

I toyed with the hem of the borrowed shirt. "Could you sit first? You standing over me is making me nervous."

His eyes traveled over my face, brows lifting. "I didn't think anything could rattle your nerves."

"Nothing but you," I mumbled, wishing I hadn't drunk the entire bottle of water. Not only would I have to pee again soon, but dryness scratched my throat with no way to relieve it.

"Why does that please me?" It couldn't be normal to move so seamlessly from serious to playful in the blink of an eye. It made my head whirl, but to my surprise, Liam obeyed, finally sitting on the edge of the bed, keeping a safe distance from me.

I had a million snappy retorts on the tip of my tongue, yet I unleashed none and chose to answer his question. The sooner I got this off my chest, the less anxious I'd feel. Or so I hoped.

"I've protected this secret, this part of me, with as much vigor as I've protected my identity as a shifter. More so, if I'm being honest." I paused, taking a deep breath. "I have a sixth sense. It's extremely rare, but some shifters are born with an extra ability. That's how I was able to stop the bullet from hitting you."

"You have magic?" A strand of golden hair fell over the side of his forehead.

My fucking fingers itched to brush it away. Twining my hands together, I nodded. "Some. It's limited. I'm not like a witch or something."

"How?"

"It's a gene carried by the maternal side of my family, passed down through generations."

"You're saying Nana has this sixth sense? And your mother?" Skepticism flickered in his eyes.

"It's a little more complicated. Nana does, but the ability can often skip a generation, as it did with my mother."

He got more comfortable on the bed, stretching his long legs out. "How does it work? Can you only create barriers like the one you did tonight?"

"I could with training and practice. I don't know the extent of my abilities. My father didn't want me using it," I explained. "Once I learned to control the power, I pretty much locked it away. Shielding myself from danger is the only thing he allowed me to learn."

"That's why the hunters want you."

"I believe so. I don't know how the hunters found out about my sixth sense. Other than today, I haven't used my power in years, ever since I learned to control it."

"I don't think they just found out about your ability. I think they just found *you*. Your father kept you hidden all these years. It's why you never came to any of the meetings, why I never saw you again. He couldn't risk you being found. But now..."

"He didn't have a choice. The treaty," I finished.

Liam nodded somberly. "To break the treaty would be an act of treason. And knowing my father, he would have taken it to the king."

I'd never heard him talk about his father. I had no idea how he felt about him. If they were close. If he respected the prince. But I didn't think so. Seeing flecks of scorn and animosity flash into the center of his eyes, I suspected Liam and the prince didn't see eye to eye. I'd sensed

tension at the summons between them, and it had me wondering...
what kind of relationship did they have?

I couldn't believe we were sitting in bed together talking about our
parents. When I imagined the heir prince and me in bed, we were doing
anything but talking.

"Your mother knows. Mine probably confided in her when they
were younger. It's why I was chosen as your mate," I said. "Your father
has long since wanted to merge our bloodlines after learning of the gene
she carries."

His head hit the headboard, dots connecting in his eyes. "That's
why he wanted her as his mate. And when she left, he found a way to
ensure our bloodlines are tied."

I nodded.

A hand went through his hair as he stared off into space, missing
pieces of his life coming together. "Now I understand the depths of his
hatred for the woman who left him. I had thought it was a broken heart
from being rejected. He never loved your mother, only desired what she
might give him."

Drawing in a deep breath, I picked at my nails. "I never meant to
bring trouble. My father was always protective, but I'm starting to see
just how much he shielded me."

"It seems both of our fathers are keeping things from us."

"Shocking," I said dryly.

Liam's arms slackened on either side of him as he twisted to face me.
"Are there others like you?"

His curiosity about my power was easier to talk about than our
parents. "I'm not sure. If there are, I've never crossed paths with another
shifter who had the sixth sense, besides Nana."

He scowled, the low golden light hitting the wink of a dimple. *So
they don't only appear when he smiles.* "It makes you wonder what else
our parents are keeping from us," he mused.

A weird sense of doom spread in my gut. "I'm not sure I want to
know."

"Hmm." His gaze landed on my face. "You're tired. I should let you
sleep."

"But you have more questions." The statement tumbled off my tongue in a rush.

"They can wait."

Again, his control struck me. How could someone possess so much restraint?

Perhaps it wasn't only sheer discipline. Faint shadows circled under his eyes. Exhaustion nagged at him as strongly as it did me.

"Don't leave," I whispered, laying a hand on Liam's forearm. I lifted my gaze, my heart thundering in my chest. "I don't want to be alone."

At first, I thought he might decline. A grain of hardness tightened around his eyes, but I couldn't be sure it hadn't already been there before I spoke. "I'll stay as long as you would like."

I couldn't believe what I'd asked. How had everything changed so quickly? The truth was I didn't just want to not be alone. I wanted *Liam* to stay.

We stared at each other, neither of us moving as an awkwardness danced in the air. This was the first time we were alone in a room with a bed. In his house. With his parents somewhere under the same roof. What had I been thinking? Am uncertainty I hadn't expected had me gnawing on my lip.

I was about to tell him what a stupid idea this was and that I'd be fine when he stood up and peeled back the covers. The bed was plenty big for the two of us without touching, yet he hesitated. A hint of a smile tugged at my lips. Somehow, the more uncomfortable I made Liam, the more entertaining it became, despite also being highly embarrassing for me. The amusing factor made it worth it.

Rolling my eyes, I grabbed his hand and pulled him into the bed. "I won't bite. Not tonight."

Liam shook his head, settling in alongside me as I snuggled down into the bed, resting my head on the pillow. "You must be feeling better," he said, his expression softening.

I wanted to turn and face him, but with my leg, I figured the less I moved it the better. As a side sleeper, it would be difficult to sleep on my back. Twisting my head on the pillow, I glanced at the side profile of his face. "You're not as bad as you want me to think." Tonight, I was feeling exposed and vulnerable, saying things I would normally hold back. Tomorrow, I would regret most of this conversation.

Liam lifted the arm closest to me and slipped it under his head. "How do you figure?"

"If there's one thing I've learned about you in the past few weeks, it's that you're strict on duty, yet you also have your own moral compass. You don't always do as you're told. It makes you intriguing... and annoying."

"You need to stop hanging around my brother so much."

Drawn to him, I inched closer, the sides of our bodies touching, but it wasn't enough. I could crawl on top of him, wrap him in a monkey hug, and it still wouldn't be close enough. This craving for him only burrowed deeper inside the longer we were together.

I lifted my hand, laying my palm on the center of his chest. "You knew I was in trouble. I don't understand how, but you came. You found me." I could think of no other way how Liam happened to be in the woods. Following me was one explanation, but I would have sensed him, and I saw him drive off in his truck, which would have put him ahead of me on the trip home.

Under my fingers, the beating of his heart quickened at my words. "I don't understand it either. I haven't claimed you, and yet..." He lightly brushed his thumb over the back of my hand.

My head somehow ended up in the crook of his arm. "What?" I prompted.

"Sometimes it feels as if we're connected."

And there it was. The thing neither Liam nor I wanted to admit, but since he had been the first to say something, I owed him the decency of admitting the truth. "I feel it too. No matter how much I try to deny it. But you're still an asshole," I added, unable to help myself.

The dark, husky chuckle warmed my ears. "Why didn't you shift in the woods?" he asked, the arm behind his head coming down around me, landing near my hip. "When the hunter was chasing you, why didn't you go wolf?"

"I was about to, but he shot me as I was shifting. Did you get his scent? Recognize him?"

Liam's fingers drew lazy circles along my side, his light touch seeping through the material and doing crazy things to my heart. "No. The bastard covered his tracks."

"Did the pack catch him?" I asked hopefully.

His body tensed. "No. He got away."

A shiver trilled through me. "Do you think there are others?"

The fingers at my hip stopped moving. "I don't know," he said, an edge of worry in his voice. "But unless my father wants to lose what he worked so hard to gain, then he's going to have to find a way to deal with the hunters. Soon."

Silence fell.

What he wasn't saying was he might not always be there to save me. That next time, the hunters might succeed.

Each time they had come closer. It wasn't a matter of *if*. It was a matter of *when*.

SEVENTEEN

The Prince of Wyoming wasn't home, but the alpha had probably already heard of my attack. Word traveled in packs faster than small-town gossip.

Liam was right. His father would step up security, meaning less freedom for me, at least until my eighteenth birthday. I wasn't looking forward to either.

Having the heir prince beside me kept my mind from obsessing. Without him, I doubted I would have been able to relax enough to fall asleep. His presence gave me more than a sense of calm. I sank into him. His warmth. His strength. His scent.

How odd that the same wolf who made me want to kick him in the balls, made me want to run for the hills, was also the one who quieted the emotional storm within me.

I'd never had a pillow as comfy as Liam. The even rhythm of his breath and the steady beating of his heart lulled me toward the place of dreams.

On the verge of falling asleep, I felt the presence of another wolf, and it tugged me away from dozing off.

The mattress dipped as Liam untangled his arm from under my head and slipped out of bed. A soft moan of protest escaped from my

lips, but, too tired to do anything but lie there, I listened as he went to the door. My eyes opened partially to see Liam leaning against the frame of the slightly ajar door. In the dark, his outline blocked my view of who stood on the other side. I didn't need to see, though, not when my other senses recognized the wolf.

Leith.

I relaxed into the plush bed, assured trouble didn't brew outside the bedroom. At least not the kind that would require me to get out of bed.

"So, you finally stopped fighting with yourself," Leith said, his hushed voice carrying into the room in a whisper.

"I don't know what you're talking about," Liam retorted, displeasure coating his response.

"She's great, you know. It's about damn time you realize it."

Disgruntled, Liam folded his arms. "Who said I never noticed?"

Leith made a snorty grunt. "It took you long enough. You're not normally so slow, bro."

"And you're not usually so interested in a girl," he retaliated, sounding a tad irritated.

"She's different." Leith wasn't typically so serious, but tonight he lacked any traces of his natural humor.

I couldn't make out every detail of Liam's face, but his expression hardened. "Are you saying you're interested?"

"What if I was?" Leith challenged. I couldn't tell if he was jesting, trying to get a rise out of Liam, and it made me want to see his face. I nearly sat up in bed before remembering I was supposed to be sleeping.

Liam let out a low rumble that I swore shook the bed.

His brother chuckled. "Chill. You're lucky Kelsey and I are just friends, because if I *was* into her, I'd move in on that girl so fast your head would spin."

The heir prince's spine stiffened. "You could try, but I wouldn't."

Leith chuckled again. "I don't get you. You reject her, yet no one else can have her. That's not how life works, Liam."

His shoulders dropped on an exhale. "I just need time to figure shit out."

"And while you do, you'll keep her safe." It wasn't a question but a demand.

A light glow brightened around Liam's eyes. "I did, didn't I?"

"Tonight, maybe, but more trouble is coming." An ominous tone blew into Leith's voice. "I know you feel it."

The aura surrounding Liam darkened. "I'd give up my life to keep her alive." The sheer conviction I heard from him surprised me, and I had to suppress the gasp that bubbled up my throat.

"Good. That's what I thought, but I wanted to hear you say it," Leith said, seemingly satisfied with Liam's response.

The older Castle shook his head. "Now that we're clear, let me get some sleep."

"Does Mom know you're spending the night in her room?" The amusement returned, chasing away any lingering tension between the brothers. It had never been my intention when coming here to drive a wedge between Liam and Leith.

I could tell it was an effort for Liam not to growl as his gaze narrowed. "She probably does now thanks to your big-ass mouth."

"Sleep tight, bro." I didn't have to see Leith's face to know he probably shot Liam an impish wink or grinned like the total shithead he was.

〉〉●〈〈

I'D HAD this dream before. I was standing on the cusp of a cliff with nothing but spiny branches, craggy rocks, and pointy thorns below me. At my back, a threat lingered in the dense woods. The same threat that had haunted me my entire life.

But this time, I wasn't the prey running in the woods.

Another wolf tore through the dark trees. Not a glimpse of moonlight peered through the clouded sky, making the forest an eerie labyrinth of darkness. I glanced behind me and then back to the ravine below, uncertainty coursing through my blood.

I had to find him before the hunter did.

An icy chill carried on the winds, the sort of cold that belonged on a cold January night as I turned away from the cliff. It ruffled my fur as dark as the bottom of the sea.

Piercing the quiet, a long, howl broke through the trees, echoing up into the blanketing clouds.

Liam.

His name vibrated in my blood. Called to me. Not to come to him but to run. To keep running. To not stop until I was safe.

But I couldn't.

How could I possibly leave him?

Just as he was wired to protect me, I was to him, and no way could I run without him.

I dashed back into the woods, my paws flying over the pine-covered floor. Despite the strength of my wolf eyes, there was no end to the darkness that stretched from all angles. It felt like I ran blindly, the darkness squeezing in on me, breathing down my neck, whispering in my ear.

Frantically running would get me nowhere. I was no closer to finding Liam than I had been when I reached the cliffs. Hopelessness raked like claws inside me, leaving scars of panic and fear.

A flash of white zoomed by the corner of my eye, and I turned toward it, seeing what looked like a shooting star flying through the branches, leaving behind a trail of sparkling dust. The particles were so minuscule, they didn't do much to combat the never-ending darkness, but I chased after them, desperate for a sign.

I pushed my body, spearing forward harder and faster to try and keep up with the trail of light before it fizzled out. The star or whatever moved through the woods with a speed I could barely keep up with. It wouldn't be long before I lost the dust completely.

I stumbled, tears pricking my eyes, that feeling of despair crashing into me harder than before. To have a flicker of hope only to have it quickly extinguished before it fully bloomed. It was like being offered your favorite piece of candy and having it taken away right as you were about to take your first bite. But a thousand times worse. Someone's life was on the line.

My spirit dejected and at the point of giving up, I finally felt those familiar tingles prancing up my spine. He was near.

But so was the hunter.

Bursting through a cluster of trees into a small clearing, I skidded to a halt. The whites of his eyes cut through the dark like a knife, glinting off the rifle he held pointed out in front of him. No matter how hard I tried, I couldn't make out a single feature on his face other than his eyes. They were the eyes of a ruthless killer.

Teeth flashed.

A low growl shook the trees, sending leaves twirling to the ground.

My chest vibrated, and it was then I realized the warning had been mine.

The hunter chuckled.

Boom!

The gun discharged.

I waited for the pain, for the slick, hot feeling of blood, for the sharp, metallic scent.

Nothing.

Yet my heart raced. Sheer terror clutched my chest, squeezing so I couldn't draw breath.

The clouds parted, letting streams of moonlight enter the clearing. A whimper pulled my gaze downward.

Liam lay motionless on the ground, his shirt soaked red right near his heart. The vital organ beat, but the rhythm slowed, and I knew in less than a minute, it would stop beating entirely. His lips formed my name as he stretched out his hand, the bright glow of his aqua eyes flickering when they met mine.

I was too late.

The panic tearing and shredding within me increased tenfold.

He couldn't die. He just couldn't.

I took a step toward him, completely forgetting about the hunter until I heard the cocking of his rifle. I lifted my eyes from Liam's to see the bastard standing over the heir prince's body. Shadows still concealed his face as he pressed the flat of his boot into Liam's gut. Blood gurgled out of my mate's mouth, dripping down the sides of his chin.

Hatred like I'd never experienced before swelled inside me, burning like a river of molten lava. I would kill him. My canines flashed as I snarled. The hunter jammed the barrel into the broad part of Liam's chest, and although I couldn't see his face, I sensed the bastard's grin.

I lunged, surging through the darkness.

The hunter squeezed the trigger.

)) ● ((

I jolted awake to darkness, and for a few stolen moments, I couldn't decipher if I was indeed awake or still trapped in the nightmare.

It was the soft bed underneath me and the white ceiling above that cleared the haze of confusion and took the edge off the fear sucking me dry.

This wasn't a new dream. I'd had recurring nightmares of being hunted most of my life. Even prior to knowing hunters existed, my nights had been plagued by being chased down and killed, in both human and wolf form. There was never a preference for one over the other; the hunters could always sniff me out in both.

My stomach roiled, a clamminess coating my skin.

A hand stroked over my hair, and the storm of emotions inside me slowly quieted.

I stilled, realizing I wasn't alone. Someone was in the bed with me, their body warm alongside me.

Liam.

His scent lingered everywhere. On the sheets. On my clothes. In the fucking air. There was no escaping him, and I didn't want to.

"What are you doing here?" I murmured, feeling disoriented.

Liam cleared his throat, and the hand in my hair fell to the bed. "You were having a bad dream. You screamed."

It all came back to me. The woods. Being shot. Liam carrying me. Bringing me back to his house. The baroness tending to my wound. And me asking him to stay with me. And finally, the vivid dream of Liam dying in my arms. Although the nightmare had been only that, I was still living in a variation of that dream.

Liam wasn't dead, but what I'd seen in my sleep could very well become reality. The closer he got to me, the more danger he put himself in.

I might have been mixed up about my feelings for the heir prince, but regardless of if I loved or hated him, I did not want his blood on my hands. Just as I wanted nothing to happen to Nana.

"Did I wake you?" I asked, turning slightly on my side. If I'd been loud enough to drag him from sleep, had anyone else heard? Had I woken up the whole house?

He shook his head. "No. I can't sleep."

Blinking, I suppressed a yawn, wondering what time it was. "Is that normal for you?"

"Sometimes."

"Did I really scream?" I had cried out in my dream, but had my unconscious body merged with my conscious mind, blending the two worlds in my head? Too fucking complex this late at night.

"You called my name. And you were crying." He brushed his thumb under my eye, dampness I hadn't noticed smearing across my cheek. "You were tossing in your sleep. I tried to wake you, but the dream had a firm hold on you. Then you screamed. I can't explain it, can't explain half the shit that happens when I'm around you, but I could hear you in your dream."

Embarrassment made me want to bury my head in his chest, but I lifted it instead, peering at him as I rested the side of my face on my hand. "So we're both in agreement that this shit is fucked-up."

Liam was impossibly delectable lying on the pillow below me. Relaxed and sexy. The image of him could have been taken directly from a magazine ad for bedding or boxers. Something provocative. "At least we found something we can agree on," he replied as the hand that had only moments ago been touching my face moved to the slope of my hip.

I drew in a shallow breath, and when I exhaled, a laugh bubbled out. Once the first one escaped, another followed, and another until I couldn't control the giggles.

"I'm glad you find this hilarious," he mumbled.

"I don't. It's just... so messed-up. Which, if I think about it, kind of makes sense because *I'm* seriously messed-up, so why wouldn't my love life be too?"

"Love life?" Liam arched a brow. "Are you saying we have something between us?"

My chest spasmed. "Do you want there to be?"

He ran his fingers over the hem of the borrowed shirt, grazing my upper thigh. "Kelsey, you're evading the question."

He wanted honesty. My eyes were drawn to his lips, and I heard his heart quicken. "You confuse me, okay?"

Liam's hand traveled to the back of my knee, lifting my leg slowly so it rested over his. "That's a good thing, pup."

I rolled my eyes, but my body had a different reaction. It had a mind of its own, pressing against him and encouraging the hand on the underside of my thigh to keep going. Higher. And higher. Until the tips of his fingers skimmed over the line of my underwear.

All sorts of warning bells should have been going off in my head, and yet only one word echoed in my thoughts: *More. More. More.* I had to have more of him.

"Does the wound still hurt?" he whispered. Something hot and feral sparked in his eyes, brightening the aqua hue of them.

"What wound?" I asked, dazed. The only thing I felt was the buzzing of electricity humming at every point his body touched mine.

His full lips curled, the scar on the bottom one winking at me. "Try not to get carried away."

I didn't get the chance to tell him it was too late.

Gliding his fingers into my hair, he cupped the back of my head as he leaned over, closing the distance between us. With the first brush of his mouth, he took the edge off the lingering nightmare. I needed to feel his warm lips on mine, needed to know he was alive. This was one way to alleviate my fears.

"Do you want to talk about the dream?" he murmured, his mouth hovering over mine, close enough that we shared the same air. He exhaled and I inhaled. I exhaled and he inhaled.

I shook my head. The last thing on my mind was talking. "I'd rather do this instead." Showing him what I wanted, I melded my mouth to his, seeing his eyes flare right before I closed mine.

There was nothing sweet or innocent about the way Liam kissed me. Or maybe it was the way I kissed him. I could no longer be sure. Perhaps it was the way we came together. All-consuming. Desperate. Frenzied.

The hand edging along my inner thigh moved to my ass, his fingers digging into the rounded flesh through the thin fabric. I moaned, and his tongue touched mine, enticing something far more potent with the taste of him, a pleasure I'd never felt with anyone.

I clung to his shoulders as the strokes of his tongue had my body buzzing, a tightening throb starting between my legs.

"Kelsey," he whispered, our mouths still fused together. It sounded both like a prayer and a curse, as if he couldn't make up his mind.

I didn't want to stop kissing him. I didn't know if I'd ever kissed anyone for this long continuously. It was as if I couldn't get enough of his lips—of his addicting taste.

Liam pushed me down onto the bed, moving with me so he lay half on top of me, his leg wedged between mine. The pillow cushioned my head, and I was grateful for the support. Kissing him didn't just go to my lips or other parts of my body. It went everywhere. My head. My fingers. Even to my fucking toes as they curled under the covers. No part of me was safe from the power of Liam's mouth, his taste, his ability to weaken me.

My fingers moved from his shoulders, trailing up the column of his neck and into his silky hair. His hands began to roam over my body in a slow exploration that had the ability to unravel me. I was the one who lacked control over everything, so it should have been no surprise that in this area, I would be the first to lose myself. The only way this didn't get out of hand would be Liam putting a stop to it. His discipline would have to keep us both from doing the forbidden until we were mated.

Sex was fine.

It was the act of claiming that we had to stay clear of until eighteen, a feat I hadn't thought would be a problem. I had stupidly believed the two could be separated.

That was before I met Liam Castle.

This close to him, this intimacy we were sharing, this heady feeling he created awakened those instinctual wolf needs to make him mine. It hit me with a force that would have knocked me to the ground. No matter how much I wanted to deny that Liam was nothing to me, wrapped up together in the bed with him kissing me senselessly, it was impossible to ignore that he wasn't just another guy.

His fingers moved confidently and expertly, and I bathed in each sensation his touch left behind like little tingling stars dancing over my skin. He was good at this. Too fucking good.

And then I started to wonder how many girls Liam had touched like this. Kissed. Murmured their name. The flash of jealousy came on swiftly but got lost in a wave of desire.

As his fingers went up my shirt, skimming close to the underswell of my heavy breasts, his mouth left mine only to cruise along the side of my jaw, moving to my neck.

I angled my head to the side, arching into the lips pressed against my throat, and my chest rose, lifting encouragingly toward his hand under my shirt.

"How many girls have you been with?" I asked, my voice breathy.

"You're not asking me this right now," he said, taking my ear between his teeth.

It seemed I was. His reluctance made my interest spike. "I'm curious."

His dick was rock-hard, pressing into me. A flash of golden heat ached in my core. "I'll give you a dozen other things to be curious about, pup." His teeth scraped along my earlobe.

I shivered.

"We should stop," he advised weakly, his lips still taunting me.

"Uh-huh," I agreed, my fingers skating the edge of his sweatpants.

He sucked in a soft rush of air. Lifting the shirt up to bare my breasts, he dipped his head, taking a nipple into his hot mouth. My back bowed off the bed, fingers pressed firmly into the back of his head, begging for more. "You have a tattoo."

I did. It was under my arm on the left side, just under my boob. Only visible if I wore a bikini or if I had my top off.

"What other surprises do you have for me to find, pup?"

My canines snapped down, bits of my wolf surfacing. Sometimes it felt as if I were two separate beings: the girl and the wolf. Other times, like now, the shifter and the girl blended seamlessly together, making it impossible for me to tell where one started and the other began. We were one in our desire for this boy. The wolf... the girl... they both didn't just desire his body. They wanted to possess him.

Claim him.

Those sharp pointed teeth in my mouth flashed, and I ran them along the throbbing vein in Liam's neck. I darted my tongue out, tasting him. The heir prince groaned, the fingers at my hips tightening as he ground himself into me.

Claim him.

Our clothes continued to be a nuisance, and I wanted them gone, but with my teeth so close to his skin, they became less important.

Liam abruptly stopped sucking, his head whirling toward the closed door. "My father's home."

The mention of the prince was like a splash of cold water. It was late —or early, depending on how you looked at it—but Liam didn't seem to find that his father was just now coming home as an oddity. "Is it a problem that you're in here with me?"

"I guess we'll find out. He's on his way upstairs."

I cringed.

"Close your eyes, pup," he murmured in my ear as he rolled off to the side, lying beside me instead of on top of me. I missed his weight, the warmth of him seeping into me. He draped an arm lazily over the flat of my belly just as the bedroom door cracked open.

I immediately slammed my eyes shut, doing my best to maintain a relaxed, natural pose on the bed, as if I hadn't a minute ago been fooling around with his son under the covers.

If the alpha hadn't come home, how far would Liam and I have gone?

Things had gotten heated faster than either my mind or body could have kept up with. One moment he was kissing me, and the next I was ready to rip his clothes off and give myself to him—ready to claim him. A fucking frightening thought. Nearly had if it hadn't been for the interruption.

I ran my tongue over the canines still dropped down in my mouth. Every ounce of power in my veins had demanded I sink my teeth into Liam and taste the blood of the heir prince. If we'd been undisturbed another minute, I would have claimed him and risked my family.

To claim Liam before either of us turned eighteen as dictated in the treaty would be considered treason, and we'd be taken to the king. Our parents would be the ones to suffer.

I didn't know if I should be cursing the prince or thanking him.

From behind my eyes, a slash of light cascaded through the cracked door. I held my breath, lying as still as possible. Liam's fingers brushed ever so slightly over mine under the sheets. He taunted me even now, and I swore his lips curved against the pillow at the skipping of my heart.

Without a word, the prince closed the door, his footsteps trailing off down the hallway.

Our eyes opened together. Bright, the depth of his gaze reached me on a deeper level. It would have been so simple to lean into him and pick up where we left off.

It had only taken one fucking night to change everything. I still didn't know what I wanted or what the right thing to do was. But it had become clear that being alone with Liam Castle was as dangerous as being hunted in the woods.

EIGHTEEN

"I should go," Liam said once his father had gone to bed. He scrubbed a hand over his face.

Readjusting my head on the pillow, I inched slightly away from him, putting even the smallest of space between us. "Probably a good idea," I agreed, wedging my shirt down near my hips.

His gaze collided with mine, and a long, intense minute passed before he climbed out of the bed. My fingers curled against the sheets, the pointed tips of my claws tearing the fabric as I watched him strut out of the room.

A whoosh of air left my lungs, and my arms flopped on either side of me.

What a fucking whirlwind of a day.

How did I go from being shot to nearly screwing up everything in less than twenty-four hours? If I'd acted on my impulses, I would have ruined not just my future and Liam's but my family's and his.

What the actual fuck had I been thinking?

And that was the problem. I hadn't been.

In the moment, all I cared about was *my* feeling. How Liam made me feel. There had been no room for anything else.

He and I alone were two sticks of dynamite just waiting for a spark. That was all it would take to blow up both our worlds—a strike of a match.

I could no longer deny that Liam was my mate. Hell, he was more than just a mate. Any wolf could have been my partner. No, this connection between us went deeper.

Moonstruck.

Goddammit.

We were fucking moonstruck.

The moon fates had to be twisted bitches to plan out such a destiny for two wolves. Our parents couldn't have known when they signed the treaty, and from Sydney's and Rowans' reactions at the summons, they hadn't suspected either as we got older.

I didn't bother to try and sleep after the heir prince left. What I wanted was a run, a way to burn off all this excess energy buzzing within me left unsatisfied. A part of me longed to finish what we'd started, and denying myself what I guessed for Liam and me was as basic as breathing hurt in a different way than being shot.

Our connection sanctioned by the moon wouldn't be ignored and postponed for long. I sensed that the longer we were in each other's company, the stronger the link demanded to be fused.

Fighting against the moon was a battle we would both lose. There were some things in the world that no amount of control could change. It would be like deciding I no longer wanted to be a shifter. The wolf was a part of my genetic makeup; no amount of plastic surgery would alter my ability to shift.

Moonstruck meant that no other guy in the world—in the fucking universe—could ever replace Liam. And once we claimed each other, our bond would be like no one else in the pack. Perhaps no one else in the world, considering the rarity of such a connection.

I needed to find out who and when the last time a pair of moonstruck wolves existed. I had questions. A lot of them.

Our lives might depend on it.

WHEN YOU COULDN'T SLEEP, morning felt as if it would never come. I lay in bed for the next few hours listening to the sounds of the house, the little groans, a tree branch tapping a window, the toilet flushing in another room, and the gentle snores of someone getting far more sleep than I was. And then finally the sun crested over the horizon, casting a warm glow behind the closed curtains.

Knowing it was still early, I rolled out of bed, unable to stay enveloped in Liam's scent, and tested my leg. No pain. I headed into the bathroom and quickly peed before sitting on the edge of the bathtub. Bending over, I hiked up the hem of the too-long sweatpants, revealing the white gauze wrapped around my calf. Dried blood stained the front of the bandage, and I began the task of unraveling the thin material.

Flawless skin lay under the dressing, not even a scar left behind as a reminder, yet instead of feeling relieved, an unsettled pit filled my stomach.

Letting the pant leg fall, I disposed of the bandage and washed my face. I had no clothes other than the borrowed ones I wore. Hopefully Liam wouldn't mind if I kept these a little longer.

I tiptoed out of the bedroom, not wanting to wake anyone up. They had already done so much for me. I wouldn't be sneaking down the hall if they hadn't saved me. I owed Liam and his mother my life. Being indebted to someone else didn't sit well with me, but I had no idea how to repay someone who saved me from death. It seemed like something that required more than a bouquet of flowers and a thank-you card.

And after what happened last night between Liam and me, I felt like some space to clear my head would be wise. So why did it feel like I was doing a walk of shame?

Avoiding was my next favorite thing to running away. Everyone had their default way of handling shit. I wasn't saying the way I dealt with uncomfortable situations was healthy, but I never claimed I wasn't a dozen shades of fucked-up. But I owned my flaws.

I made it halfway down the hall when I heard voices. Moving to the stairs, I slowly descended and paused at the bottom step. Liam and Sydney were in the kitchen.

"Mom," Liam groused as if he wasn't thrilled with their early morning discussion.

Sydney picked up something off the counter, the edge of the item scraping lightly over the surface. A cup or plate perhaps. "You understand why Kelsey's different now. If you'd brought any other wolf home with that injury, we would have had a different outcome. Her abilities stopped the silver from spreading into her blood. She contained it to the wound sight."

I had?

"You and Kelsey became something important the night of the summons. If your father had been there last night... if he'd seen what you did..." Her voice trailed off, but I could hear the raw emotion she tried to suppress for her son's sake while also instilling the importance of what she said.

I'd thought about the way Liam's touch counteracted the pain and agony that ebbed and flowed through my leg much of the night. The only thing that made any sense was it had to be a byproduct of being moonstruck.

Due to its rarity, my knowledge of being bonded by the moon was next to nothing, other than whisperings and rumors passed down in stories. None of it was concrete or real. There were no books on the subject, and although there might be a forum or two on the subject somewhere on the internet, it would be difficult to find.

Liam and I were doing this moonstruck business blind. The only way it would be a hundred percent confirmed was once we were mated. Full moon or not, the evidence would be marked permanently on our bodies. That much I did know.

A sigh breezed through Liam's nostrils. "You don't have to tell me. I know."

Was it wrong of me to eavesdrop on their morning coffee conversation? Probably. Was I going to stop? No.

Quietly sitting on the step, I continued to listen.

"You understand why I asked you to protect her now. Things are only going to get worse," Sydney advised, a grimness carrying in her tone. "And I meant what I said. You can't trust anyone. Not your friends. Not the pack."

"I've kept my promise," Liam replied. "Even when she was being a pain in the ass."

She laughed lightly. "That personality trait runs in the family. Her mom was a lot like Kelsey at this age."

"Have you talked with Cecilia?" Liam asked.

Cecilia was my mother's name. I assumed he was referring to her.

"I called her last night. She's understandably worried," Sydney retorted, and my heart sank.

My mother knew I was in trouble, that I'd been hurt, yet I hadn't heard from her all night. I tried not to be disappointed, but *trying to not feel* didn't work out so well. Liam had shattered the shield around my heart, and now I felt so fucking bare to everything and everyone.

I had to rebuild that shit. Quickly.

"We knew this day would come," Sydney continued. "But the two of you grew up too fast. I know it's been hard. It is for me as well. But it doesn't change the fact that we have a leak within the pack. Nothing else makes sense. You must do everything in your power to protect her. Not just for Kelsey's sake but yours as well."

"Do you really believe someone in the pack has betrayed us?" he inquired.

"I want to be wrong, but it doesn't hurt to be cautious." I could tell she truly believed someone from the pack was feeding the hunters information. That was how they'd found me.

A chilling thought.

"I *will* kill them," the heir prince vowed vehemently.

"You and Kelsey seemed to be getting along better."

"That should please you."

"It does. But... I want you to be happy, Liam."

"I'll be happy once we catch the traitor and kill this hunter."

A shadow appeared over me, distracting me from the conversation in the kitchen. I tilted my head back, seeing a grinning Leith. He cleared his throat and sat down on the step beside me. "Anything interesting?" he whispered, sliding those twinkling aqua eyes to me.

Does everyone in this house get up at the crack of dawn? When the fuck do these people sleep? I turned my narrowed gaze on him. "Nothing new."

A single brow rose. "Really?" he mocked. "Since you got here, it's been nothing but interesting."

I threw my elbow into his side, only causing the smirk on his lips to widen. "Do you ever do anything else besides cause trouble?"

Leith gave me a casual shrug, leaning his elbows on the step behind us. "Not really."

Liam came out of the kitchen just then, spotting Leith and me sitting on the stairs. "Seriously?" he said, troubled eyes volleying between us as if he didn't know who to scold first.

I volunteered and stood up. "I know it's early, but any chance you can give me a ride home? I need to check on Nana." I didn't like her being in that house alone when the hunter was still out there looking for me. If there was a traitor among the pack, then there was a good chance the hunters knew where I lived. If they went there...

Eyeing his brother and me, he put a hand on the banister. "Leith, I need your keys."

While Leith ran upstairs, I gave Sydney a quick hug and thanked her profusely for everything she'd done for me. I politely refused her offer for breakfast, but she did manage to get me to agree to a cup of coffee on the go.

My fingers hugged the mug as I climbed into the Jeep. The brisk October morning air kissed my cheeks, making them a bit rosier than usual. Yesterday's rain had brought fall with it, the change in the atmosphere noticeable. The leaves were bolder and brighter in color—cranberry, gold, rust, and various shades in between. The storm swept many of them off the trees, scattering them on the ground. A curling mist hung in the woods bordering the Castles' property, and an owl hooted from a white picket fence post.

Much like I walked out of Liam's house feeling like a different person, the world also felt to have changed overnight.

"Are you cold?" he asked, breaking the silence stretching between us as he started the engine.

Hoodie weather was definitely upon us, and a tinge of sadness hit me in the chest for the loss of those hot summer mornings and long star-dusted nights.

Before I could tell him I was fine, despite my arms being wrapped around myself, Liam took off the football sweatshirt he wore, handing it over, leaving him in just a white T-shirt. "Put this on," he ordered.

The maroon hoodie had gold writing across the chest, the River-bridge High School colors.

As he backed out of the long driveway, I glanced at the charming white house Liam had grown up in. The front porch wrapped around both sides, baskets stuffed with mums dangling from the covered roof that rang the length of the porch. Stone pillars flanked the steps. The windows were all large and inviting. It was the kind of home where you curled up beside the logged fire on winter nights, popped popcorn, and watched movies. Cozy and safe.

That was precisely how it had made me feel last night.

Or perhaps the real reason had been staying under the safe roof as the heir prince. It might not have been the house at all but the wolf who lured those feelings of security.

I glanced at Liam after tugging the hoodie over my head and slipping my arms into the soft material. Spending so much time being surrounded by his scent, I'd grown used to the woodsy hints mixed with his soap and skin. They still made me feel things, just not quite as sharply as before.

It didn't make me want to run.

If fact, I hugged the hoodie tighter to me as I studied his features.

Fuck me.

Am I falling for the heir prince?

It was one thing to acknowledge that he was my mate. It was something else entirely admitting I had feelings for him that weren't born of hate and resentment. But to be fair, it was the idea of Liam that I disliked, not the guy himself. I came here with my mind made up about him, not giving him a chance because I didn't want to be forced into something not of my choice.

To my great annoyance, the real Liam, underneath the facade he presented to the world, wasn't a bad guy.

Despite my acceptance that we were tied together by the moon, I hadn't dissected my feelings for him. I'd just barely wrapped my head around the moonstruck thing and actually accepting our destiny as mates.

I could only come to terms with so much shit in a day.

The whole *feelings* shenanigans would have to wait.

"What are you thinking about?" he asked, pulling me out of my head. He glanced at me before his attention shifted back to the road in front of us.

"That you're too good-looking for your own good," I lied, which wasn't technically a lie. He was attractive. Too fucking attractive. So totally not a lie. It just wasn't what I'd been mulling over.

His eyes narrowed. "Nice try. That BS doesn't work on me. First, I already know I'm fine as fuck. And second, you're not one of those chicks who get hung up on looks."

"And you know that how?" I asked, employing a dose of sarcasm.

Those full lips morphed into a lopsided grin that reminded me too much of his brother. "Because you didn't instantly fall at my feet."

Taking a swig of my coffee, I rolled my eyes. "Wow. That's something I would expect Leith to say."

"Where do you think he gets his charm from?" The heir prince was on a fucking ego roll this morning.

I snorted. "I'll let you know when I figure it out."

Liam wasn't the one who used humor to distract. I found this side of him nice, and it only made him hotter, if possible. But he'd been right. Looks were never the most important trait to me. I wanted a guy who made me feel good, and Liam knowing I needed a distraction added points to his rating.

It seemed as if we'd only been in the car a minute when he steered the Jeep into the driveway leading up to Nana's house. I hadn't realized how close we lived. A few miles at most, meaning only a handful of houses separated us. We lived on the secluded side of town where each home had five or six acres of land, an essential feature for wolves, giving us the ability to run freely in our backyards. Most of the homes in this area were owned by shifters.

He pulled in behind my RAV4 and put the vehicle in Park.

I blinked.

Holy shit. My car.

Until seeing it, I'd completely forgotten that the dumb thing died on me in the school parking lot, the sole reason I'd been in the woods yesterday after detention.

I turned to Liam. "Did you do this?" I asked, indicating at the car.

His gaze followed mine. "I had one of the guys from the shop install a new battery and drive it over."

When the fuck had he had time to do that? "How did you know?" I had trouble recalling if I'd mentioned my car troubles yesterday.

"It's not a weird ESP thing, if that's what you're thinking," he replied, referring to his ability to somehow know when I was in trouble. "I figured there was a reason you were walking in the woods yesterday after detention. I had Riven go back and check the parking lot. He saw your car."

Seemed like a reasonable explanation. "Don't start being sweet. I don't think I can handle it."

The straight line of his lips turned down, forming a very Liam-like frown. "I can assure you that no one has ever referred to me as sweet."

I smiled at the seriousness in his features. "Lucky for you, I don't like sweet guys."

An intensity glowed in his wintery eyes that enraptured me. Just when I thought things between us had mellowed, it took one look like this to amp up the heat.

Did he want to kiss me?

I had such a hard time reading his face, interpreting what went on behind those eyes. A fine line between desire and coldness shadowed his features. Did he want to pull me closer or push me away?

Everything was happening so quickly that I understood all too well the conflicting emotions.

I reached for the door as Liam said, "Don't come to school today."

I glanced over my shoulder. "I hadn't planned on going."

"I'll pick you up Monday." I opened my mouth to decline, but Liam cut me off. "It's not an offer. Be ready by seven."

Simply fantastic. "What about dinner this weekend?"

"Shit," he cursed under his breath. "I forgot. I'll come get you on Sunday too. Here..." He fished his phone out of the cupholder and handed it to me. "Put your number in. I'll text you this weekend and make sure you're still feeling up to dinner. My mom would understand if it's too much."

"Is it weird that we haven't exchanged numbers until now?" I asked, taking the phone and entering my contact info. I handed the device back when I finished.

Liam's lips twitched as he stared at me. "I don't give out my number to just anyone."

I couldn't stop the snort. "Yeah. I'm just your mate."

The dimples in his cheeks appeared, and my heart skipped. "Don't get clingy on me, pup."

"In your dreams, princeling," I replied, hopping out of the car and chiding my weak heart. Who knew I had a weakness for dimples?

Liam waited until I was inside the house before backing out of the driveway. I stood in the entryway and listened as the roar of his engine disappeared, a silly grin on my lips. If I could have seen myself, I would have looked like one of those girls I made fun of for being hung up on a guy.

I made it two steps into the hallway when Nana appeared from the kitchen. Her eyes immediately misted, and I hated the worry I'd caused. She pulled me into a long, hard hug, a strength in her thin arms that defied her age. I let her squeeze me for as long as she liked. She was the closest thing I had to home here, and a pang of emotion hit me in the chest.

As she stepped back, her fingers framed my face, and those sharp violet eyes, so like mine, ran over me. Then she let loose a curse. "I warned that bastard what would happen if he didn't protect you."

I blinked. It took me a moment to understand who she referred to. The alpha. Liam's father. "I'm okay. Liam..."

"Something's changed," she murmured, her eyes studying mine. "You realize the truth now."

"What truth?" I needed her to be a bit more specific.

Nana kept her arm around my shoulders, guiding me into the kitchen. "Your souls are knitted, interwoven by the moon fates."

I sat down on one of the stools as she fussed with the coffee, pouring me a fresh cup. "You knew before the summons?" I guessed.

She set the mug in front of me, along with the cream and sugar. "I had my suspicions," she confirmed, nodding. "But I wasn't sure until I saw the two of you together. The energy between the pair of you is unlike any I've felt."

Sensitive to other people's energy, her powers were more developed and honed than mine were, even if she rarely used them. Her abilities were limited to just shifters, and only a fraction of what she was capable of.

I added sugar, cream, and a dash of cinnamon to my coffee. "Why didn't you tell me?"

Her smile was soft. "Because you, my dear, are like me. We need to figure things out for ourselves. Only then can we accept them. You're strong-willed and need to see and feel things for you to believe them."

She wasn't wrong. I'd come here with a preconceived notion, a chip on my shoulder, and a shitty attitude. I never would have accepted that Liam could be someone deeper than a mate. Hell, I hadn't even thought that a possibility.

"Normally, having fate take my choices away would make me angry, but he saved my life because of this connection we share."

"Liam will be the only one who saves you," she said, a far-off look in her eyes.

Nana had the true definition of sixth sense. Clairvoyance, or what she called divination, the ability to see the future, but she rarely used the sight anymore. It was dangerous to know too much, especially about one's own life or those you loved. She'd known for quite some time how my grandpa would die, and nothing she did over the years changed the outcome. After his death, she locked that part of herself away.

"What have you seen?" I asked gently.

She blinked, her eyes clearing, a smile touching her lips meant to soothe me. It didn't. "Not much, dear," she assured.

"Nana."

Her sigh was heavy, the forced smile vanishing. "I only know that your Liam will face a familiar foe. Someone he knows. He'll have to choose between protecting you or betraying them."

My Liam. The way she referred to him as mine made my heart skip.

"Lovely," I grumbled. "Why are the fates so twisted?" I mumbled to myself, but nothing spoken out loud in front of a wolf was ever for one set of ears.

Nana brushed strands of my long hair behind my ears. "Because we give them purpose. Life is nothing but a bunch of intricate knots that we must unravel. Some are bound tighter than others."

"I hate puzzles."

She chuckled.

NINETEEN

N ana and I spent the day together on Friday enjoying tendrils of the sun as we tended to her gardens barefoot, letting our toes sink into the cool earth. We harvested herbs for dinner, plucked flowers for the house, ate sandwiches on the swing, and made fresh blueberry muffins for afternoon tea.

It had been too long since I'd had such a carefree, magical day. Any time Nana had come to visit, our days were much like this. The time with her unlocked so many warm and good childhood memories. She made the ache of homesickness that still clung to my heart bearable.

I let her fuss over me. Too many times I caught a glimpse of sadness she tried to hide behind smiles. She wasn't the only one who could pick up energy, but my skills were weak compared to hers. I knew enough to sense that something troubled her. Perhaps it had since I'd gotten here if I'd cared to pay attention and hadn't been so absorbed in my self-pity.

On Saturday, I texted Hope, asking if she was still free to go shopping. After the attack, which every shifter at school had heard about by now, she expressed her worry, wanting to make sure I was okay. I assured her I was fine and in desperate need of something appropriate to wear in front of the baroness. Surprising myself, I wanted to show Sydney who I really was, not the girl full of spite or drenched in blood.

Hope picked me up, and we headed to the only shopping plaza in town. The nearest mall was an hour away, but downtown Riverbridge had a bunch of boutiques that would have to do.

We found a parking spot in front of a charming pizzeria that looked as if it had been a part of Riverbridge for decades. When we stepped out of the car, the scent of baked dough wafted with the wind. Warmer temperatures greeted us than yesterday, the sky a cloudless blue. A perfect day for some retail therapy.

God knew I needed a range of therapy, but today, swiping my father's emergency credit card would do.

Downtown Riverbridge could have been a scene plucked from a postcard. It gave Stars Hollow from *Gilmore Girls* vibes, complete with a white gazebo in the center of downtown, decked out in autumn decor. Strolling down the brick pathways, I craved hot apple cider and pumpkin-iced donuts. In the distance, mountains climbed into the sky, and the foothills were brimming with trees. The town square hosted restaurants, novelty shops, a used bookstore, and even a quaint shop that sold wolf lore, figures, paintings, and such. I couldn't help but drag Hope inside for a peek around. I came out with a white wolf charm I couldn't say no to.

Did I buy it because it reminded me of a certain wolf?

Yes. And I wasn't even sure why.

Hope glanced over her shoulder, not the first time.

Tucking the little box housing my charm into my bag, I glanced at Hope. "Are you looking for someone?"

"You're not worried *he* might be out here watching you?" she asked as we made our way through the town square to another store, fallen leaves crunching under our shoes.

The hunter had crossed my mind a time or two. "He probably is, but as long as we're in public with other people around, I don't think the hunters will try anything."

She didn't seem convinced. "No back alleys, got it?"

That I could agree to.

We poked through racks of clothes. "Do you know what you're looking for? Are we going for casual? Or something dressier? A flash of leg, perhaps?" she asked, holding up a short black flared skirt that would have been cute with a pair of over-the-knee boots.

"You tell me. They're your aunt and uncle. Which would impress them more?" I asked, shuffling through a row of dresses without actually paying attention to the designs.

"We're impressing them now?" Hope's brown eyes sparkled. She wore flared jeans and a cropped sweatshirt just short enough to flaunt the gold hoop in her belly button.

I moved to a selection of sweaters, thinking about the cooler air. "Your aunt did save my life."

"Yeah, she's pretty awesome. It's my uncle you need to worry about. He's harder to impress. Alpha complex." She grinned over another skirt as she held it up for me to inspect.

My lips twitched. "Fucking alphas. They're all the same."

She replaced the skirt after I shook my head. "Speaking of alphas... you and my cousin seem to be getting closer," Hope fished.

I wondered what she'd heard. Staying at Liam's house was enough to spread a slew of rumors throughout the school. "Leith is great," I replied, shrugging.

Hope rolled her eyes, abandoning the skirts to stand beside me. "He is, but that's not the cousin I was thinking about. But now I'm curious. All kidding aside, if you had to pick between them, would you choose Leith?"

I chewed on the corner of my bottom lip, taking her question seriously. "Two days ago, I would have answered without hesitation."

"And now?" she prompted as if she couldn't wait another second for my response.

"I don't know," I confessed. "If my decision had no outside factors, no repercussions, it might be different, but I can't deny that I'm attracted to Liam."

A glint moved into Hope's eyes, and her devilish expression reminded me a lot of Leith's. "How attracted?"

Sighing, I turned from the shelf of sweaters and meandered toward the front of the store. Nothing here had caught my eye, but it also could have been that Hope was distracting me with thoughts of the heir prince. "He makes me want to kill him. The problem comes in when I can't decide if I should kiss him before I wring his neck or after."

She wrinkled her nose, making a sour face as she followed alongside me. "Definitely before. Kissing corpses is so not the mood."

I pushed open the door. "Good point. I'll keep that in mind tomorrow when Liam gets under my skin."

A crafty smirk touched the corners of her lips. "Oh, he wants to get under you all right."

The sun warmed my cheeks but wasn't the cause of my pinkened color. Hope's insinuation made me shake my head with a coy grin. "What about you and Gunnar? Is anything there?" I inquired, shifting the conversation off me.

Hope's limp wasn't always noticeable, but today she seemed to be favoring it more than usual, and I wondered if the weather played a role in its stiffness. "I want there to be, and it isn't from lack of trying on my part."

Hanging out with her, going shopping, and spending more time talking reminded me how much I missed having friends. I was glad to have met Hope. She might be the only girl in Riverbridge High who didn't hate me or want to steal my mate.

"What's Gunnar's deal?" I asked, curious about the boy she'd had a crush on for so long.

We hooked around the corner, heading for the next stop. The wind blew pieces of Hope's golden hair behind her. "You think for as long as I've known him, I would have Gunnar figured out. I don't."

Love was never a simple thing. "And guys think girls are complicated."

"No shit," she agreed before gently chuckling.

We shopped for another few hours and ate Chinese food out of the white cartons on a park bench near the gazebo. With our bags in tow, we headed back to Hope's house to watch a movie. This was turning out to be the quintessential girls' day. And I was living for it.

Tess, my best friend at home, and I used to do self-care Sundays once a month, where we did things like get our nails done, go out to eat, shop, grab a coffee, spend the afternoon in a local bookstore, and binge reality TV. The list went on. Over the years we'd done so many activities together that Sundays became a ritual—it was our day.

Hanging out with Hope did make me miss my old life, but it also gave me hope—pun intended—that things in Riverbridge could be fun. That this could be my home. I just had to open myself up to the idea of change.

I texted Nana in the car, letting her know I would be home later than I thought. Her response came as Hope drove up her winding driveway. Dropping my phone into my bag, I got my first look at the beta's home. It was nowhere near as big as Liam's house and far less daunting, but like most of the homes this side of town, it was tucked away in the woods and similar to Nana's. However, instead of a charming craftsman aesthetic, the exterior had a rustic cabin design, all-natural with honey woods and river stones.

A fluffy white pooch greeted us at the door, her tail wagging like she was on speed. "This is Peach," Hope introduced, plucking the little dog off the floor. She nuzzled her face into Peach's neck, smothering her with kisses. "She's a cuddler, not a fighter."

I held out my hand, letting Peach familiarize herself with my scent. "Good to know. And she doesn't have a problem with wolves?" Dogs were usually okay one-on-one with a wolf, but when you got multiple wolves, they were timid and wary.

"Not anymore," she reassured, grinning.

I followed her into the open family room. "Thanks for your help today. It's nice to know there's at least one girl in Riverbridge who isn't a massive bitch."

She set Peach down, who trotted over to the couch and took up her spot in the middle. "Oh, I'm definitely a bitch. I just think our bitch energy meshes."

"Either way, it's nice to have a friend," I said, sinking into the cream-colored couch.

"Same."

While Hope grabbed us drinks and popcorn from the kitchen, I scanned through the list of movies, looking for something to watch. With Halloween only a few weeks away, a spooky or supernatural movie seemed fitting.

Hope bounced back into the room holding a bottle of chilled champagne and two glasses. "How about a toast?" She set the crystal flutes on the oversized coffee table. "To the guys who don't know what they're in for," she wickedly suggested.

I was tempted, the mischief in Hope's expression contagious. "I probably shouldn't," I feebly refused. It had been a while since I had a drink. I wasn't a big party girl. Well, not exactly true. The problem lay in that I had too much fun at parties. I didn't know when to stop, and the only way to ensure I didn't end up passed out on someone else's bathroom floor was to avoid alcohol altogether.

"You need to loosen up. One drink," Hope petitioned, and my resolve weakened. "It'll help you sleep tonight."

And that did it. The recurring nightmare flashed in my head. Undisturbed sleep would be fucking epic. I could only imagine not waking up with bags under my eyes, or with fear pumping in my veins.

I reached for the glass, not needing further persuasion, and waited for Hope to pour us each a small amount. "Cheers," I toasted, clinking my crystal flute against hers and downing the bubbly contents.

One turned into two.

The movie played in the background while we talked, giggled, snacked on popcorn, and, of course, consumed champagne. By the time the credits rolled at the end of the movie, it was almost ten o'clock, and Peach snored happily, sprawled out in the same spot as when the movie started.

"I should probably go home," I said.

Hope and I glanced at the empty champagne bottle and giggled. Neither of us could drive—a bit problematic.

"You could always stay the night," she suggested as she scratched Peach's exposed belly.

My phone buzzed before I thought too deeply about her offer. I pulled it out of my pocket. The device automatically unlocked at the sight of my face. I had a text message from an unsaved phone number.

> Six o'clock

That was all it said. Just a time.

Liam. A dry laugh bubbled out, the champagne making me feel a little too good and brazen.

> Now

I texted back, the stupid grin on my face widening.

> ???

He responded.

> I need you now

I started to type, then amended it to...

> Can you pick me up now? I'm at Hope's

I sucked on my bottom lip, halting the stupid smirk that wanted to appear. I'd give anything to see the heir prince's face right now.

His reply came back a minute later.

> I'll be there in ten minutes

He didn't question why I needed a ride.

Glancing up, I noticed Hope watching me. "Let me guess. That was my cousin. You get this starry sparkle in your eyes whenever he's mentioned."

"It might have been him. But I got a ride," I told Hope, a ridiculous grin curling my lips and excitement dancing in my belly. "Thanks again for coming with me today. I haven't had this much fun since I got here."

Her grin matched mine. "My cousin's in so much trouble."

TEN MINUTES LATER, the rumble of a car came down the road, headlights swinging into the driveway. I waved at Hope in the doorway as I walked down the lighted pathway, doing my best not to stumble on my own two fucking feet.

Feeling damn proud when I got to the car, I opened the door confidently and gracefully climbed in. My boot slipped on the Jeep's footrail, and I tumbled into the seat, the packages clutched in my hand falling to the floorboard. I tried to salvage a fraction of dignity and shoved my dark hair out of my face, righting myself in the seat.

Liam said nothing, just watched me with that perpetual frown he wore too often.

"Your car smells good," I said, my voice sounding dreamy and a little far off.

He blinked. "Are you drunk?"

I shook my head and then held up my hand, pinching my thumb and index finger together but leaving a small amount of space. "Just a little," I said. "It's more of a buzz," I clarified.

The heir prince scowled before leaning over me. I had no shame and inhaled the scent clinging to his skin. He tugged the seat belt across my chest, and our eyes met. Neither of us moved for a heartbeat, his mouth only a whisper from mine. I dragged my lip between my teeth, drawing his focus.

The seat belt clasp clicked into place, but he didn't lean back. "Fuck," he murmured faintly, his lips barely moving.

I wanted him to kiss me, and I could see from the churning of emotion in his eyes that he wanted that kiss, too, which confused the hell out of me when he sat back in his seat, taking his warmth with him.

Slightly annoyed, I dropped my head onto the back of the seat. As the Jeep left Hope's house, I twisted my neck toward him, unable to stop staring at him.

"How's your leg?" he asked, his gaze sliding over my face like a caress.

Shivering, I clenched my thighs together, trying to ignore the happy tingles spreading between my legs. "Like I'd never been shot."

The roads were barren, making it seem like only Liam and I existed in the world, a feeling that happened often when we were together. "Do I want to know how you ended up drinking at Hope's?"

"It wasn't planned. Besides, it's your fault," I pouted, my bottom lip sticking out slightly. We'd been in the car for like a minute, and my whole damn body buzzed with electric need. I wanted him. It would be easy to blame the alcohol, but I was sure that even sober the desire wouldn't have been any less intense. It didn't help that the moon was so bright and beautiful tonight.

"Like I thought. It's better I don't know."

"Pull over," I suddenly said, no longer wanting to suppress my ache for him. I was done fighting. Good thing? Or bad thing? Who knew? My best and worst ideas came after drinking.

Confusion had his brows furrowing together. "What? Why?"

"Because I want a moment alone with you." The best part of living in the woods—privacy. So much privacy. We could run naked down the road, and no one would see us. Probably.

Thinking about Liam naked was going to get me in trouble, but the booze loosened my already questionable restraint.

Sandy hair toppled over his forehead, and my fingers itched to brush the strands aside. "We are alone," he stated the obvious.

I rolled my eyes. "We are, but you're focused on driving." I wanted him focused on me. Entirely on me. No other distractions.

His foot remained steady on the gas, driving the Jeep ahead on the road. A speck of worry leaped into his eyes. "Did something happen?"

"If you pull over, I can explain it." Was that a dirty tactic? Yes. But I wasn't above using them to get what I wanted, and the moment I stepped foot in the car, I'd decided I wanted him.

Blowing out a long breath, he jerked the Jeep off to the side of the road. The tires kicked up gravel as he hit the brakes, killing the head-lights a moment later and submerging the interior in darkness. He turned in his seat. The only light came from the crescent moon, a ribbon of its soft glow hitting the side of his face. "Kelsey, you're not making any—"

I unlocked my seat belt and pressed my mouth to his.

His lips remained still, but only for a second as his mind caught up with his body, and then he was kissing me. His lips moved seductively and unhurriedly over mine, leaving me breathless. It was as if he had all the time in time in the world to savor my mouth, to worship my lips with his. I had anticipated that punch of lust and hungry desperation. Both lust and hunger were present, but more tender and less savage.

I wanted this softer side to never end, but I could already feel the promise of combustible desire invading my body. Tiny sparks skittered into my stomach, and I gripped the front of his shirt.

I had to have more.

I had to have *him*.

I didn't know how I ended up in his lap, but when I opened my eyes, I stared into the depths of the most compelling aqua eyes. I felt myself drowning. My body melded into his, warmth seeping into me.

"What are you doing?" he asked, eyes narrowing despite the silky texture of his tone.

"Testing something." My eyes brimmed with wickedness and delight, my favorite combo. I lifted my hand, needing to touch him. It wasn't enough to be straddled on top of him.

He grabbed my wrist before my fingers reached his face. "Kelsey." The warning lingered in the single word, and I ignored it, much to his displeasure.

Displeasing the heir prince amused me and kind of turned me on. Then again, everything about him produced a sexual reaction within me.

He scowled. My nipples hardened.

He growled. My center ached.

He flashed me his dimples. I nearly orgasmed on the spot.

I couldn't imagine what my body would go through having him inside me. Since Liam first kissed me, every touch, every heated shared look, intensified my reaction. If things progressed, I was afraid I might implode, yet the fear hadn't stopped me from climbing onto his lap.

Someday, he would lose hold of that control, and I wanted to be the wolf who made the heir prince snap.

Lifting my other hand, I ran the pad of my finger down the scar on his bottom lip. He flinched, and my gaze darted up, surprised he would be self-conscious of a minor flaw. "You know, this scar makes you a thousand times hotter," I murmured.

No trace of amusement danced in his eyes, nor were there any signs of the coldness that usually lingered in his expression. Heat burned at the centers of his irises instead. Vivid. Fiery. Wild.

If I got too close...

I wanted to get burned. Somehow the risk seemed worth the reward.

He held my gaze, and a desperate craving spread into my lower belly. Liam's eyes darkened with a feral need that had my breath stuttering in my chest. "That doesn't matter to me."

I angled my head to the side, our lips aligning. "It doesn't, does it? You really don't care about how attractive other girls find you."

"Just one."

"Wow," I whispered, my lips curling. "Lines like that don't normally work on me, but why did I find that so sexy?"

Fingers curled around the back of my ass, pressing into the jean material. "Because you're drunk."

"Perhaps," I agreed, nipping at the scar on his lip. "Or because you mess me up inside." Alcohol made me too honest.

"If we're going to survive the next few months until you turn eighteen, pup, you're going to need to learn to control your hormones."

"Fuck control. Don't you ever just want to let go?" I purposely wiggled my hips against him, and he sucked in the smallest of breaths at the softest part of me rocking against the hard length of him.

"Never." A long heartbeat passed. "Until I saw you."

His answer pleased me too fucking much. "Could you take me without claiming me?" I asked, the question born out of both genuine curiosity and temptress want. Something about Liam turned me into a seductress. I had little experience, yet my body and my mouth knew what to do, what to say. It had never been like this with Huntley. Perhaps it was our connection that made every kiss, every touch, every whispered word between us like a siren's song.

We were exploring uncharted territory. No guidebook for moonstruck mates existed that I knew of.

"Kelsey," he moaned, fingers threading into my hair. "I didn't want to want you."

"The feeling was mutual. But now?"

"Now I'm going out of my mind with wanting you." The fingers in my hair tightened almost to the point of pain, but I fucking loved it. I wanted more than anything to see Liam lose control, to see him lose himself in me.

I was flirting with a dangerous game, but fuck me if I didn't want to play with fire.

"So what's stopping you?" I provoked.

"Kelsey." My name tumbled from his lips in a part moan and part growl.

Then he was kissing me—like *really* kissing me, not like the sweet kiss we shared moments ago. This was nothing like that. His lips branded me—marked me as his. Hunger drove the kiss deeper, and as our tongues tangled, slipping from my mouth to his, I felt the sharp points of his fangs.

My pulse thrummed, and I rocked against him again, seeking a small amount of relief from the ache that throbbed between my legs. But once wasn't enough.

Liam's mouth grew greedier, his touch rougher as his hands came behind me, guiding my hips closer to him and grinding against me.

"I want you," I murmured, but what I really meant was I wanted to claim him. Every time he started kissing me, touching me, that possessive instinct to make him mine rose like a damn storm inside me, and my canines dropped down, preparing, tempting, begging me to pierce his flesh.

All I needed was to mix my wolf saliva with his blood and I would mark him as mine. The two would combine, and any wolf would be able to smell my scent on Liam.

"Fuck, you're gorgeous."

Something in my chest squeezed, my breasts tightening and pressing into him. "Can you smell how much I want you?" Certain emotions gave off scents, desire being one of the strongest smells.

On a growl, Liam's lips yanked off the column of my neck. Through my shirt and bra, his teeth grazed my nipple, turning the pebble into a hard bullet. Heat and lust slammed into me. I held my breath as he applied a tad more pressure, and a whimper escaped my lips.

My head fell back, and I cursed my clothes, wanting to be free of them. I had to have his hot mouth on my skin, had to feel the texture of his tongue.

Liam thrust against me, the muscles in my pussy clenching and jerking with a need so strong, I wondered if it would kill me.

"I knew the second I saw you that you would torture me. Every day, pup. Every fucking day I thought about making you mine. Even when I despised you," he murmured. Then his mouth crashed into mine. Liquid lust pooled in my core, my body overheating. I trailed my fingers to the nape of his neck, nails digging into his skin. The desire within me was so raw, it overwhelmed me.

The crescendo built, and I pressed my palm to the driver's side window as we ground against each other. I knew I wouldn't last much longer. I screamed into his mouth as the shuddering climax ripped through me. I'd had orgasms before, but not like this, not this explosive, and neither one of us was naked. What the fuck did that say?

The tremors continued to rack my body, and it was a fucking effort to keep from collapsing into him. Hungry eyes latched onto mine. Conflict churned in them. His jaw flexed, and I watched him struggle with what we both wanted.

I saw the second he made up his mind and I lost.

Perhaps lost wasn't completely accurate. I had just experienced the most mind-blowing orgasm of my life. A small victory, but not altogether a win seeing as, despite the pleasure, it wasn't enough. Not nearly enough.

And if I didn't do something now, he would pull away from me. I sensed the change, felt it underneath me.

No. I shook my head as I reached for him.

"Don't," he muttered, jerking his head to the side, out of my reach. He dumped me back into the passenger seat, putting what felt like an ocean of distance between us. "Stay," he ordered with such sternness, I flinched, sinking against the seat when all I wanted to do was close the space he'd erected with the cold freeze of his eyes.

How had things gotten so twisted?

How the fuck had I fallen for him?

Oh, right. I never really had a choice.

Folding my arms, I sat rigid in the seat as Liam drove the last mile to my house, stewing. My irritation inflated with the silence that took up space in the car like a third wheel. When the Jeep rolled into my driveway, I slid my eyes to him, but the heir prince didn't meet my gaze.

"Liam—"

"The next time you need a designated driver, call Leith," he snapped, cutting me off. The vehicle hadn't even come to a complete stop when he hit the unlock button on the doors.

I collected my bags from off the floor. "You're a dick," I spat, not completely sure what the hell happened.

How could someone be so fucking hot one moment and then so cold the next that I thought his breath might be capable of frostbite?

Aqua eyes lit up the interior cab, piercing through the darkness like shards of ice. "I need you to hate me, Kelsey. Go," he growled. "Or I won't stop, and both of our families will suffer."

With narrowed eyes, I glared at him for a hard second before bolting out of the car and slamming the door shut.

Hating him had always been easy.

TWENTY

My love-hate relationship with Liam Castle seemed like an endless carnival ride I couldn't get off, leaving me dizzy to the point I might be sick.

He drove me absolutely fucking mad.

I despised him.

I liked him.

I hated him.

I desired him.

I loathed him.

And so the cycle went.

Now I had to go eat dinner at *his* house with *his* parents.

God, why had I called Liam of all people last night to pick me up? And then fully embarrassed myself by throwing myself at him.

Someone shoot me now.

Wait. Someone already had.

Liam and I hadn't spoken since last night, and I spent the majority of the day contemplating whether or not I should cancel this dinner. Then my mother called. A quick phone call to remind me of my duty.

Would it be awkward to see the heir prince after nearly begging him to bang me, only to be rejected?

Fuck yes.

I shimmied into the simple black dress I'd bought with Hope. It had a balance of both casual and sophisticated, giving me a more mature look yet still youthful. I wanted to be taken seriously. I wanted to come across as confident. I wanted to be seen as the future baroness.

Walking down the hall into the kitchen, I followed the scent of burning incense, my heels clicking on the wooden floor. Eucalyptus and chamomile tickled my nose in a calming manner. I was in desperate need of both. It was like Nana knew what I needed more than I did.

She stood sorting through a variety of dried herbs scattered over the counter, along with a half dozen bottles of oil. Her attention shifted from her work to me, violet eyes clearing and then dancing with happiness. "You look beautiful," Nana gushed, coming to stand in front of me and tucking a fallen tendril of hair behind my ear. "But you always do."

"It's the dress." For once I wasn't wearing combats, tattered jeans, and gothic graphic tees. "I kind of miss the boots, though," I admitted, glancing down at my sparkling feet. "I'd forgotten how uncomfortable heels can be, but I do appreciate the height."

Her smile never wavered. "It's not the clothes that make you beautiful. It's your heart, your kindness, your spirit, and your soul."

I made a funny face, my nose scrunching up. "Have you been sniffing the herbs again?"

Her laugh chimed through the kitchen. "I'll wait until you leave to break out the good stuff. Your mother called."

I didn't altogether suppress the eye roll. "I talked to her."

"She just wants the dinner to go smoothly."

Leaning against the counter, I mindlessly drew circles in a stash of dried herbs. "Then she should attend instead of me. Nothing in my life goes without a hiccup, and I like it that way."

Nana hooked a finger under my chin, guiding my focus back to her face. "You and me both, dear. How dull otherwise."

I smiled, happy to have a woman like her at my side. If my mother had been here, the level of stress would be an almost palpable thing in the house. "I'm glad I take after you."

"Karma." She winked, returning to fuss with her dried herbs. "He's almost here."

I glanced down the hallway toward the front door, a line creasing my forehead as the rumble of an engine came from down the road. My shoulders rose as I took a visible deep breath, my heart fluttering in my chest.

I wanted to hold on to my anger from last night, but the prospect of seeing him in a few minutes filled me with a bubbly excitement I didn't want to feel. If only I could pop each one of those thrilling bubbles until I felt nothing.

Nana placed a hand on my shoulder. "Don't worry. He'll take care of you."

But who would look after the heir prince?

She mistook my anxiety, and I didn't correct her.

Waving goodbye, I took off down the hall. *One night.* I just had to survive one dinner. It couldn't be that bad. Not with Leith and Sydney there as well. I should be grateful his family would be there to distract me.

Of course, I had to get through the ten-minute car ride it took to get to his house.

A lot could happen in ten minutes.

I could kill him.

Or... I could do the one act forbidden until I turned eighteen. Claim him.

It was a toss-up at this point.

On wobbly legs, I left the house, but I lifted my chin, faking confidence with everything I had. I would not let Liam think he got to me.

He waited at the passenger side of the truck, door open, and every ounce of steel nearly left me when our eyes clashed. My legs continued to move, but they had gone on autopilot. I was no longer conscious of my movements. The hammering of my heart was difficult to ignore, though.

Liam broke contact only to let those frosty eyes glance at me up and down. My resolve mentally might be strong, but my body rebelled, warming under his leisurely perusal.

Fuck him. And his ability to strip me bare.

My only satisfaction came from knowing that, despite the stone exterior, inside, Liam had to be feeling something similar to me.

God, why does he have to look so good?

And shit, don't get me started on his damn scent.

You can do this, Kelsey. Just get in the damn truck, and don't breathe for ten minutes. No big deal.

If only I was a fucking mermaid and could hold my breath indefinitely.

Staring into the fancy new truck, I told myself it was stupid and silly to mourn the loss of his other one, the one that had been totaled by the hunter. And yet a grain of sadness appeared within me. I was sure this truck was fantastic, new car smell and all, but I missed the smell embedded in the seat's fabric. Though in time, this one would be equally as intoxicating.

"You didn't need to pick me up. I could have driven myself."

"Tell that to my mom. She likes to think she raised boys with manners." Liam held out his hand to help me inside his car.

I stared at his extended arm. *Don't think about his fingers or how they feel. Those thoughts are banned.* "Well, I don't plan on being the one to burst her bubble." Ignoring the gesture, I hoisted myself into the cab of the truck.

He shook his head and closed the door behind me.

We didn't talk. I refused to look at him, staring out the window as the blurring landscape flew by. It forced me to take a moment to appreciate the view, something I hadn't done lately. Even that took effort. Pulling my awareness away from Liam proved challenging, but there was nothing quite like Riverbridge in autumn. I could lose myself in the painted foliage. There was something absolutely breathtaking about the horizon of mountains, the way the sunset hit the tops of the trees, and seeing a herd of elk grazing in a foggy field.

Liam parked his truck behind Leith's Jeep, and I quickly reached for the handle before he could open my door.

Click.

The door locked, and I pinched the bridge of my nose. I did not want to play this game with him again. "I'm not in the mood."

Liam's frown deepened. "Do you plan on giving me the silent treatment all night?"

"Just until dessert," I replied dryly.

He gave me a long, unreadable look and then shrugged like it didn't matter what the fuck I did. "Have it your way."

I spluttered a snort of sorts. "Don't worry. I can play my part if you can play yours."

Manually unlocking the door, I let myself out, jumping to the ground like I did that shit in heels every damn day. I slammed the door shut behind me and started to strut up to the front porch.

A hand grabbed my elbow, spinning me around just a tad too fast. I lost my balance, reaching my other hand out to steady myself on Liam's chest. His heart raced under my palm. "Kelsey, I—"

The front door opened. Sydney stood in the doorway, smiling. "Oh, good, you're here. Come in. Dinner is almost ready. Liam...," she prompted, standing off to the side to let us in.

He released my elbow, shoving his hands into the front pocket of his black jeans. I adjusted my dress, smoothing down the front of the skirt, and walked inside the house, not checking to see if Liam followed. I didn't need to look. I felt his eyes on me.

Slipping out of my heels, I left them in the entryway and trailed after Sydney into the family room, where Leith sat on the couch. He glanced over his shoulder and grinned when he saw me.

"I just need a few more minutes. Make yourself comfortable," the baroness said warmly.

Liam leaned against the wall as I went to sit beside Leith, the harmless Castle. "Hey, sexy," he greeted, extending an arm behind the back of the couch and moving in close to me. "Promise this will be an interesting night and not as dull as most of our dinners."

"I find it hard to believe that any dinner would be a yawn with you here," I remarked, holding back my amusement.

He smirked. "True. You look stunning, by the way."

"Leith," Sydney called from the other room. "Stop hitting on your brother's mate."

Leith rolled his eyes. "I'm just getting to know my sister-in-law better. Not a crime."

"Knock it off," Liam warned, arms crossed. He hadn't budged from the wall, staring at his brother and me like he was an overlord.

The hand resting on the back of the couch toyed with one of my curls. "See? The fun's already starting." Leith gave me a side-eye before shifting to Liam. "Did you two have a fight? I'm sensing some tension. Other than sexual tension, that is."

My jaw dropped. "Leith," I hissed, my cheeks pinkening. "Your mother," I mouthed.

He tugged at the end of my hair. "Can also feel the fuck-me-now energy."

Oh. My. God. I am going to die of mortification.

"You're seriously cute when you blush," he commented, further embarrassing me by pointing out the obvious.

"Knock it off," Liam barked, coming to my defense.

"Boys," a deep voice said, startling me. Rowan darkened the doorway near Liam, looking formidable. The open room suddenly became cramped and too small to house three male wolves.

Rowan Castle was a bear of a man. Standing or sitting, he made me feel tiny. The wolf within me shrank at the alpha aura he commanded when he entered the room. He might have smiled, his lips forming the action, but it didn't reach his eyes. Those remained cold and calculating. I'd even go as far as to say shrewd, all of which were common traits for the wolf in charge of a pack.

But the scope of Rowan's responsibilities went beyond Riverbridge. As the Prince of Wyoming, it was his duty to govern all the packs within the state. He also had to report to the king, both an honor and a burden.

The sleeves of his lightweight sweater were rolled up, showing fore-arms that I estimated were bigger than my thighs. It stretched tight against his chest. "Dinner is ready." Amber-ringed eyes glided over to me, the smile still in place. "Kelsey, we're happy to have you. Not just in our home but in our pack."

Swallowing the lump in my throat, I found my voice, forcing the polite response out of my mouth. "Thank you. Your home is lovely as is your town." *My mother would be so proud.*

"I'm glad to see neither of my boys has run you off yet." I swore I caught a flash of his canines as he spoke, but if they had been there, they were gone now.

My eyes flicked to Liam as he ran a hand through his hair. The heir prince's jaw was set in a scowl. He was on edge, but I couldn't figure out if I was the cause or something else. Our eyes locked for one long, terse moment before I broke contact and glanced back at his father, molding my mouth into a light smile, which ended up being difficult. "Did my parents tell you I'm a runner?"

Rowan chuckled. "They might have mentioned it." Something close to humor danced in his eyes.

We all joined Sydney in the dining room. Tall, tapered candles flickered on the table covered with platters and bowls of steaming food. Fancy dinnerware lay over a pressed tablecloth. Rowan sat at the head of the table, but not before he pulled out a chair for me beside him. Sydney sat across from him at the other head.

Liam and I glared at each other over the flickering candles. Sydney glanced from her son to me, picking up on the change of temperature from the last time she'd seen us together.

The heir prince and I seemed to be destined to only have two switches, hot or Cold. And tonight, we were freezing each other out.

"I'm sure the change of schools has been difficult. Have you settled in?" Sydney asked, striking up a conversation as the platters and serving bowls were passed around. Her gentle nature put me at ease, my shoulders relaxing.

"I'm still adjusting," I admitted, taking the bowl of seasoned green beans Leith passed to me. "It's my last year. I want to focus on studying."

"Have you thought about what you want to do after high school?" Rowan asked.

"College, I guess. To be honest, my mind's been distracted with the move and... other things."

Leith snickered.

I kicked him under the table, and Liam coughed across from me.

I had meant hunters, not what Leith was thinking.

"Ouch," Leith grumbled, rubbing at his shin, having no sense of propriety. I glared at him, but he only grinned.

Trouble. The youngest Castle was trouble.

Liam scowled at his brother, eyes darkening with the promise of violence. I had the urge to grab on to something for support in case one of them flipped the dining room table.

As flustered as I was, I couldn't help but find Leith funny. The annoyance didn't last long, and my lips twitched.

Sydney gave each of her boys a single look and then returned to filling her plate. "And my sons have been welcoming?"

Leith snorted, and I stiffened beside him, sensing nonsense was about to spew out of his mouth. He never disappointed. In hindsight, I should have kicked him again. This time before he opened his mouth.

"Does flaunting other girls in her face count as welcoming? Or shoving his tongue down her throat at the most inappropriate times? If so, then Liam has been the picture of welcoming."

"Jealous?" Liam retaliated without batting an eye. "Could it be that you wish it was your tongue inside her mouth?"

Well, fuck. This was not the kind of dinner conversation I was accustomed to having.

My cheeks went from pink to red, and I dropped my forehead into my hand, wishing I could crawl under the table at their crude words. It was as if they'd both forgotten I was still in the room.

"Who says it already hasn't?" Leith sneered with a grin meant to provoke.

I gasped, my gaze shooting up. The food on my plate remained untouched, my tongue too flabbergasted to have a retort ready.

The prince shook his head at his sons. "I'm not sure either of you is fit to be her mate. Or alpha."

Sydney gracefully put down her fork. "Kelsey, I apologize. I'm appalled by their behavior, of how they're treating you. I promise that is not how I raised them. Now, someone tell me what is going on."

Leith poked around at the mashed potatoes on his plate. Liam fingered the knife on the side of his silverware, staring hard at his brother.

"I'm sorry. It's my fault," I spoke up, drawing all eyes in the room to me.

The expression on Sydney's face softened a fraction, and she sighed. "I find that hard to believe knowing my sons."

"I came here mad at the world and determined to make Liam hate me and, in doing so, made some mistakes I'm not proud of. It was never my intention to cause strife between any of you."

"This thing between Liam and me was going on long before you showed up, Kels," Leith said.

Liam's jaw flexed for a second, his eyes locked in a hard stare with his brother.

"Rowan," Sydney prompted her husband, looking for him to say something and back her up.

Rowan's fork paused halfway to his mouth. "She's quite beautiful, but fighting over her is pointless. The treaty has been signed."

"Then tell your heir to start treating her like a baroness and not like all the other girls he uses and tosses away," Leith said through gritted teeth.

A growl vibrated in Liam's throat.

"There will be no growling at the table. From either of you. Is that clear? You might be the heir prince, but I am still your mother." Sydney's voice came out stern and firmly.

Our plates started to grow cold, but I sensed this was an overdue conversation. Rowan sighed. "Not being able to have a choice in a mate is a burden Liam and you both face. It's not an easy thing to come to terms with. None of us blame you for feeling trapped and angry."

I fumbled with the napkin across my lap. "I appreciate your understanding."

Resting his arms on either side of his plate, Rowan pointedly looked at his sons. "We can deal with this later. Let's try and enjoy a nice meal. Save the fighting for after dessert."

And somehow, we managed to do just that. It took a minute or two, but the tension between the brothers slowly lifted. Despite Liam and Leith arguing, neither seemed to hold grudges long, at least not with each other.

I thanked Sydney for the dinner, dreading having to get in the car with Liam again. I wished I had asked Leith to take me home, but that would be awkward too.

"What the fuck was that?" I asked, giving Liam what I hoped was a seriously saucy glare when we were closed inside his truck.

His eyes narrowed. "Nothing you need to worry about."

Outraged, daggers shot from my eyes at the irritating playboy. "You embarrassed me. Why were you and Leith fighting tonight? And don't tell me it had to do with me."

His eyes blazed, remnants of anger lingering in them. "Is that so hard to believe? That my brother might actually care about you?"

"Not in the way you're suggesting. Has a girl come between you before?"

"We're not talking about this," he replied coolly.

I bristled at his tone. "Oh, so you want to go back to not talking." I folded my arms across my chest. "Fine by me." I snapped my head away from him, eyes boring through the window. Ten seconds went by. "No. Fuck that. I want to talk," I said, whirling back to face him.

"No one's stopping you." Disinterest coated his voice, all part of his ruse, which really only made me more intrigued.

"Who was she?" I demanded, frowning.

Nothing. Dead silence.

Liam jerked the car around the next turn, tossing me slightly in the seat. Why did I want to keep poking the bear?

"It can't be Brina." I snorted, running through a list of girls at school who were also shifters. "Leith can't stand her. Does she go to Riverbridge?"

He glanced in his rearview mirror. "You aren't going to stop, are you?" The tattoo winding out his forearm moved with his hand as he turned the steering wheel.

I'd always been a sucker for a guy with tats.

"I'm great at peeling back the layers."

"You keep talking and your mouth will get you in trouble."

"In case you haven't noticed, I'm already in trouble." I leaned over the center console, my seat belt stretching across my chest as I whispered in Liam's ear. "Do want me to show you what else I can do with my mouth?" My lips curled.

He stiffened, drawing in a breath. "Sit back down." Grit coated his voice.

I laughed, easing back into my seat. "Thanks for a memorable evening. Let's never do it again."

We were in front of my house, and the truck rolled to a stop. "Sunday dinners are a ritual in my family."

"Fucking fabulous. Can't wait to see what happens next Sunday."

Why did all our conversations lately take place in a vehicle? The autobiography of our life should be titled *Highway to Hell*. Or *Heaven*. It depended on Liam's mood. Or your outlook, because the way the heir prince kissed made me feel as if I could go in either direction. His mouth was both Heaven and Hell.

And that was the underlying problem—all the sexual energy between Liam and me.

I reached for the door, half expecting the lock to click, but Liam had a way of keeping me on my toes. Like lightning striking, his fingers dashed into my hair, coiling and twining around the dark tendrils. Sharp points of pain spiked at my scalp, but I didn't feel pain. Not the kind that hurt. This was the sort of pain you begged for more of.

He yanked me around, our faces suddenly close. "The day you turn eighteen, pup. I'm not just going to claim you. I'm going to possess all of you. I won't be gentle or patient, so prepare yourself. That's if you don't kill us both before then. Do what you want with that information." He released me as quickly as he had shoved his fingers into my hair and took hold of me.

Every nerve ending in my body was electrified by his vow and the sheer possessiveness not just in his eyes but every part of him. The twist of his lips. The hardness of his shoulders. The raw, untapped emotion and pure, feral control.

As much as I loathed him, I could also appreciate what a fucking spectacular specimen Liam was. The prince he was. The alpha he would be. And the wolf he commanded.

"Is that a promise?" I asked, my breathing a little heavy.

"Fucking hell, Kelsey," he groaned, a hand falling to his forehead. "I can't figure out if I'm cursed or lucky as hell. I've never met a girl like you."

My lips curled. "I'm one of a kind—an original."

His eyes glowed incandescently. "Your fucking scent is all over my truck. I can't get rid of it."

"Good," I said smugly. "I hope you drown in the scent of me."

Liam blinked before the deep, husky laugh rumbled in his chest, doing ridiculous things to my belly. Dimples flashed on either side of his mouth. His head dropped back against the headrest, and he turned to face me, our eyes intersecting. "I don't know if I should be more worried about you or the hunters."

My lips twisted, empowered that I drove him as crazy as he drove me. The female wolf within me purred. My gaze dipped to his lips, the scar as tempting as his dimples. "Me neither," I said before opening the car door and jumping out.

TWENTY-ONE

S even o'clock Monday morning was too early to be arguing with
the heir prince. He showed up in my driveway while I was
applying my mascara. I dropped the tube and ran to the window
with both excitement and annoyance at the sight of Liam's truck.

A plume of smoke billowed from the exhaust. He could have at least
texted me before showing up. I knew why he was here. As long as the
hunters were loose in Riverbridge, I had a guard, a wolf to shadow me. I
wondered if Liam volunteered or if his father had commanded it.
Perhaps it was the promise he made to his mother that propelled him to
protect me.

It didn't matter.

My fingers curled against the curtain. Since the heir prince thought
he could just show up when it pleased him, then he could damn well
wait until I was ready to leave.

Forcing myself to dawdle, I finished getting ready and moseyed into
the kitchen for the only thing that would get me through the day, especially after another sleepless night. If I had that dream of Liam getting
shot by the hunter instead of me again, I might shoot the heir prince
myself just to make the nightmare end.

A ghost of a smile tugged at Nana's lips as she peered over her coffee at me. "How long do you plan on making that boy wait?"

A double meaning hid in her question. She didn't mean for just today but fully accepting our situation. And although I thought I'd come to terms with him being my mate, that didn't mean a part of me wasn't bitter and angry still.

"I haven't decided yet." Maybe until I had Liam on his knees. That was the baroness inside me, the side that believed I was as strong and merciless as any male alpha.

Liam handed me a cup of iced coffee when I got into his truck. "My mom" was all he said.

I graciously took the extra dose of caffeine, as I had a feeling the cup I downed before coming outside wouldn't be enough to get through this day. Who knew the baroness was so maternal? It also made me wonder how the hell Sydney and my mother were best friends. Or had been. I honestly didn't know where their current relationship was or if they even had one.

The baroness and Mom struck me as opposites. My mother worried too much about her hair, her clothes, and her image to consider things like cooking, baking, or remembering that her children needed to eat. She wasn't a bad mother. She just wasn't what society labeled a homemaker. Sometimes Mom acted more like my best friend. My father, regardless of all his duties, loved to cook. It was how he decompressed after a hard day, along with a glass of wine.

That was something my parents had in common—their love for wine.

"You okay?" Liam asked, yanking me out of my head, where things had been steering toward emotions I didn't want to deal with this early in the morning.

Blinking, I rolled the ice in my cup, noticing we were already at school. He had let me marinate in my thoughts, uninterrupted. "Yeah. I'm fine." I looked at him, a small smile on my lips. "Tell your mom thank you for the coffee. You're lucky, you know. To have a mom who cares enough to give you iced coffee before school."

"And you don't? Have a mother like that?" he clarified.

I lifted my shoulders in a small shrug. "My dad would. But not my mom."

I hadn't been fishing for sympathy, and I was pleased that his expression didn't tip that way. "Leith or Hope will give you a ride home after school. I have practice."

"And you don't want me to watch?" My voice came out intentionally serious, but I was joking.

Liam's expression was wreathed in confused curiosity. "You like football?"

My lips tilted. "No, but I do like guys in tights."

"Funny."

Today was my first day back since being shot. Only the other shifters at school were informed of the real reason for my absence, and it had nothing to do with the flu. It had only been a few days since I took off in the woods and abandoned my car, yet somehow, as I stepped out of Liam's truck, it felt as if weeks had gone by.

I scanned the parking lot, feeling as if was on display. Too many eyes were on me. "It feels like the entire school is watching us."

Liam came to stand beside me, unfazed and paying no attention to the stares. "Because they are."

Hugging my laptop to my chest, I wrinkled my nose. "Why?"

He held my gaze unwavering. "I drove you to school."

I was still waiting for the big revelation. "And?" I prompted sourly. "I don't see what the big deal is."

Those long legs began to strut across the school lot. "I don't drive girls around," he stated.

I blinked, my feet struggling to keep up with him. "Ever?"

"Ever," he confirmed, point blank, no hesitation.

Liam giving me a ride today made a statement. He was basically announcing to the school that we were together.

Not exactly true. Hell, I didn't even know where we stood. "Oh. Fucking wonderful."

"Go to class, and don't leave campus," he warned, halting as a car zoomed by, nearly running over a group of girls a few feet in front of us. "A few of my boys will be watching."

"Wow. You had to go and ruin this thing we had. Now I want to kick you in the dick. I can take care of myself, or have you forgotten what I can do?"

He was walking again, down the path that led to the front entrance. "And yet you still allowed yourself to get shot."

Dickhead. "I was protecting my identity. A lot of good it did, though." I still ended up revealing how different I was. Not just to the hunters but to the heir prince as well.

"You won't even know they're watching," he assured me, though I didn't believe him.

"I might not see them, but I can still smell them," I huffed, put out. This wasn't going to work for me. Order or not, I hated being leashed, and that was how this felt, like Liam or his father—hell, like both of them were trying to put a collar around my neck.

I wasn't sure how to handle this overprotective Liam. The heir prince and I weren't even dating officially, and we already needed couples therapy.

The bell rang just as we stepped foot inside the school, ending any further discussion on the subject.

I marinated over the idea of being babysat all morning. Between each class, just like Liam had informed me, a shifter trailed me. Some were way less obvious than others. And then there was Riven Hayes, who made no attempt at all to disguise what he was doing. He was waiting outside my art class when it ended.

"Hey, little rebel," he greeted, smug as fuck. That seemed to be a trait all of Liam's friends had in common. Riven had a bit of Leith's carefree attitude but was more of a playboy than Leith was.

"Don't you ever get tired of being Liam's guard dog?" I said tartly, not bothering to wait and see if he followed.

Riven shrugged, his pace matching mine as we meandered down the hall. I had lunch next and was in no real hurry. "Why would I when I get to follow around a girl as hot as you?"

I shot him a glare that promised violence.

"I miss the digs," he said, twinkling mossy green eyes looking me over in my blue jeans and soft blue sweater. No black today. I kind of missed it.

"You're about to be missing a vital limb if you keep flirting with me," I replied with a sickly sweet smile.

The asshole's lips twitched. "I flirt with everyone."

I rolled my eyes, dodging a girl who dropped her phone in front of me. "Way to make a girl feel special."

"Liam would literally kill me if I actually made a move, you know."

"You should be worried about what I would do to you."

Riven chuckled, the boyish grin on his lips widening. "I told Liam you'd be a kick-ass girl. I had a hunch."

"Did you? Are your hunches often right?" I asked with a sarcastic lilt.

He winked. "Always."

We turned the corner into the hallway that led to the cafeteria, and I came face-to-face with Brina the Bitch. It crossed my mind to just keep going and bulldoze right past her, but the expression on her pinched face looked as if she had something she wanted to say to me.

I groaned inside. A confrontation was the last thing I needed before lunch. Get between me and a meal and we'd have a problem. I'd skipped breakfast this morning, and my stomach screamed at me to eat something.

"Uh-oh," Riven muttered under his breath, anticipating trouble just as I had.

Brina flipped her strawberry locks over her slim shoulder. "Smooth move, playing the sympathy card to get close to Liam. Getting shot. Brilliant, but it won't work, you know. He can't stand you."

How the hell she thought getting shot was a ploy to get close to the heir prince fully escaped me. Or maybe she was implying that I took advantage of the situation and played up my injury. I had to wonder how well she knew Liam to believe he could be swayed by some tears and a quivering lip.

I arched a brow, a mocking smirk curling at my mouth. "Funny, it didn't feel that way when he had his tongue down my throat Friday night, or when I woke up beside him Saturday morning."

Riven chuckled beside me.

The look in Brina's green eyes was priceless. I would have killed to have captured it on video so I could relive the moment over and over again.

Her mouth opened, but before she could spew utter bullshit, I took a step forward, getting in her face. "And just so we're clear, Liam and I are not a *thing*. He's *my* mate." I didn't mean to sound so damn possessive and cringed inside. *Get a hold of yourself, Kelsey.*

Jealous rage burned in the centers of her eyes. She wanted to hit me, and I dared her with my stare to try me. Lifting her chin, she replied, "I guess we'll see." A challenging gleam danced in her villainous gaze, and I wanted to run my claws down her pretty, flawless face.

"Go make trouble somewhere else," Riven ordered, stepping between us.

I frowned at the sudden change in his tone. Gone was the flirty boy. This guy looked scary as hell, his expression dark and fierce, not someone you messed with unless you wanted to end up with a black eye and a bloody lip.

Brina snorted as those awareness tingles started in my belly. Liam was close.

"What's going on here?" His voice sent my heart cartwheeling.

I looked just past Brina's shoulder to see Liam scowling.

The smile that crossed her lips sent chills down my spine. Spinning, she lifted on her tiptoes, wrapping her arms around the heir prince's neck and planting a kiss on his lips.

I saw red.

His arms remained at his side, body stiff and unmoving. The longer Brina kept her lips pressed to Liam's, the bigger a fool she looked.

The bitch had three seconds to back off him, or shit was about to get feral up in here.

One.

Two.

Fuck it.

Patience was never my strong suit.

My hand dashed through the air toward Brina's hair. I had every intention of grabbing a hunk and yanking her away from my mate, but a hand locked around my forearm, halting me.

Eyes glowing, I whirled on Riven.

"Don't, Kelsey," he murmured in my ear. "She's trying to get you to lose control. Don't give her the satisfaction."

He was right, of course, but it was so hard to not let the wolf free and give in to the need to fight for what was mine.

I gasped.

Holy crap.

I had just referred to Liam as *mine*. It didn't matter that it was only in my head but that I firmly believed it inside. How and when had that possessiveness snuck up on me?

Liam ripped her away from him, his hands tightening on her shoulders. Eyes hard and completely devoid of emotion, he lowered his voice drastically as he said, "You try something like that again and I'll let Kelsey tear into you."

Brina's mouth dropped open before her beautiful face twisted into something wicked. Her gaze flicked to me for a second, seeing Riven still holding me back. "You've changed," she spat at Liam. "You used to be fun."

"Yeah, well, you're still the same. Once a bitch, always a bitch," he said plainly.

Oooh. That hurt, but no less than she deserved. Her desperation was starting to show, and in the end, it would be her demise. She would ruin herself.

It was hard to keep the grin of gratification off my lips.

Now that we had the attention of half the student body, the murmurings started, and it would only take a few minutes for all those videos and pictures to circulate throughout the school and beyond. If anyone doubted that Liam and I were a thing, this would have sealed the deal.

Brina stomped her heel into the ground, her fingers curled into fists. "You'll regret choosing her. I promise you. She's going to destroy you."

A promise? It sounded more like a threat.

Cheeks burning with embarrassment and anger, Brina tore out of Liam's hold, tears pooling in her bright eyes. Her head dipped, a curtain of strawberry hair falling over her face.

I moved to step in her path, wanting to hurl a few words of my own, but Liam grabbed my other arm. Between the two wolves, I wasn't going anywhere.

A curse breezed past my lips, and I turned to confront my mate. "You better do something about her or I will," I told him. "And tell your dog to release me or he's going to feel the sting of my teeth."

Shaking his head at me, the heir prince's features softened. Not entirely, but enough to know he was trying to bank his anger. "We need to talk. Set some boundaries." He gave a silent command with his eyes to Riven, and a moment later, the fingers on my arm lifted.

Liam still had a hold on me, and, feeling on edge, I narrowed my gaze. "I don't like boundaries, *princeling*."

He started to usher me through the crowded cafeteria. Dragged might have been a more appropriate description, as I wasn't exactly a compliant companion. "I don't like titles or disobedient bitches." His tone was low, but not enough that every shifter in the room hadn't heard.

My laugh brimmed with snark. "Oh, you're so fucked with me, then. To think you're going to be stuck with all the things you don't like for eternity."

We made it into the hallway where I'd just come from, the sounds of the lunchroom rising at our departure. "There's just one problem, pup."

I raised my chin, ire flashing in my eyes.

He flipped me around the corner, his body trapping me against the locker. "I like all the traits I despise *on you*."

It sucked being reminded exactly what it felt like to have the hard length of him pressed into me. To have his lips worship parts of my body. To be kissed with that arrogant, asshole mouth. "You're more messed-up than I thought."

"Isn't that what makes us the perfect match?" he asked, his head tilted to the side like he did when he was about to kiss me.

God, I even recognize his moves.

"Did we ever really have a say?" We were essentially born for the other.

His eyes darted to my mouth. "No."

My breathing quickened, my heart rate accelerating. "I thought you wanted to talk. Set those boundaries you're so fond of."

"I do, but first..." He moved to claim my lips, but I twisted my head to the side, not falling into the trap. Not that it mattered. His mouth wasn't deterred, and he kissed my cheek, then my jawline, running his teeth up the edge of my face.

Well, shit.

Before I let myself get swept away, which only gave me seconds, I flattened my palms on his chest and shoved. Gaining a few inches but not enough space. The bastard was strong, firm, and goddamn unmovable. His hands remained pressed against the locker, boxing me in.

"I'm not doing this back-and-forth with you. You want me. You don't. You're the last person I want to play games with."

Liam's eyes went from stormy to wide. His body stiffened, and he whipped his head to the side.

I heard it then. The whizzing of something sailing through the air.

"Fuck," he muttered as his body spun, cocooning himself around me like a shield.

That was my damn move. I was the one with the powers, not him. But instinct made the heir prince protect me over himself.

I understood that feeling well.

As he took us to the ground, I released my power, praying I wasn't too fucking late.

Someone screamed. Metal groaned. And the distant thud of a weapon hitting the lockers pierced the air. Fear slammed into me, and although only seconds ticked by, it felt as if we were moving in slow motion, each tick a fucking lifetime.

Peeking from under Liam's arm, I gawked at the dagger embedded in the locker where we'd stood, a folded white piece of paper pinned to the metal.

"Are you hurt?" Liam asked, thrusting me back to see for himself.

I shook my head as his attention spun in the direction from which the dagger had hurled. My gaze followed, and I caught a glimpse of a black hoodie streaking by and disappearing around the corner. Liam's body jerked into motion. He was on his feet, bolting down the hall after him.

Son of a bitch.

Surging to my feet, I ripped the dagger out of the metal, snatching the folded paper, and took off after Liam. My boots pounded on the tile, but he had a head start, and the bastard was fast. I managed to keep him in sight as he raced through the school, going toward the main exit. The front doors were swinging shut as Liam and I approached. He burst through the exit, me a few seconds behind, nearly bumping into him.

Why did he stop?

I glanced down, seeing a discarded black hoodie on the stone pathway. And because it was a lunch period, the school grounds were scattered with students, going out, coming back, or just hanging about to eat.

"Fuck," Liam swore, frustration and anger darkening his expression, his aqua wolf eyes glowing. "Fuck," he let fly again, kicking invisible dirt and rocks.

I wasn't sure why, but I shoved the slip of paper into my back pocket. I wanted to read it first, then decide who to share it with. "He's gone. Did you get his scent, at least?" I asked, catching my breath.

"If I had, I'd be tracking him right now," he snapped. "I was too damn distracted by *your* scent."

My increased heart rate from running slowly returned to normal. "How's that my fault? You were the one all over *me*."

He raked his fingers through his hair. "Exactly. I can't think when I'm around you."

I shouldn't feel good about him once again implying in a backward way that this was my fault. But I did. "How does this asshole keep getting the jump on us?" I got that distractions were a factor. Liam and I were still getting used to this unusual link between us. There was attraction. And there was whatever happened to our bodies. It was attraction on crack. Still, I couldn't help but feel as if we were always one step behind, a trait neither Liam nor I was accustomed to. Wolves normally had the upper hand in most situations.

"I haven't figured it out yet," he said through gritted teeth. "But I'm more certain than ever that you aren't safe anywhere."

"You think?" Sarcasm was a natural defense for me.

Liam's jaw tightened, just fractionally. "The hunter's a student, walking among us. Hell, he might even be one of us," he replied coldly, scanning the faces of our peers. Our friends. Our family.

"A wolf? Have you ever heard of one of us hunting our kind?" The theory both shocked and shook me. The idea of a shifter being the hunter seemed preposterous, and yet... I could understand how he came to the idea.

His eyes locked on to me. "No, but I've also never seen a wolf with the power you possess within you, pup."

"Touché," I mumbled, a combination of disbelief, horror, and what-the-fuck in my expression.

꒐꒐●꒑꒑

I WAITED UNTIL AFTER LUNCH, when I was alone in a girls' bathroom stall, to pull out the crumbled paper. Tearing open the folded sheet, I stared at the bold letters written in...

Holy fuck.

Is that blood?

What a sick asshole. Meant to scare me, obviously. As if the bold words weren't enough to chill my veins. It was animal blood smeared on the paper, but still, no less gross. I nearly tossed the freaking thing into the toilet without reading the message.

The words were blood red against the white background.

His life or yours. Next time, I won't miss. And you won't be there to save him.

How original.

This jerk got an F for creativity. The whole thing screamed budget-rated film. I crunched the paper into a ball, my fingers closing around it.

He was right. I might not always be around to use my powers and protect us both, but there was one way to fix that.

The hurdle was Liam would never agree, but I was a firm believer in "If there's a will, there's a way." And I would find it. I couldn't have my mate die before we had the chance to actually *become* mates.

Twenty-Two

The next few days passed uneventfully. A routine fell into play between Liam and me. At school, we rarely spoke to each other, despite being hyperaware of the other's existence. I hung out with Hope, Leith, and Gunnar mostly. The shadowing continued, and I grew to enjoy Riven's and Colsen's company in the hallways. They were the only shifters who made no attempt at hiding their intentions. Perhaps it was because they were the heir prince's closest friends that they were comfortable getting to know me.

My hope of desensitizing the way my body reacted to Liam by spending more time with him was an utter failure. The exact opposite seemed to be true. The more we were alone together, even for those few minutes to and from school each day, kept me on edge. But I could also admit it was the only time during the day when I felt complete.

I actually did show up to one of Liam's football practices after school, mostly out of curiosity. Sports were never my thing, unless you counted shopping as a sport. Hope and Gunnar came with me.

"What are the chances of my car being tampered with last week?" I asked Colsen as we descended the stairs to the first floor. We both had coed gym class together. I just threw the hypothesis out there, totally

expecting him to think I was crazy. But ever since Liam suggested the hunter could be at school with us or even a shifter, I couldn't let what happened in the woods last week go. What was the probability that the hunter would have known I'd be walking in the woods if they hadn't tampered with my car?

Despite being taller than practically everyone at school, he still had muscle on his thin frame. Colsen had a genuine smile that could melt the coldest of hearts. It took me ten seconds in his company to feel like we'd been friends for years, unlike Riven, whose flirtatious nature I had to spend the entire time combating.

Colsen's dark eyes gave me a quizzical look. "A hundred percent. Didn't Liam tell you?"

"No," I retorted, my face tightening into a frown. I hated secrets, and it somehow felt as if Liam had purposefully kept this little bit of information from me.

Why?

Colsen draped a casual arm over my shoulders, which were more like an armrest due to our dramatic height difference. "Look, I'm sure he had his reasons. Liam doesn't do anything without a good cause."

"And what reason would that be?" I asked, hoping he had some bro insight and would spill the beans.

He shrugged, his face a mask of secrets he would die to protect. "Believe it or not, he's actually a decent guy. If I had to guess, it was because he wanted to be absolutely sure before jumping to conclusions. And so you don't freak out," he added.

We approached the locker rooms, the potent stench of BO, sweaty mats, and dirty uniforms assaulting my nostrils. I wrinkled my nose, wishing I could ditch. "Too late. I'm never driving that car again."

Colsen grinned. "Good. I think Liam enjoys chauffeuring you around. It gives him an excuse to see you."

I snorted. "He has a weird way of showing it."

"Trust me, rock star. The only person Liam is lying to is himself. We all know our heir prince. He says one thing but means another."

"How very fucking confusing."

He shot me a wan smile, tugging on a piece of my hair. "So are you. There has never been a girl who's unnerved him like you do."

"Thank you," I said with a mocking bow of my head, then slipped into the girls' locker room to change and prepare for the class that was my personal hell.

🌒🌑🌘

BY FRIDAY, I realized it had been days since Liam and I had a proper disagreement. Things between us were, dare I say, pleasant, and somehow that made me uneasy. Uneventful wasn't my life in Riverbridge.

A bubbly Hope came over to my locker between second and third period, looking like she'd just consumed a gallon of coffee, going on and on about some party coming up at the end of October.

It had been months since I'd been to a party, and her excitement started to rub off on me until I found out who and what the party was for.

Liam Castle's eighteenth birthday.

I'd known the date of his birth since I'd found out about the treaty. The digits were permanently etched into my memory bank, and it made sense that he would have a party. Eighteen was a big deal, but Liam never mentioned anything to me.

Did that mean he didn't want me there?

"You're coming, right?" Hope asked after gushing about it for the past ten minutes. I didn't think she'd taken a single breath until now.

We went through the double doors leading into the courtyard together. The fresh air filled my lungs, chasing away the stagnant air from within the school. Traces of the river were carried by the autumn winds, rustling the trees. "Would you allow me to say no?"

She swung her bag onto the ground beside one of the benches and sat down. "Of course not. Of all the people in this school, *you* have to be there. You're his mate."

I dropped beside her, grabbing my water from the side pocket of my bag. "Not yet," I reminded her. "I'm just a girl everyone sees as an outsider. Not everyone's as welcoming as you."

"If I'm considered welcoming—which no one has ever called me that, by the way—then you're fucked."

"She has a point," a voice said from behind us, a shadow loomed over us. A moment later, a pair of arms wrapped around Hope's neck. Gunnar grinned. "She definitely doesn't have a welcoming bone in her body. Why do you think I'm her only friend?"

Like the first time I'd met Gunnar, I was struck by his human ability to be so damn stealthy. He'd managed to sneak up on two wolves undetected. As if I needed to prove my senses weren't on the fritz, I inhaled, taking in Hope's and Gunnar's scents. I separated Hope's, isolating the notes of Gunnar. Cedarwood, a tang of orange, and... something else. Something smoky I couldn't quite place.

My phone buzzed in my pocket, pulling my attention away. I fished it out as Gunnar came to sit next to Hope. She scooted in closer to me. The text flashed across the black home screen, and my heart sank.

Have you made up your mind? Your life for his? Halloween. Midnight.

Was he crazy? The festival of Samhain? All Hallows' Eve? The one night when the veil between our world and the other side was the thinnest?

Yeah, fuck no.

Next, he was going to tell me to come alone and meet him at the graveyard. Did he think this was a plot for a horror flick?

I did a lot of questionable and dumb things in my seventeen years, but this...

I cursed the heir prince.

I cursed the stupid moonstruck bond.

I cursed this gift that made me a target.

Scowling at the message, I read it again.

How did the bastard get my phone number?

I snapped my head up, keen eyes scouring the courtyard, uncertain why. It wasn't like the hunter just hung around waiting for me to spot.

Or did he?

He could be any one of these faces. Hiding in the shadows, watching while he toyed with me. Stalkers liked to spy on their victims, and this guy definitely qualified as a stalker in my book.

But other than Hope and me, not another shifter lingered in the courtyard. They were all human, which didn't jive with the hunter being a wolf theory.

This shit drove me crazy. Not knowing anything about him. How he constantly escaped us. The fact that he could mask his scent. He was unusually fast for a human, too, only supporting the wolf theory. These were all things I'd expect from a seasoned hunter, not a high schooler. And even the best of hunters wasn't this good. Or so I thought.

I'd listened to many of my father's conversations with his beta and guards. The topic of hunters was a common subject because of me and came up frequently. His guards gave weekly reports on any activity in our area. I had assumed prior to coming to Riverbridge that all packs operated under the same proceedings.

"Is everything okay?" Gunnar asked.

"For real, Kels. Your face just went ghostly white," Hope said.

I blinked, shoving my phone back into my pocket. They were both staring at me. "Yeah. I'm fine. Just my mother nagging me."

"Wait until you meet *my* mom," Hope replied, rolling her eyes.

"I can account that she's, in fact, sort of scary," Gunnar added, leaning forward so his elbows were propped on his knees.

"I was just convincing Kels here to come to Liam's party on Halloween."

Gunnar's expression lost all amusement. "God, is it his birthday already? Let me guess, he's doing another themed Halloween bash," he said dully, his voice not showing a fraction of excitement. Not like Hope.

She bumped him playfully with her shoulder. "You secretly like getting dressed up and pretending to be someone else."

"Yeah," he agreed unabashedly, a flicker coldness of passing over his face. "But I don't secretly like Liam Castle."

>>●((

THE TEXT HAUNTED the back of my mind all day, distracting me. I still hadn't shown Liam the note I found, but as I chewed on the hunter's threats and his demands, I knew what I was going to do, despite the danger and risks.

I couldn't ignore him. He'd proved more than once how capable of a hunter he was and had the opportunity to kill me or Liam on multiple occasions. But Liam had never been his interest.

I was.

And I needed to handle him.

The threats and intimidation tactics weren't the only thing that weighed heavily on my mind. My sleep continued to be plagued with nightmares. After having the same fucking dream again and again, night after night, I was afraid it was more than just a nightmare but a premonition. Was it possible that my powers were manifesting in my dreams, warning me?

I started to wonder if my sixth sense was magnifying into other areas as I drew closer to my birthday and becoming an adult wolf. What if they weren't dreams? What if, like Nana, I was being given glimpses of the future—a possible outcome. Nothing about the future was set in stone, but that didn't mean it was always easy to change or alter. The universe had a way of righting itself.

As the days passed by, the texts increased, as did the hidden slips of paper. In my locker. Shoved into a pocket of my bag. Left on the desk of my next class. The bastard had a creative side, I'd give him that, just not with threats.

I continued to ignore them. Praying. Hoping. Until...

Hope came barreling around the corner in an almost-empty classroom, out of breath and her eyes wild, big, and red as if she'd recently been crying. "Did you hear?" she panted, skidding to a halt by my table.

I'd just finished digital art class and was shoving my laptop into my bag, nearly dropping the fucking thing at her sudden appearance. "Hope? Christ, you scared—"

"Liam was shot," she rushed out before I could finish.

In situations like this, disbelief came first before the severity of it sank in. I drew back as if I'd been struck. "What? No, that can't be."

"You know I would never lie or joke about something this serious. Not with all the shit going on."

Fear like I'd never experienced clambered inside me, and I swayed, reaching out to a chair for stability. Dots of white swirled behind my eyes. "Like actually fucking shot?" I asked, almost unable to get the question out. They kept getting stuck in my throat.

Her head bobbed up and down rapidly as she grabbed my arm. "Come on. Let's go."

I didn't even ask where. I would have followed Hope blindly into the pits of Hell without blinking.

She dragged me out of the room, and then we raced down the hall to the stairwell together. "What happened?" I demanded, my feet flying over the stairs.

"I don't have all the details, just what I heard from Riven. He was hit with an arrow during archery. The teachers are saying it was an accident," she spilled in a rush of words.

"But you don't believe them?" Her tone held skepticism.

She shook her head as we reached the first floor. "No, and neither do most of the shifters."

Stay calm.

Stay focused.

It might not be that bad.

This is Liam, for God's sake.

That fear continued to shred my insides, and I wasn't sure why my heart sped like it would tear out of my chest at any second. It was as if I loved Liam. I barely tolerated the jerk. Okay, maybe I liked him more than a little, enough to want to kiss his face off and sink my teeth into every ounce of flesh on his body. But seriously, that was all.

Shit.

Two shifters were stationed outside the main office where the nurse's station was. I only recognized one of them. Colsen.

Tingles danced on the back of my neck the closer Hope and I got, and I didn't stop running until I stood in front of the guarded door. Pinning Colsen with my eyes, I reached to shove the door open, but the other shifter blocked my attempt. The last thing I wanted to do was waste time with bullshit.

I didn't bother to look at the wolf whose name I didn't know and turned my full focus on Colsen. Anger zapped through me, and I let my eyes shine, flashing pieces of the baroness I would eventually be. "If you know what's good for your balls, you'll let me pass."

Hope was right there backing me up. "Don't be a dick, Colsen. Do you know what will happen when Liam finds out you prevented his mate from seeing him?"

He finally showed signs of wavering.

"Let me fucking pass," I ordered, adding a growly texture to my voice, sounding way too animalistic, but I didn't give a shit.

Colsen shifted, rubbing the back of his neck as he considered.

"Move," a voice demanded behind me before Colsen made up his mind.

Leith flanked my other side. His scent hit me before the warmth of his body. I tilted my head a hint to the side, and never had I seen him look more like Liam than he did at that moment. Hard jaw. Cold eyes. Coiled muscles.

"You better hope my brother doesn't find out about this," Leith snapped at Colsen and the other shifter.

"That's what I fucking said," Hope added, crossing her arms.

Taking my hand, Leith escorted me past the two guards and through the door without sparing either wolf another glance. His anger trembled into my fingers, and yet like Liam, Leith possessed impressive restraint. His grip stayed gentle against mine, whereas I clung to him as if I would trip or fall at any step.

"Is he okay?" The question heaved from my mouth as Leith guided us through the office, bypassing the lady behind the front desk without a glance. Hope remained hot on our heels.

"I'm sure he's fine. If he wasn't, I have a hunch you would know," Leith stated.

The panic still coursing in my blood didn't make me feel at ease. I couldn't tell if the feelings were worry for the heir prince or because his injury might be severe.

As the three of us stormed down the narrow hallway, the sharp iron scent of blood hit my nostrils.

Liam's blood.

I'd seen it, smelled it time and time again in my dreams, but nothing prepared me for the real thing. The tang knocked me in the chest, my heart jolting.

Leith nodded at Riven, who leaned against the wall and flung the nurse's door open without knocking.

Liam's head lifted, along with the nurse attending to the heir prince's shoulder. He was situated on a chair, his shirt halfway off, exposing part of his abs and the wound.

I ignored the dark stains as I quickly ran my eyes over him. He had the arrow in his hand, toying with it between his fingers. Our gazes locked, and he saw the worry shaking in me. A tense moment hovered in the air, neither of us saying anything.

"See? Not dead," Leith said, breaking the silence.

The scowl on Liam's lips darkened at his brother.

"Dad's going to flip when he finds out you let a hunter shoot you," Leith said.

Nurse Leslie gave the brothers a terse look. She was one of the few staff members who were shifters. "A hunter at this school." She tsked, shaking her head of graying brown hair as she tossed away swabs of bloody cotton. "Lucky our young prince has such acute reflexes or this wound could have been serious." Behind her cat-eye glasses, her gaze slid to me in the doorway with a smudge of accusation.

She blamed me.

Or at the very least believed I was partly responsible.

And she wasn't wrong.

This was my fault. The only reason the hunter went after the heir prince was because of me. I refused to turn myself over, to walk peacefully into his cage. And after that...

I refused to let myself think about what came after the hunters had me in their possession.

Liam snapped the arrow in half, the crack drawing the nurse's gaze from me. I looked at him, noticing the sudden working of his jaw. He'd noticed the way Nurse Leslie had judged me, and by his expression, the heir prince was pissed. "The information doesn't leave this room."

The nurse flinched at the power vibrating from Liam's tone.

Leith rested his back on the wall. The small room couldn't house all of us plus the nurse, her desk, a patient bed, and Liam. "Might be hard. I'm sure half the shifters in this school have heard about the incident," he replied.

"I'll take care of it," Liam stated, slowly easing his shirt down over his arm. By the end of the day, he wouldn't need the dressing the nurse had attached to the wound.

"What about them?" Hope asked, nodding toward the three wolves standing guard.

Grim-faced, he stood, making the room feel suddenly smaller. "They're loyal only to me. As are you, I hope, cousin."

Hope rolled her eyes. "I'm the least of your worries."

Four sets of eyes lifted to Nurse Leslie.

She let out a little squeak, her chair on wheels rolling back an inch or two. "Oh. You know it's my duty to report any unusual disturbance at this school to your father."

This definitely qualified as unusual, but Liam showed no deterrence.

"He put me in charge of tracking down the hunter. Any information goes directly to me. I'll be the one to tell him what happened. It comes from me."

"As you wish," Nurse Leslie submitted after a few moments of hesitation.

Liam stood, adjusting the hem of his shirt. "I've been suspicious that the hunter walks among us at Riverbridge. After today, I'm certain, which is all the more reason that this needs to stay under the radar. Am I clear?"

My phone vibrated in my back pocket, and I took a step out into the hall, Riven lifting a brow at me. I shot him a sour face before turning my eyes down to check my message, then immediately wished I'd ignored the notification. I stared at the unknown number—at the message I'd been dreading but knew would be coming.

> I warned you that you wouldn't always be around
>
> But I will be

Prick!

The feeling that had just begun to settle in me after seeing Liam safe vanished like a snowflake on my tongue. Any color I had left in my cheeks dissolved, and with it came a cold that permeated straight to my bones.

A warm hand touched my hip, a cluster of tingles seeping past my clothes. "What is it? What's wrong?" Liam's breath brushed against the back of my neck.

I immediately tensed, my thumb hitting the button that locked my phone screen.

Play it cool.

Exhaling, I forced my body to chill out and turned around, praying some of the color had drifted back into my face. "You got shot with an arrow," I stated the obvious. Absurd to think I could fool him with a bit of snark.

Liam shook his head. "That's not it." His head tipped to the side, eyes studying me too keenly. They made me want to squirm. "You're hiding something from me."

He wouldn't believe anything I said if I didn't look him in the eyes, so I gave him a dead-hard stare. "Yeah, how much I hate you." The excuse came out pathetic and weak. He saw right through my sad attempt at using my attitude as a shield.

"Since we both know that's a lie, try again, pup."

I gulped at his snarling expression, and yet it only made him more attractive. The text had me unnerved as much as I hated to admit it, and here was Liam demanding answers from me, giving me no time to think. I said the first thing that popped into my head. "You need to stay away from me."

He stepped closer, a hand moving to my waist as if I might bolt. And I wanted to. "I can't do that."

"Try," I said in part plea, part fear, part anger, part desperation. My emotions were a complicated woven tapestry inside me.

"I know what you're doing."

Did he really, though? He assumed I was pushing him away for his own safety, and I was, but that wasn't the whole reason.

I was going to catch this bastard. I was going to put an end to this hunt. I was going to win the game. And no one else would get hurt.

He had made his point.
I got the message. Halloween at midnight.
The bastard was mine.

TWENTY-THREE

"Y ou need to keep your distance," I replied to Liam. Before, it had been a warning. Now it was the only way he lived. If he continued to stay by me, the hunters would kill him to get to me.

It wasn't just him. The hunters would use anyone close to me. Hope. Leith. Nana.

I couldn't let anyone suffer for me.

"All of you," I added as I took a step away, Liam's hand falling from my waist. I glanced to Hope, Leith, and even Riven.

The heir prince's hand wrapped around my wrist, yanking me back, closer than I was before. "Don't let him force you into isolation. You have an entire pack here to protect you."

Didn't he understand? It wasn't me I was worried about.

I shook my head, wiggling my trapped wrist but unable to break free. "Maybe I should just leave."

"You're not leaving," Liam said darkly, the muscles in his neck twitching. When I didn't say anything, only stared into his eyes, letting him see the stubbornness of my chin and the determination set in my features, his expression finally changed. "Don't leave," he growled lowly,

almost a tinge of panic under the rumble. The hand holding my arm dropped, falling to his side.

I had to do this. No matter how much it might hurt to walk away. "I'm glad you're not dead," I said and walked off.

And he let me.

Sort of.

One of his guards trailed behind me.

I headed to the bathroom, the only place Liam's friends didn't follow me, but Hope could.

She didn't this time.

Relieved to find the bathroom empty, I locked myself behind a stall and dug out my phone, glaring at the unknown number, my back against the steel wall divider. If I did this, there would be no coming back.

I'd never killed before.

Contrary to what people thought, wolves normally didn't go around attacking humans, not unless they had a damn good reason or a few screws loose like this hunter. But of course, like most species, there was always one bad apple. Packs had rotten apples too. So did humans.

In my book, this hunter was a spoiled apple that needed to be tossed. I just had to find the guts, courage, strength, and power to take him down... and live.

No big deal.

> Fine. Halloween. Midnight. But only if the attacks stop. No one else gets hurt

I typed.

No one else but you, asshole.

I skimmed over the message, taking a deep breath as my finger hovered over the Send button.

Sayonara, motherfucker.

I sent it.

I checked the time. Classes had already started, and although I could probably get a late excuse, I wasn't in the mood to be in a room full of people.

I wondered how long I could hide in the girls' bathroom before a guard would bust in. Regardless, I would rather risk detention than go to class. I opted to leave the bathroom and headed for the roof stairs in search of fresh air.

A shadow followed, but I paid little attention to the wolf, an easier task when it wasn't Riven or Colsen. He gave me space, and for that I was grateful.

The hunter's response came as I reached the roof, stepping outside.

> Until Halloween, then
>
> No tricks and you'll get a treat

My ass.

An absurd snort breezed through my nose as I glared at my phone screen, my face contorted in disgust.

The guard stayed at the threshold, watching the stairwell. His brows lifted at my sudden outburst.

Clutching the phone, I raised my arm in the air, seconds from tossing the device over the edge. My fingers twitched, a surge of anger, regret, and resentment swirling within me. I wanted to chuck my phone, never see another unfamiliar number or text from that bastard.

How tempting it was, but it would take more than not having a phone for the hunter to stop chasing me.

I gazed at the spot Liam had tackled me to the ground when he thought I'd been about to jump. Why did that moment feel like years ago?

Dropping my hand, I leaned against the ledge and screamed. I didn't give a shit who heard me, or that the scream ended in more of a howl than a human cry.

🌒 🌘 ● 🌒 🌔

A WEEK TURNED into two since Liam had been shot, but I couldn't tell the difference from one day to the next.

He'd said I couldn't isolate myself.

He was wrong.

I could.

But it wasn't a place I enjoyed being. I'd never been depressed before. Not really dark depression. I'd had days where I felt down or shit got to me, especially if I was on my period, but nothing I couldn't climb out of.

The closer Halloween approached the deeper the darkness inside me grew. Every bone in my body wanted to see Liam, even if we did nothing but fight and snap at each other. I just longed to be in his presence. As much as I wanted to blame that ache on the moonstruck link between us, I knew it was more.

I liked the bastard.

His arrogance. His moodiness. His protectiveness. His fucking ass.

He might look like a dream, but he often acted like a nightmare, and it was that dark side of him that pulled me.

I didn't need a good guy who always abided by the rules.

I needed someone who would stand by my side while I broke them all.

Each time our eyes connected, it felt like lightning struck within me. So much tension and magnetism zapped between us, I worried the sparks would become unbridled flames. The entire school would be doomed. We would burn it down.

The heir prince stopped picking me up for school, a responsibility he had Leith do instead. I couldn't deny I'd felt disappointment the first day Leith's Jeep showed up in my driveway instead of Liam's truck, but it would have only made shit complicated and awkward.

Funny thing, the disappointment never went away. Each morning for two fucking weeks, it appeared.

Leith did his best to put a smile on my face, but I wasn't in the mood for laughs or harmless flirting, and I knew he could tell that when I did manage a grin, it was forced and difficult to retain.

Liam wanted to maintain his control, and to do that until December, he had to avoid temptation. I wanted to shatter his control. But I also didn't want him dead, so... therein lay my dilemma.

But really, it was his pride that made him stay away. Or perhaps it was respect because I'd asked. Who knew?

I had all these thoughts and ideas in my head, uncertain which path was the right choice.

Loneliness ate at me the past few days. Wolves were meant to be a pack, and I'd started to get a sense of what it felt like to be a lone wolf. I didn't like it.

Not that my friends didn't try. Avoiding Leith and Hope at school was hard, but making excuses for after school and on weekends I could do. They caught on quickly, but there was one event Hope refused to let me back out of.

Liam's party.

I had one night of unrestrained freedom before Saturday, Halloween night, when shit got real. I told no one about the text or my secret scheduled meeting with the hunter. Not even Nana, but knowing her gifts, she could have very well already seen. If she had, she gave me no indication. No more warnings. No pleadings not to go out.

For tonight, I planned to let loose, hang out with my friends, and basically have all the fun I'd been missing the last two weeks.

One night. I thought I deserved one evening before the night of my first kill.

And I would kill the bastard, even if it meant letting him think he won. I could play dirty too.

Leith and I were meeting up with Hope and Gunnar at the party. I didn't know if I should give Liam a gift or not. What did you give to the wolf who was your mate? Any idea I thought of fell flat.

"Hey, stranger," Leith greeted as I slid into the passenger seat of a BMW M3, a much flashier ride than Liam's truck and cozier than the Jeep, but it fit Leith. Speedy. Sleek. Sexy. All things that reminded me of the younger Castle. Even the custom paint job reflected his vibrant yet playful personality. It was one of those colors that changed depending on the reflection of light.

I could admit that, as I glided onto the soft buttery leather seat and closed the door behind me, I felt like a badass. The short black-and-white plaid dress, the distressed tights, and the killer platforms only added to the level of confidence I felt. It was like waking up from the dead and breathing in the fresh air of life.

What had only been part of a persona before—the clothes, the attitude, and the heavy makeup—actually became a part of me, and I loved it. Loved the way I felt. Empowered. Sexy. Daring. Bold.

I needed all of it. Just the boost required before going into battle.

Leith's eyes ran over my attire. "I'm glad to see she's back. I was rooting for hardcore Kelsey. She's kind of iconic and sexy as hell." He grinned, flashing me a single dimple on his right cheek.

Warmth bloomed in my chest at the compliment, and I winked. "Thanks. I thought she deserved a comeback."

"Oh, I can tell tonight's going to be fun." Leith punched the gas, and the sleek car lurched down the road. "You're in a mood, and I am so living for it. I can't tell if my brother's a lucky bastard or in so much shit."

I loved the way the engine slightly vibrated the seat underneath me. A different kind of power that I appreciated. "Both."

"You're going to kill him, Kels. You know you're going to start a riot in that dress."

"Perfect. Just the vibe I was going for." Leith could make me so relaxed and hyped up at the same time. "Is it even a party if there isn't a brawl? We're fucking shifters, after all."

"Good point."

"Do your parents often let you guys throw parties?" I asked. My parents never would have allowed an unsupervised teen gathering. "Like, this isn't a big secret that I'm going to have to remember never to mention, is it?"

"A few times a year. The adults have their soirees, and we get to have ours. Pack comradery or some bullshit. It's just an excuse for us to get shitfaced. You're spending the night, by the way. No one is going to be in their right mind to drive."

My grin widened. "Perfect."

He noticed the slightly wild mischief in my eyes. "Oh, fuck. What are you planning?"

I shifted comfortably in the seat, crossing my legs. "Let's just say it's my little birthday gift."

He shook his head, his foot pressing farther down on the accelerator, giving the car some speed. "Kels, I love you, and I can't believe I'm even saying this—it goes against everything I stand for—but don't do anything stupid. Like the kind of stupid that gets the attention of the king. Or my dad."

I wished the BMW was a convertible so I could toss my head back and feel the rush of the wind over my face. "The only attention I plan on getting tonight is from every guy at the party."

"Shit," Leith muttered under his breath as he took the turn with one hand on the steering wheel. "If Liam heard that, he would make me take your ass home right now."

"And that's why you picked me up."

"God, I'm going to have to keep an eye on you tonight. Remind me to tell Hope."

I laughed for the first time in two weeks, and the smile on my face was genuine. "Only after you've had a drink with me."

Leith grinned back, matching my energy, a trait I adored about him. "Deal. How high is your tolerance? For future reference. I need to know what I'm getting myself in for."

"I don't know. I guess we're about to find out."

Rolling onto Silver Creek Lane, I gaped at the sheer number of cars parked on both sides of the road. And off the road, for that matter. The lawn had become a parking lot. There was absolutely nowhere to fucking park.

"Um, Leith? Who are all these people?" The pack didn't have this many teenagers in it. Even if they'd all brought a friend or two, it still wouldn't have added up.

He slowed down the BMW, maneuvering through the narrow road thanks to all the traffic. "Looks like someone sent out an open invitation to Liam's party."

"I think the whole school showed."

Scowling, he said, "I think you're right. Liam's going to be pissed."

My eyes rolled. "When isn't Liam pissed?"

Leith grinned at me, his car purring as he revved the engine. "True."

Five minutes later, we found a place to park, but it was a hell of a walk to the house in heels, even platform ones. Leith met me on my side of the car, giving me another appreciative once-over, and let out a whistle. "Because I can't have you breaking an ankle before my brother gets to ogle your fine ass..." Taking me by surprise, he dipped down and hauled me over his shoulder.

"Leith!" I shrieked. "Leith," I protested again as he started walking, my whole body bouncing with his movements. "You better put me down," I demanded, but the laugh that came out made the words weak, and my laugh only grew louder and longer as he took off in a jog across the lawn.

I gave up after that and just let go, allowing myself to have fun, to not worry about anything else.

Holy crap, did it feel so good to laugh, to not worry about being attacked or stalked from the shadows. So far, the hunter had made good on his word, and that meant I had more than twenty-seven hours left of stress-free teenage fucking fun.

Leith didn't set me on my feet until we reached the front porch. As I turned around, readjusting the hem of my skirt, Riven stood grinning at me.

He leaned on one of the white columns, eyeing me from under the brim of his baseball hat. "About damn time you showed up, rebel."

I did a little curtsy. "I didn't really have much of a choice."

"You don't have to worry," Riven boasted confidently, assuming my hesitation about coming tonight had to do with the hunter. "We got this place heavily secured. He would have to be a dumbass to show up tonight with a house full of shifters."

The dumbass might be a shifter. He could be in there right now, partying alongside us. But he would have to be either utterly reckless or stupid to try something surrounded by the pack.

"Is the birthday boy inside?" I asked, raising my voice. The good thing about being a wolf was everyone could hear you over the music. The downfall was loud music was extra loud with amplified hearing.

Riven's grin spread, touching my shoulder and steering me toward the front door. "He's been waiting for you. Don't let him tell you otherwise."

Leith shoved Riven in the chest, and then his hand slipped into mine before I got swallowed up by the sea of bodies. He pulled me through the hallway to the back of the house, where the drink station was set up. The double doors that led to the porch were open. A patio heater flamed at each corner of the deck.

"What'll you have?" the guy behind the bar asked with a smile.

I glanced behind him, scanning the expansive liquor selection. It looked like they had every type available. "Whatever you can make that's sweet and strong."

Flipping a glass, he said, "I got you."

"I'll have the same," Leith said when the designated bartender raised his brows at him.

I watched as he mixed some liquid together in a shaker along with ice, gave it a few good tosses in the air, and poured the contents into two solo cups. Leith took both drinks and passed one to me.

"To every idiot dumb enough to give you a second glance tonight," he said, lifting his cup.

Unable to stop the smirk, I touched the rim of my glass to his and took a healthy swig, not thinking about taste, only how much I could consume.

Back home, I'd never been huge into the party scene. I mainly only went when my best friend, Tess, dragged me. Thinking about her made me remember Hope. *Where the hell is she?*

The main reason I came tonight was because she begged me to. If she blew me off...

I checked my phone to make sure she hadn't texted me. Nothing.

"Everything okay?" Leith murmured near my ear. His hand went to the small of my back as he stood just slightly behind me. He applied light pressure, guiding me away from the heart of the party. We went through the open doors outside to the backyard patio. Lights were strung around the perimeter.

"I was checking on Hope. She's supposed to meet me here."

"She's always late," he said, brushing off my concern. "You'll get used to it. Don't worry. Hope never misses one of our parties."

His reassurance helped ease that blip of panic that started to form in my belly. I sat in one of the patio chairs closest to a heating tower and took another long drink of the concoction in my cup. I wrinkled my nose as the burn of alcohol went down, coated by the sweetness of Coke.

Two girls came over to talk to Leith. Or should I say flirt with him.

Not interested in their exchange, I glanced out over the yard, taking in the various faces, most unfamiliar, but there was one familiar feeling I couldn't shake off.

I felt his eyes on me before I found him in the crowd. The tingles started before I'd stepped foot inside the house, and now they were doing the happiest of fucking happy dances in my belly. No longer able to ignore the pull, I let my gaze move directly to the heir prince. I needed little help locating him; the link between us made sure of that.

I'd hoped for a few moments to catch him unaware, when I could just look at him without meeting his intense gaze that sucked me. No one could deny that Liam was hot as fuck, and unlike the other girls who gaped and gawked, appreciating the dark, brooding shifter, his eyes were on me.

A thrill twirled through my chest, and excitement overrode the thread of disappointment. In a messed-up, ironic way, I envied those girls and their ability to admire his looks without his knowledge. Or perhaps he knew but chose to disregard them.

Lost, I tumbled into the depths of his deep eyes. The moon sat high in the night sky, and although it wasn't a full one, the glow seemed to radiate on my skin. My eyes flicked down to the wrist holding my cup, spurred by the sudden warmth that emitted from there. A pleasant sensation, like a lover's kiss. I nearly shuddered until I saw the faint outline of a crescent moon, so faint I had to squint and blink to make sure I wasn't seeing shit.

I quickly glanced back to Liam, searching his arm, but even with my damn wolf eyes, I was too far away, the mark too faint. But the expression on the heir prince's face told me everything. He'd seen it.

The frown on his lips pulled harder at the corners, and I wondered what I would have to do to catch a glimmer of his dimples. He sat by the circular firepit, surrounded by a group of people, including the bitch on his right. Brina. Two of her friends were there as well. Seeing the smug smile on her face, I regretted allowing my eyes to drift from Liam's.

Before the end of the night, there was a good chance I would smash her perky nose into the ground. If she laid one pointy red nail on Liam—

I was up and out of my chair, my chunky heels hitting the pavement. A second later, a hand wrapped around my wrist and yanked me back into the chair. I whirled on Leith. "What the fuck?" It was a miracle I hadn't spilled my drink. Then again, there wasn't much left to spill.

The girls who'd been surrounding Leith glared at me before moving on, murmuring among themselves. I didn't give a shit. Not about them. Not about what they had to say.

"How about we finish our drinks before you start kicking every girl's ass who looks at my brother," he suggested.

"I wasn't..." Huffing, I slouched into the chair and swore. "I'm not going to last an hour."

"The booze will help. I promise." Leith grinned, flashing a solitary dimple.

Somehow, I doubted it, but I tipped my cup back and drained the contents. "I need a refill."

He laughed. "You're going to get us both in so much trouble."

Me? He was the one pushing liquor into my system, but truthfully, I didn't need much convincing tonight.

Lifting his arm, Leith gestured for someone to bring out two more drinks. "I know it's difficult to see her throwing herself at Liam, but the difference between the two of you is that she *has* to try, and you simply don't."

It was true. I needed to relax. And not let someone like Sabrina Thompson get to me.

The second drink helped. As did the next few. I might have gotten a little too relaxed. The drinking games started, the alcohol seemed to never run dry, and I completely forgot about Hope.

Of course, I couldn't forget Liam if I tried.

Other than the heated-exchange-of-glances-game Liam and I continued to play, we hadn't spoken a word to each other—not that we needed to. I could all but hear his voice in my head and see the mixture of amusement, annoyance, desire, jealousy, and impatience flipping through his expression.

Those same emotions mirrored mine.

As the party picked up, Brina and her friends started dancing—if you could call their moves dancing. It took everything in me not to hurl.

After a song or two, others joined in, and it wasn't long until the entire porch became a rave. I didn't know where the fuck the bubbles came from, but I lifted my head to the star-strewn sky and let the little fragile, soapy circles pop on my face.

Leith watched me, and when I met his gaze and smiled, he nodded toward the music. "Come on, sis." Setting aside his drink, he stood up and held out a hand.

"What the hell. Why not?" I liked to dance, and doing so under the moonlight with my body warm and buzzing on liquor was an offer I couldn't refuse.

I placed my hand in his and let him pull me into the crowd of moving bodies. The thing with parties, they tended to be a sensory overload for shifters. So many scents all stuffed into a space. Even with the cool evening breeze blowing into the valley, I could still pick up a dozen different perfumes and colognes. Not to mention the various degrees of sweat.

Leith and moved to the beat, our bodies grooving together as if this was something we did often. He surprised me. The guy could dance. He easily matched his movements to mine, and I laughed, tossing my head back, feeling lighter than I had in weeks. The music. The warm buzz. The smoky air. The moon's luster.

With Leith, everything between us was effortless, and I couldn't help but think how easy it would be if it had been his name on the treaty beside mine instead of Liam's.

The smile on my lips dimmed. Leith and I were comfortable. Safe. If there was one thing I didn't want in my life, it was predictability. That reckless part of me I could never really control sought excitement and danger—just not the kind of danger that got me shot.

There was no other choice for me but the heir prince, and it was him I wanted to be dancing with.

My gaze sought him out.

Reclining in one of the padded chairs, he held a beverage that I had yet to see him drink. Riven and Colsen sat on either side of him, chuckling about something stupid Riven had said. They both had a few empty bottles tucked under their chairs.

Everyone seemed to be having fun. Everyone but Liam, that was.

Why did his damn scowl tug on my heartstrings? Why did I want to make him smile? See those dimples flash on his defined cheeks? Why did I want to walk over and kiss him?

Brina caught me staring at Liam, and the bitch narrowed her spiteful eyes.

I didn't like the malicious light that crossed her pinched features.

Giving me a smug grin, she flipped her strawberry locks and shifted her focus on Liam. The gall of this skank. In any other circumstance, I might have admired her tenacity, but not tonight. With a deliberate movement that made me want to rip her hair out, she moved her body so it blocked my sight line to Liam, all the while still swaying her hips in a provocative manner.

The jeans she wore hugged her hips, and with her hands raised in the air, she flashed a glimpse of her flat belly.

This was going to be a problem.

Leith saw it, too, and swore under his breath, a barely audible sound over the music. "Kels," he started, but I was already moving. I felt his shadow behind me, weaving through the dancing bodies. "Kels!" he called again, but red-hot anger rang in my ears.

My fingers dashed out, the flowing strawberry hair only inches from my reach. If I could just wrap my hand around—

Someone stepped into my path, latching onto my arm and spinning me around, away from Brina. At first, I thought it might be one of her friends running interference, or perhaps Leith had caught up to me.

It was neither.

I blinked at Riven.

He smirked, his auburn hair messy in a way that made it look deliberate. "If you're looking for trouble, little rebel, I'm right here."

Snorting, I attempted to conceal the grin that wanted to curl on my lips. Why the fuck did I find Riven so damn amusing? With a flip of a switch, he'd managed to bank the fire that had been burning within me. Fucking talent. "You're trouble indeed."

"Watch yourself," Leith warned from behind me. "Don't push him too far. He's likely to snap tonight."

Riven hadn't released my arm, and he made no indication to do so. His mossy green eyes moved to Leith. "Just because he wants to be an ass on his birthday doesn't mean the rest of us have to suffer. Besides, you can't be the only one she dances with tonight."

Leith shook his head and stepped back. "It's your fucking funeral, Riv."

Riven winked at me, guiding my arm up to his shoulder. "We all have to die sometime."

I brought my other hand up, resting it on the opposite side of his neck. "You did that on purpose."

We started to move, and although the music was an upbeat tempo, Riven kept me within arm's length. "Did what?" He feigned ignorance while giving me his signature shithead grin.

I tilted my head to the side as I regarded him. "Stopped me from killing her."

He wasn't as good a dancer as Leith, but he wasn't horrible either. Perhaps a bit more sensual. "Possibly," he retorted.

"Did Liam tell you to interfere, or do you have a thing for the wicked bitch?" I asked, my nose wrinkling in aversion.

"Neither. I just thought Leith was boring you."

Over his shoulder, I caught Leith flipping off Riven behind his back.

"What happened? Why is Liam in such a shitty mood?" I asked, recalling what he'd offhandedly mentioned about the heir prince being an ass.

He, of course, tried to be coy again. "When isn't he?"

I gave him a pointed look.

Riven rolled his eyes. "Fine," he sighed. "It might have something to do with you. You test our prince, and he doesn't quite know what to do with you. And keeping you safe is turning out to be a full-time job."

My lips formed a straight line. "I don't need his protection."

Taking one of my hands from around his neck, he spun me into a twirl, and I nearly ran into three people. "Just dance, rebel."

The whole time, Liam watched me from against the wall, his features darkening with each passing glance I stole.

I didn't know what the fuck got into me. I had to put the blame on the drinks, but Liam needed a damn push. Someone had to add a bit of flare to this party. I couldn't just let him sit back and brood. I was going to give the heir prince a nudge, incite some emotion, and give him what he really wanted—what I saw flash in his eyes for a few seconds each time our gazes met before he had the chance to mask it under a frown.

Closing the space between Riven and me, I let our bodies brush as my hips swayed. He jerked back, not exactly playing the willing participant as I'd hoped. "What are you doing?"

I'm not deterred. I'm a girl on a mission.

"Getting his attention."

He put his hands on my shoulders, attempting to keep me at a safe distance. "And trying to get me killed in the process."

I lifted a brow, spinning out from under his hands and moving back into him. "Leith warned you."

Riven shook his head, a knowing light entering his eyes. "If it's not me, it'll be someone else."

"Better it's you, then."

"If I get a broken nose, you owe me."

I grinned. "It'll heal."

"Still hurts like a bitch. Especially from Liam. The thing with restrained control like his, when he lets it free, he holds nothing back." A shudder rolled through him as if he was remembering the sting of Liam's fists.

"Perfect," I replied with a twist of my lips.

Riven, being more perceptive than I gave him credit for, picked up on my slightly devious mood. "What are you up to?"

"Snapping his leash." A bit too much elation might have laced my voice.

A slash of moonlight highlighted the side of his face and the peculiar expression on his features. "Why?"

I ran my fingers down to his chest, muscles firm under his shirt. "Because it's his birthday."

The patio didn't offer much room to move to begin with, and the crowd outside dancing had grown. People were sandwiched in. Some drunk idiot who obviously didn't know who I was came up behind me. His fumbling hands went to my hips, fingers digging a little too hard for my liking when he found his grip.

Before I had a chance to react, Riven shoved the guy in the chest. "Get your fucking hands off—

Douchebag stumbled a step or two into someone behind him but then bounced back and swung at Riven. The shifter easily stepped out of the way, and then Mr. Handsy was on the ground, blood spilling from his lip. A dark, foreboding shadow loomed over him.

Liam had hit him.

"Get out of here," the heir prince growled, a sound that vibrated well above the music level. The party paused, everyone glancing to see what the commotion was.

Why do I always seem to be caught in the middle of these things?

The guy on the ground spat a mouthful of blood. "What the fuck, man? We're just having fun," he argued, shoving to his feet.

Liam got into his face. He had an inch of height on him, but the guy outweighed Liam. It didn't matter, though. He wouldn't be a match for the heir. Few were.

Liam's aqua eyes flashed brightly, his jaw tightening. "Not with her you're not." The heir prince's gaze flickered to Riven standing behind the guy, giving him a silent command, and then Liam grabbed my hand, hauling me out of the gathered crowd. People parted like the fucking Red Sea for Liam, even those who didn't owe him respect.

We reached the sliding glass doors to the house, and I dug in my heels, but I didn't pull my hand out from under his hold. I liked his damn touch too much, even one that wasn't gentle. "What's your deal? You haven't said two words to me all night, and now you think you can just haul me—"

The rest of my words were swallowed by Liam's lips.

TWENTY-FOUR

Nothing about the kiss, nor the iron grip he had on me, was sweet or soft. Before practically the entire school, Liam branded me, his mouth taking mine, demanding I give in return. My back pressed into the glass doors as I shoved my fingers into his hair. The sexual tension that had been building and building since I saw him that first day at school snapped and crackled in the air between us.

He cut off the kiss as quickly as he'd taken possession, leaving me dazed and disoriented. My chest heaved as my insides churned in a mess of fuzzy feelings and so much more that I didn't have the energy to untangle.

"What are you doing?" What I wanted to ask was why he'd stopped, but with all the people around, I was glad my mouth had chosen to reword my thoughts.

Liam's gaze was stuck on mine as he shook his head. "I don't fucking know. And that's the problem." He grabbed my wrist, ignoring the whistling and whooping crowd as he tugged me inside the house.

I didn't ask where we were going, didn't care as long as he didn't let go of me. Unable to stop myself from glancing over my shoulder, I

glared at Brina. Smiling, I flipped her off and heard a few chuckles as Liam zigzagged us through the kitchen.

Upstairs, he flung open a bedroom door—his bedroom. The entire room taunted my senses, the smell of him everywhere. On the sheets. Imprinted in the keyboard and desk. Clinging to the floors. Drifting from the closet. In the damn walls.

He halted at the threshold, glaring at the small group that had gathered in his room. "Leave!" Liam ordered. "Get the fuck out of here before I do something you'll regret," he said coldly when they didn't immediately move into action.

Grumbling, the lot moseyed out of his room, taking their drinks and party favors with them.

The door hadn't even clicked shut behind the last person when Liam whirled, taking my lips in another wild, possessive kiss that curled my toes.

He gave me no time to think. Impulse took over, and my fingers plunged into his hair. His hands moved to my waist, dragging me against him roughly.

One night. I was giving us both this one night before shit hit the fan tomorrow. He didn't need to know that.

Walking me against the wall, Liam slipped his hands up my arms as he reached for my wrists, trapping them over my head. The hunger that woke within me might have ravaged the world, and I wouldn't have cared.

"I'm done giving you space," he snarled, his eyes running over my face, taking in the heat in my cheeks and the sight of my swollen lips.

My wolf purred inside me at his admission. "I can see that."

He hardened against me, and I moaned as his lips covered mine again.

It was hard to believe Liam and I had ended up here.

I'd rejected him.

He'd rejected me.

And yet nothing could stop the cosmic pull of fate. It was beyond our control. All I could do was hold on to my heart for as long as I could and pray Liam didn't shatter me into a million tiny pieces. He had the power to do so if I gave in, surrendered to the magnetic pull of him.

Not that I thought either of us had a choice.

But perhaps if I made the decision to jump in fully, it wouldn't be destiny but me. Honestly, I didn't know. The whole fucking thing confused me now. But if I was honest with myself, there was one thing I *was* sure about: Liam. And how much I wanted *him*.

I could have kissed Liam until the end of time, but there was another side of me—the wolf—and she wanted more than to just kiss the heir prince. I should have realized a whole lot sooner how dangerous it was for me to be alone with him. I lacked Liam's discipline, and I was about to make an irreversible mistake.

Or perhaps *mistake* wasn't quite right, depending on your point of view.

My canines descended, and I ran them over his lip. Before I thought about the fallout, I sank the points of my teeth into his fleshy, soft lip. A second later, a drop of warm blood hit the tip of my tongue, and I realized I'd fucked up.

He stared at me from under half-lidded eyes gleaming with desire. "Did you just bite me?"

It was too damn late for regrets. There was no going back.

Besides, I didn't want to, because that single bead hadn't been enough. I had to have more of him. Taste more.

I crushed my lips to his, his blood smearing onto my mouth, my tongue.

Nothing I could do would stop what I'd unintentionally started. Or perhaps it hadn't been so unintentionally. "You're mine," I breathed.

"Kelsey," he growled, drawing back and staring at his blood on my lips.

I licked it off, my eyes closing as the taste of his power tingled through my system.

And then I sank my teeth into the lower part of his neck just above his shoulders. Something heady and electric charged within me, and then the thread that linked Liam to me pulled him tighter and tighter as I marked him, claiming the heir prince as mine.

His body shuddered, a ripple of power and consuming lust.

The change started—the link that would bind me to him. A tickle moved inside my chest, swiftly morphing into a hum that vibrated every crevice of my being. It became a wildfire burning and crackling in my veins. It went so much deeper. Past flesh, muscle, and bone, embedding and attaching itself to my soul. There was no pain, only pure, breath-taking pleasure.

I relished each new sensation, loving the empowered feeling Liam's alpha magic gave me. The bond glowed brighter and bolder, and I couldn't fathom how it could get any stronger when he claimed me.

"You're mine," I gasped, my head falling back against the wall.

My heart synced with his. Even my lungs felt the shift, my breathing a mirrored reflection of his. Pine and mint filled my nostrils in a more heightened way than they ever had. From this moment on, there would never be another wolf or man for me. None as vital or as impenetrable. It was more unyielding than any magic I'd wielded before.

"You don't know what you've done." His eyes flickered with such tortured emotion, need and control clashing in battle.

Why was that so attractive? Fuck, I could sense the ribbon of power that tied him to me. It was beautiful. Scary. And so damn sexy.

My gaze wavered from his for just a second to see the marks I'd left on his neck. "I do. It was my choice." I bit down on my lip, drawing a few droplets of blood to the surface.

Liam groaned. "Don't do this, Kelsey. You know I can't. Not yet." He brushed the pad of his thumb down the column of my neck, sending a shiver through me.

For the first time, I could feel as much as see the emotion, the tight knot he held on his power. He desired me, that much I could tell, and although some part of me understood what he was saying—the reason-able part—she was buried so far under desire and the high of claiming him that all I heard was rejection. Again. And it pierced my heart. "You don't want me?"

His fingers fisted in my hair, forcing me to look at him. "Are you fucking kidding me? I've never had to use so much self-control to stop myself from claiming you right now."

I didn't think anything could penetrate the luminous bond. I was wrong. "I don't understand."

"You're not eighteen," he whispered.

"Why does that matter? I don't have to be eighteen for you to claim me." Even as the argument flew out of my mouth, I knew what he said was the right thing, the right choice. My recklessness wasn't allowing me to see clearly. I was all feeling right now.

It was then I realized that Liam balanced that heedless part of me. He *was* my voice of reason when I had none.

He pressed his forehead to mine. "No, you don't. But I'm not going to give the king, the council, or your parents a reason to invalidate my claim on you. The treaty states that I have to wait until you're eighteen, and despite my father's reasons for making this alliance with your family and the king, *I* want you. Not because my father commanded it. My body, my soul, my wolf—they want you because you're meant to be mine. Neither of us likes the conditions in which we were brought together, but I can't deny that you're my mate. You're so much more, Kelsey. And I think you know it as well. You're mine. And I'll be damned if I let anyone take you from me. I'd like to see them fucking try."

Shit. Oh shit.

What was I supposed to say to that?

My chest rose and fell rapidly, my heart ready to burst out of it. He hadn't told me he loved me, but neither had I, and yet his admission had been somehow more powerful and moving than any impact those three words would have had.

I didn't know what to do.

Not with Liam.

Not with what he'd just revealed.

I lifted on my toes, reaching to caress his cheek.

He held up a hand, warding me off. "Don't. If I touch you again, if you come any closer, the thread on my control will snap. I'm barely hanging on. Everything about you is driving me mad."

"I want to touch you, to comfort you. I've never met a wolf with the kind of control you have. You won't break the treaty." My hand fell above his heart. "Trust me."

"Kelsey," he groaned like he was in physical pain, eyes so damn bright they lit up the entire room.

"Liam," I whispered.

"Foolish pup," he muttered right before I took possession of his mouth again. His tongue slipped between my parted lips and caressed my own.

My mate. Mine.

Hands braced on either side of my hips, he lifted me off the ground. I wrapped my legs around him, and he walked us to the bed. Without untangling us, he laid me on the mattress, my back pressing into the soft comforter. Giving in, he sighed as he trailed the pad of his thumb over my bottom lip. "I've tried to stay away from you. I'm done trying."

Thank God.

"It's about damn time, princeling," I replied, tracing my nails down his back until I got to the hem.

Hovering over me, those stormy, passion-filled eyes held mine. "I can't stop. Not now."

My fingers made quick work of tugging his shirt up. "If you stop, I will rip your balls off with my teeth. You don't want my teeth anywhere near your balls," I threatened, partly serious.

Liam grinned, flashing his dimples. "You're wrong, Kelsey."

Clothes quickly disappeared. I savored the feel of him pressed into the length of my body, skin to skin. My fingers splayed over his chest of muscle. I was going to devour him. He was like oxygen—I needed him to survive.

His eyes brazenly surveyed every inch of my body in such a way that it felt like a caress. I shuddered. Dipping his head, he flicked his tongue over my skin. I made a noise that was caught somewhere between a moan and a purr.

Bodies flushed and greedy for more than soft kisses, I rolled my hips against him, against the hardness pressed into me. He groaned into my mouth, slowly pulling his lips from mine to kiss my neck until he found my nipple, taking the bud into the hot folds of his mouth.

I wanted every damn inch of him.

There was no going back now. I had claimed Liam. He was mine, and the consequence of my actions was a one-sided bond. If Liam changed his mind or decided not to claim me, I would suffer. Greatly, always pining for the wolf who'd rejected me.

A massive leap of faith I'd never imagined I would take first.

What the hell happened to me?

Liam Castle.

That's what.

A lot could transpire in a few months.

But I couldn't think about all the possible aftermaths of my choice. It was done. It couldn't be undone. Repercussions be damned. I'd deal with them. *After* I dealt with the hunter tomorrow.

But first, I wanted one perfect night with my fucking mate.

My mate.

Softening the kiss, he changed the angle of his mouth, gentling the caress of his fingers.

What the fuck is this?

I was supposed to unravel him, not the other way around.

Worshipping every part of me, he made his way down my body like I was a fucking feast he couldn't stop tasting. His head dipped between my legs. The first lick of his tongue sent me into the stars. My back bowed off the bed slightly, and I moaned.

Oh God.

My nails dug into the sheets, fisting the material between my fingers. He tasted and teased, and when his tongue slipped inside me, I nearly climaxed instantly. One more second and I would have fallen over the edge, tumbling into unimaginable bliss, but the heir prince pulled out, keeping me suspended in consuming passion.

Our eyes connected as Liam propped himself over me, gaze drenched in wild desire. I thought I'd been prepared for this moment, but now... My heart raced as he pressed himself between my legs, fear blooming through the cloud of desire encompassing me.

It was normal to be a little scared and apprehensive your first time. I'd never done this with anyone, never been this close with a guy, this intimate.

What if I—

All thoughts vanished as Liam pushed inside me, filling me slowly with the length of him. I had no room for anything other than this rush of emotion.

He inched deeper, and I flinched at the sting of my virginity breaking, but the pain was quick. My body adjusted to the size of him, but then Liam stopped moving.

His eyes found mine. "You should have told me, pup," he whispered, his breathing uneven.

I didn't want him to stop. The ache between my legs only magnified with him inside me. Those internal muscles clenched. "Would it have made a difference?"

Liam groaned as my core clenched around him. "No."

I moved my hips, unable to stay still. I needed the friction, the movement, or I would go mad. "Then stop complaining."

"I'm not. You're mine now, pup," he promised, pulling out and slipping back in ever so slowly.

Not entirely, I wanted to say. Not completely, but I understood what he meant. I'd always been his, even when I didn't want to be.

Beyond words, my hips caught on to the movement, and I matched his strokes. I'd never understood how people always said they felt closer to someone after sex. Now I fucking got it. I'd never felt closer to anyone in my life as I did at this moment with Liam.

It wasn't only the physical aspect of having him inside me. The bond made every touch, every kiss, and every shared breath brighter. The claim I'd formed glowed like an eternal candle within me that had just been doused with gasoline.

The tension between us had gone on for too long and sent me reeling into that peak before I wanted it to end. Either that or Liam was that fucking good. My fingers grappled with the sheets. I climaxed with his name on my lips. Seconds later, he followed me over the edge, growling my name.

Our breathing was rough as he remained on top of me, his cheek resting against mine. My nails leisurely roamed over his back, not ready to stop touching him. "Happy birthday," I whispered, my lips curling into a feline smile of pure satisfaction.

The heir prince lifted his head, plucking a lock of hair off my face and keeping it between his fingers as they trailed down the long black strand. "You're going to be the death of me, pup."

A flash of my dreams whirled through my mind. I wanted to tell him to not joke about death, but I refused to ruin this fucking perfect moment between us. I snuggled against him instead, trying to put the thoughts of his death out of my head.

Liam shifted to the side, tucking me into his arms. For the first time since I stepped into his bedroom, the sounds of the party filtered in from under the door. Sleepily, I was content to never move, but the outside world had other plans. My phone buzzed, interrupting my lazy happiness. I ignored the incessant vibration of my phone, but the damn thing wouldn't shut up.

Groaning, I rolled out of Liam's arms. *This better be fucking important, because if not, I plan on tearing whoever keeps texting's fingers off.*

The hard part was finding my clothes. I scanned the bedroom floor, following the buzzing and searching for the glow of the screen. Locating my dress, I dug in the front pocket and retrieved the pestering device. As I sat back down on the bed, Hope's name popped up on the screen with like six messages from her.

I quickly unlocked my phone, the light illuminating my horror-stricken expression as I read through the texts.

> I need help
>
> Kelsey?
>
> Hello? Where are you?
>
> ???
>
> ???
>
> Come alone

TWENTY-FIVE

The last message chilled all the warm and fuzzy feelings right out of me. The hunter hadn't kept his word, and the bastard had Hope. He was using her to lure me into a trap. I should have known he wouldn't possess a shred of honesty or trust to his name.

"What's wrong?" Liam asked gruffly, slowly sitting up on the bed.

Fuck my life.

I could lie and go alone as planned, but I'd be risking Hope's life, something I wasn't willing to do. I had no choice but to tell Liam, to involve him—the person I wanted to protect.

More so now. Liam was my mate.

My mate.

Holy shit.

That word used to scare the hell out of me.

I squeezed my eyes shut for just a second, then shifted on the bed, angling toward him. Looking at the heir prince now, it still scared the fuck out of me but for different reasons. His life was a part of me now. If anything happened to him...

It would destroy me.

I didn't want him to come with me, but I also knew from this new

connection tying him to me that Liam wouldn't budge. If I went without him, he would only follow.

"It's Hope. She's in trouble," I said. Guilt gnawed inside me, munching away like a ravenous rat. What kind of shitty friend was I? While she'd been abducted by the hunter, I'd forgotten about her, claimed the heir, and then had sex with him.

If he hurt her, I'd show him the true meaning of pain.

"Kelsey." He inched closer to me and stared me intently in the eyes, his hands framing my face. "You need to calm down."

Only then did I realize the walls, the floor, and the windows were rattling. I was doing that.

I nodded, taking a long breath, but it did little to ease the panic grappling and scratching in my chest. Yet somehow, from just staring into his eyes, the room slowly stopped shaking.

"Good," he praised. "Tell me what happened."

My fingers closed into a knot, nails digging into my skin, a tether to keep me from spiraling. "He has her. We need to go," I pleaded. We were wasting time.

"Okay." Liam nodded, understanding. He edged to the side of the bed, pulling his jeans from the floor.

We quickly dressed, and I started rambling off everything. Well, almost everything. I left out the bits about our prearranged meeting for tomorrow night and stuck to the basics of the hunter harassing me.

"You never told me he was leaving you messages, texting you," Liam barked, halting from his search for his car keys to glare at me.

"No," I said quietly.

He reached for my hand, intertwining our fingers as he snatched his keys off the dresser. "We'll deal with that after we get Hope."

"Liam, if he hurts her..." The floor under my feet became unsteady again.

The heir prince grabbed both of my shoulders, squaring me in front of him, his eyes burning bright in the dark. "We'll find her," he vowed with such conviction that I believed him.

My phone had become a ransom in my hand. "He wants me to come alone."

"The fuck you will," he growled, anger darkening the aqua glow of his eyes. His wolf was so close to the surface. "I'm not letting you go anywhere near him by yourself. Not even to save my cousin. I should tie you to the bed and leave you here. I'm still considering it."

"Liam," I cried. "She's my only friend here."

His hands fell from my shoulders as he raked his fingers through his hair, taking a step back. "And I wasn't lying when I said we'll find her. Grab your shoes. We need to go. Text him back and tell him you're on your way."

I tucked my shoes under my arm and did as he suggested, my fingers fumbling as they flew over the screen, swearing as I mistyped a single word over and over again in my haste, finally getting it on the screen.

Where?

The three dots appeared as the hunter typed his response on Hope's phone.

The old bridge on Wells.

I relayed the location to Liam, who grunted in response, which I assumed meant he was familiar with the bridge.

We rushed down the stairs. The party raged on in full swing, everyone completely oblivious to the horror unfolding. Someone called Liam's name, but I was too focused on Leith, spotting him in the middle of a group, dancing with another guy. His eyes connected with mine, spying his brother next to me and the state of my hair. He lifted a brow, seeing where the two of us had just come from upstairs.

The brow went from curious to confused to suspicious, all things I wanted to avoid. Leith couldn't be involved in this. No one else could. It went against every fiber of my being to tangle Liam in this mess. If anything happened to him because of me, I didn't know if I would ever recover. I definitely wouldn't forgive myself.

Forcing a smirk edged with attitude, I prayed it would be enough to fool Leith, make him second-guess what he thought he saw on my face seconds ago. I wanted him to believe it had all been an act—a joke to mess with him.

I didn't know how convincing I was, but Liam took my hand, pulling me through the crowded hallway to the front door. With all the fucking people stuffed inside, it had been hard to breathe, but now, I greedily gulped the crisp evening air, desperate to be rid of the slew of scents assaulting my nostrils. We had no time to waste.

Liam jogged to his truck parked on the lawn, tugging me along. "Fuck," he cursed, halting in front of it. "I'm blocked in."

Sure as shit, dozens of vehicles surrounded his truck from literally all sides. The only way to get out would be to run them over—and it might have been capable of plowing over a few compact ones.

I snapped my eyes to his. "Leith's. He parked down the block on the side of the road."

The heir prince smirked. "Good thing I have his spare key. Let's go."

We ran across the lawn, leaving the sounds of his birthday party behind us. "You can't alert the pack. He'll know," I told Liam, opening the passenger door to Leith's car.

"Only until we know Hope's safe," he conceded, displeasure at the corner of his eyes.

I slid into the seat, quickly closing the door behind me and tossing my shoes in the back. "Okay," I agreed, rubbing my hands up and down my thighs. They were cold and clammy.

Liam started the engine. "Leith hates when I drive his car," he said, peeling off the side of the road, tires spitting up gravel.

"I wonder why," I replied dryly, my fingers moving to grip the sides of my seat or risk being tossed around like a rag doll.

The moon was always a sense of comfort for me. I peeked out the window, searching the sky for a glimpse of hope. The dense, moody clouds were shrouding the moon, and it made me anxious as hell. "Can't you go faster?"

His glare cut across the car at me. "Not without killing us."

"Liam," I nearly sobbed, the panic and anxiousness having become a living thing inside me. I couldn't think. I couldn't breathe. I couldn't do anything but wait.

And that was the problem.

My wolf wanted action. She wanted blood. She wanted the hunter's heart.

The heir prince's fingers flexed, unflexed, and flexed again on the steering wheel. "I know. Kelsey, I know. She'll be okay. She's tough."

I was tough, yet the bastard managed to shoot me. What had he done to Hope? How had he gotten to her? A million questions ran through my head, most of them not pretty, but I had to shove everything aside and kick out my fears if I wanted to outsmart this prick. All I had to do was *not* get kidnapped.

No big deal.

Chewing on the end of my nail, my canines scraped over my skin. The apprehension within me had my wolf on edge, ready to spring forward at any given second. Not a good idea inside the small confines of a sports car.

After what felt like hours but in reality was only minutes, we finally approached the designated location. Liam cranked the steering wheel with one hand, turning the car into a nature reserve, ignoring the Closed After Dusk sign.

A small parking lot sat off to our left, and Liam whipped the car over the gravel road, dirt and pebbles spinning off the tires. We came to a dusty, sudden stop alongside the only other vehicle—Hope's.

My heart thundered in my ears as I rushed out of the car, not waiting for Liam to kill the engine. I listened, praying I'd pick up the signs of human life, but it was difficult to hear anything over my fucking pulse. I didn't smell anything out of place. Not altogether surprising since the hunter was known to mask his scent. Tonight would be no different.

Dashing to the other car, I peeked inside the windows, begging any god who would listen that I would find Hope inside, but it was abandoned.

A warm hand enfolded mine. "The bridge is this way," Liam advised, his voice low and guarded.

Foreboding, dark and thick, slunk into the pit of my gut. Something terrible would happen tonight. My skin crawled with the awareness of not being alone but being unable to locate where the threat stemmed from. We were walking blindly into a trap, and I didn't know how to stop it or prevent us from being caught. Or worse, fucking killed.

Power rippled from the heir prince as we stepped onto a trail, leaving the parking lot behind us. Liam suddenly yanked on my arm, shoving me behind him. I was about to lash him verbally when the sound of a gun cocking had me freezing. His hand became a rock against mine, tightening. Instinct had my claws extending.

Pressed against his back, I glanced over his shoulder. From the dark crevices of the woods, a pair of eyes appeared. Human eyes. And yet... there was something off about them. A reflection or a shadow. I couldn't figure it out.

"I knew you wouldn't come alone. Hello, little prince," the owner of those eerie eyes said.

That fucking voice. I knew that voice.

Recognition clicked. I took a step back, my head shaking in disbelief. No. It couldn't be. I had to be wrong. He wouldn't fucking do this. Not to Hope. If it had only been Liam and me involved, I might have considered it possible. But Hope? Would he actually hurt the girl he loved? Wolves might be able to hide or conceal their feelings, but humans... No, they didn't have the ability or the knowledge that such a thing could be done.

Not unless, of course, they knew about shifters—about our abilities.

"Gunnar?" I hated that my voice quivered, but I couldn't stop the ripple.

Liam stiffened at the whisper of my voice, and through the bond I created with him tonight, I felt the truth sink in. "What the fuck?" he swore, rage flaring in his tone. "This has to be a joke."

From the darkness, the hunter stepped fully out from the trees, and despite the moon being obscured behind somber clouds, there was no mistaking his face. The dark hair. The eyes, usually so sad, now almost black and brimming with malice. And the scar high on his cheek below his lower lashes.

It was Gunnar.

How the fuck?

Who is this guy?

How has he been able to deceive so many people for so long?

I had thought about who the hunter was time and time again, sketched a picture of his face in my head, heard his voice in my dreams, terrorizing me with promises of pain and death, hurt, and agony. It wasn't me who feared those threats. It was who might suffer in his quest to capture me.

"Afraid not," Gunnar sneered at Liam. "This works out better. I can't have you hunting for me once I leave with your mate. Orders. You understand."

Teeth bared, Liam growled at him, a deep rumble that echoed in my bones. I tried to move to the heir prince's side, but he refused to let me, keeping me shielded by his frame. The fact that he stood between the hunter and me might have been endearing to some but made my heart stop.

I shook my head, my mind still refusing to believe what my eyes were seeing.

"You're a hunter," I snarled defiantly, snubbing my nose in the air, the reality of our situation settling in.

"Surprise," he replied sarcastically, waving the gun he held in the air.

My eyes flicked to the rifle stuffed with silver bullets. The same ones I'd been shot with. The same ones I'd see in my nightmares, piercing Liam's chest.

"Does Hope know who you really are?" I asked, praying I could distract him with conversation until I came up with a plan, something I now realized Liam and I should have formulated on the way here. I'd been too distraught to think clearly.

Contempt twisted his face, like it was my fault his identity had been compromised. "Not until tonight, when you made me take drastic measures. I had hoped to keep her out of it."

He'd been lying to her, to everyone, for years. "You promised no one else would get hurt," I pointed out to him flatly.

A manic smile appeared on his lips. "I lied. I'm sure you're familiar with the gesture, seeing as you lie about who you really are every day."

The muscles on Liam's back went taut, his fingers tightening against mine. "Cut the bullshit. Where's my cousin?"

Gunnar tsked. "Not so hasty. Let's talk terms first."

"Fuck your terms," I spat, letting my wolf eyes cut through the darkness over Liam's damn broad shoulders. He wasn't giving me a fucking inch.

"I bet you're amazing in bed," he crooned. "So fiery and hot."

It was said to provoke the heir prince. He succeeded.

I thought Liam would shift right then and there, and I even braced for the sight of his wolf exploding, but he just lunged for Gunnar.

The air tremored—the power of his wolf.

I had no other choice. I couldn't risk Liam being shot or him ripping Gunnar's jugular out. Not before Hope was safe. Not with my nightmares looming in the back of my mind, this scene too fucking familiar.

What had been a humming seed inside me bloomed into a world of power, flooding my veins. I expelled that power, erecting a wall between my mate and the hunter.

Gunnar's gaze met mine over the barrel of his gun, his expression like a tunnel of evil, dark and frightening. A slow smile crossed my lips. He might have inside information about the pack, might have studied wolves and their weaknesses, but he didn't know shit about me, about what I could do, what I was capable of.

He'd only seen a slice of my gift.

Liam tried to put his fist through the invisible shield and roared. "Kelsey!"

The shield shimmered, a coil of silverish light in the dark, but it held. As long as my power thrived, it wouldn't break, but there would come a point of depletion. I wasn't an endless well of power, but I did feel stronger tonight.

The heir prince kept his focus on the hunter, but his words were for me. "I can't kill him if you keep stopping me, pup."

"We need Hope," I said adamantly. In the two seconds it had taken me to throw up the barrier of magic, Liam had made it halfway to where the hunter cockily stood. Gunnar still had his gun pointed at Liam.

"She's not far. I can smell her," Liam said, his eyes trained on Gunnar despite the wall that separated them.

"Me too," I agreed. He didn't mention that he could also feel her fear and anger. Hope was pissed, but I sensed those emotions through Liam.

"I'd always envied those wolfish senses." Something in his voice and expression smacked of spite and hatred. It stirred suspicion within me.

"Funny how your own DNA can be deceived when something goes awry. I've been right under your nose for years, and you never suspected. Perhaps you're not as good a wolf as you think."

My mind worked over his words, knowing there was something important hidden in what he was trying to tell us.

Liam figured it out first. "You're part wolf," he said, taking a step back.

"Some might say that. I have pieces of shifter traits, except for the one that really counts." As if to demonstrate the truth of his words, he let his eyes flash bright through the dark.

Well, fuck me. This didn't make sense.

And then it clicked. "You can't shift." I didn't like the space that separated me from the heir prince, even if it was only feet. I moved cautiously, taking a step toward him and then another.

"No," Gunnar confirmed the worst outcome for a shifter, and it was painfully obvious that he held some form of resentment at the lacking ability. "But I found uses for the abilities I do have. Turns out that not being able to shift prevents other wolves from picking up any traces of wolf I might have."

It was rare, like extremely rare, for a wolf to be unable to shift. "How did you become like this?"

I didn't understand Liam's question at first. I assumed one of his parents was a shifter—that was the usual way these things worked—but the more I thought about it, the more I realized how off Gunnar's traits were.

A cruel, humorless laugh. Gunnar lowered his gun, leaning on it like a cane. "Not in the traditional sense. I must admit, you're making up quickly for all those times you didn't give me a second glance."

"You were made," Liam said, extending his arm behind him, reaching for me.

What in the backcountry bullshit? Made? Is that even a fucking thing?

The heir prince seemed to think it was.

Holy hell.

I clasped our hands, my soul jumping for joy at the connection to my mate.

"That's a friendly way of looking at it. What I went through felt more like having my body ripped apart from the inside and then slowly, torturously stitched back together as something new. Remade."

"Sounds delightful," Liam replied dryly. "You can spare me the details because honestly, I just don't give a shit. It doesn't make a difference. You're not walking out of these woods alive."

Gunnar flinched, a flash of ire in his dark eyes that dimmed slightly. "You might be right. One of us will die tonight. It remains to be seen who."

Foreboding slammed into me with such force that it rendered me breathless for a moment. "Why did you pretend to be Hope's friend all this time?" I asked.

Gunnar strolled up to the edge of the barrier, then reached out, testing the strength. I winced, my power flinching as what felt like a cold nail raked down my neck. His lips twisted. "Something to pass the time, get information until my assignment arrived."

My wolf growled, a flash of white teeth. "How long have I been your target?"

He gave a leisurely shrug. "Always. Since I could walk, I've been training for the day you came to Riverbridge."

I was unsure how long I'd be able to hold up the shield. We needed to move this along. Stalling wasn't helping anyone. My jaw clenched so tight, my canines ground into my bottom lip, drawing blood. "Why the fuck didn't you just come find me? Why wait until I came here?"

Gunnar sighed, the first sign he was getting bored with the conversation. "My turf. It gives me an edge. And I had orders. You had to be on Riverbridge pack soil."

"Who? Who in our pack is a traitor?" Liam demanded.

Nothing about this guy was the Gunnar I knew. He wasn't broken or sad. He wasn't weak or timid.

The hunter raised a brow. "Impressed. I didn't think you'd figured it out yet. It's a shame I still have to kill you."

Wrong. Fucking. Answer.

I bristled and hissed, "Not until I see Hope." The shield flickered with my burst of anger.

"Is she always this demanding?" he asked, studying the shield as if he was just waiting for a moment of weakness to shatter my defense.

Liam bared his teeth, growling.

"I'll take that as a yes." Gunnar waved his gun aimlessly in the air. "Fine. She's by the bridge. I didn't hurt her. In an hour or so, she'll wake up tired and groggy but unharmed. Now, enough with the party tricks."

He was right. I couldn't hold this barrier all night, no matter how much I wanted to keep Liam away from Gunnar. "You're a prick. How could you do that to her? I know you care about Hope, or you're just an exceptional actor."

Gunnar began to walk the perimeter of the shield, testing its boundaries by tapping his gun against it. "My feelings are irrelevant. I'm not being paid to care about anyone."

"Who's paying you?" Liam questioned, but it came out as more of a command.

The sneer on Gunnar's face gave me a mess of bad feelings. "I bet you would love to know, but if I want to get paid, their identity needs to remain anonymous."

I snorted. "Let me guess, you don't get paid until you deliver me?"

"Hunters have trust issues," Gunnar replied.

One of many issues, I suspect.

Liam's face contorted with wrath, and I knew the moment I dropped the barrier, he would go straight for Gunnar.

"I'm going to fucking kill you for this," I seethed.

Gunnar sighed. "Don't the threats of murder ever get old?"

"Not when you enjoy it. And I will enjoy tearing into you."

"I can see why he has a thing for you. You're just the little prince's type. Bloodthirsty."

"You're a fool to come alone." Liam's words were sharp, each syllable a blade's cut.

"Who said I'm alone? I learn from my mistakes."

At the first howl, I thought Liam had called the pack.

With the second howl, I realized it wasn't our pack.

Gunnar had brought his own.

Rogue wolves.

TWENTY-SIX

L iam went as still as death.

At least six rogue wolves that I could see. Perhaps more waiting deeper in the forest.

Rogue wolves often formed small packs of their own after being kicked out or abandoning their born packs. How had Gunnar found them? Or perhaps the more important question was what had he promised them in exchange for fighting on the wrong side?

The barrier cracked like a spiderweb, spreading and splintering until the pressure snapped, and, like glass shattering, my ward crumbled.

Fuck.

"Kelsey," Liam said in warning, holding out an arm for me to stay back.

Nodding, I understood. He had to call in reinforcements. Even with my extra abilities, six rogue wolves and a hunter would be a challenge, but one I would gladly accept if it meant saving Liam's life. Though half of his guys were drunk at his house. The elders were at a council meeting with the king, and those left would take ten or fifteen minutes, possibly longer, to find us.

Liam burst into his wolf, pure white fur covering every inch of his

muscular body. The fact that he could shift and Gunnar couldn't was a big "fuck you" in his face. The heir prince knew what he was doing.

It was an entirely different experience feeling the shift through our bond, but one I couldn't appreciate. Not now.

Gunnar swung his gun like a bat straight at Liam as he barreled toward him. The heir prince ducked, the gun swooshing over his head. Liam didn't stop and went right for Gunnar's leg, sinking his teeth into the flesh of his calf.

Gunnar didn't make a sound, but his fists tightened against the pain.

I should shift. I knew I should shift.

But something held me back. I'd already used a great deal of my power holding the shield for as long as I had. To shift would use another chunk I didn't know if I should waste. Fighting in my wolf form would be more practical, but what if I needed my power and depleted it by shifting?

Shit. Shit. Shit.

Panicking, I didn't know what to do, but I couldn't stand here and do nothing and let Liam fight off a pack of rogue wolves and a hunter with a gun.

Three wolves descended on the heir prince. His eyes glowed like living embers at the center of a flame, fierce and bright.

They clashed, a brutal snapping of teeth and snarling of fury. The other three stayed at the outer rim of the woods, keeping us boxed in. If we tried to run, they would give chase.

I had no intention of running.

I had to go for Gunnar.

I came here to kill him.

And that was what I was going to do.

Gunnar! The guy Hope trusted. Her best friend. The guy she was in love with.

It doesn't matter who he is. He's a hunter, nothing more. He was never a friend.

Shoving my feet off the ground, I ran. Not away. Not to safety. Toward my enemy.

Gunnar limped out of the way as Liam took on three wolves, blood soaking through his black pants.

I had to move quickly. Now was the time to strike, while he was slightly impaired. But I had a feeling the injury wouldn't hinder him long. Something told me that healing might be one of the traits he'd received from whatever fucked-up experiments he'd been through to become like this.

I hurled a blast of my power at him, and the iridescent bubble whirled through the air, hitting Gunnar in the chest and knocking him off his feet. Only once before had I used my power as a weapon instead of a defense. Seeing it leave my hands and knock into Gunnar made me want to do it again. And again.

Particularly since it didn't seem to render him stunned for longer than a heartbeat.

"What other tricks do you have up your sleeve, little wolf?" he asked, jumping to his feet like a fucking ninja. Not shoving to his feet or even scrambling. The prick literally moved almost like he was a wolf. Confusing as hell for my brain to understand how to fight him.

"How about we find out?" I said, throwing my hands out on either side of me, a flash of light filling my palms.

Liam sank his teeth into the side of a rogue wolf's throat, his paw coming up and slashing him across the face. He tore him to ribbons, swipe after swipe. A tortured howl rang through the forest as Liam raked his claws over his eyes.

"Run! Kelsey, you need to run," Liam's voice pleaded in my head. It was the first time his words had ever been spoken through our bond, and he was telling me to run.

"I won't leave you."

"You must. I won't let them have you."

"If I leave, he'll kill you. I would rather be taken than have you die, Liam. You can't ask that of me."

"Kelsey."

"You'll find me. No matter where I am. You will find me."

"Kelsey, no!"

But it was too late. I'd made my decision. For Liam's life, I would trade mine.

A cruel smile formed on Gunnar's lips as he faced me, his gun on the ground at his feet. Not that it mattered. The asshole withdrew a pair of daggers from behind him, strapped to a harness or some other bullshit hunter gear. "No hard feelings. I hope you understand. I'm just doing my job."

We circled each other like two crows stalking their prey. "Someone's balls finally dropped."

Faster than any human was capable of, he heaved a dagger at my chest. I smelled the silver blade as it sang through the air and sidestepped its path seconds before it would have hit me. The dagger whizzed past, and I flung another blast in response.

"Leave Liam alone, or I will make this difficult for you every step of the way," I spat. "Call them off."

Not that the heir prince wasn't holding his own. The snapping of bones echoed through the trees, followed by a wolf whimpering right before his head lobbed to the side, neck broken.

One down.

Five to go.

Twirling the other dagger in his hand, Liam pondered my demand. "Fine, have it your way, little wolf—"

I hit him in the face with a blast, right smack-dab in the center, not giving him a chance to whip the blade at me.

He wiped the blood trickling from his nose. "You little bit—"

I sent off another sphere of power. This one hit him on the shoulder, but the jerk kept his hold on the weapon.

"Kelsey! Go now. Run!" Liam ordered, seeing the same opening I did, but we had very different ideas.

Could Liam hold off the rogue wolves until the pack arrived? I didn't dare risk a glance in his direction. As long as I could feel him through our bond, then he was alive.

My eyes stayed trained on Gunnar. My feet kept moving, slow steps as I led him away from Liam. "I told you I wouldn't make this easy. Call off your hounds."

His lips thinned. "And then you'll go?"

A rock tumbled down the uneven ground under my feet as I moved in closer. If I could get my hands on the gun... *Just don't look at it.* "I guess you'll just have to try me," I retorted.

"Or how about you don't fight, and I let Hope live," he countered, eyes flaring. He held up his hands in a gesture of truce we both knew was bullshit. The dagger in his grip glinted off his eyes.

"You wouldn't fucking dare," I spat at the threat on Hope's life.

"Try me," he mocked, and then the son of a bitch backhanded me.

My head snapped to the side; a ringing buzzed in my ears along with the sharp stinging of pain on my cheek.

Liam let out a howl of pure rage.

Why the fuck hadn't I thought to bring a kitchen knife or some other kind of weapon with me?

Because I was used to fighting with my teeth and claws. And I had magic.

Pain radiated throughout my face, but I forced myself to push it aside just in time to see Liam break free and barrel toward Gunnar.

Kill him. Kill him. Kill him. The wolf within me was very vocal about what she wanted. Holding her back until the right moment presented itself was damn fucking difficult.

Patience, I whispered back.

One of the wolves on the hill howled, signaling to the other two at their guard posts. In the distance, Liam's pack raced toward us, but they were still so far away.

With two rogue wolves hot on his heels and the other three racing down the hills, the heir prince evaded their snarling and snapping jaws as he sprinted toward me.

Gunnar grabbed me while my eyes were drawn to Liam, a fatal mistake that might cost the heir prince and me both. He spun me in his arms, pressing the blade across my throat. The metal sizzled against my skin, and I hissed between clenched teeth.

At the glimmer of silver so close to my neck, Liam dug his claws into the ground, coming to a halt despite every muscle in his body screaming at him to protect me, to save me, to kill Gunnar. If I breathed too deep, the blade would cleanly pierce my flesh.

The rogue wolves were upon Liam again. He rammed into the side of one and snapped at another as the others surrounded him, closing ranks.

Gunnar wasted no time, satisfied the heir prince would be detained long enough for him to persuade me to move. "Let's go, little wolf. You and I are going for a walk."

My eyes beseeched Liam to stand down, to not try anything stupid enough to get himself killed.

"*Let me go,*" I projected into his thoughts.

Liam growled.

"*Trust me.*"

Gunnar's rogue wolves flanked Liam on all sides as he and I began to move. He eased the blade a fraction off my throat, giving me a bit of room to walk without slicing myself open.

"He'll follow," I stated the obvious, forcing my feet to move, regardless that each step grew harder. I didn't care about the rocks and twigs digging into the tender arches of my feet. "He'll find my scent. He'll track us."

Keeping his hold secured around my neck, he guided me with his body and the jerk of his arm like I was a fucking horse. "I'd be disappointed if he didn't. So would you, I imagine. He's your mate, after all. Rejecting him didn't really work out, did it?"

Since he seemed to have all the wolf senses besides shifting, I assumed he smelled my claiming on Liam. "Can we just not talk? The sound of your voice makes me want to rip out your vocal cords."

A cold laugh brushed against my ear. "So violent."

"You have no idea," I muttered, counting each step. We weren't headed in the direction of Hope's and Leith's cars, but he did keep us parallel to the road that wound through the park. Did he have another car stashed up ahead? "So what happens after you turn me over? You collect your reward and split?"

He flinched behind me. "Something like that," he replied, no longer amused.

"And you'll just forget about Hope?"

"I thought you didn't want to talk," he tossed back at me.

I told myself to drown out the sounds of Liam fighting, the brutal hits, the gnarly growls, the clashing of claws. Until I could no longer feel his heartbeat alongside mine, I had to focus on Gunnar. "I changed my mind."

"Just like a woman," he sneered, adjusting the knife to a more comfortable and yet threatening position at the side of my throat.

I bared my teeth. "Your mother must be so proud."

"Dead. Both my parents are before you go and draw some kind of conclusion about me having daddy issues."

"Do you know what they're going to do to me?" My stomach tightened into a ball.

He shrugged. "Probably the same shit they did to me... but worse," he added.

"Can't fucking wait." We needed to be far enough away from Liam that he wouldn't get hurt. Just a few more feet—

Liam leaped off the edge of a cliff, his aqua eyes gleaming like an animal in the night.

Are you fucking kidding me? He couldn't have waited another minute or two?

The world suddenly went into slow motion like some damn cinematography tactic. I was aware of two things at once.

I'd underestimated Liam's ability to kill or a least render five rogue wolves immobile.

And Gunnar had a handgun.

The hunter's arm extended, pointing the slim barrel at Liam as he descended to the ground.

"No!" I screamed, whirling on Gunnar. I went for the gun just as the first shot pierced the night, altering his aim, but was it enough?

My ears rang with the sound, and a lick of cold brushed down my spine as the sharp smell of blood hit my nostrils.

Fear became a wild, thrashing thing inside me as I searched the woods for the heir prince. Too damn close to the nightmares that kept me up, I let out a sharp breath when I found him. The bullet had grazed his right shoulder.

Fury exploded within me. Flashes of my dream blended with the picture in front of me, blurring the edges between the two realities. My vision wavered, and my breathing became a little difficult. Now was not the time to have a fucking panic attack, or perhaps it was.

Something snapped inside me.

I blinked, clearing the nightmare from my memory.

Spinning, I flattened my palms on Gunnar's chest and discharged a punch of power into him, sending him flying backward. His wolflike reflexes kept him from landing on his ass a second time.

Crouched on the balls of his feet, a hand steadying himself on the ground, Gunnar lifted his head at me. He might not have been able to transform into a wolf, but the look he gave me was truly lupine.

My nostrils flared as I squared my shoulders and faced him. Liam let out a roar that shook the forest and came to stand at my side.

I was wolf.

I was power.

I was death.

Magic sparked off my skin like little electric stars.

This ended now.

Him or me.

Gunnar lifted his gun as he shot to his feet, and I cut the last tether holding my gifts in check. From head to toe, I shimmered in an iridescent glow, my skin glittering like diamonds.

As Gunnar pulled the trigger, I cast my power. It moved through the woods like a phantom wind, splintering the bullet into dust as it passed by, never faltering or changing course. I didn't know I could do such things, but I didn't have time to marvel at the awe of it.

Hot, prismatic magic slammed into Gunnar, shoving him against a tree. Stunned, his expression twisted into something of horror. "I can't move!" he screamed, my power leashing him, cuffing his body so he was pinned to the trunk despite his struggles. The muscles in his face and arms flexed and tightened as he tried to pull himself away from the prison I'd bound him in. He remained frozen, under my control. Except for his fucking mouth. "What did you do to me?"

I thought about how I'd suffered after he shot me. All the anxiety I'd had for days, wondering when he might strike next. The endless dreams of him killing Liam. Every ounce of fear, anger, and alarm bubbled to the surface. I wanted it to end. I was tired of looking over my shoulder. I wanted to bask in the bliss of being mated. Normal shifter shit.

With Liam shadowing my movements, I strode up to Gunnar, who was pinned to the tree, and let my wolf crawl out of her cage just enough to make my eyes glow, my canines drop, and my claws extend—enough to do some damage. I lifted my hand and traced a nail down his cheek, breaking the skin. "You fucked with the wrong wolf."

"Go to hell," he hissed, spittle falling from the corner of his mouth.

I snorted. "Original. How about we play another game? Truth or dare? You go first. Truth." I shoved a pointed nail through his throat while Liam guarded my back. Blood sprayed onto my face as Gunnar gasped, his mouth frozen in a tortured cry. "Who told you about me?" Blood ran down my hand, dripping onto my forearms.

Now he suddenly remained tight-lipped. I waited for a breath, and when he didn't answer, I tightened the noose of magic wrapped around his throat and inserted another nail.

He choked, eyes widening as he struggled to breathe.

"Who?" I demanded again. "Who did this to you? Who ordered you to kidnap me?"

Gunnar grinned, his teeth stained red with his blood as he gurgled, "His father—the prince."

What the fuck?

To be continued in part two
LIAM, Moonstruck Mates Book Two

READ MORE BY
J.L. WEIL

ELITE OF ELMWOOD ACADEMY
(New Adult Dark High School Romance)
Turmoil
Disorder
Revenge
Rival

MOONSTRUCK MATES
(New Adult Paranormal Romance)
Kelsey
Liam

DIVISA HUNTRESS
(New Adult Paranormal Romance)
Crown of Darkness
Inferno of Darkness
Eternity of Darkness

DRAGON DESCENDANTS SERIES
(Upper Teen Reverse Harem Fantasy)

Stealing Tranquility
Absorbing Poison
Taming Fire
Thawing Frost

THE DIVISA SERIES
(Full series completed – Teen Paranormal Romance)
Losing Emma: A Divisa novella
Saving Angel
Hunting Angel
Breaking Emma: A Divisa novella
Chasing Angel
Loving Angel
Redeeming Angel

LUMINESCENCE TRILOGY
(Full series completed – Teen Paranormal Romance)
Luminescence
Amethyst Tears
Moondust
Darkmist – A Luminescence novella

RAVEN SERIES
(Full series completed – Teen Paranormal Romance)
White Raven
Black Crow
Soul Symmetry

BEAUTY NEVER DIES CHRONICLES
(Teen Dystopian Romance)
Slumber
Entangled
Forsaken

NINE TAILS SERIES
(Teen Paranormal Romance)

First Shift
Storm Shift
Flame Shift
Time Shift
Void Shift
Spirit Shift
Tide Shift
Wind Shift
Celestial Shift

HAVENWOOD FALLS HIGH
(Teen Paranormal Romance)
Falling Deep
Ascending Darkness

SINGLE NOVELS
Starbound
(Teen Paranormal Romance)
Casting Dreams
(New Adult Paranormal Romance)
Ancient Tides
(New Adult Paranormal Romance)

For an updated list of my books, please visit my website:
www.jlweil.com

Join my VIP email list and I'll personally send you an email reminder as soon as my next book is out! Click here to sign up: www.jlweil.com

ABOUT THE AUTHOR

J.L. Weil is a USA TODAY Bestselling author of teen & new adult paranormal romance, fantasy, and urban fantasy books about spunky, smart mouth girls who always wind up in dire situations. For every sassy girl, there is an equally mouthwatering, overprotective guy.

You can visit her online at: www.jlweil.com or come hang out with her at JL Weil's Dark Divas on FB.

Stalk Me Online
www.jlweil.com
jenniferlweil@gmail.com

9 781954 915282